A first novel by: Richard L. Wren

Mr. Wren is retired from a highly successful insurance career, during which time he was in demand nationally as a motivational and Estate Planning speaker.

In his new career as an author, he describes himself as tall, dark, handsome and a liar. A fourth generation Californian, he's a sailor, father of four beautiful and supportive daughters, and husband to one of the best wives of all time.

He lists as his advisors: a retired, very experienced FBI agent, a semi-retired Hell's Angel leader, a retired Oakland, California Police Detective, Marta Tanrikulu, a very patient editor and Nancy Blackman, an inspiration.

Watch for his next book, "JOSHUA'S REVENGE."

Casey's Slip

CHAPTER 1

For once I wished there was a gale blowing. I could take a couple of reefs in the main, put up a storm jib and ride the hell out of a gale. Even in waters as dangerous as these just outside the Golden Gate. Three hundred miles of open ocean sailing from San Diego to San Francisco and the engine chose to conk out here. Now I've got no wind, no motor and a rough ocean. The notorious dog patch is looming on my starboard quarter and I'm being pushed toward the rocks and the bridge by the following sea. In an hour or so I'd be in real trouble if I couldn't fix the engine. If I ask for help and got towed in it'll cost me my whole ferrying fee and probably more. Time for action.

I had to slow the boat down, get below and fix the motor. I needed a sea anchor, quick. Something large that would sink. A mattress! Handy and quick. I ducked below, grabbed the nearest one, shoved it into the cockpit, secured it to the stern cleat with a spare line and tossed it overboard. In a matter of moments I felt a jerk as it reached the end of the line. I checked the horizon for shipping and found one outbound ship far to my port side and another just emerging from the North Bay, heading for the bridge. That one could be dangerous. It looked like a tanker. They move fast, are ponderous and have the right of way over something small like me. If I was drifting under the bridge at the same time she came through, I could be crushed. The other was a little aft of me and represented no danger.

As I slid down the companionway, I wished I'd insisted on polishing the diesel fuel. Something I usually do before taking off on any open sea passage. Diesel fuel, when left standing for any length of time can become contaminated with bacteria and need cleaning. Private boat owners are notorious for letting this happen and consequently often have problems like mine. The solution is to have a professional come alongside your boat with high pressure pumps and filters to clean the fuel.

Like a dummy I'd let this owner convince me his fuel was fresh and okay. After dozens of sailboat deliveries up and down the California coast I should have known better. Now I was stuck with the consequences.

"Okay Casey, you know what to do, get to it." I said to myself. "Get your tools and your squeeze bulb and do it."

With luck I could remove and replace the fuel filter, re-prime the engine with the squeeze bulb and get her running again. If, on the other hand, I had to bleed the lines I was SOL.

Below deck, working on an engine, the boat tossing and corkscrewing, it's hard not to get seasick. Add to that the nearing danger of shoals and the fact that you're completely responsible for someone else's boat and you begin to get nervous.

When I glanced out the porthole, I could see the San Francisco end of the Golden Gate Bridge getting nearer and nearer. I didn't have much time.

I found the tools and the spare filters and with some sweat and a couple of skinned knuckles, eventually had the new filter installed. Then came the big test, would it work.

If it didn't I wouldn't have enough time to dismantle the fuel system and bleed the lines. I'd have to call for help.

I pumped the squeeze bulb until my hand was cramping, saw that the glass bulb looked full and decided it was now or never. The bridge was getting closer and closer.

Crossing my fingers I pushed the starter button. She cranked and then cranked again. Over and over she cranked and nothing happened. Would the batteries hold up? Nothing happened.

I switched hands and resumed pumping. The glass bulb was full, the filter was working, why wouldn't she start? Using the starter, the battery had to turn the engine over enough times to draw fuel in for ignition. If the batteries died, so would I. I could only try the starter button again and hope. She ground on and on until with a gasp, she caught. The satisfying rattling clunk clunk sound of the diesel filled the cockpit.

I quickly looked around to get my bearings and saw that we were safe. My watch told me it'd only taken about 17 minutes to get the engine running again; it'd seemed like an hour.

In order to get the sea anchor in I left the engine in neutral. The damn mattress may have saved my life and the boat, but I hated it while I was struggling to get it back aboard. Of course the mattress was completely ruined, soaked with salt water. Replacing it would come out of my profits. Without self tailing winches, I never would have gotten it in. I probably should have just abandoned it, but that wouldn't be good stewardship of the open seas.

I made a mental note to tell Mitchell, the owner, what an asshole he'd been. Down in San Diego, he'd assured me over and over that the fuel was fresh and clean. Owners lie, and he was a typical owner. That wasn't the only thing that'd bothered me. When I first met him, he'd been furtive. We'd had to meet away from the dock and he went to the boat to make sure no one was around. He'd had a bandage over one ear and a honey of a black eye. It looked like he'd been beaten up pretty good, but he said it was from an accident. I was pretty sure that was a lie too. He also made me promise that I'd ferry his boat single handed and not let anyone on the boat.

I was really suspicious, maybe the boat wasn't really his? But his ownership papers were clean and up to date and he paid me cash in advance including flying me down from Oakland, so I'd taken the job. San Diego to Oakland and almost there with just this one big hiccup, however there's always something.

With the engine purring along everything fell back into place. The wind picked up a little and seas smoothed a little. Keeping the dog patch well off to starboard, I had a relaxed motor sail under the Golden Gate Bridge, past the "Rock," under the Bay Bridge and down to the small marina on the Oakland side of the bay. I was able to go wing on wing the last hour or so and started straightening up the boat while under way. I'd been winding down, beginning to feel the pressure lifting as I coasted in toward the slips.

Pulling the boat into the dock area, sails furled, barely underway, I glanced at the notes the owner had given me. The numbers on the page had gotten slightly smudged. I was looking for a slip number that could be either a seven or a nine. Both slips were open. I was faced with your classic either/or situation.

The dock was empty – no one to help me there. I flipped a mental coin, slid the boat into slip #7, jumped off the boat, put a single line around a cleat and tried to find a dock master. When I looked around at the line up of old boats berthed nearby I quickly gave up hope of finding a dock master. This whole dock was pretty decrepit with not a sign of life anywhere.

Over on the next dock I thought I saw movement and headed that way

I had to walk off of my dock, cross over to the next dock and walk out to where I thought I'd spotted some one. On the way I passed a bunch of really old sail and power boats, a couple of fishing boats and one old tug. No people at all until I came to what looked like a 40 foot yawl. There was a guy there, at the stern, his back to me.

He was leaning over, feet on the dock, deep into the engine wearing only pants, no shirt and a mile wide expanse of skin. On top of that, his pants rode a little low on his backside, exposing a generous amount of crack. He certainly didn't look like your usual yacht owner duded out in clothes from West Marine, – more like a stevedore, and a big one, at that.

"Can I ask you a question?" There was no sign he heard me. I tried again, louder. "Can you help me?"

"God damn it, can't you see I'm busy? What the hell do you want?" came back in a low rumble.

"I just ferried a boat up from San Diego and I might've put it in the wrong slip. Can I leave a note with you?"

He uncoiled out of the engine space and turned out to be about six-foot-three and big, as in *real* big. No pot belly, just a gray haired, massive chest topped by a beard and piercing blue eyes in a tanned and wrinkled face. A long gray pony tail hung out from under a Greek sailors cap shoved on the back of his head. I judged him to be over sixty, but in great shape. His body looked a lot younger than his face. Holding a large crescent wrench in his greasy hands, he pinned me with his eyes. He wasn't smiling.

"Come again?" he rumbled. "Couldn't hear you with my head in the engine."

"Can I leave my name and cell phone number with you? I just ferried a boat up from San Diego and I might have put it in the wrong slip" I repeated. "I'd be happy to come back and move the boat if I did. I'm only about fifteen minutes away on my bike."

"Okay, which slip?" he said. I pointed out the slip and gave him my boat delivery captain's card. I was happy to get away from him; I've met his type before around the waterfront. They're kind of social outcasts. Live on their boats, have a kind of gang mentality and often have a short fuse and a long temper. This guy looked like one of those and on top of that was huge.

Back on the boat I cleaned out my gear, hosed the deck and hull with fresh water, draped the ruined mattress over the cabin, lifted my folding bike off the foredeck, set the combination lock and headed for home. Home being my small apartment near Lake Merritt. On the way I stopped at the laundry mat where I left some dirty clothes and picked up 2 local newspapers. Then on to a quick Chinese dinner. I read both papers during dinner and caught up on my craving for politics. Not much had changed in the four days since I'd seen a paper.

One headline was about a State Senator rumored to have been caught with his hand in the till and another one was about a senator being caught with his pants down, literally. As soon as I read the headline, I bet myself that I knew who one of them was. I expected it to be Senator Goldberg, an old timer who somehow or other kept his position as his party's whip, year after year after year. I was really surprised to find it was Goldberg that was denouncing and excoriating another Senator. Of course the denounced Senator was from Goldberg's opposing party. The crime the Senator was accused of was taking bribes from a big California land broker. Senator Goldberg was hogging the news for all it was worth. Business as usual.

I found myself dozing and decided it was time to catch up on lost sleep. At sea you catnap. Eventually it catches up with you and you need a good nights sleep. I'd been at sea solo for five nights; it was time for a good rest.

My plan was to sleep in late, then head over to West Marine and get the latest copy of Latitude 38, the best west coast sailing magazine ever. I had an ad running in it and another ad posted at West Marine. With luck, I'd get another delivery job quickly, I sure needed the money.

Things never work out as planned. I was wide awake a little before six AM. Way too early to go out for breakfast, I'd make do with some instant coffee using my hot plate and read the ads for used sailboats. Coffee in hand I must have dozed until my cell phone rang. I jumped up, spilled my coffee, found the phone and answered. "Yeah?"

"CASEY!" the voice roared. "GET YOUR SORRY ASS DOWN HERE LIKE RIGHT NOW OR YOUR GONNA HAVE MY WHOLE GANG ON YOUR TAIL!"

I glanced at my watch, 6:15 A.M. It was still dark outside. Got to be a wrong number I told myself.

"I think you got the wrong Casey," I quietly responded and started to hang up.

"FOR CHRIST'S SAKE, I KNOW I GOT THE RIGHT CASEY AND THE RIGHT NUMBER, YOU ASSHOLE. YOU JUST GAVE IT TO ME LAST NIGHT," he bellowed.

A light dawned. "You the guy I met last night down at the docks?"

Now he lowered his voice and became even more threatening. "You bet your sweet ass I am, and I'm telling you right now, get off the damn phone and down here fast."

"What's wrong, did I put the boat in the wrong slip?"

"Jesus H. Christ. Are you stupid or something? Do I hafta send some of my gang up there and beat the crap out of you? Who the hell cares what slip you put it in?"

"Is there something wrong with the boat?"

"Shut the hell up and listen. I'll make it real slow and simple for you."

In short staccato sentences he said, "Some guy's been murdered on your boat. The police are here. They want to blame it on me. I told the police about you. They want you here, I want you here. Is that simple enough?

"A murder?"

"Finally, you got it. Now get on your little bicycle and get down here right now or I'll have my Devils drag you down."

"Okay, okay. I'm on my way."

Murder? Police? Devils? What the hell's going on?

At the bottom of the stairs, Mrs. Perkins, my landlady, blocked my way. Not on purpose, she was just standing there.

"My goodness Casey, you're up early. Did I hear your phone ring a little while ago?"

She's old, inquisitive, very nice and has excellent hearing.

Thinking fast I said, "Yeah, kind of an emergency on one of the boats, they need me as quick as possible."

"Oh that's too bad dear. I've got some fresh crumpets you could have for breakfast. Are you sure you don't have just a wee bit of time for me?"

"I'm really sorry I gotta rush." I couldn't afford to alienate her, she was the perfect landlady.

I sidestepped her with apologies, and rushed to my bike.

As I neared the end of the street leading to the marina, a news truck with antennas on it whizzed by me. This was beginning to look like a big deal.

I skidded to a stop next to a bunch of police cars. It was just coming up daylight and there was a pretty good sized crowd between me and the docks.

The crowd didn't want to budge. I had to force my way through. I'm not a real big guy, but I'm stronger than I look. My dad always says I have a swimmer's body. Long lean muscles and fairly slim. I'm also a little taller than most at six foot two and could see over the heads of the crowd.

"Excuse me; excuse me that's my boat down there." I worked my way through pushing my bike before me.

When I got up to the front of the crowd, the police held me back, forcibly. I tried to get one of them to pay attention to me.

"Sir" He ignored me. I tried again, louder.-"SIR," he glanced around. "I think they want me down on the dock. Something about a body on my boat"

It took several attempts to convince him I was wanted on the pier. Finally he barked something into his radio and got permission to let me and my bike through.

My next hurdle was a barricade of yellow tape at the entrance to the docks and a few more policemen. I finally spotted my friend (friend?) from the previous night and caught his eye. He nudged the cop next to him and nodded towards me. The cop had me brought over.

"This the guy you're waiting for?"

Ignoring the cop he glowered at me and said, "It's about time you got here! Get the hell over to that cop by your boat and tell him what happened."

"But I don't know anything about a body," I started.

"Shut the hell up and talk to the cop."

CHAPTER 2

Most of the group around the boat had their backs to me as I approached them.

"Sergeant," I called out. He whipped around.

"Who the hell are you? What the hell're you doing down here? Somebody get this kid out of here." Was the sergeant's greeting.

"It's my boat" I replied.

"Your boat? Then who the hell's the dead guy and what the hell is he doing on your boat?"

"It isn't really my boat."

"You just said it was. Make up your mind."

"Well, I put it here, but I don't own it. I just ferried it up from San Diego for the owner last night."

One of the other police said "he's the guy Smitty said was his alibi."

The sergeant immediately bristled. "So you're in this with Smitty, I should've guessed. You part of the Devils?"

"I don't even know what the Devils are."

"Don't give me that crap. You're a friend of his and you don't know about the Devils?"

The cop that'd brought me over said, "Smitty said he just met him last night when he sailed in."

The sergeant again, "You just brought this boat here last night? Where from"

"Like I said before, direct from San Diego."

The sergeant wanted me to tell him the whole story, about how I'd been hired to bring the boat up and who owned it. I didn't tell him about my suspicions about the boat owner or about his bruises and bandages.

"Where'd you go after you left the boat and are there any witnesses to prove where you were?"That scared me.

When I told him about leaving the note with the big guy with the pony tail, he didn't believe me.

"You expect me to believe a cock and bull story like that? You drive a big Harley like him? How long've you been in the gang?" Question after question.

The entire time the cop was quizzing me, the motorcycle guy was glaring at me over the cop's shoulder. Geez, here I was, literally caught between a rock and a hard place, and only a half hour before I'd been happily sleeping my cares away at home.

"Honest to God, it's true."

"You're telling me you left the boat last night and it was locked up and you never came back and you never met Smitty before last night?" he said in a tone of disbelief while his eyes drilled through me.

"Yes sir."

"I think that's bullshit. Let's see if you recognize the body," the sergeant finally said.

I'd never seen a murdered body before and would just as soon have skipped the opportunity, but the cop kept a firm hand on me, pushing me toward the cockpit.

Once he had me where he wanted me, he pulled the blanket away from the face and, surprise, I did know him. I took a closer look to be sure.

"That's the guy who hired me to sail the boat up here,"

Another long pause. "So you're telling me you had a connection to this guy in San Diego and now you're both up here and he's dead and you're mixed up with a known criminal and you had nothing to do with it?"

"Yes sir."

"You think I'm some kind of an idiot?"

He turned to the cop that'd brought me down and said, "I think he killed the owner in an argument about his fee. Cuff him and take him up with pony tail."

The cop grabbed my wrist and painfully twisted it in a rough way that made me fall to my knees. As I fell he put his knee in my back, yanked my other hand behind me and put the cuffs on.

I was in a lot of pain. It felt like he'd dislocated my shoulder.

I complained. "What the hell?"

"Shut the fuck up. You want special treatment? You're gonna get it." With that he shoved his hand under my arm, pulled me up to a standing position and dragged me off the pier.

"Clear the way, clear the way," he yelled. He obviously was enjoying my pain as he frog walked me up the ramp.

I noticed a number of people taking pictures; people were yelling "who's that?" "Is he the murderer?" "Are you arresting him?"

I stumbled and the audience quickly retreated. The officer kept saying "no comment, no comment." I assumed that my picture would be in the evening papers.

Back up on land I found myself standing next to the motorcycle guy. He wasn't looking too happy. I hadn't noticed until then that he had his hands behind him, as in handcuffed, just like me. He also had a uniformed policeman standing behind him, with his hand on his gun butt. The crowd had formed a large open circle around the three of us. Even knowing I was innocent I felt guilty.

Turning so I could see the cuffs, he said, "Just my luck that goddamn sergeant in charge hates my guts. First thing he says when he got here was that he's sure I'm involved in some way, that he's gonna take me down. Hadn't even looked at the body yet when he slapped the cuffs on me. I don't need this shit," he continued. "What the hell've you got me into?"

"I haven't the slightest—" I started, when he interrupted me again.

"So what'd you tell the cop?"

I told him that I'd identified the dead guy and that it was the boat owner. Then I asked him how the body had been discovered.

"One of the live aboard's that'd gotten up early to take a leak." He paused, stabbed me with his eyes for a minute, then said,

"The dead guy's the boat owner? The guy that hired you?" Another pause. "You're in this up to your ears, aren't you?"

"All I did was deliver the boat and leave," I tried to tell him. "I didn't have anything to do with whatever's happened since."

"Nuts to that," he said. "It's your boat, your owner. Sure as hell, you're involved. No wonder he cuffed you. Did he say he was arresting you?"

"Arrest me? God no. I told him I was in bed all night and my landlady would probably tell him that."

"You sleep with your landlady?"

"No, no. She's old, like eighty or so. Her room's below mine and she can't sleep at night. She hears everything. If I sneeze she shows up with a Kleenex. He just said he had more questions."

"That's not much of an alibi, but it's better than mine. Slept alone on the boat all night. That damn Horning's gonna use that against me, last thing he told me," he went on, "was that he was going to use this murder to put me away somehow. I don't think he can hold me, no way. As soon as these cuffs are off, you and me are gonna compare notes and try to figure out what's happened." Then he added, "Before the freaking sergeant railroads me."

The last thing I wanted to do was spend any time with this neanderthal. He was big, he had a gang, he looked dangerous and he might be a murderer.

"Do you think he'll arrest us?"

"Horning? Hell yes. He always goes off half cocked. What'd he say to you?

"He said he thought I probably murdered him. He thought we had a fight over getting paid."

"Did you?"

"No, no. Like I said, I was in bed all night. I can't go to jail, I gotta see if I have any jobs lined up."

"Horning'll probably try to book us, but he ain't got any evidence, just a bunch of suppositions. We'll get right out. But forget about your damn jobs, you're coming with me."

"I can't."

"I wasn't asking. I'm *telling* you what you and me are gonna do as soon as the cuffs come off. Get it?" Again the threatening growl.

I'm standing next to him, handcuffed, surrounded by police. He's bigger'n me and has a gang. I didn't argue. I figured I'd go along with him 'til the first chance I had to split. I nodded.

"As soon as some brass gets here, they'll probably overrule the asshole sergeant and let us go, you'll see."

We stood around for a couple of hours watching a number of both uniformed and non-uniformed police come and go. Finally a black and white van pulled up and the body bag was loaded into it. By that time a gaggle of reporters were trying to get past the yellow tape. Even a TV helicopter was hovering overhead.

Shortly after, the Sergeant came up off the pier and told the cop holding us to take us in. Speaking to my pigtailed friend he said,

"Smitty, I got you now. I'm taking you and your buddy in on withholding evidence in a murder case and resisting arrest charges."

Before I could object, Smitty (I'd deduced that was his name) let out a roar, "Horning, you son of a bitch, you know damn well I didn't murder no one, and neither one of us resisted nothing'"

The sergeant sneered, "Prove it" and to the cop said, "Book 'em."

The cop read us our rights and shoved us into the back seat of a police car. He had trouble with Smitty because he was so big. When the cop put his hand on top of Smitty's head to push him in it was a struggle. He wasn't made for the normal car sedan.

Smitty was fuming mad. For a while he just glared at the back of the drivers head. Finally he turned to me and whispered some questions.

"Did they tell you how he was killed?'"

"Yeah, they said he'd been shot."

Smitty said, "That's what they told me, too. They wanted to know if I owned a 9 millimeter semi-automatic. They were pretty sure of the gun used, they said, 'cuz the bullet went clean through him. Said the slug wasn't in the boat, and they were gonna search underwater and see if they could find it. Lots of luck to them," he continued, sarcastically. "There's so much old metal and junk down there, underneath these old boats, they'll never find a single bullet. Though I wouldn't be surprised if they found hundreds of them."

Still handcuffed, we were marched into the police station and a jailer had us searched and relieved of all our personal items. Nobody asked us anything.

A jailer took our thumb prints, asked us if we had a special medical problems or were members of any gangs and put us into what Smitty said was a holding cell.

"What was that all about," I asked Smitty.

"We ain't been booked yet, all that was just preliminary stuff."

"What about the gang question?"

"They don't want a turf war to start in a holding cell. They'll separate gang members." He paused, "You got any priors?"

"Arrests?"

"Yeah, you got any?"

"No, nothing."

Two hours went by before the jailer showed up again. This time a full set of prints were taken. We were booked under suspicion of murder and resisting arrest. I was numb with fear. I'd never been in jail before for anything. I felt that my life was being taken away from me. I had no control over what was happening and nowhere to turn.

They read us our rights and searched us thoroughly again, including a cavity search. After that we were led to a dormitory and told that we had a right to make one phone call.

Smitty said, "Congratulations, you're now in jail."

"You know why you're here?" he whispered.

"I haven't the slightest," I began and he interrupted me.

"Keep you're voice down. Some of these guys might be snitches. The reason you're here? It's because, like you said, Horning has a theory that you did it. He'd told the desk sarge that it looked simple to him. His theory was that the dead guy hires you in San Diego and tells you he'll meet you here and pay you. Up here you two get in an argument over the bill and in a fit of anger, the owner pulls a gun. You probably wrestled over it. You're younger and stronger. You get the gun and kill him. Maybe it was an accident but sure as hell, you did it. And you know what? it sounds reasonable to me too. I know sure as hell I didn't do it. Anyway, Horning said that amounted to probable cause and he could arrest you."

"I didn't kill anybody. He'd already paid me. Before I left San Diego."

"Can you prove that?"

"Yeah, I got a receipt."

"Show me."

"The Sergeant's got it; he got the owners address off it."

"You're dead. That piece of paper'll never see the light of day. Not with Horning running the case, he's crooked'er than a corkscrew. As far as I'm concerned, I think there's a good chance you did it."

"I didn't. I was in bed when you called."

"Don't prove nothin'. Look, I've had lots of run ins with Horning before. He's gonna make it as rough as he can on us. He's a vindictive prick and right now we're at his mercy. A couple of years ago he kept me hidden in a jail cell for two weeks before I could get an attorney to get me out. You got an attorney to call?"

I realized I didn't. Who the hell could I phone? Not my parents, they wouldn't have the slightest idea of what to do. It began to sink in that I was really a murder suspect. No alibi, no friends, no money, I may end up in prison for something I didn't do.

"What about bail," I asked.

"You don't know from nothin' do you," he said. "You don't get bail until after you're charged with the crime. We're stuck in here until Horning convinces an investigator that there's enough evidence to justify charging us. He'll probably take his own sweet time to do that; we may be here several days.

"So what do we do?"

"We wait. I called my guys, so I'll have someone working for me. I don't know about you. In the meantime, pick out a cot and make yourself as comfortable as you can, this is home for a night or two at least. You better stick close to me to be safe. You blue eyed, young looking blondes look pretty attractive to some of these guys.

I looked around. There were nine guys in the dorm, including us. About 12 double decked cots and one toilet and wash basin. Several of the guys looked dangerous, tattoos and attitudes. I thought I'd stick as close to Smitty as I could and hope for the best. Nobody spoke to us. I took a top bunk above Smitty, crawled up, covered up and tried to think.

Eventually I fell asleep and had horrible dreams. In my dream I'd been convicted of murder and was facing execution. I woke up early covered with sweat. Quietly I looked over the side of my bunk to see if Smitty was still there. He was, laying on his back arms crossed behind his head, wide awake, looking at me.

"You look like shit." He greeted me.

"I feel like shit and frankly I'm scared."

"Relax. You gotta go with the flow or you'll go nuts in here. There's nothin' you can do until you face the arraignment. Unless you got someone to call."

The day went by very slowly. We had some old tattered magazines and paperbacks to read and nothing else. I couldn't get interested in anything, my mind kept returning to my quandary.

Early mid afternoon the jailor came in took Smitty and me out of the dorm. No explanation to either of us just walked us over to a courtroom. As we entered I saw lieutenant Horning in the back of the room, arguing with a guy in a suit. As we were brought in the guy in the suit left Horning and walked up to the judge.

"What's going on?" I whispered to Smitty.

"I don't know', but he's from the D.A.'s office."

The judge conferred with the district attorney for a moment or two with his hand over the microphone and then turned in our direction and said,

The investigator from the district attorneys office has concluded that there's insufficient evidence to hold or charge Mr. Smith, therefore direct that he be released from custody under penal code 849b without charges.

For a moment, I thought I was free.

"Mr. Alton will be returned to his cell and held under the original charges, pending further investigation."

It took a second for what he said to register. I was going back to the cell, alone without my protector.

Smitty spoke to me as they were returning his valuables. "Be careful, I'll get you out."

Be careful? My protector leaving shortly after he'd warned me about the possible sexual tastes of some my cellmates? I had no idea how to accomplish that but had little time to worry about it as they hustled me out of the courtroom and back to the cell.

"Where's your buddy?" was my greeting. The jailer answered them. "He's out," he volunteered, shoved me into the cell, slammed the door and left.

"Now what?" I thought. I sidled to a front corner of the cell and slid to the floor, hoping they'd ignore me. They didn't.

Luckily for me, Smitty had been partially wrong. They didn't want my rectal virginity, they wanted my clothes.

The mean one, the one with all the tattoos admired my jacket in a very direct way.

"Gimme' your jacket!"

I gave it to him, along with my favorite jeans and began to shiver, sitting in my underwear on the cold cement floor. I was afraid to move, to call attention to myself. I spent the night like that, outnumbered nine to one. The jailer came by several times, shone a light on me and chortled.

Finally dawn came, and the lights. Guards showed up and didn't leave, I felt a little safer. None of the guards commented on my semi nudity. I ignored the MacDonald's-like muffin served to us for breakfast and clung to the bars, hoping for reprieve.

Mid morning I was yanked out of the cell, led to the charging desk and had my papers returned.

"What about my clothes?" I demanded.

One of the jailers disappeared for a few minutes and then returned with my jacket and jeans. Nobody commented about their absence.

"You're free, get out of here."

Out in front, Smitty was waiting for me on a motorcycle, along with a couple of other bikers.

"Get on the bike with Red," Smitty ordered, pointing to the tall red headed biker. "We need to hash this thing out. Either you murdered the guy or you're gonna help me find out who did and you're not getting out of my sight until I find out which."

I got mad. "Dammit' Smitty, I need to go home. I need a shower and clean clothes. My cellmates stole my clothes and wore them all night. I got 'em back but they're filthy. You may be used to spending a night in jail, but I'm not. I have to check my mail and my phone. You can get along without me for a few hours."

"Hey Red, the kids got a little spunk." Then to me, "Seems to me you're marooned with us, we got the wheels. Here's what's gonna happen. First you come with us. You can clean up at the warehouse. Then I'm going to quiz you about this dead guy and then we'll see about you going home. If you do go home, one of the gang's going with you. You're mine until I get Horning off my tail, got it?"

First I'm a captive of the cops; accused of murder, now Smitty and his gang won't let me go. They're taking me to a warehouse? I desperately need to figure out a way to get away from this gang.

CHAPTER 3

Red told one of the guys to double up with another guy; he had to use his bike to take me to the warehouse. The cycle he pushed me toward was huge. I'd never been on a motorcycle before, and I wasn't wild about getting on this one. He casually mounted it and told me to climb aboard behind him.

I did, feeling like a big jerk. I didn't know what to do with my feet or hands. Reaching around he grabbed one foot and shoved it into a metal stirrup and told me to do the same with the other foot.

"Wrap your arms around me and hold on." Easier said than done. His chest was so massive I couldn't reach all the way around him. Speaking into the middle of his back, I told him so.

"Shut up and hang onto my pockets." Concise and to the point.

He kick-started the engine, rolled the bike forward a couple of inches, nonchalantly booted the kickstand off the ground, let the clutch in and we were off. I had no idea where he was taking me, but I was going. It was a little like being on a bicycle – except for the acceleration. Actually, it wasn't at all like being on a bike. I really had to hang on. Every time he turned his head his ponytail swiped my face.

Riding along my brain was trying to catch up with my body. Kidnapped on a motorcycle with a motorcycle gang chief, without a clue as to where we were headed, my employer's been murdered and I'm a suspect in a murder case.

On the face of it, I suppose it could make it a lot of sense to a cop. 'Course I knew it wasn't true, but others might not. It seemed like the sergeant was locked in on Smitty and me, and ignoring the facts. If it wasn't for the D.A.'s office dismissing the charges on Smitty, I might still be in jail. He hadn't talked about the murder at all in jail, just whispered that the place was probably bugged. As far as I was concerned, in spite of his protestations of innocence, my driver made a much better suspect than I did.

I'd heard a lot about motorcycle gangs, 'specially here in Oakland. From what I'd heard they'd be much more capable of murder than a boat bum. Jesus, I wondered, is this guy the murderer? Is he taking me someplace to murder me?"

I got a quick answer to one of my questions. We went about a couple of dozen blocks and pulled into a warehouse full of motorcycles and a lot of guys in leather jackets and boots. Smitty parked his bike with the others, threw his leg over, walked to the gang and left me sitting on the rear seat, all by my lonesome.

Now he was mad. "Fat lot of good you guys were. Me and the kid here sat in Horning's stinking jail all night and you guys didn't do nothin'?"

A chorus of denials. "We sure as hell did, Smitty," one guy replied. "Wasn't nothin' we could do last night, they wouldn't let us in to see you. But we showed up this afternoon as soon as we heard about the arraignment and we had your attorney on the way."

He seemed mollified. "Okay, listen up. We're all going' up to my place, including the kid here." Grabbing me by the arm, he shoved me toward Red. "Red's gonna take you up to my house on his bike." Not a request, an order. He tells Red to fit me out with a helmet.

"Where'd you come from? And how come I'm taking you up to his house?"

"Do I call you Red?"

"Everyone else does, why should you be different? So why am I taking you up to his house?" He handed me a helmet and led me to a bike.

"Red, I don't really know. We're both under suspicion for murder and he says he thinks I did it. He says he won't let me go home and he asked someone named Red to take me someplace. What do you know?"

"What murder?"

"Some guy down on the docks, your sergeant's trying to pin it on Smitty. And me," I added.

"Horning? That'll be a bunch of BS then."

"I hope to God you're right, he's got me roped into it too. Smitty says we're in this together, that's why he's dragging me along."

"Sweet Jesus, that's a load. You and Smitty against Horning."

In an abrupt change of subject, he turned to me and smiling, said, "Bet you can't figure why they call me Red." I figured this was a kind of standing joke. Everything about him was red. Orangey-red hair, same color small mustache, even his arms looked red. When I looked a little closer, I could see fine red hair on his arms making them look red. His complexion was red. The only things not red were his blue eyes. I'm no expert, but he didn't look like what a biker should look like, not to me.

He turned out to be a real nice guy, Red did. A retired mechanic at an auto plant, he spent a lot of time with the gang, but went home each night to his wife and family.

He took me over to his bike and told me to do exactly the same with him as I had coming over on Smitty's bike. He wanted to know what my name was.

"Casey," I told him.

"Last name?"

"First."

"Nickname?"

"Nope. That's my name."

"Like in Casey Stengel?" I immediately liked him. Not many people remembered Ol' Stengel,' the legendary baseball coach.

"Ever heard of Casey at the Bat?" I asked. "Of course" he replied. "You're named after Casey at the bat?"

I told him how my dad loved baseball and how he'd memorized the poem. And that'd been where my name came from. "Last name's Alton," I said finally.

"I'll call you Case," he announced and climbed on his Harley. I climbed on behind him. It was much easier than it'd been with Smitty. Red was much, much thinner than Smitty and I could reach around him easily. Also, Red didn't have a ponytail to tickle my face.

I'd been hearing the guys refer to themselves as devils and hogs. I asked Red about it. He said the club name was "The Oakland Devils," and that they sometimes called themselves hogs because the type of cycle they drove was sometimes called a hog.

Like I said, Red seemed like a nice enough guy, but I was still worried. Looks are sometimes deceiving. Hanging around the waterfront, I'd heard of this motorcycle gang. Not a bunch to fool around with. In fact, downright dangerous. The kind of outlaws I'd always tried to avoid. But I had no choice, they had me.

I asked him about Smitty. "Is he dangerous?"

"You bet. Don't get on the wrong side with him. He can be dangerous as hell. If you really cross him your life ain't worth a plugged nickel."

Accused of murder, handcuffed, jailed and kidnapped by a psychopath with a murderous gang of devils. What more could happen?

CHAPTER 4

We took off with several other bikers, headed generally toward the Oakland hills, further and further away from my home. They were all traveling relatively sedately, probably trying to not attract attention. After a while the bikers started peeling off in different directions. Finally it was just us, heading toward the hills.

We wound round and round the crooked streets of the Oakland foothills. Suddenly Red came to a stop and killed the engine.

"From here on we coast," he said.

"Coast?"

"Yeah, coast!" he answered. As if it was a stupid question.

I was completely mystified as we coasted silently down a short hill, then turned into a driveway and an open garage.

As we climbed off the bike, Red told me why coasting in was required. Smitty had an agreement with the neighbors. They knew he was a biker, with a lot of biker friends. He'd gone to them first, before he bought the place, trying to nip any problems before they arose. He and all his friends would coast in and out so as not to disrupt the peace and quiet of the neighborhood, he promised them.

"So far its working and it's been a couple of years," Red said.

Quite a few Devils were already there by the time we arrived, and more kept coasting in.

Red led me to a room behind the garage which looked like the world's largest rumpus room. It had multiple sofas, several TVs, even a small kitchen. The kitchen had the biggest refrigerator I had ever seen. There were lots of sofas and overstuffed chairs, even some recliners, nothing hard. A few bar stools stood facing a small bar, off to one side.

Every guy had a beer in his paws. I did a quick head count. Nine guys, nine beers, plus Red and me. I was thoroughly outnumbered.

Red asked me if I wanted a beer or anything. I settled for a Pepsi, thinking it would be a good idea to keep my wits about me. Red made a general introduction of me to the group, who immediately started kidding me about the Pepsi.

Red smiled, but then told them to lay off of me. "He's Smitty's guest." He told me "grab a barstool, we'll wait for Smitty,"

I was beginning to wonder what had happened to Smitty when he came down the stairs from an upper floor. He walked straight up to me, ignored the rest of the gang, and said, "We need to find out a hell of a lot more about this freaking murder. If you didn't kill him and I didn't, who killed him and why? Was there anything on the boat worth murdering for?"

I decided to tell him about how furtive Mitchell had been in San Diego and about his bruises.

"I think he'd been beaten up by someone. I also think he was trying to keep the boat a secret, he was real careful when we went to it. And something else, he made me promise not to let anyone aboard the boat except me, no matter what."

"So maybe there's something on the damn boat that he was keeping secret?"

"I sure as hell didn't see anything."

"Did you look?"

"Course not. That'd be like rifling through someone's purse. When you deliver the boat to the owner and he finds out you went through his private papers, you get bad publicity. I'd never do that."

"Well la-DE-da for you. How stupid can you be? Suppose he's got a stash of cocaine on board, you don't wanna know about that? I think we better look. There was something on that boat that your owner was murdered for. Think about it."

"I kinda' have. I lived on the darn thing for most of a week and was all over it, stem to stern. I didn't see anything suspicious, 'course, like you said, I wasn't looking for anything either."

"See, that's it. You weren't looking for anything."

CHAPTER 5

Red interrupted him and said, "What the hell happened yesterday. What got your guts in a knot?"

Smitty'd forgotten how pissed he had been when we'd pulled into the warehouse. He hadn't told them anything.

It took several minutes for Smitty to recap everything that had happened since I'd brought my boat into his marina last night. When he got to the part about his being cuffed by the sergeant there were a lot of "who the hell does Horning think he is?" and "screw him" type remarks. Smitty told them to knock it off.

"What we need to do is figure out who did it and why before the sergeant figures out a way to frame me. And Casey here, too. If he's telling the truth he's in as much trouble as I am. If he ain't telling the truth then maybe he murdered the guy and we'll pin it on him."

Turning to me he said, "That clear to you?"

I shrugged my shoulders.

He continued. "I'm not going to tie you up or anything, but we're gonna keep an eye on you twenty four seven. Don't even think about trying to get away. Got it?"

I was beginning to get pissed off by his continuous threats. "For god's sake, how could I get away? I don't know where I am and I don't have any wheels."

"That's the whole idea." He abruptly changed the subject.

"If you didn't do it, then I'm convinced there is – or was – something on the boat that could be the key to the murder. The cops

Have searched it, but I'm thinking that you know boats a hell of a lot better than they do. So you're gonna search it," he said to me.

I'd assumed that he was going to drag me along in a kind of passive role, to clear Smitty maybe, or maybe for ideas or something. Now he wants me to burgle a police crime scene?

"Tell you what we're going to do. I'll sneak you on to the dock and you'll sneak on to the boat and give it a thorough search."

"Isn't that against the law, what if I get caught?"

"Listen, asshole," he said, "Of course, it's against the law. Who cares? Here's what's gonna happen. You'll search and I'll be the lookout. ."

He was silent for a second or two, then announced to all assembled, "Well, that's settled."

Everyone agreed but me, and I was outnumbered, about a thousand to one. On to the life of a burglar.

Smitty told me to go home and get the combination to the boat. "Red'll run you down to your digs. Grab some dark clothes. You and he can meet me at the docks at eleven sharp."

Escape immediately flashed into my mind. Maybe, with only Red watching me I could get away. Trouble was where could I go? Maybe a friend's house? Maybe I could pick up a quick charter and be safe at sea. I'd have to wait and see.

As if could read my mind Smitty told Red, "Don't let him pull any tricks on you, keep a close eye on him."

He had Red deliver me to my apartment at a little after ten that night. Nobody spoke to me all afternoon except to tell me to help myself to some pizzas they'd ordered. I was never out of anyone's sight, even in the bathroom. At my apartment, Red said he'd wait outside.

Smitty'd ordered me to dress in dark clothing. "Think what you'd wear if you were a successful cat burglar." What I often wore on boats should be okay, I thought. Dark jeans, denim jacket, black watch cap. All I needed was to blacken my face and I could pass for a pro.

I tried to figure out a way to escape. I thought about the back door, maybe I could sneak out and get away. Taking a bag of garbage as a subterfuge, with my backpack under my arm, I tiptoed down the stairs to the first floor and the back door. Carefully and quietly I opened it and started to walk through. Suddenly a hand appeared out of the blackness and Red said, "I'll take that for you, where's the garbage can?"

Totally thwarted and outsmarted, I returned to my room and tried to read a recent edition of Latitude 38 while I waited for 11:00 to arrive.

One of the stories in the mag. had some pics of a trip down to Baja. I thought a girl in one of them looked like my ex-girlfriend. I had to rummage up a magnifying glass to make sure it wasn't her.

It wasn't, but it got me thinking about her. We'd grown up together, and everyone, us included, thought we'd eventually tie the knot. We were very close for many years and I was completely loyal to her, having rather old-fashioned ideas about fidelity. Unfortunately it gradually became obvious that my ideas of fidelity were different than hers, and we split. Since then I'd been off girls. I guess the love of my life for the last couple years had been the sea. 'Once bitten, etc.

I tried to read but couldn't concentrate.

Eventually, it was time to go.

CHAPTER 6

As I opened the front door, Red materialized out of the dark and stood beside me. It was really, really dark. It took only a few minutes to get to the dock area, there was a heavy cloud cover, and the short pot holed street leading to the dock itself had no street lights. It was also really, really quiet. The only noise we heard was from a cat I flushed that snarled and spat at me. He apparently wasn't accustomed to sharing his midnight haunts with anyone.

When we got to the docks I turned off my flashlight and started waiting for Smitty. No sooner was the light off than a dark lump next to the dock ramp went "psst.". Guess who.

"Let's get going," Smitty whispered. "Red, you stay here. I'm taking him down to the boat.

"Okay," He whispered back. "Watch him; he tried to sneak out the back door at his apartment."

They talked about me like I wasn't there. "That's bull; I was just taking the garbage out."

"Carrying a backpack?"

He had me.

Smitty led the way down the ramp and onto the docks. I noticed lots of noises I'd never noticed before. Every step we took rocked the dock. Squeaks, bumps and splashes followed every step. We sounded like an army. A big army, so much for stealth.

We made it to the boat without causing any alarms to go off or lights to switch on. It was to our advantage that this was a really old, casual dockage. Newer marinas had locked gates at the tops of fancy aluminum ramps leading down to the docks with dock masters on duty around the clock. Some of them had motion detector lighting systems. It would have been much more difficult, if not impossible.

Smitty boosted me up onto the boat and I made my way to the cockpit. Just as I'd imagined, there was yellow police tape all over the hatch. There was another hatch forward of the mast but I knew it was locked from the inside. It was the cockpit hatch or nothing.

The tape was sagging a little, maybe because the night was damp and the tape was stretching. It looked like I might be able to stretch it a little more and wiggle through without breaking anything. I unlocked the hatch, took off my jacket, tossed it over to Smitty and made my way in.

Inside was darker than it had been outside. I couldn't connect the batteries and use the lights – that'd be too noticeable. All I could do was put my hand over the lens of my flashlight and make as complete a search as possible. I didn't know where to start. The whole cabin looked like it had been tossed. Not just searched, really tossed – mattresses ripped open, bunks torn apart, every compartment emptied. Even the bilge had been stirred up. It hurt me to see it. The cabin had been a beauty and I'd left it spic and span.

What knowledge of boats did I have that might help me find something that the cop's ham-handed approach had missed? As I thought of it, it seemed odd that the police had been so ham handed. In the movies they always search carefully and take pictures as they go. This looked like it'd been tossed by someone that didn't care about preserving evidence. Maybe the murderer had come back? Maybe he was still on the boat? The only place he could be was in the forward bunk area, behind a curtain. What should I do? I thought I should get Smitty to say something. Anything. Let the guy in the forepeak know I wasn't alone.

"Smitty, can you hear me? Say something!"

"For Christ's sake, what's going on?"

"Nothing, just wanted to make sure you were there."

Emboldened, I yanked the curtain apart and lit up the forepeak with the flashlight.

Empty. I could get on with the job.

"It wasn't easy to think calmly with the loudly whispered messages like "found anything?" and "hurry the hell up" I kept getting from Smitty.

I tried several spots with no success and was about to give up when noticed something that seemed a little odd to me. A boat hook. To the best of my memory the boat hook had been secured to the cabin top when I left the boat. I remembered because I was struck by how securely it was fastened. If I'd needed it, it would have been difficult to loosen in a hurry.

Now it was lying on the settee. Had the searchers moved it? Why would they have done that? I'd been moving it around in order to search places, now I looked at it carefully. The boat hook was made of aluminum. Just a long tube with a hook fixed to the end of it. I shook it. It didn't rattle but the hook seemed a little wobbly and then came off in my hands. Looking closely I could see the screws that held the hook in place had been removed.

"AHA," I quietly said to myself. From outside, Smitty was still egging me on to hurry. I couldn't see anything inside so I held it upside down and shook it. One piece of paper fell out.

"I got something, I'm coming out."

I stuck the piece of paper in my pocket, wormed my way back out through the yellow tape and handed the piece of paper to Smitty.

He was pissed. "For Christ's sake, this is all you found, a lousy little piece of paper?"

I tried getting a little pissed back at him.

"Look, if you don't think I tried and probably did a better job than the police, then you do it."

Interesting. He cooled down a little.

"Anyway, I got the paper. Maybe that's what you're looking for."

"A single piece of paper? I don't think so." He was silent for a minute then, "Follow me." That's all, just, follow me.

He led Red and me over to his boat. Below decks, lights on, he smoothed the paper out and read it to himself. "Just a bunch of numbers and short notes. Doesn't make any sense to me. Here, you look at it," and he handed it to Red.

Red agreed and handed it to me.

I took one look and immediately knew what it was. Studying at sea, I'd used the same method. It was a list of page numbers and short notes about what was on each page.

"Give me a minute or two; I think there's something worthwhile here. Look, the numbers are listed in numerical order but lots of numbers are missing. I think the numbers are page numbers. I think there was a notebook rolled up in here and Mitchell had made a record of pages he wanted to remember. He was establishing a pattern. Look at the notes after each number. Like the first number on our page, number

2. Right after the number 2 there's a dollar sign and then the number one thousand and there's a name. .Then the next number is 5 and after it is dollar sign 3,000 and another name. It goes on and on like that. My bet is that there was a notebook hidden in the boat hook and Mitchell was reading it and making notes about information on the pages listed."

"Why would anyone do that?" Red asked.

"Yeah, and what could be in the pages that'd be worth killing for? Let me see that page again," Smitty said. After a few minutes, he said, begrudgingly, "It's possible. You might be right. But that doesn't help us much. The paper's just a hint; we need that book to find out what this's all about."

"I think I know what it's all about." I interjected. "Think about it. The paper lists dates, names and amounts. I bet the books a record of blackmail pay off. I bet Mitchell had stolen the book, hidden it in the boathook and hoped that no one knew about his boat. He'd been reading the notebook and making his own notes. Maybe he was trying to blackmail the blackmailer and that's why he was murdered."

"Wait a minute. Why didn't he take the paper along with the book?"

"It was down deep in the hook, maybe it fell out of the book?"

A long silence.

Finally, "I suppose it's possible. That means that the book's gone and we're back at square one."

More silence. Then from Smitty, looking directly at me. "I dunno'. I think that's too convenient for you. I still think you're involved somehow. How do I know you didn't take the book yourself? Maybe you found it on the way up and this's all a smokescreen?"

"Sure. And why would I find this piece of paper and give it to you?"

Red broke the next silence. "That makes sense to me Smitty. And if he didn't do the murder, someone else did. Maybe we can check around and see if anyone else saw anything."

A long silence ensued during which Smitty stared at me. It made me squirm. I was sure he'd decided to toss me to the wolves; it was just a matter of when and how.

Suddenly he looked away from me and jumped to his feet.

"Okay. Here's what we're going to do. First, and at least for now we'll assume someone else murdered Mitchell. But we'll keep young sailor boy here with us at all times until something turns up that clears him. No exceptions."

Turning to me he said, "You try escaping again, we'll find you and you'll be in deep shit. Got me?"

CHAPTER 7

"If you didn't do it then I'm thinking it wasn't an accident that the owner and his killer were both at the boat at the same time." Smitty said.

"Too much of a 'coincidence. The murderer had to have been waiting around for a day or two, expecting the boat to show up. Then he'd have had to wait even longer for the owner to go on board, find whatever it was and start to leave."

He turned to me. "Okay, sailor boy, where could he do that and not be noticed?"

I thought for a minute or two and asked, "Could he have hidden on one of the other boats?"

"Not possible," he said derisively. "I've been on my boat for the last several days. I would've noticed any strangers. But that gives me an idea. He had to be somewhere he could keep an eye on the docks. Someone must have noticed him. It's a pretty tight-knit community down here, stranger's would've be noticed."

"I dunno; there's no other place he could hide, no empty buildings or anything."

"Well, assuming the guy had been driving, he could have been sitting in a car waiting for the owner to show up in his car. There's only a couple of places he could have done that."

Red said, "I don't see how that can help us, whoever he might have been, he's long gone by now." and poured us each a cup of freshly brewed coffee he'd been nursing along.

"Ah, but it does," Smitty responded. "Let's see, there's only two streets leading to the docks. If I wanted to cover both streets, there're a number of places I could park and keep an eye on both of 'em. If he was here for more than a few hours, somebody must have seen him.

What we need to do is ask every business within a several block area if they've noticed any strangers recently."

Red looked at me and said, "Sounds like an awful lot of work without much chance of success to me."

"Smitty wheeled around and asked, "You got a better idea?"

He didn't.

"Look," he said, "I know it's a long shot, but it might work. And, we've got the crew to do it. In the morning they can canvas that whole area in no time, fan out and cover the whole damned neighborhood before the days out." He glared at both of us, daring us to argue with him.

After a moment he said "well, that's settled then," and told Red, "You go on home; I'll keep an eye on Mr. Casey here on the boat tonight."

I was still being treated like cattle. I wasn't asked for my opinion on anything, they talked about me like I wasn't there and ordered me around like they owned me. Nobody asked me to stay the night; I was just informed that I was.

He rustled up some blankets for me and I spent the night on the settee. I was fairly comfortable sleeping in my clothes, wrapped up in blankets, on somebody else's boat. Hell that was about what I did every night on deliveries.

The next morning dawned clear and bright. I know 'cuz Smitty was shaking me awake just as dawn broke. He told me to freshen up. That meant running up to the onshore heads, using the facilities and washing up. For a minute I thought about just keeping on running and getting away, 'til I remembered that Smitty had my wallet. No tooth brush, no comb, no underarm deodorant, I wouldn't be able to "freshen up" very much.

Just as I got back from the head he returned with two guys. I recognized them from the day before so we didn't need any introductions. Smitty said they were live aboard's too. I couldn't remember their names but we'd at least met. Smitty spent a few minutes bringing them up to date on what we'd done last night, then briefed them on his new plan. As soon as they understood what he wanted them to do, he got the ball rolling.

"Okay. You two get back to your boats and call all the guys. Get 'em to meet me at the warehouse by – let's say nine-thirty. Most of the businesses 'round here don't keep real regular hours, so there's really no point in starting much before ten. And tell the guys that they're probably gonna be tied up most of the day. They'll probably have to wait 'til noon or later before some of the businesses are open. That'll give us time to grab a quick bite on the way over to the warehouse. Get going. We'll wait for you over at the restaurant."

"You're gonna ride with Me." he told me. "It's breakfast time."

Suddenly I was more than ready for some eats. The four of us went to a mom and pop restaurant on the way to the warehouse and had a truck driver's breakfast. It wasn't a tourist spot. Most of the customers at this hour were either truckers or from around the docks. Almost everyone knew Smitty. He took the opportunity to ask if anyone had noticed any strangers hanging around over the last few days, but got no nibbles.

When we got to the warehouse, Smitty said that most of the guys were there and that we should get going.

"I want every single business, house, store and anything else in the area canvassed. I want you to ask if they've seen anyone or anything at all suspicious in the last few days. If some of the places aren't open yet, keep going back 'til there's someone there to ask. Don't come back here till you've covered every place, unless you get something. What I'm 'specially looking for is a man, maybe a woman, who was kinda' just hanging around for a couple of days. Anything out of the ordinary."

With that he told them to huddle up and decide who was going where, on their own. There were over a dozen Devils there. I felt like Smitty was exaggerating – it couldn't take long to cover the area he'd outlined, not with this much manpower.

Turned out, I was wrong and Smitty was right. Lots of the businesses weren't open yet and the gang had to go back numerous times to finally catch someone in. But by early afternoon most of the guys had returned, empty handed.

The guys kept coming in and going back out, trying to catch the businesses when they opened.

Because I came with Smitty, I was pretty well accepted. No one volunteered much information about Smitty, except that he'd been in the gang forever, and even though he'd "retired" from active leadership of the gang, he was without question "the boss."

I still thought it was a waste of time to canvas that particular neighborhood. Most of the businesses down there were borderline. Just making a living, not very neighborly. I couldn't see them volunteering much.

CHAPTER 8

Some of the guys were coming in saying that this was a huge waste of time. Smitty pushed them to keep going.

A little after one thirty, one of the guys returned saying, "I think I got something."

"Let's have it," Smitty said.

Expectations weren't very high. So far, they'd been coming in with nothing but disappointments.

"Okay," the guy said, "like you told me, I kept going back to my places over and over, and finally it paid off. About a half hour ago, I went back to that little restaurant over on the next street and found the owner in."

"Get to the point" Smitty said.

"Okay, okay. The owner said that a guy he'd never seen before had eaten dinner there a couple of times within the last day or so. What struck him as odd was that, after he'd finished his dinner, the guy had ordered sandwiches and a thermos of hot coffee to go each evening."

"That's it! He had to be sitting in his car all night." from Smitty. "What else did he notice?"

"Nothing else, just the dinners, lunches, and coffee to go"

"Bullshit," Smitty barked. "I'll bet my bottom dollar he knows more than he's telling you. I want to talk to him."

With that he grabbed my arm and jumped on his motorcycle with me close behind. He singled out a couple of the Devils and told them to follow him. On the way, Smitty said, "I'll get something out of that restaurant owner if I have to beat the shit out of him to get it."

At the restaurant, a whole new Smitty emerged. Nice as pie, he told the owner, a Chinese guy, he needed to know anything and everything he had noticed about the stranger.

At first the owner said he'd told everything to our guy earlier in the day. But Smitty kept pushing. Finally he asked if he'd noticed the car the guy was driving. It turned out he had, but it wasn't of much help. A dark blue sedan, that's all he knew. He did say that he thought he'd seen the same car parked up at the corner several times.

Smitty nodded. "That's the place I'd have parked to keep an eye on both streets," he said. "Did he use a credit card?" No dice. The guy paid cash, no charge records. It was beginning to look like a blind alley, except it kind of proved Smitty's theory.

But just as we were halfway out the door, the owner said he remembered something else. He said he'd tried to be friendly to the guy because of his patronage. He'd asked him if was going to locate in the area. The guy, he now remembered, had said he was just passing through – and was staying at the Seaside Inn, just down the street.

Again Smitty nodded. "I know where it is. Not much of a place. Sure doesn't attract the tourist set." The owner agreed.

We got as complete a description of the stranger as we could. Another ride on the back of Smitty's bike. Smitty did know where the place was, and it only took a few minutes to get there.

A half block from the place, Smitty hand signaled to the other guys to slow down and make a quiet approach. He yelled over his shoulder to me that he knew the owners, that it was a family run business. He didn't want to scare them.

In the parking lot he told the guys to stay outside, that he and I would go in alone. He wanted them close by in case the guy we were looking for was still there.

We went in, Smitty taking the lead.

A woman I'm sure the Devils would describe as "a tough old broad" was manning the desk. She and Smitty exchanged nods of common recognition, then Smitty launched into a story, saying we were worried about an acquaintance of ours who'd been staying at their place recently.

"We had lunch with him a couple of times at the restaurant over near the docks. We were supposed to meet him again, but he never showed."

"What's his name?" she replied.

"See, that's part of the problem. The only thing he told us was that his nickname was Blacky."

"Gosh, I don't see how I can help you without a name."

"How about a description? Would that help?"

"Maybe, normally, but I've only been here since noon today. My brother's been on duty the last five days."

"Can we talk with him? We're really worried about Blacky."

"Will's not here now," she told us, scratching her mop of gray hair. "He's gone home. He's probably in bed by now."

"Could you please try and get him on the phone. I know it's a nuisance, but we really need to find him. I can describe him over the phone to your brother, or you could, and he might recognize him. We could at least find out if he just checked out or what. Please?" Smitty had a whole repertoire of ways to be persuasive. She relented and phoned her brother.

Good thing for us, he was still up and wasn't upset by the call. She described the guy to her brother, and he immediately knew who we were talking about.

"He says you must mean Mr. Richards," she told us. She listened for a moment while her brother filled her in. He left yesterday," she repeated. "He never signed out, just never showed up after night before last."

"You tell Will we really appreciate it," Smitty said. She passed along the message and hung up.

Smitty thanked her over and over and then said, "Just to be sure, can you check his address for us?"

She said, "Sure," and went into a drawer, dug out his registration card and handed it over the counter to Smitty. No way could he have gotten that type of information from a Holiday Inn, only a mom and pop type operation like this. Smitty jotted the info into a notebook, then handed the card back.

Now he had his full name, address, phone number, even his credit card number. If it wasn't all phony, he had him.

CHAPTER 9

Smitty used his cell phone to call the warehouse and tell them we'd found the guy's name. "He lives in Richmond." He gave them the address.

"See if anyone had a friendly cop in his pocket and find out if the address we got is real and for chrissakes, don't let them know why we're asking, Make up some good reason why you want to know. Maybe like he owes you money."

It only took a few minutes to get back to the warehouse, where we found all the Devils waiting for us. Smitty said, "It's only three-thirty. I think we've got enough time to get out to Richmond and see if we can catch this guy!"

Just then one of the guys came out from a back room and said, as far as the cop he called could find out, the address was real and up to date.

"Okay," Smitty said, "Let's go!"

"Hold it, Smitty. Not so fast," said another guy. "We might have a little problem."

"Yeah? What's that?"

"There's a cop car been parked around the corner. It looks like your friend the sergeant's keeping an eye on us. We need to check on him before we take off."

"Shit," Smitty said. "He's really out to get me. Somebody go check."

It didn't take long for a couple of the guys to take a stroll around the block and report back to us that they didn't see any cop cars at all. If there had been a cop keeping an eye on Smitty, he seemed to be gone.

Once more, Smitty said we should get going. He told the gang to follow him to Richmond. He said he had an idea about grabbing the guy, but needed to check something on the way.

"Casey," he barked, "If you can ride a bicycle you can ride a motorcycle."

"What? Whoa! Wait a minute." I started ticking off the first reasons that came into my head. "I don't have any experience, I don't have a license, I don't have a helmet and actually, I'm not even that good on a bicycle." That covered it pretty thoroughly, I figured, but Smitty wasn't buying.

Ignoring me entirely, Smitty turned to another of his gang and said,

"Dave, give him a quick lesson and bring him along. Keep an eye on him; he tried to get away once." The guy grabbed my elbow and told me his name was Dave. He was the one who'd asked me how I knew Smitty, earlier in the day.

I told him I wasn't kidding. "I don't know anything at all about driving a motorcycle. I've never even been on one as a passenger until yesterday."

Somehow, I had to get out of this.

Ignoring me entirely he said, "First thing, you don't drive a motorcycle, you ride it. Hell," he added with an annoying smirk, "I taught my wife to ride in one lesson. If I can teach her in one lesson, I can teach anyone. That's probably why Smitty put you in my tender lovin' care. Don't worry about it." Easy for him to say. "Really, Smitty's right. If you can ride a bike you can handle a hog. I'll get you started, and then you just follow me and do everything I do. No problem, I promise."

He told me to follow him into a back room, unlocked a huge locker and trundled out what looked to me like the mother of all motorcycles. He assured me that it was a "kiddy bike," that it'd be a snap for me. He showed me where the throttle and brakes were and cautioned me against giving it too much throttle too fast. Okay, I was accustomed to brakes on the handlebars, but throttles?

"All right," he said, "climb aboard." Actually it was easier to get settled on the motorcycle than on a bike. It was lower to the ground than the seat on my bike. That helped.

When I was settled, he showed me the clutch and said I could start the engine as long as I was in neutral even though the kick stand was still down. That made sense to me. I was looking for a kick starter when he told me that this model could be started just by turning the key, just like a car.

I switched on the engine and Dave told me I was a natural. Then he said, "The rest is easy. Like I said, just watch me and do what I do." With that he straightened his bike up, took the weight off the kickstand, used one leg to balance the bike and kicked the stand up. I did the same.

He let his clutch out and smoothly went a few yards and stopped. Gradually, oh so gradually I let out the clutch, lurched forward a couple of yards slammed on the brakes and almost hit Dave.

"Perfect" Dave said, "Let's go!!"

And we went! He was smooth; I wasn't. Not too bad on the straight-aways, but turning was a real problem. There was so much power, I tended to over-steer. I ended up making a series of short jerky turns instead of the smooth turns that Dave handled easily.

It reminded me of my one attempt at skiing. Every one was "carving turns." My turns were a series of lurches, punctuated by falls. I was doing the same thing now. Not the fall part, at least not yet – the lurching thing.

I flashed onto a line from my dad's and my favorite poem. "The outlook wasn't brilliant for the Mudville nine that day." I didn't think my outlook was too brilliant right then either. The motorcycle was scaring me. I hoped I could somehow stay on the beast till we got to Richmond. Just as I was beginning to think I'd tamed the beast a bit, Dave headed up a ramp and onto the freeway.

At least I wouldn't have to shift now, but Dave was going much faster. Keeping up with him and dodging the other traffic put my heart in my mouth. All I could do was follow and not think. Then he began to weave his way through the traffic. I had a new problem – I couldn't make the turns like he did and kept getting caught behind and between cars. He slowed down to accommodate me, probably remembering what Smitty'd told him about my escaping. He shouldn't have worried. I was so busy trying to avoid getting killed; the thought of escape never entered my mind.

It seemed awfully fast to me. I didn't dare take my eyes off the road to consult my speedometer. Later, Dave told me he was barely crawling along, doing fifty.

Eventually he signaled a move over to the right lane to take an off ramp. I had two lanes to get through in order to take the same ramp, and I made it. Only one driver let out a long blast on his horn and I was off the freeway. One stop at the bottom of the ramp, a left turn on to city streets and I thought the worst was over.

It wasn't. Now I had to start and stop, balancing the bike whenever I stopped at a stop sign or signal. And crossing streets after a stop was really scary. But somehow I was able to keep up with Dave. He did have to stop and wait for me a couple of times, and I did catch him rolling his eyes at one of my more graceful maneuvers, but we made it.

Finally, Dave waved at me and pointed ahead to a Safeway store parking lot where I could see a bunch of the gang gathered together. A couple of them waved at us. I guessed I was supposed to follow Dave into the lot and park.

He did and I didn't. He glided and I crashed. Fortunately I crashed into a bush and didn't do any damage except to my credibility. I got a few snickers but no nasty remarks. I bet Smitty had something to do with that too.

CHAPTER 10

Smitty told the rest of them to hang out here for a while and wait for him to return.

He told me to hop on his bike and asked me if I knew where Point Richmond was.

"Yep, been there lots of times. Why?"

"There's a bike shop there. I need to use his computer. The owner said his place was near an old hotel in the middle of town. Think you can find it?"

I knew approximately where the place had to be.

"Should be a snap, it's really small."

"Have you ever used Google Earth?" Smitty asked me.

"Sure, lots of times."

"Don't they have satellite pics of the earth that you can zoom in on and pick out your own house, like up real close? We do that to Richards' house and we'll know all about it before we even go there, right?"

Before I could reply I heard him mumble to himself. "These young farts think they know so much."

Sure enough, the shop had a computer, and sure enough, Google Earth turned out to be just the ticket. We got pictures of the house, front yard, back yard, side fences, neighboring houses and streets. "Terrific," Smitty said. "We've got enough men to cover all the entrances and exits, probably even the windows." I supposed that one of the men he was referring to was me, but I wished it wasn't.

We zipped back to the Safeway parking lot where Smitty outlined the specifics of the house and assigned one or two guys to each door and window. After making sure that everyone knew exactly where the place was and how to get there, he cautioned them about coasting in.

"We want to surprise him, not scare him," he coached "We'll scare him after we're in."

He told me he wanted me on his bike with him. I think he was afraid I'd lose control again and spoil the whole surprise party. He was probably right.

We coasted up to the place, got off the bike and stood talking to each other as if we were just a couple of locals. The other Devils had stopped a block or so away and were converging on the house from several different directions. I could see them out of the corner of my eye 'cuz I knew what to look for. They were kinda' sauntering, trying to blend in, trying to not be too conspicuous. To me, frankly, they looked like a bunch of elephants in a tea house. We could only hope that our suspect wasn't watching.

After a couple of minutes, as soon as he judged that all the Devils were in place, Smitty surprised me again. He left me on the sidewalk, took Red with him, calmly walked up to the front door and knocked.

Nothing. A minute went by. Smitty was about to knock again when the door opened.

"Yeah? What d'ya want?"

"Mr. Richards?"

"Yeah, that's me."

With that Smitty shoved the door aside, grabbed the guy by his arm and marched him into the house. Richards was tall and skinny, totally unprepared for the two to them, and was easily handled.

After all the preparing and planning it was over in a second. Smitty called the gang in and told them to search the place. In a few minutes they reported back that as far as they could see, there were no guns or weapons of any kind in the house.

Richards was tied to a kitchen chair. Smitty pulled up another chair in front of him, turned it around backwards and straddled it, his well muscled arms crossed across the back. The guy was scared. A gang breaks into your house, ties you up and searches the place. The tattooed leader is huge and strong and treats you like dirt. Who wouldn't be scared?

Smitty stared at the guy for a few minutes and said, "D'ya know who we are?"

"No, sir."

"Ever heard of the Oakland Devils?"

"Yes, sir."

"Well, you're now entertaining the Devils, and we're real unhappy with you!"

"For god's sake, what'd I do?"

"We know you shot that guy on the boat in Oakland, and that it was probably an accident."

I looked at Smitty in surprise. I thought we had pretty well decided it had been a planned murder. Smitty leaned back in the chair, front legs off the floor, the very picture of nonchalance.

"We're pretty sure it was an accident," Smitty continued, "but the police think it was a premeditated murder. Unfortunately for you, the guy was a friend of ours, and the cops have no idea who you are or where you are. Question is: shall we turn you over to the cops, or keep you and you help us find the guy what hired you? Just to sweeten the pot a little, if you help us, we may not be quite so unhappy with you"

It looked to me as if Richards was more scared of the Devils than he was the cops. The Devils were in his house and the cops weren't.

"Look, I'll tell you everything. I've got no loyalty to Carpenter. You're right, it was an accident. Carpenter told me to lay in wait for someone to come onto that boat, no matter how long it took.

Smitty held up a hand, "hold on a minute. Who's Carpenter?

"He's the guy you're after. The guy that hired me. All I was supposed to do was stake out this guy's boat and wait for the owner to show up. He said it should only take a couple of days. I was to follow the guy on to his boat and get whatever papers he had. Carpenter told me, whatever it takes, get the papers. I didn't know the guy was gonna fight. I ended up slugging him. I got what he wanted and ran, I never shot him."

"You work for this Carpenter?"

"Hell, no. He hired me as a private eye. To be honest with you, I'm not really a private eye. I mean I'm not licensed or nuthin'. I never heard of him before this job. Now I wish I'd never heard of him at all. He paid me two grand up front and promised me another two grand when I got the papers. No, I don't work for him. I never even seen the guy."

"What 'did you do with the papers?"

"There wasn't any papers, just a small black notebook. So I took all his identification off him and stuffed them in with the notebook and mailed 'em, like he told me to."

A notebook! I'd told Smitty that's what I thought it might be.

"How do you know Carpenter's name?"

"That's where I outsmarted him. He sent me a big envelope to mail the stuff in. It was addressed to a post office box, but the envelope it came in had his return address on it. No name or nuthin', but as long as I had the address it was easy to get his name. I can prove it to you. I've still got the two grand he sent me when he got the notebook. In fact it's still in the envelope it came in."

Terrific. It looked like we had the name and address of the guy that hired Richards. Smitty still wanted to know what was in the notebook.

"Honest to God, I don't know," he said convincingly. "It was wrapped in brown paper. It felt like a small notebook but I never opened it except to stuff his ID into it."

"You gotta do better than that," Smitty said. "Don't tell me this guy Carpenter sent you down there without telling you some way to ID the right notebook."

"Honest, I'm telling you the truth. He said a small paper-wrapped package. On top of that he, made me swear not to open it, and I didn't. And honest, it was an accident. I really didn't mean to hurt the guy."

That's when Smitty's demeanor abruptly changed. He'd been fairly cordial to Richards up to that point. He stood up and jabbed his finger in Richard's chest. "That's real bullshit, pal. First off, you didn't 'accidentally' club the guy. You shot him in the chest. Secondly, he didn't have a gun. You used your own. Third, it was cold-blooded murder. You deliberately waited for him to get the package out of the boat and then you shot him. We can make a lot of points with the cops by turning you in. What'd you do with the gun?"

Richards broke out in a sweat and started looking evasively around the room. Everywhere he looked there were Devils staring at him.

That *really* scared the guy. Trapped in his home by a dozen or so murderous bikers, threatened with arrest? Premeditated murder's a tough charge. I was thinking that the guy probably had some previous convictions against him, that he'd be up against the third strike law on top of it all. Third time caught and it's automatic jail time or maybe worse.

"What d'ya want? I'll tell you anything I know. Don't turn me over to the cops. Honest, I'd rather take my chances with you guys than the cops."

"What else can you tell us about this guy Carpenter?"

"All I know about him is his name and address. Outside of some rumors. I heard he's a big shot in Sacramento, that he can get things done for a price. That's it."

Smitty was silent for a minute or so, then, "What did you do with the car?"

"What car?"

"You know damn well what car. The car that belonged to the guy you murdered. Don't get cute with us. Trust me; we're way worse news for you than the police'd be. You don't want us for an enemy. Right now you're skating on pretty thin ice."

"It's down there. I was told to drive it a few blocks away and leave it unlocked with the keys in it and it'd probably be stolen."

Smitty shot me a look out of Richards's sight and raised his eyebrows. I thought he was thinking the same as I was. In my mind that definitely made it premeditated murder. Both him and this guy Carpenter. If he'd been instructed to get rid of the car after the deed, that was the only conclusion.

"Okay, that's it then," Smitty said to the rest of the guys. "We're through with this guy but we need to put him on ice somewhere. Anybody got an idea?"

Red spoke up, said that his sister and brother-in-law would be happy to have him as a guest for a few days if there were a few bucks in it for them.

Smitty agreed to that and said, "Let's get the hell outta here." He told Red to use Richard's car to take him to his sister's house.

"Keep him handcuffed to something real solid like a pipe or something. And Red, you stay with your sister and make sure they know this guy's a murderer and they got him locked up secure. Make damn sure! Tell your brother in law to stay in the house and not leave your sis alone with this guy. Tell him I'll make it worth his while.

Then he told me I could take Red's bike back with the gang. He had a lot more confidence in my ability than I did. Red looked kind of stricken. Smitty had a lot more confidence in me than Red did, too.

"What about the bike Casey rode out here?" Red asked.

"Just leave it at my friend's place, we'll get it later."

"Saddle up and meet me at the house," Smitty told everyone. "Red, get there as soon as you can. Sailor boy, you follow me."

The ride back to his house was fairly uneventful. I'm sure he went really slow just for me – or maybe he was more concerned for Red's cycle? At any rate, I was able to coast in without hitting anything. I was thinking I was getting the hang of this thing until Smitty turned around to watch my last half block.

He shook his head. "You could never be a Devil, not riding like that."

CHAPTER 11

"We're in luck," Smitty said, "The address for this guy Carpenter is nearby, up in the hills of El Cerrito. Anybody familiar with El Cerrito enough to know where this street is?" and he gave the address. Nobody did but one of the guys said that most Oakland maps included El Cerrito, or at least part of it.

Sure enough, it was there and the street was pretty easy to find. It was a short street backing up to a golf course, way up in the hill area.

"Now it's gonna get more difficult. We need to find out who this guy is, and what's more, we've gotta find out what was in the package and why it's so freaking important to him. Important enough to get some guy killed."

He continued. "I think this guy Carpenter's guilty of murder. He's the one that told Richards to get the package at all costs. In my book that makes him guilty of murder."

"Why don't we just turn the guy in, after all he confessed." I asked.

"Hell no, are you crazy?" Smitty explained reality to me, patiently, the way you would to a college freshman.

"First off, the damn sergeant's in charge of the case. Every thing'll end up in his hands. Second, he's so biased against us that he wouldn't believe us, no matter what we said or gave him. You know what he'd say? He'd say we planned the whole damn thing ourselves and set Richards up as the fall guy. No way in hell he's gonna listen to us. Best thing we can do is just stay as far away from him as possible."

Smitty stopped and rubbed his head like the subject was giving him a headache.

"And don't forget," he went on, "we've both violated a direct police order by leaving Oakland, so no way we're going to him. What he doesn't know won't hurt him. As far as Richards is concerned, we'll just keep him outta circulation till the time's right. Then we'll see if we can get around the sergeant somehow. Eventually Richard's gonna take the fall."

Smitty thought for a moment. "We need to find a way to get the package and its contents from Carpenter, if we're ever getting to the bottom of this thing. The only way I can think of is to get into his house and search the place. Find the package. I know that sounds crazy but I can't think of anything else. I'm gonna google his address and see where he lives."

A little while later he came back. "I can't tell enough about the place to figure out what we're up against," he told us. "It looks like it backs up to the golf course, but I can't tell where his property ends and the golf course starts. Somebody has to go up there and take a good hard look around to see what's what."

Once again I tried to insert a little reason into the plan.

"Why? Isn't that just asking for more trouble? If this guy is as important as Richards says he is, he'll probably have staff and security up the kazoo. You'll all get caught and thrown in jail for burglary on top of murder."

Everybody ignored me.

Smitty presented a preliminary plan, in two parts. First we needed to find out whatever we could about Carpenter.

The second part was definitely more risky. It involved breaking into the house and searching for private papers, including the missing package. The gang favored this part of the plan more than the first. Actually they were visibly excited about it, rarin' to go.

Smitty brought them back in line.

"We do nothing until the house and all the surrounding properties have been thoroughly cased," he said. "No way we break in to the place without a good plan. We have to find out how many people are normally in the house, and if there's a time when nobody's in the house. If the place is almost empty, you know, just a cook or a cleaning lady – Maybe we can create a diversion that'll get us in."

He singled out Dave and told him to take a small, quiet bike and check out the address in El Cerrito. Dave was to take his time, act casual, like he belonged there.

"Find out what the house looks like, how close the neighbor's houses are and particularly, what the golf course looks like. See if you can get on the course and see what the back of his house and the backyard look like. If you can, talk to a neighbor. Get a feel for how many people are there. Try and find out if they're ever routinely out of the house. Take off, like now!" Dave was up and out the door in a flash.

"Now, you guys, relax. Grab a meal, take a nap, something. We're not doing anything or going anywhere until Dave gets back. Casey, you're staying too, like it or not," Smitty added, just as Red walked into the room.

"Wouldn't put any money on him likin' it," Red said dryly.

I sure a hell wouldn't like it but with Richard's confession, I was off the hook for murder. At least in Smitty's book.

CHAPTER 12

The guys were okay with me. I wasn't part of the gang but Smitty vouched for me. I guessed that kind of made me acceptable. I followed Red up to the kitchen. Most of the guys were already there making all different kinds of sandwiches and drinking beer. I settled for a diet Pepsi and a peanut butter sandwich.

Smitty came in and made a sandwich too. He told me to finish mine, then go upstairs and find an empty bedroom, "one of the small ones."

"You're gonna stay with me until we get this thing wrapped up."

By that time I knew better than to argue with him so I headed upstairs where I found three small bedrooms that looked like they weren't being used. Thanks to Smitty I didn't have any thing to put in there. All I had were the clothes I was wearing.

I turned the bed down and messed the covers up so the room looked like it was occupied and went back down to the kitchen. I wondered if I'd ever see home again.

Smitty'd said it might be a couple of hours before Dave got back, but he wanted all the gang to stick around and be ready if he needed them.

He was right. A little after five in the afternoon, Dave got back.

"Like you suggested, Smitty," he reported, "I took one of the quiet bikes and a handful of empty envelopes on the way out. Had an idea on how to talk to the neighbors.

First I checked out the numbers on the houses, then put a phony number but the right street on one of the envelopes. After that I started ringing doorbells and telling them I couldn't find this address. They tried to help me and it was easy to start a conversation."

Dave looked around at his audience and said, "Pretty sharp, huh?"

Smitty: "Get on with it."

"Then I went over to the golf course. They wouldn't let me on. I even offered to pay, but no way could I get on the course, legally. It turned out their security's as full of holes as Swiss cheese, so I just started walking the back nine and pretty soon I was right behind Carpenter's house. Nobody challenged me. A couple of the golfers looked at me funny, but nobody stopped me. It was a snap. I even drew a small map of the yard and the back of the house."

He ripped it out of his notebook with a flourish and handed it over to Smitty.

"So, what's the deal?"

"Well, first the good news about the house. The neighbors both said it was a strange household. Apparently the owner's a single guy, maybe in his fifties. Nobody's ever seen any women over there. Not at all sociable, never talked to any of his neighbors. Lots of speculation about him on the block. None of the neighbors had ever been in the house, but they'd seen bunches of contractors coming and going when he first moved in last year, so they figured he'd made a lot of interior changes. They said they were sure that Mr. Carpenter – they did know his name – had at least three employees at the house, maybe more. One's a chef, one's his driver and they didn't know what the other guy did. They said that his driver was really big. That's how they both put it – 'really big.' And one lady said that he and Mr. Carpenter were always gone on Thursdays. Left early in the morning and were usually gone 'til late Saturday."

"The driver and Carpenter are usually gone on Thursdays? So there'd probably only be two people there at most on any Thursday night?" Smitty asked.

"Right. On top of that the backyard looks like a cinch way in. There's a big lawn with a few shrubs for coverage. It's an old house with a large, screened-in back porch, up about four or five steps. Inside the porch is a really old door, and four windows, I think. You can get to the back yard over a fancy zigzag fence of stacked logs from the golf course. It's maybe three feet tall. That's all there is between the golf course and his yard except for some bushes."

"Terrific," said Smitty, "Even better than I was hoping for. Tomorrow's Thursday. We go in tomorrow night. We don't have to have any qualms about breaking and entering, the guy's a murderer. Fact is, based on what we know about him; I don't think he'd want the police up there any more than we would. It looks like this thing's gonna take longer than we thought, though, so we all better plan on being here at the house or nearby for several days."

A little bit hesitantly, I raised my hand.

"Smitty," I said, "what about me?"

He shot me a look that clearly said "Yeah, what about you?"

"I don't have any clothes, just what I've got on."

"Well, yeah, you do look a little raunchy. Don't worry, – I already thought about it. I'm having one of the guys stop by your place and pick some stuff up for you."

He wouldn't even let me pick up my own stuff. I gave up. I threw my hands up in mock surrender. "Okay, okay," I said. "I'll get my keys for him"

"Nah," Smitty said. "He don't need a key, not for your place. Anyway, he's already gone."

CHAPTER 13

Smitty asked the guys to gather around. When he judged that we were all there and paying attention, he began by telling them how much he appreciated their friendship and support, and had over the years.

"You all know I retired from the active leadership of the gang right after my wife died," he said soberly. "On her deathbed she made me promise to quit doing the violent stuff as a favor to her, so I did. Since then I've enjoyed nothing more than having a beer with you guys, and you've been my best friends. There's really no reason why you should still help me when I need it except for old friendship, and I want you to know that I really appreciate it."

His statement seemed odd to me. He'd been bossing these guys around the same way he did me. The Devils reacted in all sorts of ways, some blowing it off with a laugh, some shuffling their feet in embarrassment over the sentimentality of Smitty's speech, some just nodding comfortably.

Of course it was all new to me. I knew several of them were married; all I knew about Smitty was that he lived alone on a boat, but evidently owned this large home way up in the hills. Now I knew he was a widower.

He continued. "Something else important. Over the last few years we've made a real effort to change our image, and it's worked," Smitty continued, getting into the meat and potatoes of what he wanted to say.

"We've worked with police Little League groups, helped them in manhunts, even co-sponsored pancake breakfasts to raise money for police and fire department benefits. I don't have to tell you, our wives and kids have benefited a lot from this. A lot of them are active in PTAs, Girl and Boy Scout troops, some local churches. I know you guys might not talk about it but the fact is our families are more in the communities than we used to be."

Murmurs of general agreement.

"So the old days are over. We can still play hard. We may still do some things that the law frowns on. But basically we're more a part of the community than we used to be. My point's this-if any of you want to bow out of this operation 'cuz it might in any way harm your family, feel free. If you do, you'll still be my buddy, still welcome on my boat for a beer. I'm promising no hard feelings, ever. If any of you want out, just don't come back tomorrow morning and I'll understand."

Smitty walked over to the kitchen table and refilled his coffee cup.

There were several minutes of whispering, nods back and forth and shoulder shrugging. Finally one spoke up.

"Screw that, Smitty. No one's not in on this. No way we're gonna let you have all the fun."

"Okay, then," Smitty said. "Here're my conditions. First of all, we don't start no violence."

There were a few collective groans.

"Don't mean we don't defend ourselves, but with Horning looking over our shoulders we can't make things worse, got it?"

"Second, we do everything my way. No questions, right?"

A few more groans, followed by some laughter and a muttered comment from someone in the back, "So what's new?" That brought on another wave of laughs.

"All right?" Nods all around. "All right! So I been thinking about getting into this guy Carpenter's house and I got some ideas."

Lew," he said pointing at one of the guys, "you know that place on San Pablo Avenue that sells used clothing, some kind of religious outfit, I think?"

"The Salvation Army?"

"Yeah, that one. Take my car and run down there right now. Buy four fairly good-looking golf bags. Also, buy a couple dozen golf clubs. Make sure some have the big heads on 'em. I want each bag to look like the real thing. Get going right now, and get back this afternoon."

"Golf clubs? What the hell for?"

"No questions, remember? Get going."

Lew got up and headed for the door.

"The rest of you, find some dark clothes that would also pass for a golf outfit. What we're gonna do is sneak onto Carpenter's property from the golf course. Not all of you will go with me, but I want you should all be ready. Any questions?"

Again, a few moments of quiet, and then a surprise question.

"How about dinner? We're sick and tired of pizzas. How 'bout we get Josie up here and have a good meal?"

"Done!" Smitty said, "I'll call her and set it up, and that reminds me, one more thing and it's a biggie. You gotta cut out all the God damn, freaking, bull-shittin', swearin' around, Josie!"

"You should talk!" one of the guys in back called out.

"I know, I know. But for chrissakes try! Okay?"

"For you, Smitty, we'll do our fuckin' best!" Much laughter.

I had no idea who Josie was, but I imagined a middle-aged, matronly Mexican cook. Still, it sounded good to me. Suddenly I was hungry, too.

CHAPTER 14

Lew had already gone. Several more took off on personal errands, but said they'd be back for dinner. The rest of the guys settled down on the various chairs and sofas and started working their way through the beer supply as fast as they could. There was a lot of talk about Smitty taking charge, just like in the old days which led to general discussion about those good old days. Some of it sounded pretty blood curdling to me. A couple of times one of the guys started to bring something up and another guy nudged him, nodded in my direction and then changed the subject.

Pretty soon the conversation got around to speculating about Carpenter, and how they could get more information about him. His neighbors had said he appeared to be pretty wealthy. Always new expensive cars around. Had his own chauffeur. Spent lots of money on the house. One of the guys said he wondered if they could find out where his money came from. He said it was too bad we couldn't get a copy of his tax return.

One of the other things Dave had said was that the neighbors thought there had been a lot more activity around Carpenter's house lately than normal.

"Probably when he found out his little book was missing," somebody said.

I asked him what he meant.

"Seems obvious to me," he said. "He was trying to get something back. Therefore it must have been stolen from him. Maybe an unhappy employee?"

That made sense to me. Smitty had just walked in the room. "I've been thinking the same thing," he said, "which leans me toward the notebook being the key."

Suddenly someone said, "I think I hear Josie's car." Everyone, Smitty accepted, made a beeline up the stairs to the front door.

I lagged behind, not getting their excitement over the upcoming dinner. We hadn't been eating too badly as it was: lots of hotcakes, bacon, eggs and coffee for breakfast, and anything we wanted for lunch as long as we made it ourselves. Like they'd said, mostly pizza for dinner. Some of the guys had ordered chicken pot pies instead of pizzas, for a little variety. Trouble with the pies was they didn't deliver.

The guys were all crowded around the front door, then quickly formed into a bucket brigade, handing bag after bag of groceries down the hall and into the kitchen.

Josie carried in the last bag. She definitely was not what I expected. No middle-aged, motherly Mexican cook was she! This cook was beautiful: blonde, green eyes, cute figure— and young! I put her in her in her mid or late twenties at the outside.

I wondered who the hell she was. Obviously she wasn't just some cook they hired occasionally. They all treated her like family. Someone's wife? But she looked too young for this gang. Maybe a girlfriend? Maybe somebody's daughter? I wanted to get to the bottom of this mystery, and soon.

She immediately took charge, calling everybody by their names. Job one: getting the food put away. I was being completely ignored. In fact, she had too much help. She started shooing some of them out. I hung back just outside the kitchen door, where she might not notice me. I didn't want to get bounced.

A few minutes later, Smitty walked in. "Daddy!" says Josie.

"Daddy?" Well, that narrowed it down a bit. Her dad? Or maybe a sugar daddy?

Smitty settled the matter.

"Hi, daughter dear," he said, poking in a few of the bags. So what'd you bring us for dinner?"

Mystery solved and was I ever relieved – until I thought about her being SMITTY's daughter and started thinking about how difficult getting to know her would be. The next question: how was I gonna meet her? I figured we'd meet, probably at dinner, but certainly not now. I couldn't even get in the kitchen, let alone near her. The thing was I didn't want to meet her – I wanted to *meet* her. You know what I mean.

"So how about hamburger steaks, baked potatoes and a green salad?" she answered her pop. She also said she'd appreciate some help.

Wonder of wonders – Smitty volunteered *me*. "I'll let you have our newest, youngest and greenest recruit. I know he knows his way around a galley. Maybe he can help in a kitchen," he said and shoved me forward.

She asked me if I knew how to make hamburger patties for steaks. I said, "Sure." She had me get two huge packages of ground meat out of the 'fridge and told me to start making patties. I'd made a few when she started laughing at me.

"Whaddya think this is, a tea party? These guys want a steak, not a measly little thing like that. Here, let me show you." She proceeded to make a burger the size of a dinner plate.

Live and learn. Should have known – I'd seen these guys wolf down a half dozen big pancakes, bacon and eggs for breakfast. Using the ones she'd made as my model, I proceeded to make a couple dozen of these monster pieces. Were there gonna be a couple dozen Devils for dinner?

When I was done she had me wash and cut six heads of lettuce into quarters for the salad. She said each guy would eat a whole quarter. She was making a dressing for the salad.

Gosh, I was impressed. She was cute and a good cook. She was also a little bossy, but in a nice way.

At the sink, elbow deep in cold water, I was washing the lettuce, stripping off any brownish leaves, quartering each head and arranging them on fairly big salad plates.

"I have to go downstairs and get the guys to set up a couple of ping pong tables with tablecloths, plates and silverware, I'll be back before you finish the lettuce."

When she came back, she set to work frying the steaks on the industrial-sized stove. She'd worked some chopped onion into the patties. The smell had my mouth watering.

Before I knew it, everything was ready. A couple of the guys came up to help her carry it downstairs.

The dinner was a huge success and Josie was right. Nothing left over. Coffee and ice cream for dessert made everyone happy.

Well, I'd met her. I'd even spent the best part of an hour with her. But I'd never had the chance to really talk to her. She just accepted me as the gang's latest recruit.

CHAPTER 15

After the table was cleaned up, Smitty said he'd need to send some of us on more errands, first thing in the morning.

"The first one may be one of the most important. Any of you guys remember those old highway patrol uniforms we bought last year, in that surplus place? If we still got them, I need them."

One of the guys spoke up, saying he thought they were still somewhere at the shop, but he had no idea where.

"Okay, that's your job. Find them and don't come back without them!"

"Second. I want someone to find some police sirens we can put on our cycles. Then I want four or five of you to get some water-based paint and paint your bikes to look like police bikes. Who can do that?"

Several of the guys volunteered for that, more than the four or five Smitty wanted. He cherry-picked the ones he wanted, then told them they had to have their bikes painted and a siren mounted on each of them before tomorrow evening.

"Can do," a couple replied. One of them wanted to know what the hell Smitty was planning. He told them he wasn't sure yet. It still depended on a couple of things. He just wanted to be ready.

"I'll tell you this much," he said. "We need to get in through the back porch. In order to do that successfully it'd be nice if there was something going on at the front of the house to distract the chef and whoever else might be there. I'm thinking some sort of a ruckus between some bikers and some cops would probably do it, but I haven't worked through the details yet. I'm open to ideas if you got any."

Silence.

"Okay, you guys got your orders for tomorrow. Let's sleep on it and see what we come up with in the morning."

I'd forgotten about Lew and the golf bags. He spoke up, wanting to know what Smitty had planned for them.

"Are they in the garage?" Smitty asked him. Lew nodded. "Good. Leave 'em there."

I decided to do what Smitty had told me to do. Get some rest. On the way up to my room I peeked into the kitchen and saw no sign of Josie. In my room I stripped down to my skivvies and shirt and laid down to think.

Outside of meeting Josie, everything was going wrong for me. Smitty was using me as a recruit and making me a part of whatever the gang was planning. His home invasion plan sounded wacky to me, we'd probably all end up in jail. Every time I suggested something that sounded normal, like going to the police with what we'd learned, they laughed at me. I was marooned up here in the hills with no way of escape. I had to think of something. With all that on my mind I couldn't fall asleep.

Finally I decided to go down to the kitchen and have some hot chocolate or something.

The house was pretty dark. I had to feel my way to the kitchen, and I realized I'd neglected to pay attention to where any light switches were. Fortunately the switch was where it should be in any proper kitchen, next to the door, so I was able to get some light on the subject.

Try as I might I couldn't find any chocolate, so I decided to just go with a cup of warm milk and hope none of the gang caught me at it. I got the stove going, found the milk, found a pan and a cup and pretty soon I was seated at the kitchen table, trying to relax.

Suddenly the door swung open, and in walked a vision of loveliness, Josie! She made a beeline for the reefer, grabbed the carton of milk and turned toward the stove. When she saw the dirty pan, she turned around in surprise and saw me. She certainly was a cool number. She wasn't nonplussed for a second.

"Hi," she said. "You couldn't sleep either?"

I, on the other hand, was a little more than nonplussed. First of all, she had shorty PJs on. She was covered up, but provocative as hell, at least to me.

My problem was I hadn't expected to run into anyone. All I had on were my underwear shorts and an unbuttoned shirt and, glancing down; I realized the shorts weren't buttoned. All I could do was pull my chair as close in to the table as possible and be glad it wasn't glass topped.

"I guess all the strange surroundings and what's going on has me a little on edge," I said, trying not to sound too lame about it.

"Dad does that to people. When he gets his teeth into something, he has a way of dragging everyone along with him."

She'd found the chocolate and made herself some hot cocoa. She asked if I didn't want cocoa instead of milk, but as I couldn't get up from the table, I told her I preferred plain milk.

She sat down across from me. I was trying to think of a way to start a conversation, when she said,

"Who are you?"

Instead of giving her my name and so forth, I started telling her the whole story. From my arrival at the dock to Smitty shanghaiing me to help him clear his name.

"Wow," she said. "Dad sure gets in some scrapes, doesn't he?"

"Yeah, he sure does. It looks like he also gets other people into scrapes too. I feel like I'm on a runaway train that's going so fast I can't jump off. Smitty doesn't take no for an answer, does he?"

"Ever since my mom died in that motorcycle accident, Dad kind of changed. He used to be terrible. Not to me – he's been a great father to me. But not very close. He provided for us really well, but his first love with the gang. About four or five years ago, my mom made him promise to quit taking chances and start being a better husband and father. He was certainly trying, but then when my mother was killed it really changed him. He started spending a lot more time with me, and he resigned from the leadership of the club."

"When was that?"

"About three years ago. Since then we've become good friends." Maybe she felt she was telling me too much. Suddenly she switched topics.

"Are you really a good sailor? Could you teach me how to sail? Do you have a sailboat of your own?"

The questions were coming fast and furious, a perfect opportunity to blow my own horn and I did so.

"Yeah, I'm a damn good sailor, actually," I told her shamelessly. "And yeah, sure, I could teach you to how to sail, and no, I don't have a boat of my own. But I do have access to lots of boats. Why?"

"I've been sailing with my dad lots of times," Josie said sort of wistfully, "but he never lets me do anything. He thinks I'm along just for the ride, or to fix a meal for us. You know what I'd like to be? I'd like to be a foredeck ape!"

She raised her arm, made a fist and flexed her muscles.

I had to laugh. "You know what a foredeck ape is?"

"Not exactly. I do know they help run the sails up and stuff. Not much. Just mainly that they're helpful and they have to be strong."

"First thing: foredeck apes are usually really knowledgeable sailors," I informed my eager student. "They're mostly used in races, where each person has a special job. Sure, you could be a foredeck ape. You'd probably be the prettiest one on the Bay."

I grinned, then wondered if I'd gone too far with the compliment, but she took it in stride.

Peering into the bottom of her cup, she asked me, "When this is all over, you think you might take me sailing?"

"Of course," I said. "I'd be honored."

By that time we'd both finished our drinks, and she said she thought she'd head back to bed.

I was still stuck at the table with my unbuttoned underwear. I couldn't reach under the table and button them – that'd really look bad. Also I wasn't sure if I was dressed left, right or center. I told her I wanted to relax in the kitchen a little longer. She left.

I thought I'd really done a world-class job of getting things off to a great start with her until, at the door, she turned and said, "By the way, what's your name?"

CHAPTER 16

"Okay, this is what I've come up with," was Smitty's greeting at breakfast. .

"The logical place to get into the house is through the back yard and the porch. I think we can sneak in from the golf course, cross the lawn and onto the porch pretty easy. The screen won't be a problem. A little more difficult will be the door or the windows. That's why I want Nips to be on the team. He used to be a locksmith," he said for my benefit, "and we may need him. That okay with you, Nips?"

Josie leaned over to me and whispered, "His mom used to call him her little nipper and it stuck"

"Anything you say, Boss"

"In addition to Casey and Nips I want Les to go because he's big and in good shape. Les, you can be our go-to guy if there's any trouble."

"You're the boss, boss."

"Enough of the "boss" shit, you guys. Let's get serious."

He continued. "We're gonna walk up the golf course late in the afternoon. We'll be the very last foursome dragging in just before dark. Dave said sometimes it's real late before the guys finish and they have to walk in at dusk. That's what we'll do. Casually walk up the course 'til we get to Carpenter's place, duck into the bushes and wait for dark."

Turning to me he said, "I might take Dave. He's been there and knows the place better than the rest of us. If he comes, you can be my caddy."

Swell. I had no idea how to carry a golf bag. And I'm starting to wonder just how heavy these bags are. I'd never played golf in my life, never even held a golf club in my hands.

Dave added. We should look like golfers. Good looking shirts and pants. And shoes – all golfers wear golf shoes. They look like regular shoes with cleats on them. I think we can get away with regular shoes. No motorcycle boots."

"Good." Smitty added. "What we're gonna do is create a diversion. Right after dark Three or four of you guys are going to start racing around in front of Carpenter's house. Run up and down the block, make a lot of noise. Make it look like your racing each other, doing stunts, whatever you want. Take turns doing wheelies or something. Just make sure it's good and noisy and lasts until our police come." Smitty made imaginary quote marks with his fingers around the word police.

"The trick is, they'll have to show up pretty quick – we don't want anybody calling in real cops on us," he continued. "They'll show up, but they'll be our guys dressed in those old highway patrol uniforms. It'll be good and dark by then and nobody will notice any difference in the uniforms. They'll race up, sirens on and start grabbing and cuffing you guys. That should get everyone's attention and give us time to break in without being heard."

The rest of the guys thought it sounded like a hell of a lot of fun, and totally plausible. I thought it sounded ingenious – and impossible.

"What about the uniforms?" Smitty asked.

"They're here. Gus found them; they look a little ratty but will probably pass in the dark."

"Is Gus here?"

"Yeah, he's in the garage, you want him?"

Gus walked in and got a big hug from Smitty. As tall as Smitty, he was just the opposite in build. Thin as a rail, maybe in his early sixties, he was dressed to the nines. Tweed jacket, dress shirt open at the neck, slacks and saddle shoes, he looked out of place. He immediately nailed me with piercing blue eyes.

"You must be the infamous Casey I've heard so much about." He grinned.

Smitty introduced him. "Case, Gus here is my oldest and best friend. We've been through a hell of a lot together." He turned to Gus, "Ain't that right?"

We shook hands and he said, "We need to talk, soon," and turned away.

Everyone wanted to be part of the wheelie gang. They drew straws then went down to the garage to start changing their bikes to black and whites.

Smitty sat down with the four of us – Nips, Les, Dave and myself –"If we go with the plan the way I see it so far," Smitty said, "we've got some real timing issues to work out. We need to get to the golf course right at dusk, while there are still some golfers out. Then we have to wait and make sure the group we follow is the last group coming in. I haven't figured out how to do that, unless we post someone further back down the course to watch for any stragglers. It'd be hard to hide in the bushes if more golfers are comin' up behind us. Next," Smitty said, ticking off the items on his mental checklist, "we have to figure a way to let the bikers know when we're ready for them to start making that ruckus out front. Even though he's a hell of a locksmith, Nips may end up having to force the door. That could be noisy. And another thing, – we don't really know how many people might be in there. Hopefully it's just two."

It seemed that I was going on the raid whether I wanted to or not. I decided I should try to make it as safe as possible and contribute some ideas.

"What about peripheral alarms? A house security system?" I asked him.

"That's another reason I wanted Les on the team. Les used to have a reputation as a pretty good second-story man. He can disarm a house alarm in seconds. Course it's been a long time, hasn't it, Les."

Les reassured him. "It's still my hobby, security systems. I stay current. I still got the touch when it comes to alarms. But I'm not a second story man any more, not at my age. I'm a first-story man now, specializing in ranch houses." We all laughed at the image.

"Dave, didn't you say you couldn't see any signs of alarms or cameras?"

He replied, "I Tossed a few golf balls into the yard and nothing happened, no alarms, no dogs. My bet? Carpenter relies on his strong-arms to protect him, without alarms. You know why? Alarms bring cops, and that's probably the last thing he wants."

"But there's another problem," Les injected. "After we're in, we're gonna have to tie these guys up or do something with them. And, we don't want them to be able to ID us. Any ideas on how we handle that?"

Nips said he had a better idea. "Do what I used to do on those rumored second story jobs. We all wear bandanas around our necks and slip them up over our faces when we go in. And we don't use our names when we're there, for obvious reasons."

Smitty spoke up. "I like the bandana idea. But instead of using names, we'll use numbers. I'll be number one. Casey, you're number two. Nips, you're three. Les is four, and number five goes to Dave because he was the last one I chose. And to make sure we don't slip up, we'll start using the numbers as soon as we get out of the car." Nods all around.

"Okay. Can anyone think of anything we've left out?"

After standing and delivering all his instructions, Smitty finally sat down. Now he stood and patted his stomach.

"Then you guys should get yourselves some lunch 'cuz I think we'll leave here about 6:30 tonight and it might be a long night. Anything else?"

No one spoke up, so we broke up our little group and Smitty headed downstairs to see how the uniform fitting and the motorcycle painting was getting on.

Dave said "I'm gonna fix up the golf bags. I bet they'll look more authentic than any of you guys as so called golfers."

Nobody took the bet.

CHAPTER 17

The gang was split up all over the house. Garage, rec room, living room. Some were in the backyard. I really had nothing to do, so I headed toward the kitchen, driven by a hunger for food and the off chance of meeting up with Josie again.

Josie was already there. I asked her it she knew what was going on.

"I've got a general idea," she told me. "I just hope Dad keeps his promise to Mom."

I told her what Smitty had said about "no violence," and she wasn't convinced.

"He's impulsive and sometimes a little bit nuts," she giggled.

"So, what's for lunch," I asked her.

"Anything you want, "just don't expect me to fix it for you. I'll do dinner, maybe even breakfast, but I do *not* do lunch. Except for myself. The reefer's full of food. Cold meats, cheeses, fruit, drinks – it's all there, so help yourself." She had a neat way of tossing her hair back from her eyes to emphasize what she was saying. I thought it was cute and fetching.

"Were you serious about going sailing with me?" I asked.

"Sure was," she said. "Why? Is there a girlfriend or something in the way?"

"No, no. I don't have a girl friend. At least not anymore."

We spent the next half hour comparing our exes.

"You know, it's nice meeting you this way," she said, opening the reefer. "Usually when I meet someone and they find out who my dad is they disappear. This way you met him before you met me."

"On top of that apparently I'm not going to' disappear, not if you Dad has anything to say about it."

"I know my Dad pretty well and just between you and me, I think he thinks you're okay. You're not going to disappear," she repeated, distracted as her hand wavered between a Coke and a root beer. The root beer won. She also pulled out a box of eggs. "I'm having a fried egg sandwich," she confided. "What are you going to fix?"

I got the message.

"Sounds good to me. Can I watch you and learn?"

"Nice try. I still don't do lunch but you can watch me and do your own."

That's what we had, together with sodas, ice cream and cookies. While we ate, a number of the gang drifted in and fixed their own lunches, apparently well aware of Josie's "I don't gotta fix no stinkin' lunches" edict.

The Devils talked freely about Smitty's plan. Josie was visibly upset when she heard about the break-in. When they realized their gaffe, the guys worried that they'd inadvertently spilled the beans to her, but she sighed dramatically and said, "Well, boys will be boys." But I could see she was worried.

As soon as I could, I told her again that Smitty had made it perfectly clear to the guys– no violence.

"But breaking in *is* violence," she said. I had no answer to that. Actually I felt the same. I told her I was being dragged along on the adventure and that I'd try my best to keep her father out of trouble. If nothing else, the idea of little old me trying to keep Smitty out of trouble made her smile.

"You're going to keep my dad out of trouble? That'd be a first!"

Josie had an interesting way of going off on what seemed like a totally off-the-subject remark every once in a while. She did it again.

"Do you like to read?" she asked me.

I didn't know how to reply. I wanted to prolong our conversation, but I was afraid of saying the wrong thing.

"Classics. Mysteries. Horror. History?" I generalized, looking for some reaction to guide me. "I guess I've got a pretty catholic interest in books, in the general sense of the word."

God, I sounded like some kind of pontificating nerd. I tried to minimize the impact by saying that my reading was limited because I could usually only take a few paper backs on my boat trips. "You know, space limitations"

She simply said, "Me too," and asked me if I'd brought any books with me.

I hadn't, being so rushed by her dad.

She said she hadn't either but told me there were a bunch of books upstairs.

"Maybe we should take a look at them," she suggested.
"If you like mysteries and gore, you'll find plenty," she went on.

Good thing she wasn't a mind reader. I'd been thinking along the lines of 'come up and see my etchings'.

"I like mysteries but not gore. Maybe I'll find something."

Upstairs we found rows and rows of paperbacks in a bookcase in somebody's bedroom. As we thumbed through them, I took the opportunity to find out a little more about her. I asked her if she lived here with her dad. I knew she didn't but hoped she didn't know I knew.

"Oh, no, I live by myself down in Oakland. I've got my own place, thanks to a really good divorce agreement. I couldn't stand living with my dad. He's one of the last living advocates of male supremacy. He doesn't know it, but he is. In fact," she added after giving it some thought, "most of the Devils are male chauvinist pigs – but in a nice way. They treat their wives and girlfriends very, very well, but certainly not as equals." She shook her head in disapproval. "They put them on a pedestal, then neglect them. In fact, did you know that there are absolutely no women members of the Devils? Nowhere in the whole world!"

This I didn't know.

"Don't get me wrong," she went right on. "I love my dad. I even *like* my dad. I enjoy being around him – but live under the same roof with him? Never! I feel the same way about the whole gang. To a man, they've been extraordinarily nice to me, but they're still chauvinists."

"Are you telling me that there are Devil's chapters all over the world?"

"Sure. Big ones. You don't read about them so much any more, but they're there."

I'd heard about the gang in Oakland, of course, even in other parts of California, but the *whole world?* Good god, what had I gotten I tangled up in?

We found a book about sailing and spent most of the afternoon talking about sailboats and sailing in general. She really was interested in becoming an honest-to-goodness sailor, not just a passenger. She actually seemed to have an aptitude for it. We got into which sail was which, and before long she could tell the difference between jibs and Genoas, mizzens and mains, spinnakers and staysails. A little more tutoring and she could tell me the difference between a sloop, a yawl and a ketch, and port and starboard.

We would have gotten into knots and lines and leeway and more, but we ran out of time. Smitty called up to us to come down to the rec room. "We're gonna have a fashion show of police motorcycles and uniforms."

CHAPTER 18

In the garage four black and white motorcycles were lined up for our inspection. They looked like the real thing to me, but I wasn't the best judge. The gang had a few criticisms but pretty much agreed they'd pass general inspection, particularly in the dark and if it didn't rain. The four guys who'd be riding them said they thought it'd work, but they too were worried about rain, and the fact that the paint had a tendency to rub off on their legs.

"So you ride bowlegged," Smitty said. "What? I gotta do all the thinkin' around here?"

The uniforms looked like no city police uniform I'd ever seen. For one thing, they weren't blue, they were khaki. The pants weren't really made for boots and cycles, but the guys had adapted them so they looked okay if you weren't too close up. The shirts and jackets looked pretty good. The helmets were great. They'd painted them uniformly black and white and they looked pretty authentic. The best you could say was they looked like official uniforms of some sort.

"Not perfect, but I think they'll do," Smitty said passing judgment.

"Okay, everybody, I think we're ready," he announced. "We've got about an hour before we should leave. Time to break up into our own groups and rehearse what you're going to do. I'll check in with each group and answer any questions.

"You rowdies go downstairs to the garage and see if you can gimmick your bikes to be noisier than they already are." He told the police group to meet in the rec room and compare notes on how the police had acted the last time they'd been arrested. Evidently they'd had a lot of experience being arrested and thought they could handle that assignment easily.

When he finally got back to our group, I had questions.

"One. What do we do if a neighbor or someone accidentally sees us or hears us breaking in?" I read from my notes. "Two. What do we do if there are more guys in the house than we expect? Three. What if Carpenter comes back while we're there? Four. What do we do with any guys we catch and tie up?"

"Any others?" Smitty asked. The other guys shook their heads.

"Casey" he said, "you're doing okay. I've been asking myself the same questions. Alright," he said, "to answer your question. "I know there's a lot of ifs in my plan, but you can't predict everything. Part of the answer is why I chose you guys. We may have to punt if any of those if-things happen, but I really think the five of us have the cool to handle just about anything that comes up. The answer to all your questions, Casey, is I don't know. We'll figure it out on the fly."

Needless to say, I didn't know Smitty the way the Devils did. They accepted his plan without a question. I couldn't do that. However I didn't have any choice in the matter.

Smitty paused, leaned back in his chair, linked his hands behind his head and calmly generaled us.

"The plan's really simple." he reminded us. "We leave at five thirty, park close to the course and wait until we get the signal the last foursome's coming in. We follow the last group to Carpenter's yard and hide in the bushes. That's it. The rest of the plan depends on what time its dark enough for us to sneak across the lawn. Everybody straight with that?"

Several nods of acquiescence and one "no problem" was the response.

"Now get rid of your cell phones. No surprise calls. I'll have mine and it's already on vibrate. I'll use it to coordinate the ruckus out front, and call for help if we need it. Now, golf clothes on and ready to leave in ten minutes, fifteen tops, okay? And relax, it's gonna work just fine."

CHAPTER 19

Five people plus four golf bags is a tight squeeze in a standard sedan. Three of us ended up in the back seat with one of the bags across our laps. Fortunately it wasn't a long trip.

Near Carpenter's house, Smitty told the three of us in the back seat to scrunch down out of sight while he drove around and looked for a good place to park. Smitty found a street about two blocks from Carpenter's house that dead-ended against the golf course. From the front seat, Smitty could see the course. He could see the fancy stacked log fence.

"It seems like a quiet street, nobody walking around, but keep your heads down, just in case.

It was getting too dark to even think about playing golf when we finally got the call that the last foursome was coming in. Smitty said to watch for them. He'd been told that one of them was wearing pink pants. Pink pants? At least they should be easy to spot.

"Now we need a bit of luck," Smitty said, checking the rearview mirror. "We don't need anybody driving by 'til we get on the course."

Luck came our way. The street was totally quiet. Fortunately, the dead end street had only one house on either side.

We exited the car, retrieved the rest of the golf bags from the trunk and snuck onto the course. The final foursome was about a hundred yards ahead of us and had no idea we were there. We walked big as life up the middle of the course as if we owned it. Smitty made a big deal out of having me carry his bag as his caddy. Promised me a good tip.

Carpenter's house, which looked exactly as Dave had described it, was easy to spot from the fairway. Dave verified that it was indeed the right house and we all melted into the shrubbery beside the course and waited for dark.

Smitty whispered, "Okay, when I judge the time is right, I'll call the guys and have them start doing their wheelies. We'll hear them, for sure. After they've been doing it long enough to attract attention, we'll start going in. Number Two'll go first because he's the youngest, smallest and the fastest of us."

Number Two. Oh, right – me! I'm going first? Why? I didn't have time to object before he continued.

"I'll go second. Number three, you go after me. I want Nips – I mean, number three in there ASAP so he can get started doing his thing on the doors right away. Four and five, you better come across in your number orders.

Once again we waited, giving me time to contemplate the problem I had with this numbering system of Smitty's. Every time one of guys called me Number Two, I had a silly flashback to when I was a kid and bathroom breaks were called going number one or number two, number two being, to put it delicately, the more odious of the two. The mind sure does funny things when you're under pressure.

I think we waited about twenty minutes. When we ducked into the bushes, we'd just had enough light to see our way in. Now it was pitch black. Smitty admitted we were just lucky there was no moonlight. He'd forgotten to check for that.

He quietly phoned the gang. "Anytime you're ready, we're ready." He slid his phone back into his pocket, then whispered to me, "Real soon now."

All too soon for me I could hear motorcycles approaching. Just cruising in, all four of them together, made a lot of noise. Then the noise ratcheted up. I could picture them racing one or two at a time, up and down the short street, practicing wheelies.

In a minute, Smitty was gonna shove me out into no man's land. What if I get shot? Did he know something I didn't know? Why did he want me to go first? Probably because I was the most expendable? How in hell did I get into this mess?

"Get ready," Smitty said.

CHAPTER 20

A couple of the guys with really old bikes had poked holes in the mufflers to make them even noisier. "With the mufflers holed out," Smitty'd told me, "they'll shake his whole house down."

Unless the whole household was deaf, there was no way they wouldn't be at the front windows watching.

"It's time," Smitty said and gave me a shove toward the fence.

Turns out, it was a breeze. No one shot at me. One step up on a lower log and I could slide over the top of the fence. Nobody had told me exactly how to get across the lawn. I figured I'd crawl on my belly, but Smitty immediately stopped that. "Stand up and crouch down," he stage whispered at me. "Walk really, really slow to the porch steps. Sudden movements are what people see when it's really dark like this."

Against my better instincts, I followed his directions. It was the longest ten or fifteen yards I've ever walked, but I made it and threw myself into the welcoming arms of a shrub which, in retrospect, I'm happy to say was not a rose bush.

One by one the others came, all without setting off any alarms, all disappearing into the landscaping except for Nips, who went directly up on the porch.

In a few minutes Nips whispered for us to come on up. He had simply opened the screen door and walked right in. The back door was gonna be a snap, he assured us as we joined him on the porch.

"Hold on. Wait a sec before you force the door," Smitty stage whispered to Nips.

"I just want you all to remember, there're probably only two people home, and they're probably in the front of the house watching all the ruckus. But we can't be positive. One might still be in the kitchen."

"I've already cased the door and given the lock a good dose of WD 40, it ain't gonna make a sound," came from Nips.

"Great. All I'm saying is, we're not breaking in, we're *sneaking in*. So, Nips, we need to open that door as quietly as possible. And we want to get ourselves inside as quietly as possible that way, if anyone's there, we can still surprise 'em. Hopefully, they're in the front and when they return to the kitchen, we can grab them without a struggle. And that's the other thing. Remember – we grab these guys without hurting them. Throw a towel over their head or something, then tie 'em up and gag 'em."

In the dim light from the kitchen window, we could barely see each other.

"Ready?" Smitty asked.

Whispered okays.

"Okay, Bandanas up." I felt ridiculous. I hadn't worn a bandana bad guy style since I was eight.

With that, he signaled Nips to go ahead and open the door, and we tiptoed in. The kitchen was empty and almost dark. Just one light on over the sink.

So far, so good.

Just then we heard sirens in the distance. Smitty smiled with the satisfaction of a plan well executed. "Ah, you gotta love it," he whispered. "Here come our cops, right on time!"

The single light over the sink barely lit up the large kitchen. We came through the door from the porch. There were two other doors, both closed. Les quietly edged one door open, it led into a dining room, empty. The other, a swinging door, had to lead to the front of the house. Smitty inched the swinging door open a little, then closed it again.

"A hall," he reported. "Bet they come back here that way. That's when we grab them. Find some towels. However many there are, as they come through the door, one of us'll throw a towel over their heads and a rag in their mouths, so they can't yell. They'll never know what hit 'em."

Smitty stationed Dave and Les behind the swinging door with towels at the ready. He, Nips, and I lined up just out of sight of the door, each of us holding a towel in our hands. We were ready… I hoped.

CHAPTER 21

Smitty whispered that he wished his guys out front would finish up and get going

"Damn those guys. They're having too much fun, taking too much time." Smitty was getting antsy. "There's been plenty of time for our cops to have made their arrests and gone on their way." We waited. Finally the street noised went away.

Shortly after that we heard footsteps coming down the hall. We could hear two guys talking to each other about the arrests and how noisy motorcycles were.

The door swung open and the first guy came through, his head was turned back as he talked with the second guy. He never saw us. Les, being real tall, sized up the situation quickly, threw his towel over the head of the second guy and got the rag in his mouth simultaneously. The first guy whipped around but it was too late. Dave got his towel over his head, rag in his mouth, and we had both of them.

We tied them up, carried them out and set them at either end of the porch, a good distance from each other. As a precaution we taped their mouths.

Then, things began to go wrong. We had just got the guys stored on the porch when Smitty said, "Shhhh. What's that?"

He was standing next to the swinging door. I tiptoed over to him and listened quietly. Footsteps, that was what Smitty heard, and I could hear them too. There was someone else in the house.

"Where the hell did he come from?" Smitty whispered.

"Now what do we do?" I whispered back.

"We need to find out who's there. I tell you what; he probably doesn't know we're here. You get on your belly and crawl up the hall and see who's there."

It's hard to argue when you're whispering. Smitty said we didn't have any time to waste and to get going.

I took off my shoes, got down on my belly and tried to slide along the baseboard to where I could peek around the corner and see who was there. Very slowly I inched my head into the room. In a moment or two I could just about see the whole room and I couldn't see anyone.

I had just started a reverse crawl out of the living room when an arm came out of nowhere and grabbed a handful of my hair. I was pulled around back into the living room and yanked up to my feet.

Facing me was a big guy, much taller than me, and he had a gun in his left hand. With his right hand, he was holding me up by my hair so we were face to face, and shaking the hell out of me for good measure. That hurt!

Whispering into my face, he said. "Who the hell are you, and where are Steve and Johnny?" I was simultaneously thinking that his breath stank, Smitty should have sent someone much bigger than me and he was tearing the hair out of my head.

"I asked you a question, asshole."

It crossed my mind that he must be the bodyguard that was supposed to be with Carpenter.

The only idea I could come up with was to answer him as loudly as I could. Hoping Smitty'd hear me and do something.

"Ow," I yelled, "that hurts!" Okay, you got me. I thought the house was empty."

He shook me harder.

"Where're Steve and Johnny?"

"On the porch. They're okay, honest."

"On the porch? What d'ya mean?"

"They're tied up on the porch. In the dark they thought I had a gun and I was able to tie and gag 'em." I spoke as loudly as I could.

Shaking me like a rag doll he said "Shut up. You're making too much noise."

I shut up.

"You're feeding me a bunch of crap. He whispered. "I don't believe you. No way could you surprise those two. You got someone else out there. I ain't afraid to use this gun, so you better tell me who the hell's in the kitchen."

He still had my hair in his hand and we were still face to face. He was quiet now but very, very menacing.

"I'm telling you the truth." I still said it pretty loudly, trying to make it sound like I was really scared by this guy. Which was easy because I was. "You don't need to use your gun on me. I'm telling you the truth, honest."

"I think you're lying, but I ain't taking any chances. I'm gonna let go of your hair and you're gonna march ahead of me into the kitchen. We'll see if you're telling the truth or not. Don't forget – I've got the gun aimed at your back and I ain't afraid to use it." He didn't need to remind me.

With that he pushed me back into the hall and toward the swinging door into the kitchen. He kept one hand on my shoulder, making me walk slowly, while he tiptoed quietly behind me. I could feel the gun barrel on my back. When I got to the door I hesitated but he signaled that I should push it open.

Standing in the doorway, I couldn't see anyone at all in the kitchen. He pushed me a little way in, then cautiously came in behind me. I still couldn't see anyone and was wondering where they'd gone when all hell broke loose.

With a loud yell, Dave came out of nowhere and crashed down on my captor. Evidently he'd managed to wedge himself above the door and dropped down from there.

He knocked the gunman down, the gun went off and I was hit.

CHAPTER 22

All in all, I'd have to say this whole plan was not going particularly well. Particularly for me. I didn't feel anything. I was just, all of a sudden, down on the floor. I had no memory of how I got there. No pain. My biggest concern at that moment was how Dave was doing. He and the gunman were wrestling for the gun and Dave was having a hard time of it.

My next biggest concern was that, as they fought for the gun, it seemed to mostly be pointed at me. I still hadn't realized that I'd already been shot. Another shot rang out, but at that moment the cavalry arrived. Our other two guys jumped into the fray and in a moment had the gun in their hands and the gunman pinned down on the floor.

Smitty looked around.

"Where'd that blood come from?" he wanted to know. Sure enough, there was a big smear of blood on the floor next to me.

"You been shot?

Weird. As soon as he asked me that, it began to hurt. Actually it more burned than hurt. I rolled over on my side. Les got down and took a look, then reported that I appeared to have a flesh wound in my right buttock. He said it was pretty long and was really bleeding.

"It's pretty deep but it looks like the bullet just gouged out a groove and passed on out."

I think in an effort to take my mind off the problem, he resorted to a statement calculated to make me laugh, but it didn't.

"It almost ripped you a new asshole."

"Thanks a lot."

"Find something and stop the bleeding," Smitty ordered. Then tie this son of a bitch up real good and put him out on the porch with the rest of the trash."

Les took me over to the kitchen sink, pulled my pants down and washed the wound with soap and alcohol. That's when it started to hurt, really hurt. He got the bleeding stopped and covered the wound with a huge home made bandage.

"Jesus Casey, couldn't you get hit someplace that's easier to bandage than your ass? I don't think I can get your pants back up over all this."

We finally got my pants back on, but the pants put pressure on the wound and the bandage, it stung like hell. Les found some Advil and gave me four of them.

Back in the kitchen, Smitty regrouped.

"Shit," he started out. "This ain't going the way we planned. Casey, you okay?"

I gritted my teeth and said, "Yeah."

"Okay, problem. Now that they've seen our faces we're gonna have to take these guys with us when we leave." For the first time I realized that my bandana had been pulled off my face by the gunman and that Dave's had fallen off during the fight.

"No use trying to clean up after ourselves anyway. With his staff gone missing, Carpenter'll know damn well that somebody's been here. We need to start searching ASAP."

Smitty made a quick tour of the house, then started assigning rooms for each of us to search. I got the library. It was on the other side of the dining room and looked promising to me.

"The most important thing we're looking for is the little black book from the boat," he reminded us.

"It's got to be real important to Carpenter, important enough to kill for. If we can find it, I bet we'll find the reason for the killing. But keep an eye out for any papers at all. If we don't find the little book let's not overlook anything else. Take your time. We've got all night. We can afford to be thorough."

I limped off for the library. The first thing I did was rather painfully sit down at the desk and take a good look around the room. It was a large room, with bookshelves on all four walls. One of the walls had a large fireplace with logs arranged in it, ready for a fire. Two windows, one on either side of the fireplace, tightly shut. A pair of leather easy chairs flanking the fireplace. A small coffee table between them. Dominating the center of the room was a huge desk. The floor was covered with several large oriental rugs.

If there was a small book hidden anywhere in there, it would probably be either in the desk or somewhere on the book shelves.

Where do I start? The logical first place to search was the desk. Okay, the desk. It looked easy, unless the drawers were locked. It certainly looked easier than searching the thousands of books on the walls.

I started on the center drawer, and of course it had to be locked. So much for easy.

There was a heavy letter opener in one of the side drawers, just right for forcing the lock on the center drawer. Inside I found letters, bills, an address book – wrong size – and some personal medical records. No diary or anything even remotely like one.

The other drawers were full of all kinds of things. Dictionary, phone book, check book, plus a bunch of odds and ends of no particular interest.

It looked like I was gonna have to look at every book in the room in case something had been hidden there. It would be slow but I had to be methodical. Start in one corner and make my way around the room. The shelves were floor to ceiling with a ladder that was used to reach the upper shelves. I was going to have to climb that damn latter with a burning butt.

I started at the top shelf. Removing a couple of books at a time, I looked behind them and between them and inside them, with no luck. I took out a couple more books. And a couple more.

I was stirring up a lot of dusk and started sneezing. About halfway down the first bookcase, it finally dawned on me. All of the books were really dusty. They hadn't been moved in a long time. I didn't have to look at every book. I only had to see if any books *weren't* dusty.

With that I started moving from bookcase to bookcase rather quickly. Most of them I was able to skip over almost at a glance. The few that were even a little questionable, I looked at carefully. When I got to the other side of the room, near the window wall, I ran into something strange.

Several of the books looked newer than the others and were at lot less dusty than their shelf mates. When I climbed up the ladder to check them out, I couldn't pull them out. I tried book after book and was unable to move any of them. They were fastened securely to the back of the shelves. How very odd!

I think the four Advil addled my thinking. Nothing popped into my mind for a minute or two.

Finally it dawned. It meant that the bookshelf in question was not really a bookshelf. But if it wasn't a bookshelf, what was it? The only thing I could think of was a door. 'A secret door. 'But to where, and how to open it?

My only experience with secret doors was in movies. There was always a switch somewhere that opened the door. 'Usually embedded in the floor under the desk or concealed somewhere in the desk itself. The other classic place was either in or on the fireplace. I chose to look at the fireplace first.

I pushed and pulled every brick, felt around the mantle, checked the firewood (real) and couldn't find anything that moved. Moving on to the desk, I started under the center drawer first. Removing the drawer I ran my fingers all over and found nothing. Next I did the same thing with the other top drawers and again found nothing.

The only place left was the floor. I crawled on my hands and knees looking for a bump that might have been a switch. Nothing there.

Frustrated, I gave the desk a huge shove. It tilted and toppled over, exposing a thin wire hanging under it. I had uncovered a wire and then broken it, all in one swell foop, as my Dad says. Good going, Casey. Well, what did they expect from an amateur?

Nothing to do but tell Smitty and get some help.

The possibility of a secret door got Smitty all excited. When I told him about the broken wire he said, "Not to worry. That's what Nips is for. Let's go."

Smitty yelled for Nips, then he and I went to the library. I suggested trying to open it by ourselves. There was another, much larger letter opener in the desk and, grabbing it, I tried to force the door open, but no luck there. Upon closer inspection we found small cracks around that whole section of the bookcase, and realized we didn't have a clue which way it might open, we didn't even know which side to try to jimmy.

About that time Nips showed up and told us to get the hell away from the door before we made it impossible for him to open.

He walked up to the bookshelf, stopped a couple of steps away and stared at it. Then he stepped up to and ran his hands all around the cracks we'd found. After a minute he said, "I think I've got it."

Smitty: "Can you open it?"

"Yep, it should be easy. You'd never be able to pry it open. Actually you have to push on it to open it. It's got a spring-loaded lock. All you gotta do is push on the left side and it will spring it open. 'Watch!"

He was right. He casually pushed against the left side of the bookcase, there was an audible click and the door immediately opened toward us. Pulling it open all the way, we saw a fairly large, sparsely furnished second office. It had a desk, some filing cabinets lining the walls, and no book shelves. This was a working office and a working office only.

Nip said, "I think the wire you broke was used to lock and unlock the spring loaded device on the door. Otherwise anyone leaning on the case would open it. You broke it and unlocked it."

Crossing over to the filing cabinets, Smitty pulled open the top drawer of one, glanced inside, then turned back to me.

"Looks like you've got your work cut out for you, Casey," he said. "Go through all these drawers. Pull out anything that looks remotely interesting. And don't worry about keeping too much. We're taking as much as we need. Plus we've got the three prisoners. I've made arrangements to get us all outta here around dawn. That means we've got several hours to go through this place, so get to work. Grab every piece of paper you find that looks useful. Stuff it all in paper bags. You've got till about four-thirty in the morning."

I found a bunch of paper bags in the kitchen and got to work.

CHAPTER 23

There wasn't much in the desk. A few pens and pencils, a dead cell phone, a telephone book, a package of Kleenex and that was it. But when I started on the files, I hit the jackpot. It was immediately obvious what these files were all about. Each one had someone's name on it, or the name of a company. They were neatly arranged in alphabetical order.

I pulled out the first one, labeled Ackerman. Ackerman, it turned out, was Harold J. Ackerman, the vice mayor of a small town near Bakersfield. Two letters in his file accused Harold J. of stealing trust fund money. Times, places, amounts. Pretty damning stuff.

Stapled to one of the letters was a copy of a newspaper article about a surprise turnaround by Ackerman on a water bond vote. Written on the article with a marking pen was "$2,000.00." It looked to me like Carpenter had used the letters to blackmail Ackerman into voting a certain way and had been paid $2,000 to do it.

Putting that file back, I started looking at one or two files at random in each section of the alphabet. There were literally hundreds of them. It was mesmerizing.

I looked through dozens of the files. Almost all of them contained records of something shameful in someone's past. Most of them were pretty trivial. Some of them weren't. There was only one inescapable conclusion. This was a treasure trove of blackmail files, pure and simple.

Glancing at my watch, I was surprised to see that almost two hours had gone by. The reading, like I said, was hypnotic. It was like reading a sleazy novel. However, I knew I had to stop reading and start packing. But how much?

I decided I'd better check with Smitty, tell him what I'd found and see if he agreed with me that we should take it all and sift through it back at the warehouse. I told him that it included a lot of odd-ball things, like medical reports and X-rays.

He said, "Just bring business papers and records, stuff that might incriminate him. We'll take it to the research lab."

We have a research lab?

"But before you start," he said, "take a look at the guys on the porch. Make sure they're still secure."

As I approached the door, I could hear scrabbling sounds. A lot of scuffling. Easing the door open, the first thing I saw was the gunman, on his feet next to the porch window. Smitty was right, they needed checking on.

The gunman had rammed his shoulder through the window and was using a piece of the broken glass to saw through the rope around his wrists. He had his hands over a piece still stuck in the window trim and was sawing back and forth. He was maybe halfway through. There was quite a bit of blood on his hands, and on the window sill.

I rushed over, pulled him away from the window and threw him to the floor. At the same time I yelled to Smitty that I needed help. Smitty appeared and in a few seconds we had him retied, this time to a pipe. He wasn't going anywhere.

His cuts were pretty superficial. A wet paper towel and a couple of band-aids for him. No aspirin for this asshole.

Smitty said it was time to start packing up.

"Bring whatever you find to the side door and don't worry about how much you bring, we'll have plenty of room, even for our prisoners."

I couldn't figure that out. He had a truck coming?

"Oh," he added. "We found a hydroponic marijuana farm in the basement, complete with plenty of indoor lighting. I found a camera and took lots of pictures. Dave and Les wanted to take it all, but I nixed that idea. Better he's found with it than us."

It took a lot of time to pack all the files into grocery bags. I wanted to keep them in order. I ended up with over a dozen bags stuffed full, then had to lug them across the house to the side door next to the driveway.

I was the last one bringing stuff to be taken away and I was surprised by the size of the pile already there. Including the three prisoners, it was a whole lot more than one or even two cars could carry away. I asked Smitty what his plan was. He sent me to the front room and told me to keep an eye on the street. He had a smirk on his face. I had a hunch that I was in for a surprise. I pulled a curtain aside and looked out.

Nothing. A garbage truck was making its slow way up the street from house to house. It looked like it was delivering new cans to the houses in the block below us. I wondered if it was gonna spoil Smitty's plan by getting here just as his ride arrived. I kept watching.

The truck kept coming up the street, dropping garbage cans occasionally as it came. I kept hoping they would hurry up and get out of the way. It was still fairly dark but that wouldn't last long. We needed to get things going, and this damned garbage truck wasn't helping.

The truck finally got to us, but it didn't drive by. Instead it backed into Carpenter's driveway. Maybe the guy was turning around? Jeez, now what? If he went only a short distance he'd see the pile of papers and stuff we were stealing from Carpenter's house. He might even think it was garbage!

I yelled for Smitty as I followed the guy's progress down the driveway all the way to the back of the house. Running out the side door, I almost crashed into Smitty, who was standing on the step, arms folded, the picture of calm. Nodding his head, he kept waving the driver further back in the driveway. The driver leaned out his window and in a loud whisper asked, "We okay on time?"

Smitty whispered back. "Perfect. Now get the hell over here and help us get this junk out of the house as fast as we can. Don't want the neighbors to get suspicious!"

That's when it hit me; something hadn't happened that should have. That garbage truck hadn't beeped once while it backed all that distance.

CHAPTER 24

Two guys jumped out of the cab, ran around to the rear and opened it. The mechanism that usually picked up the cans and dumped them inside the truck was nowhere to be seen. The inside of the truck was empty and clean as a whistle.

With the driver and his helper helping the five of us, the loot and our captives were inside the truck in a short time. The driver and his helper jumped back in the cab and closed the rear opening, ready to go.

"Good going, guys," Smitty said. "About as much time as it would have taken you to sneak a cigarette. Now, get going. We'll meet you at the body shop."

They took off and I was left wondering what the body shop was and how in hell Smitty'd been able to arrange for the garbage company to help us.

Looking around at the general mess we'd left in our wake, Smitty announced that it was time to leave, the same way we got here. "Grab your golf bags and let's get back to the golf course before any golfers show up."

"We don't clean up anything?" I asked. "Not even my blood on the kitchen floor?" I had visions of crime scene technicians taking samples, slides, microscopes, databases. I was a regular blood donor. They'd know it was mine in twenty minutes.

"Relax, Casey. Carpenter won't be calling the cops," Smitty said. "He'll be down there on his hands and knees cleaning it up himself. This guy's in so deep, last thing he'd ever want is cops. He won't even be able to call in Merry Maids."

We made no effort to hide our tracks. It'd be entirely obvious that the house had been ransacked. We just walked out the back door, across the yard, over the fence, down the golf course and out to our car. It was just barely light and foggy as heck.

"Just made it." Dave said.

"Just made it? What does that mean?" Smitty asked.

"Believe it or not, there'll be guys playing already, but they're all at the beginning of the course, what they call the front nine. We're at the back nine, the end of the course, that's why there's no one here."

"Now you tell me. Anyway we're okay!"

We literally piled into the car. We had made the trip back from the house somewhat casually, but the moment we were at the car, everyone was in a hurry to get away, everyone but Smitty. He stepped in behind the wheel, took his good time fastening his seat belt, pulled away from the curb, and drove away quietly, indulging the neighborhood speed limit of twenty-five.

Down the hill and toward the freeway. When we got there I expected we'd be taking the on ramp and heading toward Oakland. We didn't. We continued straight ahead, under the freeway and toward downtown Richmond. A few blocks later, we turned toward a commercial area below the freeway near the waterfront.

We passed a wholesale meat company, a backyard furniture outlet and several similar businesses before coming to a large metal building with a sign on the front of it. HOGHEAVEN TRUCK BODY CO., INC. Smitty pulled up to a huge metal door, honked his horn, the door rolled up and we drove in. The inside of the place looked big enough to house a football field. Along each side of the building were trucks – a lot of trucks in various stages of remodeling or repair. In the back were a bunch of large machines making a hell of a racket.

"How d'ya like it?" Smitty asked me.

"What is it?"

"We build and repair truck bodies. One of the biggest and best shops in the whole Bay area. The devils own it. We don't particularly advertise that we own it, but we don't keep it a secret either. We're just like every other business – we have to bid on jobs like everybody else, but we get our share."

Looking down the rows of trucks I could see several garbage trucks being worked on. Now I knew where our truck came from. Seeing me eyeing them, Smitty confirmed my supposition.

"Yeah, we borrowed one of the trucks we're working on. What nobody knows don't hurt no one."

As I walked toward the garbage trucks I could see that the one we'd used had been almost emptied, but I didn't see any sign of our three prisoners. I turned to Smitty.

"And our—?" and hesitated.

"Guests?" he said. "They're safely stored in back for now. We'll be taking all the paperwork up to my place so we can go through it all and see what we've got. That treasure trove you found makes me think this thing is a hell of a lot bigger than I'd imagined. I haven't the foggiest idea what to do next, except to keep digging and see what we see."

"One thing we do know though," I said. "We know Carpenter's mixed up in this thing to his eyebrows, and that he's the guy that ordered the killing."

"You're right," Smitty agreed. "I just don't know how to use what we've got yet. But first things first. We'll take a good look at his records and then decide."

Without the three prisoners, we were able to get all the papers loaded into two cars and headed back to Smitty's house. As fast as Smitty drove, the Devils on their bikes were there before us.

Smitty backed into the garage and we all lined up to unload the papers.

"Just dump the stuff here in the garage first," he decided. "Then we'll gradually move it into the rec room, sorting it as we go. Keep all the papers from each room stacked separately. In case some sort of relationship develops. You know, like if we find something interesting and want to refer back to where it came from, we can find it."

This whole operation was turning out to be pretty damn successful. I was really impressed with Smitty's generalship and resourcefulness. In a rare burst of confidence in me, Smitty told me that I was to oversee the examination of all the papers and I would probably need help. My first thought was of Josie. Would he let her help me?

The stack of papers was getting higher and higher. It was going to be a big job. A thought occurred to me.

"Smitty, maybe the notebook isn't as important as we thought it was, at least now."

"Why's that?"

"I'm thinking that the book just referred to all this stuff that he thought was safe in his house. You know what I mean?"

"You're thinking that if we have everything from his house, it doesn't matter what's in the book?"

"Exactly."

Smitty took out his bandana, unfolded it, and blew his nose.

"Jesus, these papers are dusty. I can hardly breathe. You may be right about these papers being more important than the book."

"It's just an idea."

"Yeah, but either way, we need to go through everything pretty carefully. I recognized several of the names you read to me. This stuff could be dynamite."

CHAPTER 25

Before starting on the papers I needed to get to the bathroom and clean up. Then I wanted to get some food into me. Funny thing, even though we'd been up all night, involved in a fight and got shot. I wasn't sleepy and the gun shot gash hurt like hell. I needed to have it washed and re-bandaged but I couldn't have Josie do it. On the way back to the house, we'd agreed not to tell Josie about the gun play. It was probably just as well as the gash was in an embarrassing place anyway.

I locked the door to the bathroom, stripped my pants off and for the first time was able to see my wound. The bandage stuck a little and by the time I'd coaxed it off, the wound was bleeding again. The bullet had made about a two inch long gash in my cheek. Fairly deep, entirely in the fleshy part of my butt and still bleeding. I was admiring it in the mirror when there was a knock on the door.

"Casey, you in there?" It was Les. "I found some good bandages and some sulfa powder to sprinkle on your wound. Let me in."

He was just in time. The bandage he'd put on before was soaked through and blood stains showed on my pants. He took a long look at the wound and let out a low whistle. "It's a little deeper than I thought, that's why it's bleeding so much. We really need a compression bandage. You feel okay?"

"I guess so, but it hurts."

"Well I'll do the best I can. I'll clean it to prevent infection and then I'll bandage the hell out of it. We can't take you to a doctor 'cause it's obviously a bullet wound and they have to report them. But it's really just a flesh wound and should heal easily. You load up on Advil and I'll try to find something stronger for you."

A half hour later, re-bandaged and loaded up with Advil, I joined the gang in the kitchen.

Josie wasn't there but she bounced in a few minutes later. When I say she bounced in, I only mean in comparison with the rest of us. Most of the guys were dragging. It appeared that she'd had a full nights sleep and was rarin' to go.

"How about biscuits, bacon and eggs, guys?" Nobody objected.

I saw my reflection in the door window and decided I looked better than the rest of the guys, maybe because I was younger. Anyway she put me to work setting plates and silverware, while she whipped up buttermilk biscuits, fried bacon and eggs and had me put a half grapefruit in front of each of the guys. That together with coffee and it was back to work.

It was difficult walking without a limp and sitting down without grimacing while trying to conceal my condition to Josie.

Before Smitty showed up I asked Josie if she knew what had happened last night. All she knew was that we were back okay, that nobody'd been arrested and that we had a bunch of papers to look at.

After breakfast, I asked Josie if she'd like to help me go through the stack of papers I had to work on.

"Would I? You bet!" she answered instantly. Talk about a hard sell. "That's why I was asking you about books yesterday. I get so bored. All I'm asked to do is cook. When and where?" I told her about the bags of papers I had and that Smitty had just told me to move them someplace and get to work.

"Let's take them up to the living room," Josie suggested. "It's quieter and a little bit away from all the rest of the guys."

"Do you think you need to ask you dad?"

"No, let's just do it. I'll clear it with Dad on the way."

The stack of dirty dishes in the sink drew our attention.

"We gotta get rid of those first. C'mon, we'll get them in the dishwasher and go."

Shortly thereafter we headed for the garage and started to pack up my pile to take it up to the living room. Smitty saw us but didn't say anything, so I took that for tacit approval. It seemed like it was going to be okay for us to work together.

As we were leaving the garage, I heard Smitty telling the guys that some of them needed to leave. He said, "There're too many people here for the job, and too many for Josie to cook for." He asked Nips, Les and Dave to stay, and for them to pick out three others.

"The rest of you guys, take off. Can somebody check on *Jezebel?* Looks like I'll be here a couple of days, somebody could even stay on the boat."

Two guys volunteered.

On the way upstairs, Josie asked, "Are you okay, it looks like you're limping a little."

Woops! Thinking fast, I said; "I think I turned my ankle a little when I ran across the lawn."

It seemed to work. Her reply was a semi-disinterested, "Oh."

We decided the best way to tackle the stuff from the filing cabinets was to keep it all in alphabetical order and go through the files drawer by drawer. Josie suggested we get a pad of paper and start listing every name we found. Then we could cross reference them every time we ran into the same name. The trouble was we had no idea what we were looking for, except that damn little book.

After the first hour, her notebook's first page was almost full.

I'd been making a separate pile of every file that had a name we recognized, that pile was getting big enough that I was afraid it was going to tip over. We quit for a Coke when we finished with all the files from the first drawer, then started reading through the contents of the files of the most interesting names.

That's when this whole exercise started to get interesting. We started opening and reading the files. Every single file had damning evidence in it, bad enough to send someone to jail or cost them their jobs or careers. Josie started to write down the evidence after each name, and it was scary. Believe it or not – okay, call me naïve – a couple of state representatives had been literally caught molesting minors. Others had stolen money. A couple had been involved in DUIs. Some of them were closet gays. Every one of them was a politician or prominent businessman. Each of them had committed crimes. As far as we could see, not a single one of them had been officially charged with anything.

It was clear to us that these were blackmail files. Each file was in a manila envelope together with proof of the crime. Some were yellowed newspaper clippings, some were in affidavit form, some were copies of records, it would take a lot of time to read them.

We decided it was time to show Smitty what we had. As I got up off the floor my wound bit me. I staggered a little and put my hand on the stack of papers for support. The stack shifted under my hand and most of it fell to the floor. Trying to gather the stack back together, I felt something hard in the middle of the pile.

"Wait a sec," I said. "There's something here." I carefully separated the pile and extracted a small black book. The five by seven inch Holy Grail. It had been buried in the middle of this stack.

I called to Smitty and told him I thought I'd found the book. He yelled back that he'd be there in a minute. Examining the book closely, it looked like a diary. It even had a small lock on it; one that looked like it could be broken into by your average curious five-year-old. I asked Josie to find a screwdriver. I wanted to get it open before Smitty got there. Heck, I'm as curious as any average five-year-old.

The screwdriver and Smitty arrived at the same time, however. Smitty took one glance at the book and the screwdriver in my hands and yelled, "Put it down! Don't touch it!" Shocked, I dropped it on the desk and Smitty picked it up – extremely carefully, I noticed.

"I saw an ad for an address book, looked just like this," Smitty said, never taking his eyes off it. "It came with a cute little special feature. If you tried opening it without the proper sequence, it'd explode in your face. Let's get Nips up here and see what he thinks." He handed it back to me. I gingerly set it down on the desk.

We all stood staring at it until Nips got there. He picked it up and turned it round and round in his hands.

"Jesus Christ Casey, were you just going to open this?"

"Yeah, until Smitty stopped me."

"He may have saved your life! Anybody got a small screwdriver?"

There was one in the desk.

"Okay everybody, back up a few feet; I don't want anyone hurt except me. These things are tricky to open without the right sequence. Maybe I can unscrew it from the back and avoid the explosion, if I'm lucky. Fortunately, the blast is pretty small. It can blind you or take a finger off, but that's about all."

"Okay now, stand back." Turning his back to us, he appeared to struggle with the miniature screwdriver for a moment then loudly yelled "OH SHIT," and tossed the book at me.

CHAPTER 26

Stunned silence! Then I yelled, grabbed Josie and dove for the floor. A moment later I raised my head and saw Nips doubled over laughing.

"Wasn't that fun?" he asked.

Rather mildly, Smitty said, "I should have known better. That's not the first time you've got me with your weird sense of humor."

I didn't know whether to laugh or cuss him.

"You okay Josie?"

"Wow, that was exciting!" I guessed she was okay.

There was a moment of silence while the three of us adjusted to this little anticlimax. Nips handed the screwdriver back to me and told me I could have used it safely. "In fact, you could have used a sledgehammer on this little baby." Nips said. "No explosive in it at all. At least not of the nuts and bolts and kaboom variety."

I wanted to see what was in the little black book, but Smitty had other ideas. He took the book from Nips and said he'd take it and look at it downstairs.

"You might also want to look at the list of files we've checked through so far," I suggested. Josie handed him the pad. His eyes bugged as he skimmed down the list.

"Casey, I'm beginning to agree with you about this book. I think the book tells the secret of the room you found. But now we don't need the book – we've got the room! I'll go through it, you two keep at the rest of the files."

So Josie and I went back to the files. After a couple of hours, Smitty sent one of the guys up to us to tell us we should quit, at least temporarily. Smitty'd decided we already had more stuff than we could probably use. That was okay with us. We'd already been saying we needed time to start researching the names we already had.

In addition to the politicians' names we had, we'd come across some other pretty interesting names as well. Many were prominent businessmen. One owned a small donut shop. Two or three were stockbrokers. Several were in management with large corporations. One was a police chief. Lots of leads to lots of people! We needed to figure where we were going.

Smitty hesitated, then said, "Casey, I think you were right. Carpenter's little black book just referred to all these files. The files are more important than the book. What I can't figure out is where all this stuff came from. Some of its years old. Carpenter got this info from somebody and that person's pulling Carpenter's strings. I'm thinking that whoever's behind Carpenter is just as much a murderer as Carpenter."

Les spoke up, "There's gotta be something in those files that'll lead us to Carpenter's boss."

"I think so too," Smitty said. "So everybody take a stack of files and let's find him."

For a short while there was a lot of silence, then some laughing started to break out, followed by lots of "wows," "I always thought so," and one incredulous "I voted for this guy?"

"Don't play around guys, hop to it," Smitty said, then grabbing Josie "I'll see if I can talk this daughter of mine into making a bunch of sandwiches for you guys."

Josie'd told me she never did lunch but she didn't argue with her dad, either. She didn't invite me to help her, so I stayed in the rec room and grabbed a bunch of the files.

The file I was most interested in was fat. It contained material about that California state senator I always thought was a crook, Goldberg. His file was more than a little juicy. One item involved a fifteen-year-old girl, a classic case of statutory rape; even though the senator claimed the girl said she was eighteen. There were letters, affidavits, etc.; all proving that it really happened. But no court case, no conviction. Reading more of the letters, it got even worse. The young lady was the daughter of a good friend of said senator. So good, the father was apparently willing to drop the whole case in return for an undisclosed amount of cash. Some father!

It was pretty obvious that Goldberg had been really important to Carpenter. There were a number of references to things Carpenter had been told to do. Oddly enough, however, I couldn't find any evidence that Carpenter had gotten any money from the senator. The records appeared to be otherwise quite complete, but nothing about him getting any money. And there were plenty of other files like this one.

It took me a while to figure out how Carpenter'd used these files. He'd been blackmailing senators to get a vote for or against a particular bill. After the vote was cast Carpenter would get a payback, in either cash or check, from the sponsors of the bill. Josie said she'd bet that he was registered in Sacramento as a lobbyist and that's how he got his money.

It was clear that Carpenter got his orders from Goldberg, but we couldn't find any money trail.

What a crock some of our elected representatives are. They do something really bad, something they can be blackmailed for. Then they allow some slime bag like Carpenter to blackmail them into voting against their constituents' interests and Carpenter makes money. Worst of all is what it eventually leads to, outright criminal behavior like murder to protect the original crimes. On top of that, there's a Senator who's sworn to uphold the law behind it all. We had paper evidence of a direct link between Carpenter and Goldberg, but nothing to prove they were crooks together. They're all crooks. They just haven't been caught.

Smitty reminded us how Richards had broken down and admitted that he'd been told to use a gun if necessary. Richards had been told, "If you have to shoot him to get the package, do it! Just be damn sure to get the package." He told the Devils he'd assumed he was supposed to shoot the guy based on what he'd been told.

Now we needed an ironclad link between Richards and Carpenter. Smitty said we'd need something in writing to convince the police that we were innocent of murder. We had the confessed shooter but we didn't know his motive. If he was a hired killer, who'd hired him? 'If Carpenter hired him, why? If there was someone behind Carpenter, who was it and was he the one who ordered the killing?

Smitty was turning into a one-man private detective agency.

A couple of hours later I found myself almost asleep in my chair. Josie was reading files, curled up near my feet. I was staring at a wall clock without seeing it. I shook myself and realized it was only three but we'd been up all night the night before.

Smitty spotted Josie on the floor and called a halt for the day.

"That's enough guys. It's been a long day and night. Grab a snack and get to bed. We'll have another full day tomorrow."

CHAPTER 27

Later that evening Smitty, Gus, and I sat in the kitchen drinking coffee.

"So what do you think?" Smitty asked me.

"About what?"

"What we're doing and if it's the right thing. Sometimes I think we're just spinning our wheels. You're outside the gang and maybe a little more objective. So, what do you think."

"Honestly? I think it's a little late for second guessing. You can't quit now. For one thing, the guys wouldn't let you."

"Maybe I'm just tired, probably should get to bed," and he lapsed into silence.

Several minutes went by and then, just as Smitty was getting up, the phone rang.

Gus grabbed it and after listening for a second said, "It's for you." And handed the phone to Smitty. "It's Moose. You know, on your boat."

On the speaker phone the guy said "there's been a couple of strangers' snooping around the docks boss. Didn't look like they belong around here. Been asking a lotta questions about anyone living on any of the boats, but they didn't get much info from anyone. There's hardly anyone here, and those that are here don't seem to cater to strangers. What d'ya want us to do?"

"You alone?" Smith asked him.

"No, there's a couple of us here on the boat. More at the warehouse."

"Are the snoopers still around?"

"Yeah. They're off the docks, but they're still hanging around."

"Okay. Somebody's gotta stay on the boat. The other one try to tail these guys when they leave. Whoever stays on board, keep your eyes open and call again if anyone shows any extra interest in my boat.

Maybe it's just a coincidence. Sometimes we get bail bondsmen or the sheriff's department looking for stolen boats down there."

Smitty stopped and thought for a moment, tapping his fingers on the arm of the chair, then said. "But they never come around at night, do they. And no locals ever case our docks, they're not gonna cross the Devils. It's gotta be out of towner's so you better be extra watchful. Okay?"

"You got it, Boss."

Smitty sat thinking. "You know," he said after a bit, "now that we know Richards was sent to kill the guy, I gotta change my mind about the caliber of people around Carpenter. The guy at the boat was a professional gunman, somewhat amateurish, but still a pro."

"But why'd he hire an outsider, when he's got his own enforcer?"

"I can't figure that out. Maybe the guys he had around him wouldn't pull the trigger if necessary. But if it was Carpenter's men down there, how in hell did he find out about me so soon?" Smitty asked

He continued, "I wonder if he's got an informant in the police department. Guess who that'd be…That God damned sergeant would drop a dime on me just to get even!"

CHAPTER 28

We looked to Smitty to see what was next. Several minutes went by while Smitty stared at the floor. The rest respected his need to think this all through. Nobody broke the silence.

Finally he lifted his head, shrugged and announced, "Council of war. Gather up and let's talk about what's happening."

Everyone came to the biker equivalent of attention.

He stared at the floor again for a moment, then continued.

"This Carpenter guy don't know squat about how much trouble he's in. We could totally put him out of business overnight if we wanted to play rough. We've got an organization I'll put up against anyone's. I want to put him out of business permanently but – and we're talkin' spelled out in capital letters here. No rough stuff. That's gonna be tough. Plus I'm convinced he's just someone else's tool. The real boss, the real murderer's still out there."

"We're walkin' a tight rope on the fringes of the law," Smitty went on, "but Carpenter's operating way outside the law. That's in our favor. We need to find out as much about him as he seems to know about us. If he's snoopin' around my boat he evidently knows who I am, which means he can find out a lot about me in a hurry. I'm too damn well known on the waterfront, plus I've been in the papers a lot."

Smitty wasn't exaggerating. I was gradually remembering seeing his name and the Devil's name in headlines back over the years. He'd been newspaper fodder a lot, most of it some years ago. He hadn't mention it to me, but I remembered he'd been arrested plenty of times. I couldn't remember if he'd ever been convicted.

I wagged a finger at him, indicating I had a thought I wanted to throw out. I sure as hell wasn't going to raise my hand, not in this crowd. I made it more like I was bidding at an auction, like when the bidder doesn't want to call attention to himself. It worked.

"What you got?"

"I was thinking, Maybe we could take advantage of someone he's been blackmailing."

"And how would we go about doing that?"

"Pick out somebody he's been blackmailing, over something fairly small. Maybe you could make him more afraid of you than he is of Carpenter. Or maybe somehow you could make his problem go away? I think if we all go through the files again as a group we can come up with somebody who fits the profile."

Smitty stared at me for what seemed like a full minute. Total silence.

"I like it. It might even work. Any other ideas?"

There were none.

"Okay then, that's it. Start going through the files and find someone for us to work on."

"Smitty? One more idea."

"Yeah, what's that?"

"We should try to find someone that has some power. Not, for example, the guy that owns the donut shop. We need to find someone we can leverage."

Because Josie and I had organized our files so well, it was pretty easy to flip through them. Within an hour, I had a list of several names that looked promising.

One of them was the one I'd told Smitty about earlier, the Sacramento politico. But his problems were so monumental; I didn't think there was any way we could get him out from under them. Besides, I had a feeling that this particular senator was involved with Carpenter, not a victim. Another was an aide to a senator. He was a possibility. His particular sin: forgery. Another was a retired army officer. The army knew he was gay, but his new employer didn't. Maybe?

However, the one I considered the most promising was a local police chief. His sin was misappropriation of funds. It wasn't a large amount, but being a police chief, it could be seriously damaging to his career. It looked like Carpenter or someone had hired outside accountants to check the department's books and found the transgression that Carpenter was holding over the chief's head.

The best part about him though was that he wasn't just any police chief. He was the police chief of El Cerrito. Carpenter's home town.

Smitty wasn't as enthused as I'd hoped. "A *police chief*? We're on the run from one police department. You want us to get mixed up with another one?"

That argument wasn't going to stop me. "Think about it, Smitty. First off, he's already in trouble with Carpenter. If we can convince him that we want to help him and that no one's gonna find out what we know, why wouldn't he want to help us? Maybe we could convince him that if he helps us, we can get Carpenter off his back. He'd end up indebted to us. How many police chiefs can you say that about?"

Smitty sat silent for a long time. He was again obviously mulling over the whole problem, starting from square one.

Finally he said, "You know, I think maybe it's worth a try. But we'd have to be real careful about it. Let me sleep on it. Maybe I can come up with a way to get to the chief. We could try."

He eyed me somewhat speculatively, as if I was some kind of new specimen he'd gotten his hands on but wasn't quite sure about. I felt that I was beginning to prove my worth to him. Hell, being able to ride a motorcycle isn't everything. Thinking had its points too!

Josie popped her head into the kitchen and announced she was on her way upstairs to bed.

Everybody was yawning. "I don't care about you guys," Smitty said, "but I'm turning in too. Josie, you gonna fix breakfast for this gang in the morning?"

"Yeah, Pops. Have a good one."

I caught up with Josie on the stairs. We talked over the days happenings for a few minutes and then headed for our respective bedrooms.

I got to rethinking what I'd suggested to Smitty. We're going to entrap and un-blackmail a police chief? And it was my idea? I couldn't sleep.

CHAPTER 29

I could smell coffee and breakfast, and so could the rest of the guys. We were in the den, hashing around yesterdays developments. Josie came downstairs and said breakfast was about ready, we'd eat in the dining room.

Smitty was issuing orders. "Red and Dave, you two stick around today. The rest of you clear out for the day. Go relax, see your family or something. Get back here by five this afternoon. We're going to figure out how to meet that chief. We'll do a lot better without you guys around guzzling beer all day."

Looked like I had a day off, kinda'. I couldn't get away, no wheels. Maybe Josie would be free too? I asked her but she said she was gonna spend the afternoon reading. That's what I did too, Latitude 38.

By five we were all assembled in the den again. Smitty held forth.

"Okay guys, we mulled over lots of ideas today. Needless to say, we don't have much experience meeting with police chiefs. Particularly to talk about him being blackmailed. We even called some other chapters for suggestions.

Finally we decided it'd be best if I simply made an appointment saying it was a private matter. That I could only talk it over with the chief. Our thinking was that El Cerrito being such a small town, the chief would be more accessible than in a big city like Oakland."

He went on. "I'll use my full name and this address so if he does a background on me, it'll be clear."

Josie had returned to the room and seated herself next to me.

I leaned toward her and whispered, "What's his full name?"

Without turning her head, whispering from the side of her mouth, she told me.

"Smith, Edgar Eugene Smith."

Smitty continued. "I'll have to explain, as carefully as I can, what our plan is. I gotta let the chief know that we know he's being blackmailed and so am I, and that's why I'm seeing him. Somehow or other, I'm going to stop the blackmailer, is there any way he can help me and help himself too? That's the general idea we came up with, anybody got a better idea?"

Silence.

"Okay, then. We'll go over the details tonight. I have to rehearse what I'm gonna say to the chief. Tomorrow morning I'll go over the whole thing with all of you. Once we've got all the kinks out of the plan, I'll call the chief and make an appointment."

After dinner was over I helped Josie with the dishes and she asked me if I wanted to go to a movie with her.

"I don't think Smitty will let me out of his sight."

"Oh pshaw. You'll be with me all the time and you wouldn't hurt lil' ole me, would you?"

I was surprised, Smitty was easily convinced. Josie said he'd told her he thought I was really helping out.

So we went to a movie. She drove and I passengered. I offered to pay, but she said that since it was her idea, it was her treat. We had popcorn and held hands. It was like a first date. In fact, it *was* our first date.

We got home early. A little after nine thirty, we had some hot chocolate and a piece of cake, took some kidding from the gang about our dating, and went to our respective beds about 10:30. This time I was out like a light. I fell asleep thinking about Josie and how comfortable we seemed to be with each other. My wound had quit bleeding but still throbbed.

About 6:30 in the morning someone started shaking me by the shoulder, giving me no choice but to reluctantly regain consciousness. It was Smitty.

"Something's happened. Get up!" and he was gone.

It didn't take long to get dressed. I already had my shorts on and I didn't have a lot of clothing to dither over. I tossed yesterday's clothes on and dashed downstairs. All the guys were there and so was Josie, all wolfing down bacon and eggs and toast, while Smitty paced back and forth, a cup of coffee in his hands.

I tried to catch Josie's eye, but she was busy. I grabbed a plate, filled it up and sat down next to Dave. "What's going on?" I asked.

"You remember who Red was" he asked. I was immediately worried by his use of the past tense.

"Sure, I remember Red. He gave me my first motorcycle lesson. What's happened? Is he okay?"

"No. It's really bad news. He was shot at his home."

"Who shot him? What happened?"

"As far as we can piece out, Red decided to go to his sister's house last night and take that guy Richards to his house instead of leaving him with her. Somehow Carpenter must have found out about Red and decided to get Richards back."

"How do we know Carpenter did it?"

"Red was still conscious when we found him. He told us 'They got Richards.' That's all he had time to say just before the cops came.

"He told the cops he'd interrupted a robbery. Told them he'd walked in on the guys, they'd slugged him and he was out cold for a while. When he came to Richards was dead they were rifling the house so he tackled the closest guy. That was when the other guy shot him."

"They killed Richards?"

"Deader'n a doornail. Red said he heard them say something about what snitches get."

"Is Red Okay?"

"The paramedics were pretty pessimistic about his chances, but Red's tough. He's been shot before and came through it. We'll just have to keep our fingers crossed. I'm just glad his wife wasn't there."

Smitty was pacing back and forth across the room. Turning to Dave he asked, "Can we visit him?"

"The Doctors said no visitors. They're not even letting the cops talk to him. One of the Doctors told me he's in a coma."

Smitty went into a rant. "Damn it, this isn't supposed to be happening. It's got to be that God Damned Carpenter again. He's been a half step ahead of us for a couple of days now, ever since we raided his house. I still think he's getting information from the cops. How in hell did he even know where Red lived? How could anyone else find him? This stinks. It really pisses me off. Red's been like a brother to me. We've been through more shit together than you guys ever imagined."

Smitty dropped himself in a chair.

"We have to make sure he gets the best care available. Dave, you take care of that," he said. "Get some of the wives to visit and help his wife, and you go to the hospital and make sure he's getting the best. I guess I have to stay here and deal with Carpenter."

Then he switched gears, from dealing with the past to the future in a blink.

"For you guys that just came up this morning, here's what we outlined last night. First thing we do is hit Carpenter where he lives, literally. We need to take his headquarters, his home turf, away from him. We think we can do that with the help of – of all people – the El Cerrito police chief! And guess what. We're going to blackmail the chief, in a nice way. Listen up."

CHAPTER 30

He certainly had the group's attention as he continued.

"Thanks to Carpenter, we've got something on this particular chief and we're pretty sure he'll want to work with us. You don't need to know what it is, but it's something we found in Carpenter's files and we can use it to our advantage. Once the chief knows what we know, and that we don't intend to use it to harm him, I'm layin' odds he'll jump at the chance to get Carpenter off his back."

Restless, Smitty got back on his feet.

"The problem I wrestled with last night was how to approach the chief. I've already made an appointment with him for this afternoon. I'm gonna tell him what I said last night about both of us being blackmailed and that I'm not gonna take it."

"Then I'll ask him if the name Carpenter is familiar to him. I'm betting he'll say yes, but probably no more. At that point I expect he'll probably clam up. He'll be getting worried about his own secret. I'll tell him that we got some very strong evidence against this guy, that some of this evidence could be incriminating against some fairly prominent local citizens. – But all we want to do is stop this guy Carpenter and get rid of any evidence he has, against anybody."

One of the guy said, "He's gonna want to know what all that has to do with him."

"I know. You're right, and that's when it'll get a little dicey, so help me with this. I tell him that some of the evidence we've been able to come by has to do with a very prominent police officer in El Cerrito, that the last thing we want to do is hurt the policeman. That in fact we think the evidence is bullshit and we can make it disappear. We're hoping the officer in question would understand this and help us help him. You all still with me?" Heads nod slowly in agreement. It sounded really iffy to me.

"All right. Assuming he gets the picture and agrees to help us, then I tell him who we are. What d'ya think?"

"What d'ya mean, who we are?"

"I'll tell him about the gang and how we're being framed and how we're trying to avoid violence, the whole enchilada. I'll convince him we can help him and he can help us be the good guys."

As usual, Smitty had his way.

The gang broke up. A couple of the guys were going to drop by to see Red, the rest scattered. I headed toward the kitchen and Josie.

She was in the midst of drying the dishes and greeted me. "Poor Red, all we can do is pray." She handed me a towel, "do you want to help?"

I did. Grabbing the towel I started drying and putting dishes away.

"I know you sail, but do you have a sailboat of your own or do you have a boat we could use? I mean, how can you teach me to be a foredeck ape without a boat?"

"Don't worry, there're a lot of sailboats I can borrow when we're through with this Carpenter business. So you're really serious about sailing?"

"No question."

By the time we finished the dishes, the house was empty and quiet, and it was mid-morning. Time for an early lunch. Grabbing a couple of sodas, we both sat on bar stools and ate some brownies Josie'd whipped up for later on.

"Do you always sail by yourself?" she wanted to know "It seems scary, the idea of sailing all the way from San Diego to San Francisco all by yourself."

"Sometimes it can be scary. But usually I have one or two crew with me. On some of the bigger boats, fifty or sixty footers, I need several crewmen to help me. I shouldn't call them all crew *men*. Some of them are crew women."

"You've actually sailed for several days with a crew of women?"

I knew what was on her mind. Everybody thinks there's a lot of sex on a sailboat if there's a woman crew on board. That sure wasn't my experience. First off, it's usually cold when I bring a boat up the coast. I guess if it was warm and clear, the owner wouldn't need me. He'd bring his boat up himself. And trust me, when you're bundled up with warm clothes and a float coat on, you don't look very sexy. Male *or* female. On top of that, most of us didn't change our clothes very often on a short trip, so we didn't smell very appealing. So much for the romantic notion of a sailor man.

I asked her a question. "You told me that your dad never let you handle anything on the boat when you went sailing with him, right?"

"Yes. I was just along as chief cook and bottle washer."

"If you go sailing with me, I'll let you handle anything to want."

She giggled and said, "Really? Anything?"

It took me a moment or two to catch on to her meaning. Then I blushed.

"You know what I mean!"

CHAPTER 31

While we ate, Smitty left for his appointment.

Later he called and talked to Josie. Said he was getting along okay with the chief, lots of interruptions, and it looked like he might be there for several hours.

Josie decided she needed a nap and suggested I could read some.

I couldn't keep my eyes open when I tried to read. When I woke up it was dark and I was hungry. Downstairs I could hear Josie sounds from the kitchen and headed there.

"Thought you were going to sleep forever. Hungry?"

"I only slept three hours. Did you?"

"Yeah, I'm just up. How about a little steak? Baked potato? Salad? You better say yes because the spuds are already in the oven."

"In that case, it sounds okay to me." Actually it sounded great to me. She told me she didn't usually fix steak for the group, "Too much trouble for that many guys and it was damn expensive."

We finished up the meal with a frozen chocolate-covered ice cream cone, sitting in front of the TV, in the living room. Just the two of us, quietly digesting our dinners and watching a travelogue about Europe. I asked her if she'd ever been.

"Where? Oh, you mean Europe? No, but I'd like to. You?"

"No, but I'd like to, too." We both laughed. The travelogues continued on and we decided we'd rather watch them than some mystery reruns.

We watched travelogues until after nine, and then I guess we both napped a little. It was pleasant. Josie had moved over to the couch and was leaning back against me. We were both really comfortable and just sort of dozed off. Like an old married couple.

I think Josie heard it first. She grabbed my arm and said, "What was that?"

At first I didn't know what she was talking about. After a moment, I heard a scraping sound from downstairs. "Is anyone else here?" I asked in a whisper.

"No," she said. "It sounds like someone's trying to get in the garage."

"Maybe it's one of the guys coming back?"

"No way. They always throw the door open so they can get their bikes in."

"Is there any way we can see the front of the house without being seen?" I asked.

"The upstairs front bedroom window. It's got a window that sticks out from the house. We can see the whole front."

It was a bay window with a window seat, and from one side of it we could see the front door and all the windows. It had drapes, and we could peek out without be seen. At first we didn't see anything or anyone. Josie studied the street-scape.

"That car looks out of place to me," Josie said. "And I think I see a couple of guys in the front seat." I squinted through my closed fist. She was right. There were definitely two men sitting there. There wasn't a street light anywhere near, but the moonlight was enough to make them out.

"I think their motor's running," Josie whispered, "and they certainly don't have their front wheels turned into the curb." Josie would make a good detective. I hadn't thought about the fact that they were parked on a steep downhill slope. "I bet they're watching the house. What do you think we should do?"

All I could think of was to keep an eye on them and see what developed. "Why don't we watch from here and see what they do. Is there an alarm system in the house?" I asked.

"No, there isn't. Dad never thought he'd need it. No one ever crosses the Devils."

"Okay, let's settle down right here and keep an eye on them. How about if I stay here, and you get us some hot chocolate or something to help pass the time."

She said, "Sounds like a plan to me," and took off.

Almost an hour and two cups of chocolate later, both doors of the car opened and two guys got out. They must have disconnected the dome light 'cuz it didn't go on when they opened the door. We could see them okay in the moonlight, but not well enough to make out their features. They both were dressed casually, khakis and a light jacket. They approached the house as if they didn't have a care in the world.

"But they must know someone's here," I said. "We had the light on in the living room when we heard that noise."

"Unless the door to the kitchen is open, you can't see the light from the front of the house," Josie said. "Besides, we only had one small lamp on, plus the light from the TV. I bet they've been watching the house for a couple of hours and never saw our lights. They think nobody's home."

The two guys walked up to the front door. The first one pulled a gun from his waist and using the butt, banged on the door. After a moment he backed up and the other one knelt down and started fiddling with the lock.

"He's not going to have much luck with that," Josie whispered. "Dad's got special locks on the doors."

I hoped they were good and special.

The other guy backed into the street a little ways and stood there holding the gun in plain view.

CHAPTER 32

"Oh god, Casey, what do we do now?"

"Call your dad's cell quick while I keep an eye on them."

Josie, on the cell phone in an instant, came and stood next to me so I could hear what Smitty had to say. He answered immediately. "This better be important, Josie, it's after eleven, he said, "I'm in the chief's office planning our next step."

"Dad – listen to me. Two guys are trying to break into the house, and they've got guns!"

Smitty snapped to instantly. "Are they in the house yet?"

"Not yet."

He told her to hold on. I could hear him tell the chief to call the Oakland cops and get someone up to his house ASAP. Then he was back on the line to us.

"What room are you in?" Josie told him. "Good," he said. "Go to the closet. Up on the shelf you'll see a locked box. Get it quick and come back." Josie motioned for me to get it.

Smitty gave her the combination and we opened it. Inside were two guns.

"They're loaded but they've got a trigger lock on each of 'em. The key to the lock's in the bottom drawer of the night stand next to the bed."

Josie had the guns out and the key in her hands in a matter of moments. While she did, Smitty asked me if I knew anything about guns. I had to say no. The only gun I'd ever fired was a Very pistol – a flare gun. Those you just point in the air and pull the trigger.

"Never mind," Smitty said. "Just stay away from them. Josie's a crack shot. You're in good hands."

"Thanks, Dad," Josie said, back on the phone.

"Josie, stay in the room," he went on. "Keep the gun handy. If they get in, stay hidden. We've got police on the way. As soon as they hear sirens, they'll hightail it outta there."

We huddled in the dark, watching the two guys. The one trying to open the door must have been a rank amateur. I told Josie how Nips had gotten through the locks at Carpenter's house much faster.

"He wouldn't these, except maybe because he actually installed these himself. He said it'd take quite a while, even for him to open these buggers."

The two were making a fair amount of noise working on the lock, so Josie took a chance and inched the window open just a smidge. We could hear them talking but couldn't make out what they were saying. One was standing ten feet down the walk, watching the street.

After a few minutes Josie said, "Can you hear that?" She beckoned me back over to the open window. We could both hear the faint sound of sirens in the distance. It took a few moments for the housebreakers to hear them too. Suddenly the guy out toward the street stiffened and said, quite loudly, "Shut up and listen."

"What is it?"

"Sirens. Coming this way!"

"What the hell?"

"Somebody must've seen us or there's a silent alarm or something. C'mon, we gotta go."

They split for the car and took off down the hill. The passenger must have caught something in the door. It was swinging wildly as they spun away. There was enough light to make out what kind of a car it was and get the license plate.

We got Smitty back on the phone. "Can you hear police yet?"

"Yeah, Dad," Josie reported. "They're on the way, and those guys took off."

"Okay, now quick," Smitty told us, "put the guns away. When the cops get there, tell them you're house sitting for your dad. Tell them I'm on vacation somewhere, but you don't know where. Tell them you think the guys thought the house was empty and it was just lucky you two were there tonight."

"They're just pulling up."

"Did you get the license plate?"

"Yeah, we did."

"Don't tell the police. Tell them that the angle made it hard to see the plate or that it was too dark or something."

"Got it," I told him. "gotta go. The cops are pounding on the door!"

Josie ran downstairs and opened the door. "You just missed them," she told the officer in the lead. "They took off in a black or maybe a dark blue sedan as you were coming up the street."

"Shit! Oh, sorry, lady. We got here as fast as we could and made a lot of noise on the way. We'd rather scare them off and lose them than have someone hurt. So tell me what happened?" Josie fed him Smitty's story, faithfully leaving out any mention of the guns we had.

"Sounds like a fairly normal robbery attempt, except for the gun part. You sure you saw a gun?" We both assured him that we'd both seen a gun.

"In fact," Josie said, "it looked like an automatic to me, not a revolver." That felt like a little more information than your average young female house-sitter should know, but nobody raised an eyebrow.

The other cops came in and said they'd been around the house and hadn't found anything. It took another half hour for them to finish their paper work, give us their cards, reassure us of our safety and thank us for calling them.

Josie immediately called her dad back. He told her a couple of the guys would be there in a minute or two.

"I can see them," Josie told him. "They're already here – just waiting for the cops to leave."

Sure enough, a moment later we heard the garage door open. They came hurrying upstairs immediately and one of them used Josie's phone to let Smitty know they were there. Then we had to tell the whole story over again.

"Well, its over," one of the guys said. "They won't be back. But we're staying here the rest of the night, so you two can get some sleep."

It was after one a.m. We'd both wound down by then, sleep sounded good.

CHAPTER 33

Smitty must have gotten in shortly after we went to bed. At breakfast he had Josie recount the events of the previous night. None of us could figure out what had happened. Who were the guys, why were they there, what were they after.

"What about the license plate number?" Josie wanted to know. Smitty said the El Cerrito Chief was going to run the plate for him even though "he was a little upset when he heard me tell you to lie to the police."

He said he and the chief hit it off pretty well. He'd been real wary at first, but gradually seemed to warm up to him. Smitty'd had a little trouble getting over the Devils part of it, but he convinced the chief all that was behind him. They already had plans to meet again right away to plan strategy. Smitty told us that the chief's name was O'Meara but we're supposed to call him Chief.

"First, this is what the Chief and I came up with. I did pretty much what I told you I was gonna do. I'd phoned ahead and asked for an appointment without saying what I wanted to see him about. I purposely got there about ten minutes early to make a good impression."

"How big is his department?" I asked. "Were there a lot of cops hanging around?"

"I don't know how big the department is," Smitty admitted. "I only saw one other cop while I was there – a desk clerk, I think. The chief and I met in his office, just the two of us. I told him pretty much what I'd planned to say."

He paused to add some sugar to his coffee.

"I can't take these all nighters the way I used to. Need the coffee and sugar pick up," he confided.

"I told him some guy was trying to blackmail me. Some guy that lived in the El Cerrito hills near a golf course. Told him that the idiot had picked the wrong guy this time, I wasn't having any of his blackmail crap. Asked him if he had any idea of who I was talking about."

He said he might have an idea. When I told him that we had a list of all the people this guy was blackmailing, he wanted to know how we got it."

"You don't want to know," I told him and added, "Does the name Carpenter mean anything to you?"

He allowed as how it might, being real cautious.

"So I went on. Well, we've got this real damaging list of some pretty well know people and the things he's blackmailing them for. We could just burn it, but ten to one, he's got copies hidden away. I could see I had his attention. But you know, he *is* a police chief. Real cautious and inclined to play it strictly by the board. He suggested that maybe we should be talking to the FBI.

I told him we'd thought of that, but that there were some names on the list we didn't want the FBI to get. Then I asked him if I could ask him a hypothetical question, off the record."

He answered, "Off the record? Okay, but if you tell me something that incriminates you, there's nothing like attorney client protection here."

"I told him I understood. Then I asked him for his opinion."

"Like, if I ran across an insignificant piece of information that some guy wanted to use to illegally blackmail a public servant, would I be morally wrong to destroy that insignificant piece of information?"

Another question from him. "An insignificant piece of information?"

"Yeah. Something meaningless, but something that could be twisted to sound bad."

"And it's never actually been used for blackmail purposes?" he asked.

"As far as I know" was my reply.

"There was a long pause, during which he stared at me. Then,"

"I'm going to assume you're correct and that insignificant piece of paper's never been used for blackmail purposes, so it's just a scrap of paper. In that case, I'd say you could destroy the hell out of that piece of paper."

"He got the message," Smitty said with a satisfied wink.

Smitty continued, "I followed with, 'Chief, can I cut to the chase? if we promise that we can get rid of Carpenter once and for all – if we can get him off my back and everybody else's and be *mostly* legal doing it, could you help us?'

But he wasn't sold yet. He hadn't seen any papers, he pointed out, just a lot of talk. I felt it was time to show him a copy of the original papers Carpenter had on him.

"He recognized it, a page from an accounting book. He'd used some money from the wrong source. It was an insignificant amount and he'd later made it right. But it could be blown up and made to look bad."

He said, "I don't know."

I said, "First, the evidence we found about you is peanuts. We can make it go away real easy. Then I took a chance and told him how we'd gotten the evidence."

He blanched and said, "I can't be a party to that."

"I reminded him that we'd done that long before I came in to meet with him. I also pointed out the obvious, that Carpenter wasn't gonna say anything to anyone. The last thing he wanted was police attention. I told him we had evidence that Carpenter was growing pot in his basement."

"The Chief wasn't sure. He told me that if he had probable cause to search the house and there was pot growing in his basement, he could nail him on that alone but basing the raid on our evidence alone, he thought it violated all police protocol."

"I told him we'd thought about that too. How about if you appoint a couple of us to your Grand Jury, don't they make investigations and stuff?"

"He shot that down in a hurry. It turns out you have to be an El Cerrito resident to be on the Grand Jury.

However he did say 'But maybe if I took my suspicions to the Grand Jury, they could *hire* you. I'll need to think about that.'

When I told him about our prisoners, he balked again. I told him that I was sure these guys were all ex-cons, judging by their tattoos and the way they talked. I told him we'd made a citizens' arrest on them and we were holding them for him.

"The chief's a real guy. I like him and he's smart. He's down to earth and practical. I usually don't have much respect for cops, but this guy's different. I think you guys'd like him. More than that, I think we can work with him."

He continued. "Okay, I told the chief, let's see if I'm right about these guys being ex-cons and I gave him the three names.

He glanced at the names, called in his desk clerk and said, 'run 'em'.

In a short time he was back, and my suspicions were confirmed.

All three guys from Carpenter's house had records. All three of them can be arrested on sight as parole violators. Then when I added that one of them had a gun on him, he was sold. I asked him if there was some way we could get our prisoners into his cells. He said he'd need some reason to pick them up; He couldn't do it just on my word. I asked him if a local business owner said he'd been threatened by one of the three, would that do?"

Smitty was on his feet now, warming up to the retelling.

"So the chief says, 'Is that true?' Sure, I tell him and explained how our garbage truck driver had been threatened by the guy, with a gun. We'll handle the driver and his boss if you'll handle the rest, I told him. I also said that we could deliver the three of them any time he wants them.

I'll need a formal complaint replied the chief.

A couple of the guys spoke up, all with variations on the same question, the one that kept surfacing like a hungry goldfish.

"Do you really think we can trust a police chief?"

Smitty's answer was, "Absolutely. First I think I'm a pretty good judge of character. I spent most of last night with him to the wee hours and I mean it when I say I like him. Yeah, I trust him. Secondly – and more importantly, he needs us. He wants out from under Carpenter. He told me he feels so bad about Carpenter he's even considered quitting his job. Yeah, we can trust him."

He turned to Josie and me and told us to get busy. "Write down every idea we've talked about, and dream up some new ones. I'm seeing him again this afternoon, so we need to get going. Get back to me by ten."

Actually, the minute Smitty had mentioned last night that he was meeting with the chief, Josie and I had started thinking about just that. I didn't tell Smitty, but the only ideas we had were ones we'd come up with ourselves. No one else had volunteered any thing at all.

One idea we had was to let the El Cerrito building inspector know about the obvious code violations we'd seen when we were there. Now that the police chief was on our side, maybe that could be done. Another idea we had was to get the blackmailing information into the hands of a friendly reporter. Maybe these ideas plus a couple more we were still working on might distract Carpenter from us, or make him move out of his headquarters for a while.

At ten we reported back to Smitty. He liked the inspector and the reporter ideas and said he'd take them to the chief in the afternoon.

Out of the blue Smitty said, "Casey, you look like hell. How long have you been wearing those clothes?"

"Well," I allowed, "it's been several days now. I've been able to wash my shorts and socks in the sink and I've been putting my pants under the mattress at night to press them a little. Why?"

"Yeah? Well, it ain't working so well. You need to get some fresh things. And speaking of fresh, don't think I haven't noticed you nosing around my Josie either! Volunteering to help with dishes after each meal is pretty obvious, don't you think?"

I was flabbergasted, to say the least. Did this guy have eyes in the back of his head?

I happen to know for a fact that when I volunteered to dry the dishes, he was down in the garage. Some of the other times he wasn't even in the house.

Then he said something that took the sting out of his previous remark. Turning to Josie he asked her if she thought she could handle one of the big bikes in the garage.

"If you can, take Casey by his place and let him pick up some more clothes."

She said, "Sure. Maybe I'll swing by my place and pick up some things for me, too."

"I may need your car," Smitty said. "That's why I want you to take a bike. Use mine. There's a pair of big saddle bags on the wall, take them too."

Sounded like fun to me. I immediately remembered how I'd had to wrap my arms around Smitty and Red, and was more than looking forward to the same experience with Josie. He told her to make sure I was helmeted and had a good jacket for safety.

"Dad, for heavens sake, don't you think I know *any*thing?" Josie said in the voice of a sassy sixteen-year-old. "I'll take care of it!"

CHAPTER 34

Josie looked awfully small on her dad's bike. She told me that his bike was called the "big Mama," 'cause of the big comfortable rear seat.

We had trouble finding a jacket to fit me. Most were too big. The smallest one we found was still large, but would have to do. I wondered what my landlady would think when she saw me for the first time in several days, wearing a leather jacket featuring a bright yellow hog with a black top hat, sporting a red pitchfork clutched in its hooves. Maybe she wouldn't be home.

Josie wheeled the bike out to the driveway and told me to mount up behind her. I climbed on and wrapped my arms around her waist. She told me to hold her tight. Out of the corner of my eye I could see Smitty keeping his eyes on us. Trying to not look too eager, I did as she directed but somewhat delicately to satisfy her dad.

It was immediately obvious that even with all the padding, Josie was wonderful to hug. I wasn't sure what to do with my head. She told me to kind of hook my chin on her shoulder so we could talk on the way.

Once out of the driveway and away from her dad's watchful eyes, my imagination began to kick in. The position we were in, me tucked in close behind her, made me think of being spooned together in bed with her. Very erotic. I tried to put that thought out of my mind and concentrate on our trip.

Yanking my attention back to the present, I had to admire how proficient she was. We weren't breaking any speed laws, but we were definitely traveling at a fast clip. Weaving in and out of traffic, she seldom had to slow down. She never missed a signal light, somehow speeding up just enough to slide through.

I gradually realized one of the reasons she was so successful was that she didn't consider herself limited by lanes. We slid between, around and beside cars. I thought she was gonna scrape my knees off on some we barely squeezed by.

She must have been told where I lived. Never asked me for directions, just wheeled up to my digs and said, "What now?" I asked her if she wanted to come up for a sec.

"Why not?"

I gathered up a few personal things. A couple of pairs of pants, a few shirts and some underwear together with a toothbrush and I was all set. Actually I threw in some deodorant was an afterthought. You know, a pretty girl? I wrapped the deodorant in a pair of sox so Josie wouldn't notice. It only took a few seconds; I had everything and was ready to leave when my landlady knocked on the door.

"Casey, do you have a girl in there?"

I may not have mentioned that my landlady was quite elderly, and generally not too nosy. Real good qualities for a landlady to have. However, she was very old-fashioned about morals. I think she would have insisted I entertain any girlfriends I had in her parlor. Ideally with her sitting in the corner in her rocking chair, knitting. I wasn't surprised by her question.

Josie looked at me and giggled.

"Oh, hi, Mrs. Perkins. We were just coming down to see you. My employer's daughter gave me a ride over to pick up some clothes."

She invited us in for tea and I had to disappoint her again.

We picked up my clothes from the cleaners and headed for Josie's place. My place was right near Lake Merritt. Hers wasn't.

"Wow, is this yours? How big is it? What – three, four bedrooms?"

"Slow down, one question at a time!" Josie laughed. "Yeah it's mine, lock stock and barrel. Thanks to my ex. I had a good lawyer, and Dad helped. You're right – three bedrooms. Two baths. Plus it has a two-car garage and a rumpus room. You want to see it?"

Her place was neat as a pin. It looked very comfortable, downright pleasant. A place that'd been lived in by someone who knew how to make a house a home. Smelled good too. I asked her if she took care of the place all by herself. She said she did.

"I'm going up to grab some things," she told me as she headed for the stairs. "Get yourself a Coke or something. I'll be down in a minute." I wandered through the kitchen and breakfast room to what must have been a guest bedroom. It reminded me of my parents' house, up near the Oregon border, spacious and comfy. Once again my imagination soared. A pretty girl, huggable, owns her own home, good cook – what more could a guy ask?

I grabbed a Coke from the kitchen and relaxed on the living room sofa. Josie proved what I've always suspected, that a woman's minute is much longer than a man's. She finally came down about fifteen minutes later. She looked great. I suspect she may have taken time to do make-up or something.

"I guess we better get going," I said. "Your dad's waiting."

"Oh, pooh! He's always in a rush. I don't let him have his way all the time. Sit back and relax," Josie said with a dismissive wave of her hand.

"Sometimes I deliberately dawdle just to annoy him. I'm going to have a Coke and maybe even some cookies before we head back. Besides, I want to know about your family. How come you quit college? You going back? How close are you to your parents? Do you see them often?"

"Whoa," I responded, "that's enough. How'd you put it? One question at a time? Not in order but here goes. My parents live near the Oregon border. They're both retired. I see them every couple of months or so. As for college, I ran out of money. My plan was to earn enough to go back, but it hasn't worked out so far."

"How come sailing? Did you grow up near the ocean, or was your dad a sailor?"

"No and no. I grew up in Kansas. My dad was an accountant for a huge company and got moved around a lot. The company transferred him to California when I was about thirteen. Based on my experience, you're more likely to be in love with the sea if you grew up in the Midwest than if you grew up on the coast. At least that's the way it worked for me and most of the people I know. I hung around all the yacht harbors during my teens. The rest is history."

We finished our sodas and Josie decided we should head back; she just had to put her leathers back on over the tight jeans she'd changed into. I counted my visual blessings.

In a short time we had the house locked up and were headed back towards what I was actually coming to think of and refer to as "home."

CHAPTER 35

"It's about time you got here," was Smitty's greeting as we coasted into the garage. "I had a great meeting with the chief this afternoon and do we got plans! But first I want to set out the rules for everyone, including you two. Everybody grab a seat."

I had no idea what this was about and, looking around, I don't think anyone else did either.

"We got a new partner. A police chief. Means we have to really toe the line. When I said no violence before I mean it even more now, in spades!"

He looked around the room again, this time looking hard at each of us before moving on to the next. Some of the guys squirmed a bit. Only when he was satisfied that he'd made his point did he continue.

"Okay. Repeating rule number one. There will be no violence started by us."

"Wait one fuckin' minute, Smitty," someone said from the back of the room. You might not tell it from his choice of words, but he did deliver this interruption with respect. "You made that rule before they shot Red. We gonna let *that* go by?"

"No, Hap, we don't let that go by. What we're going to do is, with the chief's help, let the *law* take care of him." This was met with silence, then a smatter of rumblings.

"Look, think about it, guys," Smitty said quietly. "Most of you are married. For some years now, we've been trying to tone down our image for the good of our families. We've volunteered for the police athletic league, helped in searches – a whole bunch of things. Because of that, our wives have been active in all kinds of social stuff and our kids are better off for it too. We don't want to mess with that, do we? Don't worry – we'll get even, all right. Just *not* with violence."

"As for Carpenter and his gang and the violence *they've* pulled so far or what he might do next, I'm not saying we're gonna be shrinking violets. We'll take care of them, but we won't start any violence. With all the street smarts we've accumulated over the years, I'm betting we can out-smart him."

"Rule number two's one you'll find real easy. I'm the boss." Laughter and boos. "I mean it. I'm taking charge of the whole thing. Nobody does nothin' without telling me about it! Anybody have a problem with that?"

He paused, waiting for any dissent. There was none.

"Okay then. Tomorrow I'm meeting with the chief again. You'll go through the papers once more. Work with Casey and Josie. The chief agrees there must be someone above Carpenter. See if there's any reference to anyone else above Carpenter. Someone who provides him with the information he's using."

That immediately rang a bell with me. I flashed on some of the really bad stuff that Josie and I had seen. Most of it contained a common thread –Sacramento politicians and that senator. We'd have to find those files again.

Josie and I headed back to our files, planning as we went. Josie came up with a great idea. She had several of the guys and me start going through all the papers looking for anything with a name or title on it. She and Gus then gave those a good scrutiny to see if they recognized any of the names.

She told us, "Don't get wrapped up in the stories, all we want are names and titles like senator or mayor or whatever."

They immediately start running into more of the stuff we'd spotted before, Carpenter acting like a crooked lobbyist. Lots of names, most with a dollar amount written beside it. Contractors, building inspectors, politicians, even some cities and counties. Gus agreed with my previous ideas what he was doing. He'd blackmail someone to get a project done and then get a kickback. He claimed the kickbacks as lobbying fees. But we couldn't seem to find a smoking gun from him to anyone else. No records of money transactions other than those lobbying receipts.

Late in the morning Josie found something. "This is it!" Josie cried. "Boy is this ever it. Look at this!"

Crawling over to me, she shoved a really fat file in my face. Inside, at the back, were a few handwritten letters paper-clipped together.

"This is it?"

"Yep. Read the letters!"

The letters were old and hard to read. Three of them. Each only a page long, signed, dated and notarized. They weren't long but they were damning. The first one was a handwritten document from a woman saying that she was a secretary in this particular politician's office. She gave dates and places where she'd had multiple liaisons with him – a married senator – over a period of about two years. She wrote that the senator had promised to divorce his wife and marry her numerous times. In her own words: "I decided to come forth with this information of my own free will after accidentally discovering that he'd been having affairs with at least two other women over the same period of time. I also discovered that he'd promised marriage to each of them."

"Double wow! That's devastating!"

"There's more! Read the other two letters."

The other two were from the two other women saying essentially the same thing, and again, each one was dated, signed and notarized. One was from a typist in the secretarial pool. The other was from a secretary in the attorney general's office. At the bottom of the typist's letter was an additional paragraph, underlined in red, separately signed and notarized: a sworn statement that the typist was a student summer worker who was only sixteen when the Senator originally seduced her. Triple wow!

Each of the letters had one thing in common. The senator had been the subject of rumors for years. Each of the three thought she was the only one. Gradually, having met one another over time, they came to realize the truth.

However, outside of the fact that the letters had been in Carpenter's possession, we couldn't find any link to him. Each of the letters was addressed, "To Whom It May Concern, and none of the letters gave the senators name. How had he gotten the letters? Who had the girls gone to with the information? How did the letters come to be kept private? And where were those girls now? Why did Carpenter have them?

Josie pointed out that the letters did one thing for sure. "The source of the blackmail information is in Sacramento. Carpenter's source or boss is in Sacramento. You know what my dad's going to say. The same thing he said about Carpenter. Even though he didn't pull the trigger himself, he's just as much a murderer as Richards. He's going to say the same thing here. He'll want to find the Sacramento guy."

"Just because Carpenter's got blackmail evidence on Goldberg doesn't necessarily mean that Goldberg's in the blackmail business with Carpenter." I suggested.

"Maybe Carpenter kept the blackmail stuff to protect himself from the senator?" Josie quietly asked, almost to herself.

"So what you think but can't prove is that Goldberg is the boss and he set a moral climate that led Carpenter to hire Richards and Richards murdered the boat owner?" I asked.

"I think so and that makes Goldberg a partner to murder." Then she added, "let's take all this to Dad, I'm really confused."

We found Smitty in the dining room all by himself. He was sitting at the table, hunched over and slowly beating the table softly with his left hand. His right hand held the uncradled phone. He looked miserable.

"Dad, what's the matter?"

"The hospital just called. Red died this morning, at seven o'clock." He looked down for a moment, then looked back up at us. "In my book, he was deliberately murdered, somebody's got to pay."

CHAPTER 36

We followed Smitty downstairs and listened in as he told the gang about Red. That raised the stakes a lot. Most of the guys were calling for instant blood letting.

Smitty waited them out. "Slow down, guys. I've known Red longer than any of you guys have, and probably better too. Red was one hundred percent in favor of my no-violence plan. You know I'm right. Red had more patience and smarts than most of us put together. Remember how he always bragged about having the patience to teach his wife to ride a bike. He was proud of that. He'd be the first to say let's get even – but legally."

He paused a moment, "What we need to do in Red's memory is work harder and smarter to avenge him."

He turned to me and said, "Casey, tell the guys what you and Josie found."

"What we've found is a bunch of letters incriminating a California state senator, dating way back. We think they've been held by Carpenter as protection against the senator. Maybe that's how the whole scheme started. The senator cut Carpenter in on the blackmail scheme in self protection. The letters show us that the information on most of the blackmailing is coming from Sacramento. It's pretty clear that someone in Sacramento provides the blackmail information to the Senator. It's also pretty clear that individual's a politician too."

"What about Red" someone asked.

"We're gonna have the best damn wake for Red you've ever seen," Smitty said. "Nips is already working on it. It'll be at the warehouse 'cuz I expect a couple hundred friends of his will come out. Nips is also taking charge of a group of wives to give Red's wife all the support we can. We'll go to the funeral as a group and give Red every honor we can."

"When's the wake gonna be? Can we bring someone outside of the gang?"

"Absolutely. Everybody liked Red. Bring anyone you want. But it's gonna be respectful, not a riot. Most of our wives and children will be there. I expect it to be dignified." Smitty waited for nods and got them.

"Now," Smitty continued, "we got a lot on our plate. I think we're going to end up in Sacramento, based on what Casey and Josie've found out. But first we'll concentrate on Carpenter, for several reasons. He's here and he's now. He knows about us and he's hurting us. So we go after him first. I think the best way is to trick him into admitting the murders using the blackmail evidence we stole. The chief agrees with me."

"So you can see, the chief and we have a lot in common," he finished. "He's a real ally for us and we have to be fair to him and also use him as best we can. What the chief wants is any link we can find between Carpenter and Richards, no matter how inconsequential it may seem. He can tap into department records to get a lot of information that's not available to us— tax records, property records, prison records, arrest records, and on and on and on. One of the things he's planning on doing is contacting his sister city of Richmond and getting Richards' house searched."

Smitty stopped for a minute, while a small smile formed on his face.

Gus spoke up, "I saw Red give the finger to a police chief once."

Somebody said, "What happened?"

"The chief laughed and gave it back. It was at a motorcycle meet."

Smitty said, "It's true. I was there; the chief had just beaten Red in a race."

Then he added, "a couple more ideas. The chief suggested we contact the *Chronicle* and the *Tribune* and see if they could find any old stories about Carpenter, or if they an obituary already prepared in case of his death. The chief was trying to get Carpenter's fingerprints so he could run them and he was also checking nation-wide records against his name.

One other long shot the chief mentioned is the FBI. If Carpenter ever applied for a government job or ran for public office, he should be on record. The chief said he had a contact at the FBI and would try that angle."

All of a sudden it was as if we'd shifted into high gear, sparked by Red's death. Smitty enlarged our field of research

"How about credit checks, "I asked.

"Good idea. We'll do that too. And I've got another idea," Smitty said. "Does anyone know if blackmailing a state senator is a federal offense? Something the FBI'd be interested in?"

Hesitantly I spoke up, "I think what the FBI can and can't do is a matter of public record. I can call them, tell them I'm writing a book and need that information. I bet they've got a public relations officer who'd be happy to tell me."

"Do it!"

Great! Carried away by Smitty's enthusiasm for his own idea, I'd just volunteered to lie to the FBI. I wondered how many years in jail you get for lying to the FBI, even if it's only a little white lie.

CHAPTER 37

Josie had taken advantage of my time with Smitty and gone to the kitchen. The guys were all downstairs talking about what we were going to do and drinking beer. I could hear some of them telling stories about the crazy scrapes they used to get into with Red. The only personal scrape I'd gotten into with Red was when he taught me how to ride a bike. But Smitty was right; he was a real likable guy.

I headed for the kitchen and found Josie sitting at the table, crying.

I sat down beside her, and took her hands in mine.

"Red?'

"Yes. I was starting dinner when, all of a sudden it came over me that poor Red was gone. The guys all seem so callous, nobody's mourning him."

"Actually they are, in their own way. They're all downstairs telling each other about personal memories they have about Red. They're celebrating his life by reminiscing about the good times they had with him. It's really kinda' touching."

"That's nice. I feel a little better," she said and dried her eyes.

"I better fix something for the guys to eat," she said.

"We got home so late and we've been so busy, and then the news about poor Red, I forgot all about prepping dinner. I'll throw something together quick and easy."

She ended up fixing macaroni and cheese. The talk around the table was about Smitty's plan. He may have convinced them that they had to avoid violence, but there was a lot of talk about what was and wasn't violence. Several also said if Smitty's plan didn't work, they knew another way.

A little later, when Smitty came back, all that talk went away.

"I've e-mailed information about Carpenter to every English-speaking chapter in the world," Smitty announced, joining us.

All over the world? Somebody had told me there were chapters all over the world, but I never imagined they were that closely linked.

"I don't know how far Carpenter's reach is, or how far back he goes. The chief's only been able to trace him back about twelve years so far. No sign of where he came from before that. He could have come from Europe, for all we know."

Josie asked her dad, "Has he found out anything about the guys that tried to break in here last night?"

"Not much. The car's registered to a corporation that seems to be a dummy of some sort. He's having tough sledding trying to find out who's behind the corporation. You know, one corporation leads to another and then another, and so on. But he's working on it."

CHAPTER 38

The guys stayed in the living room for quite a while, talking mostly about Red. Josie and I talked for a little while in the kitchen, then headed for bed.

As I was undressing I heard the house phone ring. I could hear Smitty answering it and then start cussing.

Now what, I thought. Must be something bad; it takes a lot to break Smitty's calm. I headed back down. Most of the guys were there too.

"Crap. That was the chief. He's had a couple of his boys checking up on Carpenter's house off and on all day. He said it looks like trouble's brewing. There's been a lot of activity at the house for the last couple hours. Several cars. His cop thinks there're twelve or fifteen men there. The cop told the chief that it looked like they're planning on going somewhere tonight. The chief said his man hadn't seen any weapons yet but some of the guys could be carrying"

"Are they headed here?"

"Don't know yet, but the chief seems to think this is where they'd be heading," Smitty said, looking concerned. "If they're heading here, maybe that's what those guys were doing here last night. Maybe they were casing the place for tonight."

"He also said his hands are tied. He can't really help us, at least not publicly. He's gonna keep an eye on 'em for us and track them if they leave, but he can't stop them."

"For all the chief knows they may be getting together for a poker party. He can't do anything until they do something illegal, so it's up to us if they head this way. The only thing I can imagine is that they think they can take over my house with a show of force and get his papers back."

He went on "I've been kinda' expecting something like this ever since the two guys tried to case the house. I got kind of a plan to nip them in the bud – without violence."

He nodded to Josie.

"It's pretty complicated and involves all of us. I don't have time to go over all the details so I'm asking you guys to do what I tell you and not waste a lot of time asking questions. Okay?"

One of the guys said, "Let's get at it." Nobody argued.

"First, somebody get on the horn and call the Richmond branch. Use my name. Outline the problem and ask them to get a couple of guys up to keep an eye on Carpenter's house for me. Tell them to keep in cell phone contact. I want to know the minute Carpenters' guys start moving. I want them to tail the group and keep us informed about where they're going.

Be sure and tell them that a couple of friendly cops are watching the place, that the El Cerrito police chief's a buddy of ours and working with us.

"Next thing is for you, Nips. Call the warehouse and get everyone up here right away. Be sure and tell them to be super quiet. Don't want the neighbors to think World War Three's broken out. And tell them to bring some iron with them, just in case. Crowd control stuff like shotguns", he added.

Somehow, shotguns and "iron" didn't add up to "no violence" in my book. What the hell was he planning?

Smitty became a whirlwind of action.

He glanced at Josie. "If he's coming with guns, he's either so scared or so mad he doesn't care about the outcome. We need to control the situation so that it never happens. You know what I mean? We need to stop them in their tracks, before they get near the house. We have to figure out a way to neutralize his weapons before he uses them."

"If there's that many coming, they're probably planning to split up and approach the house from different directions, coming up each street," one of the guys offered

"I think you're right. Okay, how do we use that against them?" He gave everyone a moment to think, but the room remained silent.

"No other ideas? Then I'm going with my plan, and we need to step on it. What I've come up with is a trick. I agree that they'll split up. We need to take care of them separately. I've got an idea that might work. Actually it has to work."

Nervous laughter.

"Those klieg lights we used last year, they still in the yard?"

"Yeah," Les spoke up. "I think there're three or four of 'em, way over in the far corner."

"Okay, take off and find 'em. They're pretty heavy, so take a couple of guys with you. I need three of them up here and operable ASAP"

"Will do. I'm sure they're there, and there's a truck to haul them in."

"Take off!" Smitty tells him. To the rest of us, he continued thinking out loud. "I'm figuring they're planning on something tonight. They haven't left El Cerrito yet, so I'm betting they'll try to force the house when they think we're asleep. Two, three in the morning. That gives us a few hours to get ready. Carpenter's been pretty lucky so far but his luck's about to run out. I don't think he's as good planner as he probably thinks he is. The murder on the boat was a mistake, the attack on Red was a mistake and the first approach to our house was a mistake. Ten to one whatever he's planning now is a mistake too."

I had no idea what Smitty might be planning. One thing's clear: the guy's devious.

While Les and a couple of the guys were pulling out, some of the other guys showed up. As they coasted into the garage, dismounted and came into the rec room, I noticed they were all carrying large duffel bags. I was pretty sure what was in them, and as it turned out, I was right. Each guy emptied his bag on the floor, very carefully. Between them, there was enough firepower to start a small revolution.

There were a lot of small arms and a few rifles, but mostly what looked like sawed off, double barreled shotguns. Smitty'd told them to bring their crowd control stuff. I guess this was it. Josie looked worried. Smitty noticed and came over.

"Don't worry honey," he said, putting an arm around her. "This is just for scare purposes. With any luck at all we won't have to fire a single shot."

Josie looked somewhat reassured – until she heard his next words.

"Okay, guys, I want you to clean your shotguns and load 'em. I also want each of you to carry a sidearm. You're all experts with guns. I'm counting on you to use your guns to scare the SOBs, not to do any damage."

"I don't like this." Josie whispered to me.

CHAPTER 39

Smitty was pacing up and down the room.

"God I hate waiting. Jesus, if those guys don't get back with the klieg lights soon, this ain't gonna work. I gotta phone the warehouse and see if they're on their way."

He still hadn't told us what his big plan was, so there was no way we could help him. Josie brought him some coffee and the guys kept peppering him with questions about his plan. He kept saying it all depended on the klieg lights.

As he waited for someone at the warehouse to answer, he kept pacing. Finally someone answered. "Did Les and the guys find the searchlights?"

"Yeah. They're on the way up."

"Did they find out if they still work?"

"They didn't plug them in, but the janitor said they work. He ran them for us at the party last year. He says they're perfect."

"How long ago did they leave?

"I'd say twenty minutes or so. Should be getting close to you about now."

Smitty hung up, looking relieved. Turning to us, he said, "Okay, here's my plan. As soon as the lights get here, we're gonna set them up outside on the streets. There are three streets converging just above our house. You'll place the lights at the head of each street coming up here, pointing down the street. Somebody go down to the garage and get every extension cord you can find. I want each light rigged so that we can turn them on all at once, on cue. Les can do that. How many guys we got here?"

Twenty-three, it turned out.

"Great. I want you to divide up into three groups of about six or seven and be ready to go out onto the streets, with your guns."

Just then Smitty's phone rang. It was one of the Richmond gang calling to tell him that the group from Carpenter's house was moving. He said there was quite a few of them, crowded into three cars. They'd just turned off the freeway heading toward Oakland.

"That's what I figured," Smitty said after he'd hung up. "They must be heading here. I bet that's why that car was here the other night. Scouting the streets. Here's what I think they're gonna do. They're in three cars. They have to come up one of the streets, maybe they'll come up all three of them. I bet they'll take one car to each of the streets coming up. They'll get within two or three blocks, park them and come the rest of the way on foot, as quietly as they can. It'll be after two in the morning. The street'll be dark. What they don't know is that we'll be waiting for them – with a surprise! When they get within a few yards of the place, we'll light 'em up with the searchlights. They'll be temporarily blinded."

"Wait a second, Smitty," someone said. "Aren't those arc lights? Don't they need like five or ten minutes to warm up? No way can you turn them on suddenly like you think you can."

"Shit," Smitty said through clenched teeth. "Shit, shit, shit. Now what do we do?"

"They ain't arc searchlights. They're surplus Navy signaling lights," came from Lew, a Navy veteran. "I was the one who went to the army surplus store and got them."

"So?"

"They've got blinkers on 'em. They're designed to be left on, but no light gets out until the blinkers are opened. They're used for Morse code signaling."

"You're sure? Check 'em out quick! If we can't surprise them, we're screwed! They're on the way here and I sure as hell ain't got no back up plan."

CHAPTER 40

In just a moment or two Lew had run outside, met the truck and confirmed that they were indeed surplus Navy signal lights. We were back in business.

"Okay, you seem to know about them, so go out and get the lights set up on the streets the way I said. They need to be pointed exactly down the middle of each street so when we open the shutters the whole street will be lit up. Got it?" Lew jumped to do Smitty's bidding.

"Okay, we're running out of time," Smitty said to the rest. "You guys divided up into three groups like I said?" They said they were.

"Okay, here's what you have to do. Each group go down a different street for three or four blocks and get out of sight. Take your shotguns along. Watch for one of the cars coming onto your street. This time of the morning there ain't gonna be much traffic. You should be able to spot them easy. When they park and get out, follow them quietly – make sure they don't know you're behind them. Carry your shotguns at the ready."

"We just walk behind them?"

"Yep. Here's what will happen, I hope. When they're close, all of a sudden the search lights'll flash on in their faces and they'll be temporarily blinded. They'll also realize they've walked into a trap. They'll turn to get back to their cars only to see a half dozen guys with shotguns waiting for them. With any brains at all, they'll give up without a shot."

"How soon?"

"I don't know when they're coming – we just know they are. So I want you guys to get going now and get into position. Make sure they don't see you when they drive up, and don't let any of the neighbors see you. Everyone jumped to their feet and headed for the door.

"Josie, I've got a job for you," Smitty told his daughter. "How well do you know the neighbors?"

"Actually pretty well, Dad. I've been gardening and stuff up here enough that I've met pretty much all of them."

"Well enough to call them at one-thirty in the morning?"

"If it's important, sure."

"Here's what I want you to do. Try to reach each of them. Tell them that you just found out that a movie studio will be shooting a movie scene on our street sometime in the next hour or so. Tell them that at first the studio was planning to shoot it without telling anyone because it would be dark anyway and they wanted the streets to be empty, but then they changed their minds. They need to use searchlights in one portion and they're afraid that everyone will wake up and come outside, or worse yet, call the cops. That's why they called you."

"Okay."

"Tell them the director said they're welcome to watch from their windows, but please don't come outside 'cuz it'd ruin the shoot. Tell them it'll only take maybe thirty minutes or less. Can you do that?"

"I can call them – but I can't guarantee they'll buy it."

"Try! I'm going out to make sure the searchlights are set up right."

I sat by Josie as she called the neighbors. Surprisingly, it went easier than she'd hoped or expected. The first lady she reached happened to be a big movie buff and was enthused about the idea from the get-go. Unfortunately, she was full of questions.

"What's the movie? Who's in it? When can we see it? Do they need any extras?" And on and on. On the other hand, she volunteered to call some of the other neighbors for Josie, which more than made up for the aggravation.

Josie re-emphasized how important it was that no one should be outside during the shoot, but they could feel free to watch from their windows. The use of the word "shoot" made me nervous, given what I was expecting, but I crossed my fingers and didn't comment.

Between Josie and her neighbor, they reached all but two houses where the owners apparently were away. She reported to her dad. "Great!" Smitty said, "We're gonna cream them – I hope!"

There wasn't anything for me to do except to watch in amazement. Amazed that anyone thought this crazy idea would work. Smitty was going to start world war three right here in the Oakland hills. Everybody but me was gung-ho for the idea, even Josie was pitching in enthusiastically. It was going to be a complete disaster and I'd end up dead or in jail.

CHAPTER 41

The guys were hidden in the street, the searchlights with their crews were at the ready, the neighbors had all been warned. Each searchlight crew had a cell phone, ready to relay Smitty's command to turn the lights on. They'd set the cell phones on shaker mode so they wouldn't ring. One shake and the lights went on. All we needed now were the bad guys. Smitty was like a football coach at half time, getting everybody revved up and anxious to get on with it.

While Smitty was outside, Smitty's cell phone rang and I answered it. It was one of the Richmond bike guys, calling to tell Smitty that three cars had turned off onto one of the streets coming up here. He said they were driving real slow like they didn't want to attract any attention. He estimated they were about fifteen minutes away.

I'd tried to tell Smitty that his plan had no chance, but he wouldn't listen. Told me to shut up and help. I'd volunteered to stay inside and answer the phone. Now I ran out to tell Smitty how close they were. He alerted his crews, then told me to get back inside and turn off all the house lights. As he was walking back into the house he grabbed his cell phone and set it on shaker mode. Then called the guys at the lights and told them, "they're coming, the next call will be to turn on the lights."

Once inside, he took Josie and me aside and ran through the drill. His comments were for both of us, but his eyes stayed only on Josie. "Okay, you two," he said. "I want you to do just what you told the neighbors to do – stay inside and watch from the windows. No argument! You know where the guns are. Get 'em and have 'em ready, just in case. My bet is that Carpenter's trying to do to us what we tried to do to him. He wants to take away our base. I don't think any guns'll be used by either side, but be careful!"

Josie whispered a question to me. "So – what do you think of Dad's plan? Really."

"its nuts!"

"Why?"

"There're so many variables – and so many guns. So much left up to chance. What if they don't use the streets? What if the lights don't work? What if they charge instead of turning and running?

"What can we do?"

"Wait and hope!"

Five minutes went by. Seven minutes. Ten minutes. Twenty minutes and still nothing.

Suddenly bright lights. All three of the searchlights came on, almost simultaneously. Just as Smitty had said, they were really powerful, lighting up the whole street for several blocks.

Like the proverbial deer in a headlight, on the street nearest to us stood six men, stopped in their tracks with genuinely startled expressions on their faces.

It seemed like a minute they stood there, though it was probably only a few seconds before they turned and bolted down the street. They only took a few steps before they stopped. Below them, equally well lit up, were our guys, strung out in a line, completely blocking the street. Holding their sawed off shot guns at the ready.

The intruders were in complete disarray. Slowly they started raising their arms in surrender. It was all over, at least on our street. We couldn't see what was happening on the other streets, but suddenly we heard a popping sound and one of the lights went out.

Less than two minutes later one of the searchlight crew came in and told us everything was okay.

"What happened to the searchlight?"

"One of their guys snapped off a quick shot and got the searchlight before he realized they were surrounded. We've got them all rounded up and we're disarming and tying them up right now."

"How many were there?"

"Eighteen or twenty."

Smitty came in. "Quick," he called, "we gotta get all the equipment off the streets and our prisoners hidden before the neighbors get too inquisitive!"

The gang rushed out, herded the prisoners inside and, with Smitty in the lead, went back out to drag the searchlights into the garage. As they were bringing the last one in, we heard an odd sound from outside.

Smitty went back out to see what is was, turned around and called back to us,

"Well, I'll be damned. The neighbors are applauding!"

With that he walked to middle of the intersection, took a huge bow and then another. What a ham! Walking back into the garage with a huge smile on his face, he waved to the rest of the houses, then came in.

Inside, he was met with more applause. He'd just pulled off a major confrontation with a military precision that was remarkable. The whole idea was his, from beginning to end. He conceived it, marshaled his troops and executed the plan to perfection. I wondered what he might have accomplished in some other life.

On the other hand, what the hell was he going to do with eighteen or twenty prisoners? That's what I asked Smitty,

He was still on an emotional high. Still having fun, enjoying the moment.

"How the fuck do I know?" He gave a little laugh. "Well, we could shoot 'em. Course we'd have to get rid of the bodies somehow and I suppose Josie'd object to that. Hell, I don't know. Give me a minute. I'll figure out something!"

CHAPTER 42

Originally the El Cerrito cop had said it looked like some of the goons were wearing uniforms. It turned out they were just khaki pants and shirts. Several had guns in their pockets or stuck in their pants.

They looked like ordinary guys, someone you might bump into on any street corner. I'd been expecting Carpenter's goons to look like – well, goons. These guys were pretty young. Some looked like they might still be in college. Our guys relieved them of their guns and patted them down just to make sure.

I wondered what kind of a bill of goods Carpenter'd sold them.

Sitting on the cement floor of the garage, tied up, they didn't look remotely threatening. If anything, they looked like they were in shock. This obviously wasn't what they'd signed up for.

"Let's empty all their pockets and see what we've got," Smitty said.

I asked one of our guys if he knew which one of them had shot the light. The kid he pointed at looked to be about sixteen. He looked frightened. In fact, as I looked carefully at their faces, they all looked young and scared.

The guys set to work, finding wallets, keys, candy, gum, smokes and various sorts of identification.

"Double check any photo IDs against the guy whose pockets they came out of," Smitty reminded our guys. "Make sure you get the right ID with the right guy. Later on, we'll get all this organized and over to the chief. He's sending fingerprint kits over to see if there's warrants or anything on any of 'them."

I asked Smitty if he'd arranged all that earlier. He hadn't.

"Nope, I just now called him. I didn't tell him anything about how we caught them. Just told him they'd walked into our trap and we caught 'em real easy. If any of these guys have outstanding tickets, or warrants, or are on probation, he can hold them. If he can't, I don't know what the hell we'll do with them."

He pointed to three of our guys, who dropped what they were doing and came over to see what he wanted.

"We need to get rid of these guys and their cars. Find the cars and bring them up here. We'll move the guys down to Richmond in their own cars.

"Josie, you go down in the morning and take Case with you. You'll have to figure a way to feed these idiots too, can't let them starve to death on us."

By that time it was after four in the morning. It took a little time to shoehorn our prisoners into the three cars and send them on their way to Richmond. Then everyone hit the sack.

CHAPTER 43

Next morning, as we were backing Josie's cycle out of the garage, a couple of the neighbors wanted to know if we knew how the shoot went last night. Josie told them that as far as she knew it went fine. In fact they'd left some of their equipment in our garage. They asked her who it was that came out and took a bow at the end. She laughed and said, "Oh that was just my dad, acting silly."

We'd come down to the body shop on Josie's cycle, but needed a car to get the groceries. There were several sitting around they said we could use. I looked at the registration to be safe. The way they had used the garbage company truck stuck in my memory – I didn't want to be arrested driving a stolen car. The one we got was registered to their company.

Josie said we needed to go to a big store. She had a list of personal things they needed. Advil, aspirin, Pepto Bismal, Tums. One guy wanted something called Smooth Move, which to my embarrassment Josie had to explain was sort of a laxative. I'd kind of forgotten the average age of these guys.

Josie drove the car the same way she rode a motorcycle, with a kind of careful abandon. Fast, but smart. The word nimble came to my mind. It had been a little scary on the bike with her, but it wasn't scary in a car. It also wasn't as satisfying either. I couldn't snuggle up to her backside in the car. I decided to bring it up.

"You know, I have to say I enjoyed the motorcycle ride yesterday much more than I'm enjoying this."

She looked at me questioningly. "Why?"

"The seating arrangement."

"That *was* fun, wasn't it?" she said noncommittally. "When this is over, we'll have to do it again. Maybe you can really learn to ride and we can go places together." Not as appealing, in all honesty, but I decided to let it go.

"Will you be my teacher?"

"With pleasure, sir."

Progress!

Josie, I noticed, was glancing repeatedly in the rear view mirror. "Something wrong?"

"Don't turn around," she cautioned me. "I think we're being followed. When I tell you, adjust the side view mirror and see if you can spot them. I'll tell you when we're making a left turn and your side of the car can't be seen. Wait, wait, wait – now!"

I quickly rolled the window down and adjusted the mirror so I could see the cars behind us from my side. "The second car back, a blue sedan. Can you spot it?"'

"Got it."

"It's been there almost since we left the garage. Turn for turn, but always a couple of cars behind."

"I've got the car but I can't make out the driver," I said. "I think there are two people in it, but I'm not sure."

Josie said she was going to make a number of turns and that I should pretend we were looking for an address. She wanted to see if they really were following us.

A couple of corners later it was very obvious that they were.

"Call Dad," Josie told me. "Tell him what's happening and where we are. Tell him I'm heading for the big Safeway in Richmond. He'll know which one it is. Hopefully there'll be a big crowd there and we'll be okay."

Smitty answered on the first ring. He told us to keep on doing what we were doing.

"I got two guys on bikes on their way"

"I'll park as near the entrance to the store as I can," Josie told him as the Safeway appeared around the next corner.

We both wanted to believe our follower didn't know we'd spotted him. He didn't drop back or anything, like he would have if he thought we were on to him.

When we pulled into the parking lot it was really full. No parking places anywhere near the doors. Even the disabled parking places were full which meant that we had to park near the edge of the lot. Plenty of cars around but very few people.

I could see the other car in our mirror, parked one row over and a couple of cars behind us. Just as I started to tell Josie that as long as they stayed in the car we'd be okay, both her door and mine were thrown open and we were confronted by two men, both holding guns.

Then the guys from the other car came strolling over, at which point they proceeded to congratulate each other on their double tailing plan. They'd let us see and concentrate on one car while the other one followed further behind and surprised us. Have to admit, it worked

In a few moments they had our hands tied and we'd been thrown into the back of the second car. They didn't blindfold us, just tied our hands. The passenger turned so he was facing us, holding his gun loosely in one hand. With his other hand, he called someone and reported, "We got 'em. On our way."

CHAPTER 44

Josie had no idea where we were going but I knew almost immediately. We were on the streets that led to Carpenter's house. I couldn't tell Josie. The guy with the gun had said, "No talking." I wasn't about to debate the matter.

Just as we were leaving Richmond and entering El Cerrito I noticed a guy on a motorcycle duck behind a parked car as we drove by. A couple of blocks further, I saw another parked bike with one of our guys sitting on it. It looked like the Devils got there too late to help us, but they'd be following us.

Our captors didn't seem to care if we saw where we were going. My imagination ran wild with thoughts of one-way rides in gangster movies – you know, when they don't care if you see where you're going because they're going to kill you anyway.

I look at our two captors. Neither resembled the picture I'd seen of Carpenter. The driver appeared to be the boss. He'd been telling the others what to do, and he was the one who'd made the phone call.

A few more turns and, sure enough, we pulled into Carpenter's driveway. I didn't want them to know I'd ever been here before, so I let them lead me in even though I knew the way. I purposely didn't tell Josie where we were so she couldn't accidentally give it away either.

We were roughly pulled out of the car and pushed into the house through the same side door we'd used to load the garbage truck. No one spoke to us. They led us through the house, through the library and into the secret room. They untied our hands. The door'd been fixed. I heard it lock after us. We were standing in total darkness.

I'd had a moment to survey the hidden room before the door closed behind us. Things were very much as before, but the desk had been righted since I last saw it. Fumbling, I managed to find and turn on a lamp. The light revealed the rest of the room I knew only too well.

No windows, just the one door we'd come through. A small ventilation screen way up the wall, nothing I could ever reach. A couple of chairs sitting side by side. About all we could do was sit down and wait.

"What do you thinks' going on?" Josie whispered to me.

"I'm not sure, but this is Carpenter's house," I told her.

"Do you think we're in any danger?" What could I say?

"I don't think so." I made a snap decision not to share my thoughts about being killed because they hadn't blindfolded us. Not useful. Also not useful was remembering that they'd killed twice already.

"I bet he's gonna try to reach Smitty through us. We should be okay," I said, trying to sound a lot more confident than I felt. "Did you notice the Devils spotting us on the way up?"

"No. Where were they?"

"The two I saw were on my side of the car, and they were definitely keeping an eye on us. At least your Dad knows where we are."

"It's all my fault. I shouldn't have stopped in the parking lot," Josie said shaking her head. "I should have just kept going. I bet I could have outraced them."

'Doesn't matter. We're here now. I'd bet we're gonna meet Carpenter. But we have to pretend we don't know who he is, that we don't know his name or anything about him. Okay?"

I couldn't tell Josie but I was really worried. It was beginning to look like Carpenter, or at least some of his goons were capable of almost anything, and killing definitely made the list. What could I do if they got rough with us? The thought of Josie being harmed sent chills through me.

CHAPTER 45

So far everything had been an adventure. I'd convinced myself that I was kind of once removed from what was going on.

Not anymore. Now I had to protect Josie. Up till now, Smitty'd had Josie protecting me, as well as acting as my chauffeur, both motorcycle and car. Now it was my turn.

"We need to relax," I whispered. "Keep calm. Conserve our strength. Sooner or later we'll have a chance to get away, either with your dad's help or on our own. But for now, there's really nothing we can do except wait. This'd be a good time to learn more about each other," I said half in jest.

"Okay, me first." To my surprise, it appeared that Josie took me seriously. Actually, I realized after the fact that I'd come up with a reasonably good idea. It'd help pass the time, and hopefully keep Josie's spirits up.

"First question," Josie said. "Why did you leave home?"

"Short story. To go to college."

"Where'd you go?"

"Junior college in Concord, for two reasons. One, my grades weren't good enough to get into Cal. Second, I couldn't afford Cal. Now it's my turn. Did you go to college?"

"Yeah. I did go to Cal., but I didn't get my degree. I majored in boys, mostly. Just kidding! I really wanted to major in oceanography or something like that. Unfortunately marriage got in the way. We met in college. He was lots of fun at frat parties, college games and stuff like that. We both thought we were in love, but after the fact, I think it was just 'like,' not love. He had lots of family money. We bought our house while he was still in college. I quit school and started playing housewife. I mean, really can you imagine me a housewife?"

"So what went wrong, if I may be so bold to ask?"

"Well, he stayed on at school, and he also stayed on with the frat parties. Eventually, among other things, he got a sorority girl pregnant and got himself in a lot of trouble with the law and her family. His family got rid of me by giving me the house they'd actually bought for him."

"Do you still see him?"

"Never! Not once! Good riddance!"

I wanted to keep her mind occupied so I asked her about her childhood, where she was born, where she went to school, her first date and so on. It was interesting. Needless to say, having a dad like Smitty created some pretty unique problems. Whenever other kids, teachers or neighbors saw something in the paper about Smitty, she'd hear about it. The kids would tease her. She said they could be real mean sometimes.

I had an ulterior motive with some of my questions. I gave her plenty of opportunities, but she never mentioned anything about current boyfriends. Finally, though, my curiosity got the best of me. "Since your divorce, do you date much?" I asked flat out.

"Nope. Like I told you before, most guys get scared off because of my dad. Would you have been scared off by him?"

"Maybe, at the beginning," I admitted. "Now, I really like him. He strikes me as tough but fair. I certainly wouldn't want him for an enemy. I've heard some stories about him that are pretty scary."

Josie laughed. "They're probably true. Though Mom used to say, 'Don't believe all the stories you hear about your dad." Then she'd laugh and say, "They're only about three quarters true."

"Actually I think they really were true. I think he did some really terrible things years ago. He was just lucky not to have been caught. I think almost all the guys did horrible things in the past. There's still a younger part of the gang that I'm glad Dad's broken with."

We passed a couple of hours getting to know each other much better, waiting for the other shoe to drop. Josie told me that Smitty had always been there when she needed him, for money and clothing, those kind of things, but she never felt close to him until after her mom died. Since then they'd become friends as well as dad and daughter.

She told me how hard it'd been for her when her mom died in a motorcycle accident. . Smitty'd taken it really hard, even blamed himself for her death.

"He said she'd never have been in the accident if it wasn't for him. Eventually he'd turned to me. From then on, we've been closer than ever before."

For quite a while, we almost forgot where we were. Josie admitted that she really enjoyed my company, but she'd held back 'cuz she didn't know who I was, fearing I just another biker type that she wouldn't want to get serious about.

"So what was your first clue, you know, that I wasn't a biker type?

"You mean outside of the fact that you're useless on a motorcycle? I guess when I noticed how shy you were. I kind of liked it. Most of the younger gang members think they're hot stuff, that they can snap their fingers and the girls'll come a'runnin'. Hah, not this girl!"

"What an education, growing up around this crowd," I chuckled.

"Well, as far as my dad's concerned, I just ignore him," Josie said breezily. We sat for a while in silence. Gradually her head gravitated to my shoulder as she fell asleep. I couldn't move for fear I'd awaken her.

CHAPTER 46

I think we'd both been dozing when I heard the door to the outer library being opened, and then our inner door swung open as well. One of our captors came in with two bottles of fruit juice in his hands. Right behind him, the other was holding a couple of homemade sandwiches. They put the food on the desk and asked if we need to go to the bathroom.

We both did. The first guy says he'd take us, one at a time. I was buoyed up by this, them wanting to treat us pretty well, until I saw how roughly they manhandled Josie and me. The closest one reached for Josie's arm and forcefully dragged her out of the room. I'd been hoping they'd be gentle on us, but they were no. They didn't seem to care if they hurt us.

When she returned, they yanked me to my feet and force walked me to the bathroom. It was outside the library, through the living room and down a short hall. I'd been in the living room but I was seeing the short hall for the first time. I really needed the bathroom, but kept my eyes open for anything else useful.

The small guest bath had a proportionally small window, but the guy kept the door ajar and I barely had time to dry my hands before he herded me back out. I did have a chance to wad up a small handful of toilet paper and stuff it in my pocket. Perhaps I'd have a chance to drop it by the door to our cell and it could keep the door from completely closing.

It didn't work. I dropped it okay, but the guy saw it and nonchalantly kicked it out of the way before pulling the door shut, I heard it lock. It hadn't been much of a plan anyway.

I remembered that the door was rigged with some sort of a spring lock. When we'd broken in, Nips had simply pushed on it and it had sprung open. Being on the inside, it seemed logical that pulling on it might produce the same result. I tried every which way I could think of, but nothing budged. It stood to reason that Carpenter'd had a way to let himself out of the room, but neither of us could find anything that worked. Maybe they'd disconnected it.

Josie asked me if I'd noticed anything on the way to the toilet that might be of any help. I had to tell her no. She gave me a big hug and told me to eat my sandwich and drink my juice, that we needed to keep our strength up.

"I agree with you," I told her and reached for the sandwich. "And I take it as a good sign, that they've been ordered to take good care of us."

We ate deliberately slowly, to make the time pass. Just as we were finishing, the two goons came in and hustled us out of our cell. No explanation. They just yanked us to our feet and prodded us out.

This time their manner was clearly threatening. Josie was scared and so was I.

CHAPTER 47

We were being dragged into the living room and told to sit down on a sofa. In a few minutes, Carpenter walked in. It had to be him, judging by the deference the others showed him. The pictures I'd seen of him must have been really old. He looked to be in his early seventies. Lean, a full head of black hair, somewhat distinguished. I had to remind myself that he was a murderer.

He walked in and leaning one hip on the corner of the desk, stared at us for a couple of minutes. No one said anything.

He was dressed in a tweed jacket, sport shirt open at the neck, slacks and loafers. Not at all what I'd expected. Not even a cigar.

"I know all about you two," he said finally. "I know you're Smitty's daughter and I know your name is Casey. I know all about the motorcycle gang."

I was surprised by his voice. High, yet gravelly. He went on for a while telling us what he knew about the gang, and Smitty's house. It was for all practical purposes, an admission that he'd done all the things we thought he had.

I gradually got the impression he was fishing for more information. He'd found out a whole lot of physical things –but he was completely mystified as to why Smitty was doing him all this harm. He didn't get it that Smitty took murder personally.

"I don't know why you guys broke into my house. All I want is my papers back."

He must think we'd just taken them, not read them. I glanced at Josie. She appeared to be on the same wavelength as me.

"As you can see, we haven't harmed you in any way. Did you enjoy your little snack? Our food isn't quite what it used to be, since I lost my chef – thanks to you guys. But we did the best we could." He didn't give us time to answer.

"I want you," pointing to Josie, "to call your father and tell him you're both fine. I want you to tell him you've been given food and drink, and that you have a message to him from me. Tell him that I mean you no harm. Tell him I'll trade you for the papers."

He told Josie to make it short and clear. "Tell him he and I can meet at the public library here in El Cerrito for the exchange tonight at eight-thirty. A public place, safe for both of us. And tell him not to bother coming looking for you. I'm moving you. Take a few minutes to compose what you're going to say and then I want to hear it."

Josie took a moment. "I guess I can say something like this? 'Dad, it's me. I'm supposed to tell you that Casey and I are okay and we're not being harmed. Mr. Carpenter says to tell you all he wants are his papers back and he wants to trade us for them. He wants to meet you at the El Cerrito library at nine tonight.' Is that okay?"

She glanced at Carpenter who nodded okay and told her to go on. "I don't know where we are, but Mr. Carpenter says he's going to move us anyway by then. Outside of being locked inside a small room, he's treating us okay."

Carpenter, perched on the corner of his desk, thought about it for a second or two and then laid down the rules.

"Sounds okay to me, just don't deviate from the script. I'm putting the phone on speaker so I'll hear both you and your dad." He handed her the phone.

Once she had the phone in her hands, Josie hesitated for a second and started to say, "I don't know if I —"

Before she could finish her sentence, one of the goons behind us grabbed a handful of her hair and twisted her head around, saying, "Don't think. Just do it." Josie fell to the floor crying in pain.

Without thinking I jumped up and grabbed at the guys arms. In a flash, Carpenter reached out and belted me a vicious chop that sent me straight back to the sofa. He was much stronger and way faster than he looked. The other guy threw a wire around my neck and pulled back, I started to choke. I thought I was going to die.

Carpenter said, "Don't kill him."

The goon loosened the wire a little, just enough to let me breath.

Carpenter was perched on the edge of his desk again, calmly watching me die.

"Dear me, Casey. Now what do I do? I don't really need you to negotiate with Josie's dad, do I? Maybe I should just get rid of you right now. What do you think?"

Josie yelled at him. "Stop it all I wanted to say was I didn't know whether to call him on the home phone or the cell phone!"

Within a moment or two order was restored. Josie and I were back sitting down on the sofa. The goon left the loosened wire around my neck. My head felt like it was going to fall off. The two goons were calmly standing behind us again.

Josie repeated, "All I wanted to know was whether to call him on the cell phone or the house phone."

"Cell phone, that'll get him wherever he is."

She got Smutty on the phone and gave him the message. He countered with a demand of his own. He'd have the papers available for the trade only if he saw his daughter first. He wanted Carpenter to have us with him and to let him see us before he'd meet with him inside the library.

Carpenter told Josie to ask him to wait a minute. He was silent for a short time, then told her to just say "okay" to her father, then hang up.

As she hit the off button, Carpenter barked out.

"You know what to do with them" to his guys, then left the room. We were taken back to our little room with no view.

The two flunkies were just as polite as they'd been before. They shoved us back into our little cell.

Josie had a headache from having her hair yanked so hard. My ear hurt like hell where Carpenter had belted me, my throat hurt from the wire and my voice was raspy. Josie gave me a big hug and said, "We're in a heap of trouble, wouldn't you say?"

I didn't know what to say. I wanted to keep her spirits up, but I couldn't help agreeing with her.

Carpenter scared me. I thought I was up against a psychopath again. I thought he was really capable of ordering me killed. I wasn't about to share my fears with Josie.

"Yeah, Carpenter's a nasty piece of work. But I think he wants Smutty, not us. Just don't aggravate him; he's got a hair trigger temper."

Privately I thought Carpenter was surely a psychopath. His vicious reaction to me and then instantaneous calmness with Josie was alarming.

CHAPTER 48

We sat on the floor, hugging each other for almost an hour, when suddenly the door was flung open. The two goons strutted in.

"Get up. We're going on a trip," they informed us.

"Can we use the toilets on the way?" Josie asks politely.

They allowed each of us a pit stop before they hustled us out the side door to the driveway where two large sedans were sitting, idling. Carpenter was behind the wheel of the front car. The two guys pushing us along opened the rear doors of the second car and shoved us in. We weren't tied up – just locked in. I surreptitiously tried the door handle but it wouldn't budge. Probably had a kiddy lock on it.

Carpenter got out of his car and walked back to our car. He leaned in the driver's window and said, "Stay close and don't lose me. I'm going to go slow and not attract attention. Can you handle that?"

He walked back to his car and took off. The driver turned to the other goon and said, "Doesn't he think we got any brains at all?"

We followed Carpenter's car. I had thought Smitty might have caught the little hint Josie had dropped about where we were. About the small room we were held in. But now we were being moved. He'd have no idea where we were after we were moved. I couldn't see any way we could get out of this mess.

At the first corner Carpenter turned right and so did we. When we got to the next corner, Carpenter continued straight ahead. As we entered the intersection there was a sudden loud crash and Josie and I were knocked around in the back seat.

Josie screamed, and the driver yelled, "What the fuck?" Everything was pandemonium.

"Josie, are you okay?" I yelled.

"I think so," she replied shakily. "You okay?"

Neither of us had seat belts on and we'd been really thrown around. I made a quick mental scan of my body, decided I was all right, and told her so.

Josie said, "What happened?"

Glancing out the window, I said, "We've been saved, that's what!"

CHAPTER 49

Smitty figured out where we were when he got Josie's phone call. He couldn't see any reason why she'd tell him about the small room unless she was trying to tell him something. The only small room without windows he could think of was the hidden office in Carpenter's house. He put two and two together and got the right number.

However he was stuck at home and was sure the house was being watched. How could he get out without being seen? The solution had been a pizza order.

The gang had ordered a dozen pizzas from the place they'd been getting them all along and Smitty'd talked the driver into letting them sneak into the delivery truck when it left.

That worked and Smitty and four of the gang had gotten away without any watchers being the wiser.

Then Smitty cooked up the idea of an engineered car crash. He told us how they'd pulled it off. He knew there were only two streets leading down the hill from Carpenter's house. He knew they were going to move us and they'd have to be on one or the other of the two streets.

Rather proudly, he described what happened. "I positioned a car at each of the two intersections and told them to wait for my signal. Then I hid up at the top of the street with my binoculars and waited for you to leave."

Smitty'd been in place for almost an hour when he saw activity around the two cars in the driveway; saw the side door open and the five of us come out.

Even from a distance, he immediately recognized Josie and me as we were being shoved into the second car. He waited until he was sure that Carpenter's car would lead the mini-motorcade. All he had to do then was to wait and see which street they took. Their choices: either straight ahead or turn right. Both of his drivers were on their cell phones, waiting for his signal.

"I waited until they pulled out and told me guys that they were leaving and that Carpenter was alone in the first car and you two were in the back seat of the second car. At the first corner they turned right. I yelled RIGHT TURN, RIGHT TURN, just as we'd planned."

He continued. "The guys knew what to do. The one at the intersection that Carpenter would be crossing had his motor running and car in gear. All he had to do was step on the gas and ram the second car. Smitty told me later this plan wasn't an original Smitty special. It was out of the police play book, a standard maneuver that police often used to stop stolen cars."

Smitty's biggest problem was that he didn't want us hurt. His plan was for his guy to hit our right rear fender hard enough to put our car into a spin, but not hard enough to flip it. By the time the driver had the car back under control, his way would be completely blocked by Smitty's second car.

It worked just as Smitty planned. The first car hit us to perfection. Our car immediately went into a pirouette a ballet dancer'd be proud of. Josie and I were thrown around like rag dolls, but neither of us was hurt.

I don't think the guy driving had ever been trained in defensive driving. He did all the wrong things. He stopped the car, opened his door and started to get out. By the time he saw the second car and men with guns pointed at him, it was too late. The guy in the front passenger seat just sat there and was easily subdued.

Ahead, Carpenter's car slowed to a stop. He started to back into a driveway as if he might turn around and come back, but then hesitated. After a moment, he put his car in gear and took off.

"Let him go," Smitty said. "We got our kids back and that's what's important."

"You two okay?" Smitty asked, as he simultaneously hugged her and shook my hand.

"Yeah, Dad, we're okay and ever happy to see you! But did you really have to scare us so much? Wasn't there some other, less dangerous way to rescue us?"

Smitty laughed. "Aren't you ever satisfied?" Then, in a quick reversal. "Did these guys hurt you at all?"

I glanced at Josie as she said, "No they were okay. There was a little misunderstanding when one of them pushed me around a little. Case jumped up to help me and Carpenter slapped him down." She downplayed the incident. I think she didn't want to inflame the situation.

"Lucky for them," Smitty said, then gave me a strange look and said, "You did that?"

Back at the body shop Smitty sent out for a huge Chinese lunch and told us about the special delivery the pizza guy had made.

A moment later he followed that with a philosophical, "All's well that ends well. Of course it didn't end so well for Carpenter, did it? He had lost two more men and another car. To say nothing of losing Josie and Casey. My daughter and my new idea man."

I was saved from making a comment by the arrival of the Chinese dinner. It looked like Smitty just told them to bring two of everything on the menu. We gathered around two large picnic tables and dug in. There was enough to feed a small army.

As it turned out we *were* almost a small army. A bunch of bikers, a couple of customers, us and the office staff from upstairs. But even with so many mouths, there was plenty left over. That went to our prisoners.

When we got our fortune cookies, mine said, "Beware of strangers on motorcycles." At least that's what I told Josie.

She said, "Humph!"

The first chance I had, I cornered Smitty and asked him what he'd meant when he said I was his new idea man. "I don't remember giving you any new ideas about what to do next," I said.

"The FBI, remember? You said you would call their PR person and find out about any federal offenses Carpenter might have committed. You need to get going on that ASAP."

It wasn't a request, it wasn't a suggestion, it was an order.

CHAPTER 50

At the top of the stairs I saw several women at computers and phones in one of the office spaces. The offices had large windows so that the staff could oversee the entire downstairs operation. Downstairs I'd heard names being broadcast over a public address system. "So-and-So, you're wanted on line two," that kinda' thing.

Smitty led us toward the rear of the building. Just past the offices, the rest of the building was walled off. He opened a door in the wall and led us into a house. Well, it wasn't really a house; it just looked like a house – made of concrete blocks and with no windows. A large living room and dining room lay directly ahead, and off to one side was an equally large kitchen. Along the rear wall were two more doors. Josie, who'd caught up to me by then, told me that the doors led to three bedrooms and two bathrooms.

"Dad used to live here before he bought the house in Oakland," she explained. "Occasionally he still uses it. More often he lets friends use it. It's kind of a hideaway."

The guys immediately threw themselves onto the many sofas and chairs scattered throughout the room. There were more sofas and chairs in that room than I'd ever seen in any one room in my whole life, other than a furniture showroom. And maybe the rec room at Smitty's house.

"The guys like it here," Josie said. "It's comfortable."

I could see why.

Another reason they liked it was quickly apparent. The kitchen was really more of a bar than a kitchen. A huge refrigerator, dominating one end, started disgorging beer at an alarming rate.

Smitty yelled for the guy's attention.

He asked them about the prisoners from the raid on his house.

"Did anybody find out what these goons had in mind for us last night?"

"Yeah," one of the guys volunteered. "They seemed to be pretty happy to rat out on Carpenter."

He continued." They were supposed to surprise us with their sheer numbers. Then they were supposed to search the house, find some private papers of his, and finish up by trashing the place."

"That idiotic son of a bitch sent a vigilante group of kids up there?" Smitty said, sounding genuinely astonished. "Armed with loaded guns? And he expected them to overpower us without a shot being fired? Jesus H. Christ, it's a wonder we weren't all killed."

Smitty turned to another guy and asked him if he'd contacted the chief with the information about the guys we'd caught.

"Yeah, I did. He was out when I called yesterday so I left all the names and stuff with the desk sergeant. Today when I called back, he was out again, but the sergeant had a message for me. Turned out that a number of them had minor records of one sort or another. A couple more were on parole. A few had outstanding warrants for things like traffic violations or worse. He told me to tell you that he could take seven off your hands at least temporarily."

"That's all?" Smitty asked. "I was hoping he'd take all of 'em"

He thought for a moment, then said to the same guy, "Sort those seven out and get rid of them. Seven down, eleven to go. Use one of the vans in the shop and run 'em over to the chief"

Dave asked if he had a plan for the other eleven.

"I really don't give a fig for the rest of the guys, but we need to do something. Anybody got any ideas?"

A bunch of silly ideas were tossed out. Strip them naked and maroon them way up the coast. Make a very convincing show of supposedly murdering one of them and tell the rest that's what'd happen to them if they didn't forget what happened.

"Then we'd only have to hold one guy," the fellow with this idea said, clearly quite pleased with his cleverness. "The guy they thought we'd murdered."

Smitty told him he'd been watching too much TV. "C'mon, get serious. The rest of these guys aren't criminals. They're probably just poor dumb jerks that Carpenter hijacked some way or other. We know by their wallets they're all local. They got wives, parents, people that'll worry about them."

Gradually a consensus emerged. It was really quite simple and seemed somehow right. A plan that would get them off our hands immediately, yet keep them quiet. And nobody'd get killed in the process, for real *or* pretend.

"Okay then, here's the plan," Smitty said. "In their wildest dreams, these guys never thought what might happen if they got caught. Their wallets were stuffed with everything from drivers' licenses to Social Security numbers, pictures of family and friends, bank cards, you name it. A couple of them even had the passwords for their bank cards in their wallets. A bunch of freaking idiots!"

"We can use all that information against them. We'll tell 'em we're making copies of everything we found in their wallets and that we're gonna keep it forever. We're also gonna destroy all their guns. On top of that, we tell them that Carpenter's a murderer and it's only a matter of time before he's arrested and convicted. They should be grateful to us for keeping them from being charged on accessory to murder charges. We'll tell them to stay away from Carpenter and his house, or else."

All eleven of them promised fervently we'd never hear of them again.

CHAPTER 51

I was still trying to figure out what to say to the FBI on my call to them, when I had a better idea. I asked Smitty if there was a computer I could log onto and do some research.

Out front in the office there were several laptops I could use. I went online to find out exactly what the FBI does. In a few moments, I was on the Wikipedia page about the Federal Bureau of Investigation. From there, it was a hop, skip and jump to what their "top investigative priorities" were.

It wasn't much help. Way above my understanding of the law. Smitty suggested we take the list with us when we see the Chief later this afternoon.

"We really need his cooperation. He says a lot of what we've got can't be legally used 'cuz it's 'tainted.' Tainted as in we stole it. He's a good guy, but he doesn't need to know everything."

Josie spoke up. "Dad, don't you think you should wear something else to see the chief. Something other than your boots and jacket? And for goodness sake, neaten up your ponytail!"

"Spoken as a true daughter. Okay, I'll do my best. You guys hang on. I'll see what I can rustle up so you won't be ashamed of me."

In a few minutes he emerged from the back bedroom, did an amazingly agile pirouette for his size, and said, "How's this?"

Light tan slacks, blue blazer, cordovan shoes, light blue sport shoes. He was a different man!

"Wow, Dad. You're beautiful!"

"The old man don't look too bad, does he? The hell with the chief. I'm much more concerned with how I look to my daughter"

"Well, I'd go out to dinner with you anytime!"

"Okay, it's a date. As soon as we get this mess over and done with!"

We left in one of the many cars parked in the repair area. It was missing its front fender but it ran just fine. On the way we passed a great looking hamburger joint, but Smitty said we didn't have time to stop.

Gus was driving, Smitty beside him. Josie and I shared the back seat. Josie hadn't said much to me since I'd asked her what her fortune cookie said, so I asked her again.

"Do you really, really want to know?"

"Of course."

Looking me right in the eyes, she slowly reached into her blouse pocket and withdrew the little folded piece of paper. "Last chance. You're sure?"

"Josie, quit teasing me."

"Okay, you asked for it. Here it is! Read it yourself." She handed it over.

I unfold the paper and read, "Everyone loves you, specially the one you're with now."

A moment or two of silence, then I whispered one of the great comebacks of my life. I blurted out "That may be one of the few times ever that a fortune cookie got it totally right!"

That potentially life changing statement went unanswered as Smitty interrupted us. "We're getting close. Just a few blocks more."

We'd been driving out the freeway from Richmond and turned off at the El Cerrito exit. Now we were on San Pablo Ave.

Smitty had called ahead and the chief was expecting us. He quickly ushered us into his office and closed the door. Smitty introduced Gus, Josie and me. He looked surprised to be meeting Smitty's daughter.

Smitty told the chief he could call us Casey and Josie. The chief told us that we could call him Chief O'Meara. So much for immediate familiarity.

"So, what's up," he asked Smitty.

Smitty turned to me and told me to take over. I pulled out the list of FBI priorities and show him the areas we thought might apply to Carpenter. He looked them over carefully, then said, "I think several probably do apply to Carpenter, but I don't see any way we can use them."

I didn't know what he meant. "Can't we call and make an appointment to show them what we have, Chief?"

"One of my closest friends is an FBI agent. We went to college together. I can tell you they get who knows how many hundreds of tips every day. Most of them are thrown away at first glance. The few that make the cut are only taken seriously if they can identify the source. If they don't trust the source, they usually reject the tip. Most tips from the general public get rejected. Too many people try to get even with someone by way of the FBI. 'And once the FBI found out your relationship with a motorcycle gang? No way they'd listen to you."

I must have looked a little crestfallen. The chief tried to soften the blow.

"It's a good idea. You just need someone with credentials to get it to them. An attorney or something."

So much for that idea – totally shot down. They might not find out how I was involved with the gang, but I'm just a boat bum and, on top of that, I'm a suspect in a murder case. Hell, I not only don't have credentials, I've got negative credentials.

Maybe Smitty had a friend who had a friend that might be credible. Except he'd still be a normal tax-paying citizen, the kind the chief said would pretty much ignored by the FBI anyway. We needed someone already in law. 'An attorney or someone in another department of the government.

Suddenly I realized I was looking at another department of government. A police chief!

"If the FBI got information from, say, a police chief, would they pay attention to it?" I asked him.

There was a long, long silence. Smitty had told me the chief was tough and smart. He stared at me and I was sure he knew exactly what I was thinking.

Finally, "No question. They'd definitely pay attention to information brought to them by a police chief. But I can't think of any way I could do that. The information you have is definitely tainted."

Another idea shot down.

He turned to Smitty. "I'm sure all four of you know about the blackmail I've been threatened with. Needless to say, I really like the idea of getting out from under that nuisance. But I can't, and won't, do anything illegal. I've even been toying with the idea that I should just resign and admit my mistakes. But that's difficult too. In part because I don't think I've done anything really wrong, and also because I think I've done a good job here."

That gave me another idea.

"Have you seriously been thinking about resigning?" I asked.

"Yes, I have," he answered forthrightly, "but I have to think of my wife and kids, too. It's going to be a difficult decision."

I told him I had an idea that might solve everything, but that I wanted to talk it over with Smitty before I told him about it. "Can you wait a few days before you make a decision about resigning?" I asked.

"Sure," he said. "As I said this is not going to be easy for me. I love the city and the job. If you can figure out a way to lose the evidence against me, and it's legal, I'm willing to consider it."

Smitty looked at me like he didn't know me, but got up and walked out to the car.

It suddenly hit me that I'd just been talking to a police chief as equal to equal for a half hour. A week ago I'd have gone to great lengths to avoid spending time with any cop— let alone a police chief.

What if he found out that I was a fraud? I'm a college drop out boat bum giving legal advice to police chief on how to talk to the FBI?? Why should he listen to me?

CHAPTER 52

Outside, in the car, Smitty said, "What's going on?"

By then, I was a little embarrassed by what I'd done. Inside I'd been carried away by the conversation and all the ideas flying back and forth. Outside, in the cold light of day, with both Smitty and Josie looking at me as if they didn't have a clue who – or what – they were dealing with, my idea didn't seem practical at all. But "upward and onwards," as my dad used to say.

"Okay," I said, thinking fast on my feet and hoping it'd all come together into one brilliant whole, "I think the chief is really serious about quitting. His honor is a real thing to him. He's holding back mostly to protect his family and because he feels a real sense of obligation to the job. His real concern is that he may yet be forced to do something dishonest by blackmail and, if push comes to shove, he'd quit before doing it."

"Yeah, I agree." Smitty said, nodding. "When he said he'd been contemplating resigning, I believed him. So?"

"What if we can show him how to turn his liability into an asset? What if we can show him a way to admit his petty larceny in a way that'll clear him and trap Carpenter at the same time?"

"Go on."

"The chief said that the FBI would listen to a police chief. He also told us he had a close friend in the FBI, someone he knew in college, and still kept in touch with."

"Okay so far."

"Suppose he went to his friend and told him he had information about blackmailing, bribery, even murder going on in his city with roots in the state capitol. Suppose he told his friend he'd found all this out because the guy had tried to blackmail him over some dumb little thing. He could admit to a questionable misuse of some police funds, tell them he'd already repaid them, and say he wants to give all this information to the FBI – but that he wants his name cleared. I keep reading how prosecutors compromise on charges in order to get information. 'Seems like it might work the same way here."

"You think the FBI would clear him in exchange for this information?"

"Why not? He didn't do anything criminal. It was such a small amount; it was more misappropriation than theft. If he wasn't a police chief, he probably wouldn't even have to worry about it. On top of that, the information he has is so inflammatory, I bet they'd give even more than that to get it."

Smitty was looking less dubious by the moment.

"I wanted to talk to you about it away from the chief because I think the idea will be received better coming from you than from me."

Smitty worked it through, looking for potential problems. Then he finally said, "I like it. As long as we're still here, let's get our asses in gear and go back in to the chief, see it he thinks he could pull it off."

On the way in, I found myself worrying about my getting in deeper and deeper with the gang. Now it was way too late for second guessing. At least we were trying to work within the law – sometimes.

Smitty presented the plan. The chief's reaction was lukewarm. Smitty told him he thought it was the only way to get the chief off the hook and trap Carpenter at the same time. "The only thing I worry about is your connection with the FBI," he added.

"Bud would probably help me all he can. But any agreement he and I were to come up with would then be kicked upstairs. Who knows what they might do? Then there's the question of the legality of the information you have."

"One thing at a time chief. It looks to me like you're at a crossroad," Smitty said. "On the one hand, you can resign in some disgrace. On the other, you can take the information to the FBI, and give yourself a fighting chance at correcting a huge wrong and getting personal exoneration in the bargain. So I guess it's your choice, Chief."

We all sat in silence for a few moments, the chief drumming his fingers on his desk.

Finally he spoke.

"Smitty, you've done a good job of painting me into a corner."

A small grin softened the statement.

He continued, "I guess it's time for me to fish or cut bait. Tell you what. Let's meet early tomorrow afternoon. I'm pretty sure my main goal is to stop Carpenter and I think your plan is feasible. But I want to talk it over with my wife tonight, so we'll meet tomorrow.

"Should work out fine. We have a funeral to go to in the morning; I'll call you when it's over."

My immediate thought was Red. Smitty had checked his e-mail on his cell phone while we were in the car. He must have received the message then.

On the way back out to the car, he confirmed my guess. The funeral service was set for eleven the next morning. Smitty said we'd better hurry back to his house. He had a lot of planning to do before then.

CHAPTER 53

He wasn't kidding. Smitty had a lot to plan, on a number of fronts. First of all there was gang protocol to arrange. Gang funerals were always held at the same funeral parlor in East Oakland. There was a certain military precision to them that had to be organized. Every motorcycle had to be spotlessly cleaned. Every Hog had to wear the same uniform. Black gang jackets. Black leather pants. White shirts and, of course, their helmets. No scuffed boots.

They would all leave from the garage in Richmond as a group, two by two, and proceed sedately to the parlor. At the parlor they'd enter, again two by two, and take seats in a special section. Very much like a military or police service. Smitty planned for upwards of twenty bikes in the parade.

He told the guys to sit in the roped off section of the parlor, but that he might sit with the widow if there was room.

Nobody was talking to me. I wanted to go to the funeral service, simply because I'd liked Red. Josie was in the kitchen preparing dinner. Perhaps she'd have an idea.

"Sorry," she told me. "They aren't going to include you at all. The Devils are an exclusive club. Even though they'll accept you as a friend, you're never really a member. Same thing with me. There are no women in the Devils. Never have been, never will be."

"But you're Smitty's daughter!"

"Regardless, only members can go to official meetings. You have to be a provisional member for a year before you can become a full-fledged member. The funeral is like an official meeting. We're not included.

"What about wives? A lot of the guys are married. Won't they want to come?

"Oh they'll come, the ones that knew Red. But they'll come separately. They'll probably car pool or something. And they won't sit with the gang."

"Boy, that's really chauvinistic! How come the wives let them get away with that?"

"It's just something they all agree to when their husbands decide to join the Devils. Joining the Devils is like a commitment."

"But you're going, aren't you?"

"Absolutely. We can go together in my car, if you want. Something else. Don't be surprised when you see a bunch of motorcycle cops show up. There's quite a history of violence at gang funerals, or at least there used to be. It got so bad the cops got to showing up to try and head off the brawls. Now they show up out of habit, I think."

"What about dress?"

"If you've got something fairly conservative, that should be fine. If we leave early enough we can stop by your apartment."

So it was all arranged, we'd go together. Josie was not looking forward to the service.

"I hope you don't mind if I cry during the service. Red was almost a second dad to me. He used to baby sit me some times. He and Dad were really close."

She was close to tears as we talked.

I'd been sitting on a stool watching her cook dinner while we were talking. She was making sandwiches on some sort of a gadget, four at a time. She'd put corned beef cheese and sauerkraut between two slices of bread, then toast them on the device. They sure smelled good. My mouth was watering.

She turned toward me.

"Do me a favor?"

"Of course, anything."

"Go to the refrigerator and get a couple of heads of cabbages, wash them and chop them up into small pieces. I'm going to make a coleslaw salad to go with the sandwiches.'

A short time later we piled up the sandwiches on a large platter for me to carry downstairs, and Josie followed with the huge bowl of slaw. As usual, beer was the drink of choice. The meal was a little subdued, I guess because of Red.

After dinner Smitty announced he was pretty sure some of us would be going up to Sacramento in a day or so.

Josie and I spent the evening watching TV on a small set in the living room. The guys were all in the rec room watching sports on a huge screen.

Something Smitty had said was bothering me.

"Why do you think Smitty said we'd probably be going to Sacramento?"

"I guess he thinks that the chief will take care of Carpenter and there's bigger fish to fry in Sacramento."

"Yeah but how will he make any contacts in Sacramento?"

"Relax; he's got lots of contacts in Sacramento. You'll see."

I tried to relax watching the TV. Spending a lot of time out to sea, I'd never gotten the television habit. After watching it for a couple of hours that night I realized I hadn't been missing much.

"You're bored, aren't you," Josie said.

Perhaps my yawns were the giveaway. We both decided we'd get to bed early. The next day would be a long one.

Next morning, after breakfast, all the guys at the house were busy shining their boots and getting ready for the funeral. Smitty told me that they'd be leaving around nine-thirty, meeting up with all the rest of the gang at the Richmond garage.

"I'm going with Josie in her car."

"That's good. Tell Josie you two can follow the procession from the garage, or you could just meet us at the funeral parlor."

I wanted to see and follow the group. Josie did too.

We left shortly after the gang did, stopped at my apartment to get my one and only sport jacket and got to the garage in time to see Smitty organizing the procession.

Even though Smitty had told them the night before about how it was always two by two, it still took a lot of yelling to get them in order. The noise was deafening the garage was big enough to accommodate all the gang and their bikes, but that many bikes in an enclosed place was more than just noisy.

Josie and I climbed up the balcony stairs so we could watch from that vantage point. I counted thirty seven bikes; it'd be thirty eight counting Smitty's. "He'll lead the procession from the right front slot," she told me. Like the first violinist in an orchestra."

I'd noticed some black and white bikes outside the garage that looked like police bikes. "They're "funeral cops," Josie told me. "They'll go ahead of our procession, to clear traffic at stop signs and so forth. It'll make the trip much faster, even though they'll be riding real slow."

Finally everyone was organized to Smithy's satisfaction. He even made a final walk up the whole line, checking on their clothing. Exactly on time, the huge factory doors were rolled up and the caravan hit the streets. As the last two left, we followed in Josie's car.

CHAPTER 54

We arrived at the funeral parlor a few minutes before the scheduled services. The Devils parked their bikes in even rows, then lined up two by two and, led by Smitty, walked slowly into the chapel. It was impressive and scary at the same time. Thirty eight big guys, all in black leather jackets and wearing dark glasses walking in unison down the aisle. A real tribute to Red.

When they arrived at the roped off section they filed into the rows, all except Smitty. He went forward, sat down next to Red's widow and gave her a big hug.

I don't remember much of the service. My mind kept wandering back and forth between my short friendship with Red and the Carpenter problem. It wasn't a long service, focusing mostly on what a nice guy Red had been and how many friends he had. There were lots of people there, even though his widow sat almost alone. Josie sniffled several times through the service.

After the service Josie told me that the gang was gathering back at the warehouse, that this too was customary. "They call it a wake."

"We should go," she continued, "but we shouldn't stay. It'll be fun for a while, but some of the guys don't know when to stop. Let's go by for a half hour or so, then leave. Nobody'll miss us. Maybe we can have dinner or something."

That's what we did. She knew a nice place on the waterfront that served a great hamburger. It was a full restaurant with a full menu, but Josie said they were famous for their burgers. We lingered over the meal for a long time, long enough to tackle dessert and coffee.

As we were leaving, she said, "All dressed up and no place to go."

"I've never been there," I said, "but I've been told there's a hotel in Berkeley that has a nice bar and a small dance floor, if you like to dance?"

"Wow!" she said. "Your mama must have raised you right. I love to dance but I never get the chance."

We found the place, had a few drinks and Josie got her fill of dancing. Most girls tell me I'm not a great dancer, but I'm enthusiastic. Anyway we both had a good time and got back to Smitty's house before any of the gang.

Next morning, as were having breakfast and listening to the news, a flash came on. The announcer said he had a news flash. The station was being advised that there'd been an explosion and fire at the 5th avenue marina, more news to follow. Smitty jumped up and said, "The Jezebel, I gotta get down there."

I remembered that the gang had two other members living at the Marina.

Smitty raced off on his motorcycle and we tailed him in Josie's car. As we headed through downtown Oakland towards the Embarcadero, Josie nudged me and said, "Look at that." Directly ahead of us, a pall of smoke was just beginning to rise up. A moment or two later, we began to hear sirens coming from several different directions.

Smitty gunned his bike and raced ahead. Later he told me that he'd been hit with a premonition that it his boat. We pulled in a minute or two after Smitty. He was already off his bike and running toward the *Jezebel,* or more correctly, what was left of her.

One fire engine was already there and more were arriving. Two policemen were trying to restrain Smitty, and we were rudely shoved aside.

Smitty's boat was literally in pieces, at least all of it I could see. As we got closer I could see that there were actually two boats in pieces and on fire. The second one was in the slip next to Smitty's, and was producing most of the smoke. The firemen had a hose rigged up, and water was pouring on the fire. Someone was yelling that there might be people on board both boats.

The firemen were having a tough time. The *Jezebel* was just about completely demolished above the water line. They were trying to hack their way through flames and ruins. The other boat was even worse. The flames rose higher and the smoke was getting even more dense.

The fire trucks had been able to get only one hose out on to the docks. The second truck had to lay a hose down from almost a block away. When they finally got the second hose operating, they quickly got control of the fires. Just then one of the firemen poked his head out of Smitty's boat and yelled,

"We've got one. Need an ambulance!"

"Shit, shit, shit," Smitty groaned. He turned to one of the guys and asked him, "Do we know who was on the boat?"

"I think it's one of the new guys. He's single. He wanted to do it 'cuz he'd never spent a night on a boat."

"Have I met him?" Smitty asked.

"I don't think so. He wasn't at the funeral or the wake yesterday."

"God, I hope he's okay"

I could imagine what might have happened. I had a mental picture of me taking a nap below decks at some of the yacht harbors. I'd sometimes stuff earplugs in to cut out the dock noises. Some one could tramp all over the decks and I'd never hear them. Poor guy.

Two firemen climbed out of the smoldering wreckage of Smitty's boat carrying a man between them. They lifted the guy out and laid him on the dock. Most of his body was wrapped in a blanket, but I could see that his left arm was severely burned.

At the same time, on the other boat, the firemen were using axes to break down the hatches and get inside. In a few moments one of them yelled.

"We got another one."

Josie and I'd moved over to the other dock where we could see without being in the way. Looking at the firemen's efforts to save lives, something struck me as odd. Smitty's boat was blown apart like from an explosion. But the other boat looked like it had caught fire from the inside. It was an older wooden boat, and they sometimes have galley fires, but what about Smitty's? I resolved to ask one of the firemen before they left if they'd noticed the difference too.

The way the second guy was being carried out of his boat, we were sure that he was dead.

While the firemen were getting control of the fire, the police were asking questions in the crowd, trying to find out if anyone knew either of the guys on the boats. We could see people pointing at Smitty. The cops made their way over to him and started asking questions.

"That your boat?" one of the cops asked.

"How's the guy they dragged out?" Smitty asked

"We're not sure. The firemen told us he was severely burned and he's on his way to the hospital. I guess you know the other guy died?"

"Yeah, from over here it looked like he was dead when they hauled him out."

"What can you tell us about the two guys?"

"Not much. The guy on my boat's a new member of the Devils. I've never really met him. I don't even know his name. If you can find Gus or in this crowd, I think he knows the guy's name and stuff."

"You don't know him but he was sleeping on your boat?" the cop asked in a clear tone of disbelief.

"Yup. I'm staying at my house right now, usually I sleep aboard. I thought it'd be a good idea having someone on the boat for security. They tell me this young guy volunteered as a lark. Damn it – why would someone blow up my boat?"

"Didn't you have a fire on the boat a week or so ago, Mr. Smith?" It was the first time I'd heard him called Mr. Smith. The cops were suddenly being very formal.

And wasn't there a murder here a few days ago? And now your boat's blown up. I find that very suspicious. Why don't you tell me why someone would blow up your boat?"

Smitty kept his calm. "I wish I knew. Maybe the kid had some enemies?"

I could see that Smitty didn't want that fire or the murder to be linked with this explosion. He wanted to avoid saying anything that would suggest our war with Carpenter.

"What about the fire last week?"

"That was probably because someone was careless with the heater or the stove. That's a problem when you let amateurs stay on the boat overnight. We were able to get it out ourselves okay."

"You didn't report it for insurance?"

"You kidding? D'ya have any idea how much it costs to insure these old boats?"

"What about the other guy in the other boat?"

"Gosh, I've known him for over fifteen years. He's had a boat here for at least that long. But he's only had his boat next to mine for the last six months or so. When I say I've known him, I can't really say I *know* him. His name is, was, Art, I don't even know his last name. I know he's divorced and has a son around L.A. someplace. You can check with the dock master's office. They'll have all that information for you. Poor guy. He loved his boat even though he hardly ever sailed it. Just worked and slept on it."

The cop finally seemed satisfied with Smitty's information and left.

As soon as the cops left, Gus came over.

"What the hell happened? You think Carpenter again?"

"Who else? But how'd they know about my boat, and why blow it up?"

I said, "Smitty, you're too darn well known. Lots of people know you were arrested on the murder night and lots of people know you live on your boat. Anybody could find that out real easy. It's pretty obvious to me that the dead kid was supposed to be you."

Gus said, "we gotta start taking this guy seriously." Just then we were interrupted by Smitty's old nemesis, Sergeant Horning. He was positively gloating.

"Soon as I heard it was your boat, I knew you'd be involved somehow," Horning sneered. "Then when I heard it was a bombing, I was doubly sure. I can't wait to get the forensics and pin this one on you. An insurance scam, right?"

"You idiot," Smitty said diplomatically. "I was five miles away when this happened and besides, it's one of my guys that was in the boat. From what your cop told me, it was a bomb all right. But as usual, Horning, you got it all wrong. The boats not insured so you can take that theory and shove it." Then Smitty went face to face with Horning and said, "Now get the hell off my back!"

Horning's face turned a mottled shade of red. "You S.O.B. You're in something up to your neck, and I'm gonna have the pleasure of turning the key on you before I'm done" And with that he walked away.

"Good riddance," Smitty glowered. "I want to find out what really happened."

Smitty found one of the firemen and asked him what his take on it was. When the fireman found out that Smitty was one of the owners, he opened up a bit.

"Your boat? That was definitely an explosion. Some sort of an explosive device, though we'll have to wait for the marshals to get here for that to be definitive. But the other boat – that was really odd. No explosion, but it was definitely a set fire. There was a strong smell of booze, much more than if someone had just been drinking. Off the record, I think that guy saw something he wasn't supposed to see and was clubbed to death. Then they used the booze was used as an accelerant to make a quick fire. They wanted to make it look like an accident and destroy the evidence, but we got the fire out so quickly it didn't work."

"What caused all the black smoke?"

"Real strange. The guy must have been using regular asphalt roofing tiles on the cabin top, didn't you ever notice?"

"Musta' been recent. I don't remember anything like that."

Smitty told me to stay at the docks and see what was left of the *Jezebel*. He thought that maybe, after everyone had left, maybe I could get near her. Josie said she'd stay with me so I'd have a ride.

As he was leaving, Smitty turned back to us.

"I have to go to the hospital. God, I hope that kid is okay."

CHAPTER 55

Josie and I grabbed a quick lunch at a Mexican restaurant nearby and got back to the boat as soon as we could. The cops were gone, but two firemen were still there. One of them knew who Josie was and was willing to let us see the boat up close, and even volunteered what they'd found so far.

"We're positive it was some sort of an incendiary device," he told us. "The stove's propane and propane floats if there's a leak. We always suspect a gas explosion if it's a gas stove, but that's not the case here. All signs point to a fairly powerful explosive originating just inside the cabin. In a way, it's lucky it was placed where it was. If it had been placed on the floorboards or in the bilge the boat would be sitting on the bottom right now."

I walked all around what was left of the boat. I could see both sides and her bow, but couldn't see her stern. The more I looked at her, the more I agreed with the fireman. Maybe Smitty's luck had turned for the better, for a change. The explosion had mostly gone upward, destroying almost everything above deck. But the hull was largely undamaged, and it didn't appear to be taking on any water. There was a lot of water in the cabin from the fire hoses but it wasn't increasing.

I turned to Josie. "I don't know if she can be salvaged and rebuilt, but we need to get her out of the water and on the hard pretty damn quick."

The fireman overheard me and told me they were through with it. The fire marshals had been there, taken lots of pictures and released the boat.

I turned back to Josie. "Why don't you call your dad and tell him what I think," I suggested. "Maybe he can arrange to get her out today."

Josie shared the phone with me so I could hear Smitty's side of the conversation. He was relieved to hear that the *Jezebel* wasn't completely destroyed, and said he'd get on it as soon as he got off the phone. "There's a lot going on today, Josie," he went on. "I need you two up here as soon as you can make it. See if you can hire one of the other guys on the dock to keep an eye on her. The last thing I need now is looters."

I'd been dreading Smitty blowing his stack all morning. He loved his boat. It had to have been a crushing blow to have it blown up like this. I asked Josie why he seemed so calm about this.

"Probably because there were so many people around. The firemen, the police, the crowds. Dad's pretty good at concealing his emotions," she explained.

Back at the house, it was bedlam. The guys were really pissed off. They couldn't understand the violence that Carpenter'd unleashed. They were all sure it was Carpenter again, and were all for immediate and harsh retribution.

All of a sudden guns appeared. Everyone there was just about ready to jump on his bike and head to Carpenter's house, guns and all. All hell was about to break loose. Smitty's boat was sacrosanct. It was the last straw.

Gus walked in. His timing couldn't have been better. Quickly taking in the state of things, he got to work defusing the situation. Once he got them simmered down several degrees, he said, "Whoa, whoa, whoa. Smitty's got a plan – Smitty always has a plan," he reminded them. "And we gotta wait till he gets back from the hospital. A short time later, thank goodness, Smitty did get back

Ignoring the gang he backed Josie and me into a corner and whispered, "Get the hell out of this thing."

Josie said, "What?"

"It's getting too dangerous. You should both go home and let us handle this thing by ourselves from now on."

"What does that mean," Josie demanded to know. "You planning on doing something drastic to Carpenter?"

"Doesn't matter – you'll be out of it."

"I'm not going anywhere," Josie said, standing her ground. Suddenly I could see a lot of Smitty in her. "And I'm not going let you forget your promise to Mom. And Casey's not going to either!"

That was news to me.

Smitty stood there, silent for a space, then finally, reluctantly, agreed to let us stay.

Gus joined us, put arm around Smitty's shoulder and said, "Smitty, I'm proud of you. You handled that asshole Horning like a pro. gotta tell ya, I was worried about your reaction to the boat burning," Gus said, shaking his head.

Josie wanted to know about the boy in the boat.

"He's in intensive care. Massive burns over a large part of his body and a broken leg. The only thing the doc would say was that he was holding his own. Apparently he'd been sleeping in just his shorts when the explosion occurred, which was too bad. If he'd had clothes on, he probably wouldn't have been burned so badly. Part of the cabin caved in on him and broke his leg."

Gus suggested we brainstorm where we stood so far. "Case, earlier you said you had a couple of new ideas.

"Yeah, I was thinking the chief's apparently going to meet with his friend at the FBI fairly soon."

Gus nodded. "Yeah?"

"Okay. Think about some of the papers we found in Carpenter's house. The stuff about being a pedophile. An underage girl. Interstate travel. Evidence he'd been blackmailing pedophiles. That means he knew of pedophiles and had concealed the knowledge. The FBI and the public would eat it up.

Maybe the chief could get Carpenter arrested and labeled as a child molester. Think that'd be humiliating enough for Smitty?"

Gus said, "He'll love it."

CHAPTER 56

Our plan had already been partly agreed to by the chief. He'd been willing to approach the FBI with a vague sort of "what if" scenario. We needed to convince him that he should tell the FBI everything, including his malfeasance. He'd have to take his chances that the Bureau would overlook his lapse of judgment.

The chief had struck me as being sincere about resigning, but I figured he'd grab at the chance to clear his record without having to resign. Problem was, could he figure out a way to tell the FBI what he knew about the murders, kidnapping, arson plus blackmailing? Everything he knew to date was from us and was, as he kept reminding us, tainted. 'Including the old hidden information about concealing a pedophiliac record.

"We need to find a way for the chief to know about all of Carpenter's crimes but leave us out of it," I summed up.

"Didn't Dad go to him as a private citizen and ask him if he knew he had a blackmailer in his city and ask for help?" Josie asked.

"Yeah, he did."

"Wouldn't it be logical for the chief to start an investigation, based on that citizen complaint?"

"Josie, that's it! He could start an investigation today. Using what we already know, he could get his own facts in a day or so. We need to go see him, right now."

"You've talked to him the most and you told him you'd be back with more ideas," Gus said. "You should call him and get an appointment to see him as soon as possible. Tell him Smitty suggested it."

The chief was more than agreeable. He said the first appointment he'd been able to arrange with his friend at the FBI was for early next week, but he could see us today. I told him we were on our way.

Gus drove and Josie and I sat in the back seat. I tried to put my thoughts in order. He didn't help my thinking much when he said, "I'm sure glad you're gonna be talking to the chief, I wouldn't be comfortable doing it."

I was more than a little worried about Gus putting the whole load on my shoulders. Josie glanced at me, gave me a big smile and patted me on the knee.

"Dad would probably never admit it, but he admires you and your ideas. He told me 'Casey's been a lotta help. Direct quote"

"Did he really?"

"Well, not exactly a direct quote. What he actually said was, 'that little son of a bitch has some pretty good ideas, don't he.'

I felt like Daniel entering the Lions' den, real nervous. I had to convince the chief that it would be legal and logical to investigate Carpenter. Then we had to figure out a way to make what we'd found usable. Then the chief had to get that to his friend at the FBI and convince him. Then his friend had to convince his superiors. On top of that, I wasn't totally sure that the Chief wouldn't yet simply decide to resign.

CHAPTER 57

At the station, Chief O'Meara was outside, waiting for us. He told Gus that Smitty had called and told him why we were coming to see him.

"We're going to a restaurant nearby," he said. "I've arranged for a private room so we can have an uninterrupted lunch and talk this whole thing out."

We quickly agreed to his suggestion. Actually, the way he put it plus the fact that he'd already made reservations really left no room for discussion anyway. I asked if he'd like to ride with us. He suggested that we go with him in his official car.

Around in back, the chief led us to a brand new Buick with no police markings.

"The city council wants me to use the city car as my personal vehicle," he explained.

"That way when I'm off duty, I'm still on duty. Inside, it's got everything our marked cars have. On the outside it's just a plain sedan, except for the antenna" I could see a portable red light and a siren attachment fixed to the dash. A little more ominous was a strapped-in shotgun next to the passenger seat.

He suggested that Gus sit in the front. I bet he figured that since Gus was the eldest, he'd be doing most of the talking. Wait until he finds out the young whippersnapper in the rear seat will be carrying the brunt of the conversation.

On the way to the restaurant we took turns bringing the chief up to date on everything that'd happened in the last two days. He hadn't heard about the explosion and fire.

"What makes you so sure Carpenter was behind it?" he wanted to know.

"Several things, Chief O'Meara," I answered.

"Enough with the Chief O'Meara," he said, still talking directly to Gus. "Let's just make it Chief!" Even my family calls me that."

"Casey, you better answer the chief's questions. After all, most of this plan is your idea." Gus replied.

From the back seat I listed our reasons.

"One. The kidnapping, the attack on the house, all these things started happening since we got hold of his papers.

"And two, things like this don't happen to the Devils. There's no rival gang stuff going on. It has to have been someone from out of town. Someone who doesn't understand the reputation the gang has.

"Okay. The restaurant's just ahead, we'll talk inside."

Looking ahead I could see the restaurant, a conspicuous tile-roofed, two-story building, painted a bright red, white, and green. As we pulled up to the front door, it swung open and a middle-aged man with an apron around his waist came over and opened the chief's door. He looked Italian to me. Wonder where he got the name Jerry?

"Hey, Chief!" he said cheerfully. "Your room's ready and waiting."

The chief led us upstairs to a cozy private dining room set up set up for four. As we seated ourselves he said, "One thing I want to get straight right now."

Now what, I wondered.

"I'm paying for the lunch," he said solemnly. No one argued. It certainly was easy for me to agree. I hardly ever argue with a police chief. Besides I didn't have much money.

He continued. "I took the liberty of ordering the lunch special for everyone. It's one of Jerry's specialties. If you like Italian food, you'll be more than satisfied."

Before we could settle down to talk, Jerry came up to see if everything was satisfactory. We assured him it was. As he was leaving, he paused at the door for a moment, looking a little nonplussed.

"What, no wine on your table? Italian food without wine? I'll send some up."

And with that he closed the door and was gone.

As soon as he was gone the chief split his gaze between the three of us and said, "Okay. What's so terribly important?"

I took the bull by the horns, cleared my throat and tried to marshal my thoughts. Inside I was a mass of jelly, telling a police chief what we wanted him to do.

"Smitty and I think what we're proposing is entirely in your best interest."

"I hope so. So what is it?"

Brusque, but he seemed interested.

"Okay, first question, Chief," I said. "Were you really serious the other day when you said that you were considering quitting because of the blackmailing issue?"

A short silence. Then, "Yes, I was. I can't apply a double standard to myself. How do I know Carpenter won't compromise my position on something important down the road?"

"Good," I replied. He gave me a rather odd look. I quickly went on. "Because that fits in with our plan to get you off the hook."

"Off the hook?"

"Yeah, Chief, off the hook." Good. I had his attention.

I continued. "If the information we have wasn't tainted would it be enough to indict Carpenter? Like if the information got untainted?

Before he could answer, there was a knock on the door and the waiter came in with two bottles of wine. The chief thanked him and said he'd handle the pouring himself.

As he was pouring, he looked at me and with a smile said, "Untainted?? At least he still had a sense of humor. Then, "is there really physical evidence against Carpenter?"

"You bet, tons of it. Some of it's even in Carpenter's handwriting."

"Okay, then the answer's yes. With those papers they could build a case against him, and probably indict and convict him on a number of charges. However, it's still problematic and I don't see how they could be what you call untainted."

"I know." I looked him in the eye and asked, "If *you* had uncovered all this information instead of us, do you think the Bureau would act on it?"

"Without question."

"Okay, Chief," I said, "we think we've come up with a plan that'll allow you to present all the information in a way that the Bureau will accept. A way that you can use the evidence without its being tainted. And – *and* – we think it's pretty much completely legal."

The chief cleared his throat, looked down, then, "Pretty much completely legal? What does that mean?"

"It means, as far as you or your department's concerned, you'll find all the papers, in his house, on your own, it's that simple."

"So somehow, the papers are going to get back into his house, do I read you right?"

"No comment," I said.

I'm sorry, Casey," he said, and he really did look sorry. "I don't think I can do this. I know it's important to you, and it might be important to me, but I just don't think I should get involved in whatever your idea is. Let's forget the whole thing.

Without the chief, nothing would work. Without the chief, we were dead in the water.

Providentially, our meal arrived just then. I desperately needed time to think.

CHAPTER 58

Nothing more was said while we ate. Josie and Gus looked at me and I shrugged my shoulders in desperation. Finally he spoke again.

"For me, it's my conscience. I'm proud of being a good police chief. I'm proud of my reputation. I'm afraid something'll go wrong and I'll end up even worse off than I am now."

"As long as we're here, can we at least tell you our plan?" I said, trying not to sound like I was begging. "We think it's damn near foolproof. See what you think?"

"And it would get all this information into my hands legally?"

"I'm pretty sure." I said. I was trying to undersell the idea; I didn't think he'd react well to my being super enthusiastic.

"Josie, ask the chief the same questions you asked Smitty this morning."

I don't think Josie was expecting this, but she rose to the challenge.

"Chief, you know my dad's reputation and history, but would you consider him – for legal purposes – as much a legal citizen as anyone else?"

"Of course."

"If he – or anyone else – came to you with a legitimate complaint about someone in your city doing something criminal, would you investigate it as a matter of course?"

"Of course."

"Even if this citizen didn't live in your city, but the supposed criminal did?"

"Yes."

"And if you had a complaint from a city department – say a garbage collector – that he'd been threatened with a gun by someone in that house, could you get a search warrant?"

"Uh…yeah. Where are you going with all this?"

"Those were the 'suppose' questions I asked Dad this morning. He thought you'd be able to answer them all with yeses, and really, that's why we're here."

I gave Chief O'Meara a moment for thought, gave Josie a nod of thanks, then took over again.

"Okay, Chief, here's our plan. Smitty will lodge an official complaint with your office about him being blackmailed by Carpenter."

A long slow nod of acceptance.

"And the local garbage collector will lodge a complaint about being threatened by an occupant of the house. It'll be an honest complaint because he'll be the actual relief garbage man for Carpenter's house, and he actually did have a gun waved in his face by one of the guys in the house."

Of course we weren't telling him that the garbage man had been part of the group that broke into the house, and the gun waiving had occurred inside the house, not outside.

"With those two complaints, can you get a warrant to search his house?"

"No problem at all."

"One more thing. We'll guarantee that every incriminating piece of paper you need for the FBI will be in the house for you to discover for yourself during the raid. We can't see how the FBI couldn't accept that. They're his papers, in his house. The fact that Carpenter thought they went missing for a few days is inconsequential, right?

"You're saying that the papers you have will somehow magically reappear in his house, in time for me to 'discover' them?"

"The way I see it, we'll be correcting something. We'll be undoing a wrong. You might say we'll be un-stealing. Is there a law against un-stealing?"

For the first time today, the chief laughed. Un-taint and un-steal? I don't want to know anything about that," he said. "As far as I'm concerned, I never heard anyone say that."

He went serious again and lapsed into a silence, apparently mulling over all the consequences of our plan. While he was mulling, I took the opportunity to study his face. He looked to be in his late forties or a real young looking fiftyish. Up to this point, I hadn't thought of him as a person, just a uniform. He didn't wear a uniform, but you get my drift. I was finally seeing him as a person. He was rather good looking, with an open face and blue, somewhat piercing, eyes and brown hair that was receding and turning grey around the edges of a military cut. A very serious man.

Thinking of him as a husband and father in addition to being police chief, I could appreciate the deep concern he had to feel for his family, let alone his city and his future. A lot hung on the decision he had to make.

I broke his silence. "There's something else you can use, Chief. Have any of the prisoners we gave you told you anything worthwhile?"

"I've been thinking about that too," he said. "They've volunteered several interesting things, and have corroborated a number of the things you told me. If I add that to what I find at his house, it gets even more damning for Carpenter."

Again, he went silent. We waited.

"I guess I have no choice," he finally said. "It is an okay plan. It's certainly the only way I can maybe get out of this mess with some honor for myself and my family."

I told him we'd have to get back to Smitty and start laying out the plan. We shook hands. He paid the bill and drove us back to the station.

In our car, Josie immediately phoned the house. Nips answered the phone and told her that Smitty was looking at his boat.

"Is he okay?

"No he ain't. The more he looks at the boat the madder he gets. He's really pissed, steaming and ready to blow. I hope you guys are coming back with some good news or he's gonna blow his top. You know your dad. He's not good at waiting for something to happen. If you can get here pretty quick with something positive to do, maybe that'll defuse him."

She got off the phone and told Gus to get us home as quickly as he could.

Smitty was waiting for us in the garage. Josie grabbed his arm and said, "Come on. Let's go up to the dining room. We need to bring you up to date on some good news."

He yanked his arm away from her and said, "Good, I could use some good news."

The chief agreed on our plan, he's going to talk to the FBI. We need to work out some details."

He looked over at me. "What details?"

"We gotta figure out a way to get Carpenters' papers back into his house so the chief can legally discover them."

"How the hell do we do that? Where'd that idea come from?" Is that another of your crazy ideas?"

Ignoring him I continued. "And you have to lodge a formal complaint about being blackmailed by Carpenter."

"You're kidding me, right?"

I went on, "Oh, yeah, the last thing. You have to get Carpenter's garbage man to swear that he was threatened with a gun at Carpenter's house."

"You finished?" he grumbled.

I looked up from my notes just in time to see him wink at Gus. He was having fun at my expense. It looked like he was okay with our list of to-dos.

"I think so. I already told the chief we'd do that. He said if we– you– could do all that, he'd do the rest. I didn't tell him about your plan to get Carpenter nailed as a sex pervert."

"And you're sure that's all you promised I'd do?"

"Yeah, Dad," Josie said. "Nothing you can't do with both hands tied behind your back."

There was one thing the chief had told us that we weren't sure we should tell Smitty. Josie and I whispered together and decided it was okay to tell him, seeing how he seemed to be in control of himself. Josie did the telling

The chief said he got some interesting info from one of the jailed guys. There's a guy working for Carpenter that's got a rep. as a bomb maker.

Smitty pursed his lips.

"He's the guy that blew my boat?"

"Probably. The chief said to tell you he'll get the guy. He should be easy to find. He's big, about six three, bald and has tats up and down both arms. The kid said the guy usually goes around in tank tops, showing off his art work."

Smitty took the news calmly. I was pleased that we'd evidently successfully kept Smitty from erupting. He sat there eying the three of us for a moment.

"You guys think you're so clever, don't you," he finally said. "I know what you're doing, you know. You're trying to keep me cool. Well, I'm way ahead of you." Josie and I exchanged guilty looks.

And Smitty wasn't finished. He pointed a finger at his daughter. "Josie, *you* stop trying to manipulate me. You forget your mom manipulated me for years. I sure as hell recognize it when I see it."

CHAPTER 59

"So what do I have to do?" Smitty asked.

"The chief said he'd need a deposition from you about the blackmail attempt. Said for you to call the station and make arrangement to meet with an officer"

As usual, Smitty delegated to me. "You call and arrange the meeting and see if the officer'll come over here for the damned thing. And while you're at it," he added, "since you get along with him so well, tell him I'm making you my liaison with him. You stay over there in El Cerrito with him and keep me posted on his progress. And have Josie and Gus go along. You can report to me here each night."

And then, totally unexpected, "By the way, you're not doing a bad job for us, so I'm putting you on salary. How does a hundred a week sound?"

How did it sound? It sounded great! I was practically broke. He handed me five twenties and I went to a phone and called the chief. He said he'd handle Smitty and would very much like Gus, Josie and me as liaison. "So you'll be out here all day? Would you three like to come to my house for dinner?"

I didn't even ask Josie or Gus, just said we'd be delighted. When I told them what Smitty had requested, that we stay over in El Cerrito, Josie was a little apprehensive. She wanted to know what her dad was planning, and why he wanted her out of the way.

First chance she got, she asked Smitty the same thing. He swore he was planning nothing.

"Just doing what the chief suggested."

"Thanks to you three, I'll be spending most of today trying to figure out a way to get this stuff back into Carpenter's house. Any idea how fast the chief can organize the raid on his place?"

Chief O'Meara hadn't mentioned a time table. I'd gotten the impression he was waiting for Smitty to deal with getting both his and the garbage company's depositions on file. He certainly wasn't going to move until he knew the evidence was back at Carpenter's.

When the three of us got to the police station, we were told that the chief had left a message, that we were to make ourselves comfortable in his office and he'd be right back.

A few minutes later, he swept in, took his chair behind his desk and invited us to sit. He wasted no time getting right to the topic.

"The reason I invited you to the house for dinner," he said, "is that I wanted you to see how important my family is to me. Also I thought it would be a good idea to get to know you a little better. For example, I know Josie is Smitty's daughter, and I know Gus has been with Smitty for umpteen years, but – how'd you get mixed up in all this?"

Obviously he was talking to me. So I proceeded to tell him the whole story, only slightly abridged to protect the guilty.

"I wonder if Smitty knows how lucky he is to have you around. Seems to me that a lot of the ideas we're using came from you," the chief observed, inflating my ego.

"On the other hand, if he wasn't around, we wouldn't have been in this mess in the first place," Gus said, deflating it back to normal.

"Thanks. I needed that," I said to Gus, then turned to the chief.

"What makes a guy like Carpenter tick? Is it just money?

"Probably. Although in Carpenters' case, I have another theory. I don't think that Carpenter operates in a vacuum," the chief went on. "Ever wondered where all his information comes from? I think someone's pulling *his* strings. From what you told me, it sounds like most of the blackmail stuff originated in Sacramento. I'd be willing to bet there's someone over Carpenter, someone in Sacramento. The guy who made Carpenter what he is today. *That* guy's the real murderer."

"Why do you think that Chief?" I asked.

"To me, it's pretty obvious. Carpenter's pretty wealthy, from what we know. There's really no reason for him to go off the deep end like he's done – unless someone's ordered him to. Someone in the state capitol's worried stiff about all these missing papers. Someone who's making Carpenter do things he'd normally not do."

"Yeah," I added. "And not do them very well." The chief nodded.

"You're a quick study, my friend. You know what I think? I think you guys are going to end up in Sacramento, and you're going end going up against a lawmaker of some sort. I can see it now: Senator So-and-So indicted on charges of something or other... I'll tell you one thing; if a senator's involved you won't have to worry about getting the FBI involved. They'll be falling all over you."

I liked the sound of that.

Just then the desk sergeant stuck his head in and told the chief they had a situation that needed him. The chief in turn asked us if we wanted to wait there or go out for coffee or something. We elected to stay put.

"Do you guys think we'll end up in Sacramento?" Josie asked after the chief left the room.

Gus said, "I don't know but Smitty seems to think we will."

A few minutes later, after some silence, Gus added, "I've been mulling over an idea about getting Carpenters papers back in his house. We gotta get him out of the house long enough to sneak the papers in, right?"

"That's the idea."

"You know how Carpenter still hasn't found his precious diary? Suppose it turned up somehow. Suppose someone got in touch with him and told him he'd found it. D'ya think he'd go after it? 'Specially if the guy wanted a reward for his trouble?"

"Like a shot!" I responded. "But what good would that do?"

"It might get Carpenter out of his house long enough for Smitty to get the papers back in and I think I got a way to do it. This friend of mine runs an antique warehouse in Alameda; he'd do it for me."

"Do what?"

"Call Carpenter and convince he had found the little black book and he wants a reward for returning it. But he can't get away from work and Carpenter will have to come to Alameda to get it. It would take most of an hour and a half to go from Carpenters house to Alameda and back. Plenty of time.

"Might work. You want to call your friend and see if he's willing?"

Gus's conversation with his friend was short. The guy said he'd not only willing to do it, but it'd be a blast and he had some ideas of his own.

"D'ya think if we hid the stuff in his basement, he wouldn't notice it before the chief raids the place?" Gus asked.

"Probably as good a place as any," I told him.

Josie suggested that Gus phone her dad and tell him what he'd told us about Alameda.

I added, "The more I think about it, the more I like it. Tell Smitty we can make it work. And we don't say anything to the chief about it, right?" They both agreed.

Gus made the call and added his own take.

"As soon as the papers are in place, we let the chief know and he raids the place."

CHAPTER 60

At the Chief's house we meet his wife, kids and dogs, not necessarily in that order. At the front door the dogs were all over us. Once we shooed them off we met the kids. An all American family. His wife was sweet and cute, obviously accustomed to having guests for dinner at a short notice. The three kids, all under nine, were tickled to have us, especially having heard about the Devils. The chief must have given them a sanitized description of the gang's reputation. Of course, I'm not really a member and neither is Josie, and Gus is the most gentlemanly member I've met so far, so he probably thinks his kids are safe.

He offered us a cocktail and suggested we talk in the living room while his wife finished fixing dinner. The kids and dogs traipsed in after us and we had a lively conversation about motorcycles for some time. One of the kids told me he was glad we were there because that meant they'd have a real dessert tonight.

The chief put up with them for a short time and then shooed them off. "Go do your homework or help your Mom set the table or something. We need to talk, okay?" he told them. Once they were gone, he turned back to us.

"I called Smitty and brought him up to date. While we were talking I asked him if it was okay for you three to stay here tonight. We've got three extra bedrooms and two guest baths. You'd be quite comfortable. Angie said she'd fix blueberry hotcakes for breakfast if you stayed."

"What did Dad say?" Josie asked.

"If you really want to know, he told me that if I'd keep an eye on you two, it was okay by him."

I looked at Josie and Josie looked at Gus and Gus looked at me and we stayed.

"So—what's going to happen when?" he asked.

"It's real simple. Hopefully, sometime late tomorrow you'll get a call from Smitty. That'll be your signal to serve the warrant."

"That may be a problem," the chief said. "I have to go before a judge to get the warrant and sometimes they're hard to corner. I don't think I'll have any trouble getting it, just finding a judge."

"Do you think we should delay the plan for a day?"

"No, I'll get the warrant. In fact I think I'll phone a couple of the judges right now and set up a meeting for tomorrow morning."

The chief's kids came in and announced it was time for dinner. The kids directed us to our seats. Evidently their mom had let them choose who sat where. They'd arranged us so that we were pretty much surrounded by the kids. We had a lot of fun and a great dinner. Nothing really fancy, just plain good— broiled chicken, green salad and some sort of rice dish.

And dessert, as the kids promised. Fresh strawberry shortcake.

I told them a little about my sailing background. Josie and Gus told them a little about the Devils. The chief told us a little about law enforcement, and his wife told us a little about the chief.

We watched the news and got to bed early. We weren't prepared at all to stay overnight. No pajamas, no toothbrushes, Josie didn't even have any make-up with her. Evidently, Angie had been warned about our lack of supplies. She had pajamas, towels and everything we needed on each bed, even toothbrushes and toothpaste. I almost expected to find a small chocolate on the pillow.

Breakfast next morning was as advertised. Blueberry pancakes and all the trimmings. Angie said she'd grown up being told to eat breakfast like a king, lunch like a queen and dinner like a pauper. I told her I'd never met a pauper that had a dinner like last night's.

"Well, you know what I mean."

The chief hurried us along, got us to say goodbye to the wife and kids, gave her and each of the kids a kiss and a hug and we left. On the way to the cars he asked Josie if he could tell her dad I'd been a good boy last night. He has a wry sense of humor. I liked him and so did Josie.

"What about the search warrant?" I asked

"The judge told me last night that based on the sworn statements we had, he'd have no trouble issuing a search warrant. I'm stopping at City Hall on the way in to pick them up, He answered.

Gus interjected, sotto voiced. "I'm ready too. I'll need a private room at the station to make my call to Carpenter.

CHAPTER 61

Gus had been rehearsing what he was about to say for some time. He and Josie and I crowded into the small room and Gus made the call on a speaker phone. Gus warned us to be as quiet as church mice.

He got Carpenter on the line right away and did a masterful job. He sounded real youthful and he talked as if he was in a hurry.

"Look, I work in this pawn shop antique place thing here in Alameda, and we get in all kinds a' crap from all kinds a' places. I don't know nothin' 'bout antiques. All I do is kinda' clean up the stuff so the experts can value them. Anyways, I always say what I find in drawers and under seat covers is mine.

"And what's this got to do with me?" Carpenter asked angrily.

"Hey, buddy, slow down. I'm tryin' to tell you!" Gus said with well feigned irritation. "If I find something hidden, I figure it's mine. So's I find this diary kinda' thing – you know, like a notebook or something, stuffed in a box of papers somebody found on the freeway and brought in. I'm like asking, this ain't no antique shit. What're *we* doing with it? I was told to just look through it quick like, and throw it away if there wasn't nothin' there. Well there wasn't much – except this here locked diary book."

There was a short pause. "Where'd you get my name?"

"It's on some of the other papers in the box. I just looked up the name Carpenter in the phone book and started phoning. You're the first one I caught home. If it ain't yours just tell me and I'll call the others."

"What's it look like?"

"It's small. And black."

"How small?"

"Real small."

"About three by five?"

"Yeah, that's 'bout right. Anyways, it looks valuable to me. *Real* valuable. Got lotsa names in it. Interesting names. Interesting phone numbers. I was gonna keep it, but then I got to thinkin' that maybe the right thing to do was to return it to its rightful owner. 'Course I 'spect a small reward."

"Small?"

"Yeah, small."

"How small?

"Oh, I was thinkin' maybe five hundred would be about right."

"Are you crazy? I hadn't even missed the damn thing yet. Why would I pay five hundred bucks for it? Tell you what, just for sentimental value; I'll give you two hundred. If I can get it today."

They eventually settled on three hundred.

The next step Gus took was masterful in order to get Carpenter in person over to Alameda.

"How'll I know you're really this Carpenter guy, just because you answered the phone? You got a drivers' license with a picture on it?"

"Of course. I'll come personally, and I'll have my driver's license with me. Picture and everything." It was obvious he really wanted the book.

"Okay, but I split at three-thirty, and it's gotta be cash."

"Give me the address and I'll be there about two, okay?"

"Ain't no address," Gus told him. "It's a huge warehouse, way at the end of Alameda where the air station used to be. Building number three-seven-five. Ask for Greg."

"Greg as in Gregory?"

"You got it. See you at two."

Wow, did it ever go good. Gus sounded just like some young dock worker or something, and Carpenter went for it hook, line and sinker.

Quickly Gus phoned "Gregory" at the antiques place and filled him in on the phone call he'd just made.

"So all I have to do is tell the truth? All I have to do is take quite a bit of time making sure for him there's no Gregory working here and never has been?

"Yeah, but he might blow a fuse. He might think you're in on it some way. You better be careful. Make sure you got a couple of guys with you all the time."

We phoned Smitty and told him Carpenter'd be out of the way by about one thirty.

He said, "That'll work. Gives us plenty of time. Oh, by the way, Josie, were you okay with the arrangements last night?"

"Yeah, Dad, they were fine," she said with a sigh.

"Enough spare rooms to go around?"

She glanced at Gus and me and smirked. "No, Dad. Casey and I had to share a bedroom."

Silence. She let him stew for a short time and then laughed. "God, Dad. I'm kidding. We each had our own bedroom, and the chief sat in the hall all night to make sure nobody left their rooms."

"Okay, okay, I get the message!" Smitty groused and hung up.

The three of us had nothing to do but wait. The chief suggested we go back to Jerry's restaurant for lunch and he'd arrange it for us and said we should try the gnocchi.

I wondered aloud as to what gnocchi was, and Josie said, "That settles it; you're having gnocchi for lunch." It looked like my lunch menu was settled, whatever gnocchi was.

A waiter led us upstairs to the same room we'd had before and told us he'd be right back with the wine. At Jerry's, it seemed we were going to have wine whether we wanted it or not.

We all three had the gnocchi. But first Jerry appeared with wine and four glasses and sat down with us. Right behind him, the waiter appeared with crusty French bread and a big platter of salamis, cheeses, olives and pepperoncini.

Jerry was a great host. I could see why the chief liked him so much. Short and a little on the pudgy side, he was dark skinned with black glistening eyes. He didn't walk; he bounced and was very entertaining.

He stayed with us while we enjoyed the wine and pretty much decimated the nibbles he'd brought. When the entrées arrived he excused himself and said he'd check in with us later. "Take your time eating. You can stay here all afternoon if you wish. Chief said he'd call you if he needed you and that you should relax and enjoy!"

Finally we were alone and it was gnocchi time. Josie told me that they were little "pillows" made from potatoes. Didn't sound good or even interesting to me, but they turned out to be delicious. All three of us were more than satisfied with our meals and lunch ended all too soon.

When we'd finished the small dishes of ice cream that seemed to be mandatory with Jerry's dinners, Gus said if we didn't mind he'd head downstairs to the bar area. "I feel more comfortable in bars than I do in restaurants," he claimed. We knew he just wanted to give us some time alone together. What a nice guy!

We decided as long as we had the whole afternoon to ourselves, we could afford to have a nice after-lunch drink and relax, as Jerry had suggested.

Drinks ordered and delivered, we started talking. We found out we both loved music but entirely different kinds. I leaned to light classical, while she was a devout disciple of jazz. In fact, Josie told me she had a pretty large collection of jazz. I had a rather small collection of light classical. I often took mine with me on boat deliveries if there was a player on board.

"We should be able to live with that, shouldn't we?" Josie said, as if it were the most natural observation in the world. I wasn't sure how much to read into that offhand remark.

What with the wine we'd had with lunch and the after-lunch drinks, the conversation flowed easily, and before we knew it a couple of hours had passed.

"Do you think you should check on Gus?" Josie finally asked me.

I found him at the bar, deep in conversation with a couple and a young lady. I asked him if he wanted to come back up with us, or if he'd like us to join him at the bar?

He told us to get lost, in the nicest way. The guy really was at home in a bar. I guess four's company, six is a crowd.

On the way back upstairs, Jerry stopped us and said, "Boy, that guy Gus can sure hold his liquor, can't he!" I had no idea if he could or couldn't, and asked Josie if she thought he'd be okay.

"Heck, yeah. He'll probably drink everybody under the table," she laughed. "We had him over at the house at Christmas. He put a major dent in our liquor supply."

We decided to go for a walk and spent the time in small talk about how each of us had grown up. After about an hour, Josie's cell phone rang.

"Hi, this is Jerry. You better get back. The chief called for you. 'Says he needs you. By the way, I hope you're not counting on Gus driving."

We got the message.

He was right. Gus was very, very happy. His friends had multiplied to seven or eight, all sitting around a table in the bar, where he seemed very much at home. He was also ready to leave.

Jerry helped us get Gus out to the car and waited to make doubly sure he wasn't driving. Actually Gus didn't want to drive. He sat alone in the back seat and talked all the way to the station. Amazingly, by the time we arrived he sounded almost sober.

CHAPTER 62

The chief said he was about ready to raid Carpenters' house and we were supposed to call Smitty. Smitty said it'd gone off like clockwork. He said Carpenter had taken off for Alameda about one-thirty and taken his ex-con bruiser with him. He told us that as soon as he was out of sight, Smitty and two other guys had driven up in what looked like a UPS van and delivered several boxes of stuff to his side door.

Smitty said that what the neighbors didn't see was that the boxes were not left at the door. They were quickly taken inside, thanks to Nips, our experienced locksmith, and tossed down the basement stairs for the police to find. He said the guys weren't there long enough to make the neighbors suspicious. A routine UPS delivery"

He said, we were in and out so fast and so quiet, if there had been someone in another part of the house, they probably wouldn't have heard us."

"So now what?" I asked the chief.

"According to my guys, Carpenter's back at his house, got there about fifteen minutes ago. Now we serve the warrant and search the premises. That's why I called. You want to tag along? You can't go in with the team, of course, but you can sit across the street in my car and watch the whole thing come down, if you want."

Josie said, "Me too?"

"Sure," O'Meara said. "And you too, Gus. If you want. There're probably only two of them and there'll be about a dozen of us. We're gonna cover the front, back and both sides, so no one can slip out. You won't be in any danger. But you have to promise not to leave my car once we get started."

Gus said he thought he'd wait at the station and have some more black coffee if the chief didn't mind. The chief winked at me and said he thought that was probably a good idea.

"First I'll take a very slow drive by, just to make certain everything is nice and quiet. You'll have to lie down in the seats when I get near, just to be safe. As soon as I'm satisfied, I'll radio my men and they'll come up and serve the papers."

"Chief, Won't Carpenter recognize you or your car?"

"Not the car – it's brand new. Hardly anyone's seen it. I'll put on dark glasses and a golfer's hat. I'll look like any other golfer trying to find the gate to the course."

As we got near Carpenters' house, the chief had us lay down, out of sight. Over the next few minutes he gave us a running commentary on what he was seeing.

"Nothing unusual yet," he reported. "His car's parked at the side, near the side door. The front shades are up but I don't see any movement. I think we're okay to go. I'm ready to radio my team. Stay down!"

I'd started to lift my head up but quickly changed my mind.

"I'll tell you when it's okay to start watching."

Several minutes passed.

"Don't get up yet," the chief said quietly. "My men are all in place. I'm going to the front door and serve the papers. I'll have three men with me, just in case. When I leave the car, count to a hundred, slowly. Then start watching. That'll give me time to get over there and focus their attention on me."

With that, we heard him open his door and leave. I started counting to one hundred as instructed, and supposed Josie was doing the same. When I reached eighty, Josie said she'd reached a hundred.

"Chief said slowly!"

"I did count slowly!"

Adding our little exchange, I figured enough time had gone by. I cautiously raised my head so I could see Carpenter's house.

"its okay, Josie. You can come up. Looks like it's going peaceably. Carpenter and the other guy are at the front door and the cops are handcuffing the goon. I can see tattoos on both of his arms. Must be the ex-con, the one they said was so brutal."

"Is he the one they said was the bomber?"

"I think they said he made bombs. I don't remember anyone saying he was the bomber, but you're right, that's the guy!"

Nobody knew what to expect, not even the chief. They were looking for incriminating stuff, wherever it was. It wasn't long before the cops discovered the secret room and the basement with the boxes of papers, not to mention a nice haul of marijuana plants. They had plenty to put the whole household in the clinker. The chief said he wished we'd been able to be there when Carpenter saw what they'd found in the basement.

"He knew immediately he'd been snookered but you could tell he had no idea how. He looked sick, like someone had just punched him in the stomach. Wait till he meets up with some of his gang already behind my bars."

The chief took us back to the station and Josie phoned Smitty to tell him how well the plan had worked.

Shortly after that, Gus called his friend at the antique place and put him on his speaker phone.

"So what happened?" Gus asked.

"We had a ball. First he drove up like he owned the place and demanded to see Gregory. I told him I didn't think we had anyone working here with that name."

"Then?"

"He insisted. 'Said he'd just talked to the guy on the phone. Told us the guy worked cleaning up new stuff just come in. I told him I didn't think so, but I'd check for him, maybe it was a temporary guy. Then I went behind the door and just waited for a couple of minutes. When I went back I had five of my buddies with me and he was fuming. I told him I'd asked everybody and there's no one here by that name. He said he wanted to see the boss. I told him I was the boss, at least today."

"Did he give up then?

"Not yet. He had a big guy with him. Tattoos all over his arms. He tried to get tough with me, but there were five guys behind me so that didn't work. He stood staring at us for a minute, then turned to his boss and told him he thought they'd been had and they'd better get back home in a hurry. Then they left. Fast! Like I said, we had a ball. It was like being in a play where we knew the script but they didn't."

I told the chief that Smitty wanted us to stay with the papers and try to get more information about the Sacramento connection.

The chief quickly threw cold water on that idea.

"Actually, you might as well head home now. First, I have to protect the integrity of the evidence," he explained to us. "I have to document the entire handling of it and make sure it isn't compromised in any way. I can't let you even near it, let alone touch it. It's what's called the chain of evidence." He stopped for a moment, looked hard at his desk, ran a hand through his hair, then looked back up at us, each of us, individually. Then he finally said, "What I *can* do is let you know the minute we run across anything that might be helpful to you. I just can't let you see it or touch it in any way."

We couldn't argue with the chief so we did as he suggested and headed home. Back at the house Gus seemed to be none the worse for his afternoon of drinking. He said he'd been thinking about Sacramento. Trying to figure out how someone got hold of that type of information.

"I don't think it'd be a senator," he said, "They don't deal in that kind of information, not on a regular basis. More likely someone in the Attorney General's office?"

"Isn't there some sort of senatorial committee that looks into illegal things that senators do?" I asked. "It'd help if we knew the name of that committee,"

Smitty had more to add. "I still think we need to go to Sacramento. I'm gonna phone Little George up there and see if he can arrange a place for us to stay a couple of nights. He can help us, he knows more about Sacramento than any of us.

"Who's Little George?" I asked Josie as we headed downstairs.

"He's like Dad, only he's in Sacramento. And, trust me, he isn't little. He's about six five, and he must weigh over three hundred pounds. Ever seen a motorcycle with a rider so huge you could hardly see the bike? It's Little George. But he's like Dad, getting up there in age and mellowing out. I like him."

Gus and the guys wanted to fix something to eat, even though it was late. We all settled for a midnight snack and hit the hay.

Next morning, after a breakfast that was pretty much a rerun of last night's snack, the phone rang. It was the chief. Smitty put him on the speaker phone, expecting to hear that they'd gotten an indictment on Carpenter or something. What we got was something else.

"You're not going to believe this," Chief O'Meara told us, sounding grim. "Carpenter made bail. Either he's got some friends in *mighty* high places or he's got enough dope on someone that they came through for him. Either way, he had a high-priced attorney here last night. Somehow or other, he got himself an early morning hearing, had bail set and got out."

"What does that mean?" I asked. "Can you still get an indictment?"

"Course I can. He's not supposed to leave town. We'll still indict him and get a second crack at putting him behind bars. Trouble is he knows now that he doesn't have me under control any more. I made it very plain to him that I wasn't going to cooperate with him, any way, any more. Now I'm afraid he's a flight risk. Now that he knows his house of cards is sliding into the San Andreas Fault, he may just take off, bail or no bail."

"What can we do?"

"I'm putting a detail on his house. If he makes the slightest move, I'll know it. My problem is I can't spare enough men to track him or try to stop him. Particularly since I'm acting on just a hunch. This could take days. Can you get three or four guys out here to help my guys? With a few of your guys on bikes and my two guys in cars we should be able to keep track of him. What do you think?"

Smitty said he'd send some guys right away.

"They've got helmet radios, don't they?"

"Sure do."

"Tell them to stop by the station on the way. We'll make sure they have the right frequency to talk to our guys."

CHAPTER 63

Smitty sent four guys up to augment the chiefs' forces and then announced to us, "We're going to Sacramento, maybe tomorrow."

"Did you find a direct link to someone there?" Josie asked.

"No, we didn't. Not a direct one, anyway. But the trail seems to stop with Carpenter, as far as where all the blackmail information actually ended up, and it's pretty obvious that he got the stuff from someone else. Every letter we find leads us back to Sacramento."

"So who's going?" Josie asked.

"So far, I'm thinking you, Casey and Gus. I've already talked to Little George about what we're doing. He's got some ideas. He says there've been rumors about a couple of senators for years. Maybe he can help us. Anyway, we're going."

That left Josie and me with nothing really to do.

She asked me if I'd heard of an old movie theatre that served pizzas and had sofas and overstuffed chairs instead of the regular seats.

"You bet! It's right near my place. I've been there a couple of times. It's fun, if you don't mind old movies."

So that's what we did. Two on a sofa, pizza and an old movie. What could be better? When we got out it was still light. Josie suggested we go to her favorite ice cream place for a cone or something, but just as we were pulling into the parking lot, the phone rang.

"I knew it was too good to be true," Josie said. "I was really looking forward to the ice cream."

She was right – it was her dad.

"Better get back here fast," he said. "Looks like Carpenter's on the move."

Josie kept right on going, through the parking lot and out, headed back up into the Oakland hills to her dad's house.

The place was a beehive of activity. Smitty was on the phone. Several of the guys were sitting on their bikes with helmets on, ready to go. Gus was the only one we could talk to.

"He's left his house. Gone to a restaurant in El Cerrito. The cops saw him sneaking suitcases into his car. We've got four bikes and two cars set to follow him wherever he goes. The chief's checking all the airlines to see if he's made reservations. Other than that, all we can do is follow him when he leaves."

"If he tries to fly out, can't he be stopped?" I asked, exasperated. "I thought the court told him he had to stay in town."

"The chief says that'd be real hard to do. They don't have an indictment yet. He says he has to be super careful and not violate any of Carpenter's civil rights in advance of the indictment and trial."

"So, what are we doing?"

"Well, we're not sure. We're pretty much on our own. Smitty says we're gonna follow him wherever he goes and somehow stop him. That's why he wanted you. He said you might have more useful ideas and that you're quick on your feet. His words. I'd say get ready to go any minute. When he leaves the restaurant, our guys are gonna follow him and feed us information on his route. As soon as we find out his general direction, we'll try to get ahead of him. Smitty's pretty sold on the idea that he'll be heading to the Oakland Airport. But it could be San Francisco. We just better be ready either way. Smitty wants us with him in the car."

Smitty walked in and interrupted us. "I'd bet real money he's headed for the Oakland Airport. What I'm afraid of is that he might get ahead of us and get away. It's taking a chance but let's leave now so we'll be ahead of him. Josie, you drive. I'll be on the cell Gus; you follow us and keep your cell phone open."

Gus, ever alert, instantly understood and agreed.

"As soon as we're sure he's heading our way, we'll get in front of his car. That way we'll be sure to get to the airport first. We'll need to hatch out some sort of a plan on the fly."

I immediately saw a snag in Smitty's plan. "How'll we know which airline he's going to if we're ahead of him? It's a long way from one airline to another."

"Do I have to think of everything? You figure it out!"

In a few minutes I had an answer. "You said we'd be in front of him when we got to the airport?"

"Yeah. That's my plan."

"Okay then, this should work." I said. "We pull into the very first terminal, as if we're picking up or letting someone out. If he follows us in, we know where he's going. If he drives by, then we follow him."

"On the other hand, he could drive into the parking lot and walk in, you know," Smitty pointed out.

"Probably not with all the luggage he had. But if he does, then we follow him into the lot and park where he can't see us. The guys on bikes can circle ahead and let us know which airline he heads for. Then we follow him."

"Okay, Then what?"

"So he gets to the airline counter and gets in line," I continued my high-wire improv. "I'm guessing he ordered tickets on line or by phone. He'll have to get in line to get them. Then I'm stuck. I don't what to do once he's in line."

"*I* don't know either. Come up with an idea!" Smitty urged.

I'd flown up and down the coast plenty of times, often at the last minute, on the way to pick up a boat for delivery. I tried to envision standing in line and some way to disrupt Carpenter.

As we got to the freeway entrance, we got the call.

"He's out of" the restaurant. Trying to look real nonchalant like. You know, paused outside and used a toothpick. Read the newspaper headlines, studiously avoided looking at his watch, before getting in his car. He's definitely heading to the freeway. Only question now is does he go north or south. Hang on."

Total silence for about a minute.

"South it is! If you're right and he's heading for an airport, it's gotta be either Oakland or S.F. I'm on his tail. I'll know pretty soon. Keep this line clear."

This time several minutes went by before he called back. Carpenter had passed the SF turn off. He had to be headed for the Oakland airport

Smitty got a complete description of the car plus the license number. He told Josie, "Go! We can poke along on the freeway and let him catch us."

Just as we pulled onto the freeway, I remembered something that happened to a guy standing in line near me in the San Diego Airport some years ago

"Smitty, is there any chance that any of our guys here might have a small amount of a controlled substance on them?"

"What the hell are you talking about? It's not time for any of that crap now!"

"Not for me, for you! No, no, not for you, for Carpenter! I've got an idea that might work, but I need a little bit of marijuana or cocaine or something."

"Shit, I don't know. Josie, get on Gus's cell and see. Jesus, I hope the chief isn't listening in on all this."

It took some time for Gus to convince his guys that this wasn't some kind of a joke, but he finally managed to round up some cocaine. I had no idea which of the guys had it, and I didn't want to know. All I needed to know was that one of them did. I also had no idea if my idea would work. I asked Smitty if Les was on one of the bikes tailing Carpenter.

"Yep," he said.

"Tell him to quit tailing. Tell him to get hold of the cocaine and meet us at the airport. Fast!"

"Yes, sir" Smitty responded. "Anything else, sir?"

Josie said, "Okay, now that we've established who gives orders to whom, would you mind telling me what we're doing?"

"Simple," I said, wishing it was. "We're gonna get Carpenter arrested! Again!"

CHAPTER 64

Smitty got Gus on his speaker phone. "Keep going as slow as you can," he said, let him catch up with you. They said he's alone, so he should be easy to spot. I'll bet he's not driving too fast either. Last thing he wants is to be stopped by a cop for any reason."

"Hell, if I go any slower, I'll get rear ended," Gus grumbled. "I'll try to spot him before he sees us. Going this slow we stand out like a broken thumb."

"Well, as soon as you see him, step on it and lead him into the airport. We'll do like Casey said, park at the first airline and let him pass. Oh, and watch for Les, too. Casey says we'll be needing him."

"Okay, boss," Gus said. "Anything else?"

"Where does the tail say he is?"

"He's still coming our way, about a mile behind us. We're still far enough away from the airport that we can speed up a little and still not be so noticeable. He's doing the speed limit, so he'll catch up with us well before the turn off."

I wanted to know where Les was.

"Les is way ahead of you," Gus said. "He took the frontage road to avoid being seen by Carpenter and he's flying! He saw you guys as he passed you. Wait, I think I see Carpenter. He's five or six cars behind us now. We better get going!"

Josie handled it perfectly. We "followed" Carpenter from five or six cars ahead of him and he had no idea we were there. Pulling into the first airline stop as planned, we let him go by, then followed him to United's stop at the far end of Terminal One. He found a valet service and, after unloading four large suitcases, had the valet service take his car. We had him.

No question, he was abandoning ship. Now we had to make my plan work. It *had* to work, 'cuz we sure as hell didn't have anything for a back-up plan.

Smitty handed a hundred bucks to one of the valet guys and said, "Off the record, for a short time?" A quick acceptance and we were inside.

We didn't know if Carpenter would recognize Smitty or Gus, but we knew for sure he'd recognize Josie and me. We stayed out of sight until Carpenter got into line. Les was waiting for us inside the doors, looking a little anxious with a pocket full of cocaine.

The United desk was about a hundred yards long, with lots of lines all going to different destinations. Fortunately we could see Carpenter walk all the way to the end, to a line for Cleveland, Ohio. Maybe it was the first ticket he could get.

I had time to outline my idea to Les. I took him aside.

"Smitty tells me you used to be a pretty good pickpocket and magician?"

"Yeah...but it's been a long time," Les said, dubious.

"Did you get the cocaine I asked for?"

"Yeah, got it right here," he said, slipping a hand into a front pocket of his jeans. He was showing it to me!

"Jesus, don't wave it around." He froze, then put his other hand in the other front pocket and rocked back on his heels. Old Mr. nonchalant killing a little time at the airport.

"Okay," I said, "here's what I want you to do. As soon as he's in line and busy dragging his bags forward, get as close as you can to him. When you're close enough, slip the cocaine into his inside coat pocket. Can you do that?"

Les looked over at Carpenter, took in his preoccupation with his four bags and the suit jacket he had on, and broke out in a grin.

"Piece of cake!"

"Okay, but you must do it right away, for the second part to work."

He gave me a swift thumbs-up, then walked away, headed for Carpenter's line. When he got there, he kind of insinuated himself right beside Carpenter. I don't think he even noticed Les. Then I noticed Les giving Carpenter a hand moving his four bags. In a couple of minutes Les walked back to us. This time he gave me the A-OK sign.

"Time for Part Two of my plan. This time it was up to Gus. We'd gone over it twice. He'd already located a cop and was keeping an eye on him so he could flag him down as soon as he needed him.

"Okay, Gus, time to go," I said. "Just to review: tell the cop–"

"–that the guy in the United line," Gus recited, "the guy wearing the suit jacket over jeans, approached me in the men's' room and offered me a hundred bucks if I'd carry a small amount of cocaine to Cleveland for him."

"Right. Then he'll probably want you –"

"I know, Casey, I know. To go with him when he confronts Carpenter. I'll have to go, but I know damn well that Carpenter'll make a big stink. The cop'll probably have backup, I should be able to slip away in the confusion."

"Right. And they won't need you –"

"– once they find the coke in his pocket." Gus gave me another sour look.

By that time Carpenter was about halfway to the counter, with six or seven people ahead of him. It was time. I gave Gus the nod.

Gus took off after the cop. In a moment, he was gesticulating and pointing. The cop turned and pointed at the United line, saying something to Gus. Gus nodded and said something back. The next thing the cop did was drop his mouth to his shoulder radio and call for reinforcements.

Next he took Gus by the arm and started toward the United line. On the way he was joined by two other cops.

The cops, with Gus in tow, worked their way through the line till they had Carpenter surrounded. Carpenter started out as the "what, me?" picture of innocence, then quickly switched to arguing with them, even trying to jerk his arm out of their grips, to no avail. By that time there were five cops there. They forced him out of the line, leaving his bags in line, guarded by a cop.

We hid behind one of the baggage carts and watched the whole thing go down. It was all we could do to keep from laughing. As they marched Carpenter toward their offices, Les lagged further and further behind, then slipped out a side door. The last we saw of him, he was headed for the parking lot.

Shortly thereafter we watched the really good part, the part where one of the cops gave Carpenter a pat-down and found a package of something in his coat pocket. What a surprise! And then, handcuffs!

The last we saw of Carpenter he was being driven away in a police cruiser.

CHAPTER 65

On the way back to the house, Smitty called the chief and told him we'd heard that Carpenter had been picked up at the Oakland airport on drug charges.

"He's in the Oakland jail?"

"That's what we heard."

"Great, I can put a hold on him as a bail jumper," O'Meara said, "He won't get out of that."

"Turning to me, Smitty said, "Casey, you did good! I didn't think it would work, but you pulled it off."

I thought we'd been really lucky.

It was early evening when we got home and Smitty announced that we'd probably head up to Sacramento the next day. He told me I'd be riding shotgun with either Gus or Josie, my pick. Gee, guess which one I picked.

"As long as there's nothing more we can do tonight, maybe we should go out for dinner and a show," Josie said, looking over at me. "And don't forget, young man, you still owe me an ice cream cone!"

I threw my hands up. "Guilty as charged, ma'am," I said. That was an idea I could really get behind.

Smitty seconded the idea and, for a minute I was afraid he would invite himself along. After a moment's consideration and a sharp look from Josie, he decided he really should spend some more time planning. He also wanted to talk to the chief again and put another call in to his buddy, Little George, up in Sacramento.

We drove over to her place, she picked up some personal things, and we went out to dinner. We had a great meal and saw a lousy movie. Because neither of us had any preferences we went to a multiplex and just chose the movie that started when we got there. Something about a guy and his girl friend trying to figure out if they wanted to get married or not. Best part of the movie for me was holding hands with Josie.

When we got back to the house Josie fixed us chocolate sundaes, complete with cherries, nuts and whipped cream.

"Now you owe me two ice cream treats." Being in debt never felt so good.

We finished our ice cream and went downstairs, where a bunch of guys were playing poker. It looked like fun to me and I thought about hanging around and maybe getting in the game. Josie saw the gleam in my eyes. "Forget it!" she laughed. "These guys play cutthroat poker, for high stakes."

There was no money on the table, just chips. She told me that the chips were worth up to a hundred a pop. I still had most of the hundred that Smitty had given me, but that was about it. I decided not to play. Besides, how long could I play with one chip.

Next morning, nobody was in a hurry.

"It only takes an hour to get to Sacramento, we have plenty of time for a good breakfast," Smitty told Josie.

A little before eleven, six of us took off for Sacramento. Five motorcycles and riders with me tucked in behind Josie for the ride, clad in borrowed helmet, jacket and boots.

Little George's house was located in a suburb of Sacramento. What was originally a tract house had been enlarged several times and now had five bedrooms. Smitty told us he'd bought both the adjoining lots so he had plenty of room to expand.

When we got to his house there was an urgent message for Smitty to call the chief.

"Carpenter's out of jail again," Smitty reported. Smitty put his phone on speaker, the chief was talking.

"It was a real foul up. Oakland got a call from the lieutenant governors office in Sacramento saying Carpenter was a close personal friend of somebody up there, and this friend would take it as a personal favor if he could arrange for Carpenter to have the benefit of the doubt. An assistant to the Oakland chief relayed the request to the local judge who let him out under home confinement. So he's home but who knows what he'll try. Shouldn't have happened but it did."

Smitty asked the chief if his counterpart chief in Oakland had any idea who in the office had called. The chief said they had no idea, that they'd only been able to trace the call back to the lieutenant governor's office. Said the call had been logged in late in the afternoon, when the LG's office would have been full of people.

The only clue they had was that it was a female voice.

As soon as he got off the phone, Smitty introduced us all to Little George. He was everything Josie had said he was. The only word that fit this fellow was huge. Hugely huge, with a grayish red beard. Every inch a Viking. I thought he'd make a great Santa Claus. All he needed was the suit and to dye his beard white. I couldn't make out the color of his eyes, they were so permanently crinkled.

We all sat down at a large dining room table, the six of us and three of them.

Smitty started. "You know what we're here for. You said you'd heard rumors about a couple of guys that might pay off. And you heard what our police chief just told us. Does any of that link together?"

"Maybe. I'm not sure who works in the lieutenant governor's office. I'll have to get help there. But you say the call came from there and it was a woman's voice?"

"That's what the chief said."

"That's where I'd start then. I can get a list of all the gals that work in his office and we can start checking them out."

One of his guys spoke up, "I can get that done," He stood up to leave.

Smitty stopped him. "What we probably need is the name of every gal that has access to his phones, not just employees."

Little George told the guy to keep going. Then to Smitty, "No, actually you don't. I know the lieutenant governors office phones are guarded. Only the staff and his personal assistants have access, and Smitty, this won't take long, it's a matter of public record. Couple'a hours, maybe. In the meantime, head over to the Senator hotel. I got five rooms reserved for you. Check 'em out."

The hotel turned out to be a grand old dame of a hotel. The rooms were large, comfortable and fancy.

As soon as we checked in, Josie called me in my room and said, "We better take a little time and buy you some decent clothes."

She said if we ate at the hotel dining room, she didn't think my jeans would look too sharp. Then she really surprised me. "It's Dad's idea," she told me. "He gave me his credit card and told me to 'get Casey looking halfway decent.' Those were his exact words."

"How much money do you think it'll take to make me look 'halfway decent'?"

"I don't have any idea, but there's no limit on his card. We can go hog wild! I'll knock on your door in ten. Be ready!"

At the door, she said she was kidding a little about spending a fortune, which I wouldn't have let her do anyway.

"I think if we can find a Penny's, we can get you looking like a million for a lot less than a million," she assured me.

It was fun. We didn't buy a whole lot. Slacks, sport coat, shoes, no ties. Josie wanted me to buy a tie, but I put my foot down, insisting instead on a couple of nice sport shirts suitable to wear with a sport jacket.

When we got back to the hotel, we ran into Smitty at the entrance to the cocktail lounge in the lobby. I thanked him for the clothes and he wanted to know why I didn't have them on. I said I'd wear them later in the evening if we ended up here for dinner.

"That'll work. In the meantime how about I take the cost of the clothes out of your pay, at a rate of, oh say, about fifty bucks a month?"

I must have looked shocked.

Then he laughed and said, "Gotcha!"

I had a hard time telling when he was kidding.

CHAPTER 66

At five, Smitty called Little George.

"You better come on over," Little George told Smitty. "We got the names of everyone in the lieutenant general's office, plus one lady's name that actually works in the AG's office but spends lots of time in both. I don't know what to do with them, so let's talk."

We piled into the car Little George had rented for us and crossed town to his place. As we pulled up, a large maroon limousine was just leaving. Obviously the car belonged to the gang – it had motorcycle decals on both front doors. We parked and walked to the front door.

Little George threw the front door open before we could ring the bell. Laughing, he said, "Didja' see my pimpmobile? I just sent a couple of the guys out for Chinese. They love to drive it. It's a blast!"

"Guess you don't believe in keeping a low profile, do you?" Smitty laughed.

"Naw – I do all my good deeds in that thing, like for the boy scouts or the PTA, you know, stuff that earns you a good rep. You want to use it?"

"Thanks, but no thanks," Smitty said, to my surprise. Then I remembered – *we* wanted to keep a low profile. "Let's see what you got."

We went back to the big table and he laid out what he had.

"There're eight ladies permanent in the office. Then there's the other lady I told you about, from the AG's office."

"AG?" I asked.

"Attorney general" Smitty said looking at me like I'd suddenly dropped three bars in his estimation. "Knock, knock. You do remember the attorney general, right?"

"Right," I said, abashed.

"So there're only nine ladies who might have made the call?" Smitty said.

"Yeah. There're a couple of other ladies who're in there once in a while, but they can't use the phone, so that's about it."

"How many guys can you round up for me to use?"

"Hell, I can get a couple a dozen if you need that many. Whatcha got in mind?"

"Can you get the home addresses of these nine?"

"Sure. It'll take a couple of hours, but sure."

"Why don't you get your guys started on that, and I'll run my ideas by you. See if you think they'll work." Little George disappeared for a few minutes, then returned.

"Okay," Smitty said. "My guess is that one of these nine has been feeding info' to whoever it is that's Carpenter's boss and been getting paid for it. That means she's been getting extra money. Maybe lots of it."

"Or maybe not," Little George countered. "Maybe someone just bribed her to make that one phone call."

"I don't think so," Smitty disagreed. "First, whoever wanted the call made couldn't ask just anyone to make that kind of a surreptitious call. It had to be someone she's known a long time. But more than that, someone had to be working in a place where they could swipe information for blackmailing purposes. What better place than the AG's office?"

"That sort of points to the lady who works both offices, doesn't it?" Little George said.

"Yeah, but we can't be sure," Smitty said. "Anyway, that leads me to my idea. Tomorrow morning, get nine of your guys to take one lady each and do some research on them."

"Research?" Little George asked.

"Yeah, personal research. Each guy goes out and rings doorbells. Calls on every neighbor in each gal's block. Asks a lotta questions."

Little George looked a bit uncomfortable with this idea. "What kind of questions?" he wanted to know.

"The kind that'd help us find someone who's living above her income. I'm betting that one of these gals has been getting extra money by lifting files from her boss's office and selling them to somebody else. And I'm betting that she'll have blown at least *some* of that money. An expensive car. Luxury trips, maybe. Who knows what, but something that'd set off alarms."

"My guys are pretty sneaky," Little George said, "but they can't come roaring up on motorcycles asking questions and not expect to be stiffed."

Smitty had to agree. "You're right. I'll rent cars for any of the guys that need wheels. They need to look respectable and drive up in a car."

"They could tell people that they're doing a background check on someone who's being considered for a big job in government," I suggested.

"Sure. That'll work," said Little George. "Goes on all the time here!"

"What do you think?" Smitty asked. "Can your guys do it?"

"Oh, it'll work okay," Little George said. "I just don't know if you'll find out what you want."

"Tell the guys to be a little pushy," Smitty said. "Like it's a really big job the gal's being considered for. Can you get the guys together by tomorrow morning?"

"Done," said Little George. "Let me get the guys organized. I don't need you here to get this rolling. Why don't you all relax back at the hotel? Are they treating you right? Are the rooms okay?"

"Perfect."

"They better be," he said. "They owe me."

"They owe you?"

"Yeah, I got rid of a problem they were having with a teen gang. They comped me the rooms."

He was right, he didn't need us around. We headed back to the hotel. As we crossed the lobby, the lady at the front desk called to us and wanted to know if we had a Mr. Smitty in our party.

"That'd be me," Smitty said, and walked over to the desk.

She handed him a message and said she'd been told to tell him it was urgent. When he opened it all it said was to call the chief as soon as possible.

"C'mon," Smitty said. "I'll call him from the room. Wonder what's gone wrong now."

We all went into Smitty's room and he got the chief on the phone. His first words were,

"Where were you yesterday morning?"

"Why, what's going on?"

"Never mind. Just answer my question, where were you early yesterday morning?"

"Yesterday morning? I was home all yesterday morning. I think we left for Sacramento about eleven."

"Were you home alone all morning?"

"No, we were all there. Josie fixed a big breakfast for us about six or so in the morning."

"Good, you have an airtight alibi."

"What do I need an alibi for?"

"Smitty, you'll never guess what's happened."

"Involving Carpenter?"

"Yep, your old buddy Carpenter got himself murdered."

"Murdered? How?"

"Well, he got out again on a home confinement and there's some evidence that the judge was compromised."

"Yeah…?"

"Last night we get a call from the golf course back of his house that some of the first golfers out in the morning had heard gun shots."

"On the golf course?"

"Yeah. Two of them. We rushed up there but we couldn't find anything. Later in the morning the fire department got a phone call from a golfer that one of the homes next to the course was on fire. That there was lots of smoke coming out of the rear of the place."

"And it was Carpenter's house?"

"You guessed it. When they got on the scene, smoke was pouring out the back of the house on the golf course side. They broke in and found a kitchen grease fire. Carpenter was lying dead on the floor next to the stove. They had the fire out quickly. Being a grease fire, it was mostly smoke, not much by way of flames."

"And he was shot?"

"Yes, twice," the chief said. "The firemen called us about the body. When we got there we found him with two bullet holes in his chest. He was dead before he hit the floor. As far as we can tell he was taken out by rifle shots from a small hill on the golf course. The shooter must have gotten there while it was still dark and waited. The only shot possible was through the window above the stove and that's what he did. Only a pro could put two shots in his chest from that distance."

Reflectively, Smitty said, "I'll be damned. D'ya have any clues to the shooter?"

"Not a one, so far. By the time we got up there, golfers had trampled all over the whole area. Judging by the time that the gunshots were reported, we're estimating he was shot about six-thirty yesterday morning. The fire department didn't get there till after ten, and we didn't get there the second time till almost eleven – way too late to find any clues on the course."

"How about witnesses? Anybody see anyone suspicious?"

"Nothing. We asked everyone we could find, and we've got a list of everyone who was on the course yesterday morning to interview. Maybe we'll get lucky, but I doubt it.'

"So, now what about the FBI investigation?

"They're here right now. If anything they're more interested."

"Jesus Christ, what's next?" Smitty replied.

"You!" the chief replied, "You and Casey. That's what might be next. Somebody's cleaning up loose ends. You or Casey might be next on the killer's list."

"You think so?"

"Why not. Somebody knew Carpenter was trying to get out; odds are that person knows about you and Case too. Don't forget this was a pro operation. You better be extra careful."

Smitty slowly and thoughtfully hung up. "Did you hear all that? Murdered! By a pro. And the chief thinks we might be next."

Everyone was silent for a couple of minutes.

Smitty called Little George and brought him up to date.

"Son of a bitch. You bring more trouble to this town," was his response. "A professional hit man's on your trail? Look, I'll send some guys over to keep an eye on you; I sure as hell don't want you killed on my turf."

How thoughtful, I thought. I've survived jail, a motorcycle gang, a psychotic cop and wild motorcycle rides, only to be killed by a professional hit man? I hoped that Little George's men were good.

CHAPTER 67

Little George recommended a nearby restaurant that he could protect and we all agreed to meet down at the bar at 7:30, on the way to dinner. At seven my phone rang, Josie asked me if I was dressed yet.

"Sure," I said. "What's up?"

"Let's meet right now at the bar downstairs. I just can't wait to see you with clothes on."

"Clothes on?"

"How about *new* clothes on? Does that sound better? Hurry up. There's something I want to ask you!"

Josie'd already ordered a drink for me. She said she wanted to try a Cosmo and had gone ahead and ordered for both of us. We found a booth towards the rear of the room.

"So how do I look in my new duds?" I asked.

"They're the cats' meow, she laughed. Now shut up and listen," she commanded, "I've never done this before and I'm a little nervous, she started."

"Is something wrong?"

"No, nothing's wrong. I just have a question to ask."

"Okay, shoot." I had no idea what I'd done.

"Do you like me?"

"Is that your question?"

"It's part of it."

"Well, of course I like you. In fact I really like you!"

"Okay. I don't know how much longer this chase will last and I'm afraid it'll be over soon and we might not see each other anymore. There, I've said it."

"We'll finish this investigation and we won't see each other anymore. That's what you were nervous about saying?" I kidded her.

"No you idiot. It's that I don't want that to happen."

"You don't want the investigation to end?"

"Casey, if you don't quit fooling around I'm going to throw my drink in your face."

"Okay, okay. Don't throw your drink. Truth is I've been thinking the same thing. I don't want to not see you anymore either."

Listening to myself I thought, is a double negative a positive?

Out loud I said, "Are we too old to go steady?"

She leaned across the table to give me a kiss. I leaned over to receive her kiss and knocked my drink over.

We both started laughing and grabbed napkins to mop up my spilled Cosmo. "Just shows what a cosmopolitan kinda' guy I am," I couldn't help saying.

Just then Smitty and the gang showed up, and of course wanted to know what we were laughing about. The fact that we were laughing over my spilled drink got nothing but stares. They couldn't imagine what was so funny. Maybe you just had to be there.

The restaurant was French and the guys were a little dubious. So when Josie explained that *pommes frites* meant French fries and that they could have them with any entrée they wanted, they were happy. All the guys, Smitty included, ordered steak and the *pommes frites* – each trying to outdo the rest in butchering the pronunciation of the words. Josie ordered a chicken dish for each of us, putting her high school French to work. Smitty conferred with the waiter and ordered a very nice California wine to go with the meal.

And when everyone was finished, Smitty announced that he wasn't about to leave a French restaurant without having a real French dessert. He called the waiter back and asked him if they had any real authentic French desserts. After registering the appropriate shock at the outrageous question, the waiter assured him that, *mais oui*, they did indeed have authentic French desserts and recommended the *crêpes suzette*. Smitty said he'd heard of them.

"They have liquor in them, right?"

When the waiter advised him that, *oui*, they did, he ordered them for all of us.

I'd had them before but these were definitely the real deal. By the time we finished the *crêpes* and had coffee, we were all complaining of being stuffed. I'd seen these guys eat a lot more than this at one sitting. Must have been the richness of the food.

I guess Little George knew the owner and had called ahead. As we were leaving he personally thanked us and asked us about the two motorcycle guys parked outside the front door. Our protection.

Back at the hotel, the guys headed to there rooms. Josie and I sat in the lobby, had black Russians and talked for an hour or so. Mostly we compared notes about where we'd been, what we thought about, our families, and a lot of trivia.

In the elevator, going up to our rooms, the thought crossed my mind that maybe this was the night we could use just one bedroom for the two of us. Nah. The thought of Smitty catching us nipped that idea in the bud.

Sure enough, next morning, Smitty was banging on our doors first thing. He would have caught us in flagrante delicto, or fragrant delicto or whatever that is. For sure.

"Get up, get up. Time for a quick breakfast and get out of here quick! Little George's up and waiting for us. I need to talk to his crew before they go out."

Little George had his group assembled when we got there.

"Look guys." Smitty had their immediate attention. I guess his reputation preceded him.

"This ain't gonna be easy. All the gals you're gonna be asking about should be at work by now. You need to canvas all the neighbors. Assure them that these questions are strictly routine. I've got a supply of clip boards and papers to make you look official. Ask if they keep regular hours. Ask if they go away on weekends. If they're married, ask about their husbands. Ask if they have a new car, or more than one. Ask if they own a boat, a vacation home, or other property they know about. If she's single, ask if she has a boyfriend. Find out where they shop and go interview the shop keepers. And for God's sake, clean up your English."

"That's gonna take all day, Smitty," one of them complained. "How we're supposed to get people to answer all them questions beats me."

"I told you it wasn't gonna be easy. Remember, act like you're government employees. Be friendly and casual. It's hush, hush because she's being considered for a big promotion and she doesn't even know she's in the running. Wear a suit or slacks and a jacket. Look the part. Keep us in touch. If you get anything at all, call us. If we get a good lead, we'll call the rest of you off. So – just do it, okay?"

The guys picked up their target names and addresses, left in the cars Little George had rented and went home to get into suits. I figured they'd look okay. They'd been picked because they could pass as a government employee – no beards, no ponytails. They'd look like genuine ordinary guys once they had suits on.

"Nothing to do now but wait," said Little George. "Can't leave. Have to be here to monitor the phones and coordinate this show."

"Supposing this doesn't work what then?" Gus asked.

"Jesus, I don't know," Smitty admitted, then tossed it off to me. "Maybe Casey'll come up with another idea. What about that, Casey?

I'd been so invested in Smitty's plan; I hadn't considered thinking up an alternative. I told Smitty that, told him I'd get on it right away, then dropped myself on a couch and closed my eyes.

Then Gus again. "But supposing it does work. What then?"

"Do I *have* to think of everything?" I heard Smitty answer. "If we find her, Casey'll think of something. Right, Casey?"

CHAPTER 68

What *would* we do if we found her? We couldn't torture her. We had to use finesse. Or maybe bribery? How could we get information out of her?

Drawing a blank, I thought two heads were better than one and decided to enlist Gus's help.

"Gus, my man," I said heartily, throwing an arm around his shoulder, "I Need your help."

Gus laughed. "Got your tail in a bind?"

""Yeah, Smitty's put it there— again."

"Well, let's grab us some coffee, find somewhere quiet and see what we can come up with."

We found an unused bedroom with a pair of comfortable-looking chairs. "Welcome to my office," Gus said and ushered me in.

"So," I said, "how do we get information out of this lady presuming we find her."

"I won't bullshit you, Casey. I have no idea."

"Okay. Let's just brainstorm it a little. We'll know she's involved in something illegal. Something she could lose her job over. That'd be leverage, wouldn't it?"

"Yeah. Plus there's blackmail and murder involved. Criminal activities I bet she doesn't have the faintest idea about."

"Right, but we don't want her in jail, we want her to talk."

"So who could offer her something worth while, or scare her enough to make her talk?"

"I've no idea. Who scares you?" Gus threw the question back at me.

"Well, the FBI, but we sure can't go passing ourselves off as FBI. The IRS?"

Gus thought about that one. "You know that might work," he said. "The IRS can threaten and they can offer settlements. What d'ya think? Assuming she's been getting lots of extra money, I bet she hasn't been reporting it. They could threaten her with jail time for falsifying her tax records, then offer her immunity if she owned up about her boss."

"Great, how do we get the IRS to do that for us?"

"We don't. We don't need the IRS to actually do it. We just need this gal to believe it's the IRS she's dealing with. Right?"

"I guess, but I still don't…"

"Let me finish. Here's what I'm thinkin," Gus said.

"I saw this movie where a guy conned his way into an IRS building, appropriated an office and used it to fleece thousands of bucks out of small business owners. We could use the same idea on her. Borrow an office in the IRS building and convince her she's in tax trouble unless she spills the beans on her connection."

"You really think we could do that?"

"I don't know, but it worked in the movie."

We decided to talk it over with Smitty. He was less than impressed. Even after hearing the whole movie described to him. He told us to find something better.

"Movies are movies. Nobody would fall for that in real life," was his comment.

We both thought it might work, in spite of him and kept working on the idea.

It was now noon and we hadn't heard anything back from the nine guys out working. Smitty had told them to keep trying and if they got to the point where they were absolutely sure they were wasting their time, they should go help one of the other guys. Half a day and Smitty was getting frustrated.

Finally, about five thirty, we got something positive. It was about the lady that worked in the AG's office but spent lots of time in at the lieutenant governor's office.

"Most of her neighbors work," this guy reported. "I had to wait till they got home to interview them. Once I was able to get to them, the rest was easy. Just about all of them were more than happy to gossip about her. She isn't friendly with any of them and nobody really knows her, but they certainly watch her."

"So what'd you learn?"

"Want me to come in and tell you there?"

"No, give me an idea now," Smitty said. Again the call was on speaker phone, a technology I was coming to really appreciate. "If it's what we're looking for, we may call the rest of the guys in."

"Okay, here's what I found. She's got a brand new Jaguar in the garage, which costs a hell of a lot more than she should be able to afford. She goes on expensive week-end trips and very expensive vacations. She loves to brag about where she's been. She's a regular weekend jet-setter– Vegas, even Hawaii. Has a mysterious boyfriend who drives a limo-like black sedan and comes by himself, always after dark. The capper? One neighbor had the license number of the black sedan. I'll bring it in with me. Is that enough?"

"Wow, perfect! That's our gal. Come on in. I'm gonna call the rest of the guys in."

Smitty hung up, then turned to the rest of us. "Did you hear that, guys? It's her. I know it's her. We got our break." Which was good for everybody except Gus and me. Smitty hadn't like our idea of what to do next, and we didn't have another one.

"Now what do we do, Gus?" I said, turning to him. "You got another idea?"

"I'm trying to remember another movie."

"You know, maybe we gave Smitty too much information. I'm beginning to think your idea might work – at least I can't think of anything else. Suppose we slim your idea down to just something that might work with this gal. Forget the deluxe, fancy con. All we need is to get her in and talk to her."

"Well damn, – sure! I like it! Let's get at it. Back to square one. Let's assume that we'll want to start on the plan by tomorrow. We've got time tonight to perfect and present Plan B – and make Smitty love it."

"And I think I've got the perfect closer for the whole idea," I said confidently.

"And what's that?"

"You. You volunteer to be the con man. You know the plan, you've got the maturity and presence to pull it off, and nobody up here knows you. And Smitty trusts your judgment."

He tried to object, but couldn't resist my logic. Let's face it – it appealed to the ham in him.

We spent the next hour fine-tuning Plan B. Got rid of just about all the hoopla from the movie. Simplified the heck out of it. All we needed, really, was to get our hands on a room at the IRS office, convince her that she had to meet with us and get her to admit everything.

Back in the front room, the guy with all the information on our suspect lady was back. He and Little George and Smitty were reviewing every thing he'd learned. The more they heard, the more they were sure they'd found the key to landing Carpenter's boss.

Little George asked the sixty-four thousand dollar question:

"How are you gonna get your hands on her and get the information out of her?

"Gus and Casey have a great plan," Smitty said without hesitation. "It's simple, straightforward and virtually foolproof! Gus, Casey, come over here and outline that new plan you developed."

Huh? What Gus and Casey was he talking about? What great plan? 'Simple'? 'Straight forward'? 'Foolproof'? Last I heard he didn't like our plan.

CHAPTER 69

So we outlined Plan B. It was almost exactly the same as Plan A, which Smitty had dismissively rejected. It was met with his instant approval. Particularly when they found out that Gus was gonna be the star.

"The biggest problem I see is the IRS office," I told them. "Somehow we have to find out the layout and if there's a room we can use. Anybody know anything about the IRS office here?"

Little George answered. "Well, it's huge. Five floors. The only time I was ever there was to the third floor on my personal taxes. The third floor was a huge room of cubicles. The lady I had to see was in one of the cubicles. There might have been offices at the back of the room but I'm not sure."

Smitty surprised me again.

"Don't worry about it," he said. "I think I know a way. Let's get some food in us and a good night's sleep. I'll need you guys up and at 'em bright and early in the morning. Oh yeah, is there a Radio Shack or one of them spy stores anywhere in Sacramento?"

Once again, Little George to the rescue, "Yeah, there's an electronics store about a mile from here. Why?"

"Tell you in the morning. In the meantime, find us a good restaurant. If you can," Smitty challenged.

"If I can? *If I can?* I'll bet I can find you the best Italian food you ever had, not ten minutes from here."

The Sacramento guys grinned like they hoped Smitty'd take the bet, but he just put on a matching grin and said, "Let's go, drinks are on me."

A spy store? Now what was Smitty up to?

Little George said, "Ain't you forgetting something?"

"What's that?"

"Your sniper. I'm sending your two bodyguards over first to check out the area. Can't have you murdered on my watch."

Smitty responded, "Gee, thanks buddy. You're all heart."

Everybody laughed, but we still waited for the two guys to call and say the coast was clear.

Little George was right. The restaurant, called simply "Joe's," was great. It was a full-menu, real Italian ristorante. They had a good-sized private dining room on one side, meant for up to maybe three dozen or so. Little George headed for it as if he owned the joint. The owner followed him.

"About fifteen of us tonight, Joe," he told our host. "Send your bar girl in while you're setting up the tables. This tall old guy," he said, pointing at Smitty,"is buying."

The party was on. Drinks flowed. Trays of salami, anchovies, olives, marinated peppers, cheeses and nuts appeared. Waiters bustled around. Tables were set, chairs brought in. Candles were placed and lit. Wine was served, and lots of it.

To the best of my knowledge, nobody ever ordered anything. Huge bowls of spaghetti were placed on each table. More wine was poured. Loaves of garlic bread came and went. It was a family style feast.

At one point, Smitty stood up and said, "Little George, I'm sure as hell glad I didn't take you up on that bet. I give this meal my 'Damn Good' seal of approval. Even if I did have to bribe you with that first round of drinks."

"First round? I thought you said you were gonna buy all the drinks?"

Laughter all around. It was a joyous, happy group of bikers enjoying that dinner.

After dinner and drinking was done, after checking with the two guys on guard duty and getting an all clear, we headed back to our hotel. On the way, Smitty told me he wanted me to reconnoiter the IRS offices tomorrow.

"And how am I gonna do that?"

"Believe it or not, you're gonna revert to what you really are."

"And what might that be?"

"An innocent looking, fairly young babe-in-the-woods as far as taxes go, sailor boy."

"I'm not sure I can pull that off any more, after being exposed to you and your gang of ruffians so long."

"C'mon, you'll love it. Besides it's the only way we can find the room we're gonna need. Don't forget, this whole thing's your idea."

"Your wish is my command, m'lord," I said with a slight bow.

As I said it, I was thinking how our rather amazing relationship had progressed. A week ago he would have told me to do it and to shut up. Now I could banter with him.

"Besides, if I get what I want from the electronics store tomorrow, you're gonna have a ball using it." Now he had me.

On that note we broke up and turned in for the night.

Next morning, Smitty had us all paged in our rooms to make sure we were up bright and early and on our way.

Smitty had arranged for us to park our car in the private hotel parking lot, out of deference to our sniper worry and Little George still had two of his guys around somewhere. In a short time we were back at Little George's place.

Smitty's greeting to Little George: "Did you find out what time that electronics store opens?"

"Good morning to you too, Smitty! Yeah, it's open now."

"Tell me how to get there. I need to see if they have what I want before we make any other plans."

Shortly after Smitty left, we got a call from the chief in El Cerrito. He wanted to know if we were making any progress. I told him we were but didn't get into any details. I wasn't sure if he really wanted to know how many laws we were skirting.

Then he said, "I've got news that Smitty'll like. Grab this morning's San Francisco Chronicle and see what it says about our old friend Carpenter."

"Good news?"

"Go get the paper and read it for yourself!"

We'd been so hurried by Smitty to get over here; nobody had thought to glance at a paper. One of the guys said he'd run down to the corner and come back with a couple. I couldn't picture any news about Carpenter that Smitty'd particularly like. Boy was I in for a surprise!!

As soon as I glanced at the front page I knew what the chief meant. "MURDER UNCOVERS LURID PAST."

The article, most of which was on the front page, went on to document Carpenter's murder at his home and the ensuing investigation. It detailed his blackmailing schemes and, more importantly for Smitty's thinking, made a big deal about his background involving child molestation. It was a long article, continued on an inside page, complete with pictures of him, his house and some of the papers found there.

Gus said, "Wait till Smitty sees this. It completely destroys any reputation Carpenter ever had."

I read the article all the way through to see if the chief's name was mentioned. It wasn't, only that the El Cerrito chief of police had been instrumental in helping the FBI break the case. I guess he was off the hook. I hoped so. I really liked the guy.

A short time later Smitty rushed into the house, eyes sparkling and all excited. Before we could tell him anything about Carpenter, he said, "Look at this! Isn't this a little beauty?" He was holding an ordinary looking fountain pen in the air like it was a prize or something.

"Looks like a pen, doesn't it?" He didn't wait for an answer. "But it isn't a pen. Well, I mean, it *is* a pen, but it's more than just a pen! That electronics store Little George sent me to is like Santa's Village. Everything they have, I want."

He handed the pen to me and said I'd be taking it with me when I went to the IRS. "With that pen, you can get all the information we need for Gus to become an IRS agent with his own office," he claimed.

He told me to uncap the end and write with it. It wrote quite nicely, but I did have one complaint.

"It's a little bulky," I said.

So he told us why it was a little bulky. "That little beauty is called a DVR camcorder pen camera recorder and it does everything its name says. It'll record up to *forty hours* of crystal clear audio *and* video, which you can download directly onto your computer! How d'ya like them apples?"

I whistled my appreciation.

"When you're at your IRS interview, you can fiddle with it, write with it, take notes, anything. At the same time you can be taking pictures of the whole damn place for Gus to look at when you get back. Go play with it right now and get used to it," he suggested. "You have to use it naturally, as if it's been yours for years. Go interview Josie and take pictures of the room. Not for too long – don't want to use up the batteries. I wanna' see the results on the computer. Anyway, go. Get used to it."

Finally Gus got a chance to shove the newspaper in front of his nose.

Smitty was ecstatic. "Holy shit! This is even better than I hoped! He's completely ruined! I mean, his reputation is! Hot damn, I love it! The perfect obit!"

I told him that it looked like the chief had been completely cleared; his job and future were safe.

Then Smitty sobered up a bit. "Jesus, at times like this I sure miss Red. And dammit, that poor kid on the boat." Turning to Gus, he asked if the kid's identification had ever been established.

Gus apologized, saying he'd forgotten to tell him. He'd gotten a call at the hotel last night saying the police had identified him and gotten in touch with his parents, who were actually foster parents. He'd been with them for several years. They had no idea who his real parents were, but they wanted to take care of all the arrangements for his burial near their home in northern California.

"Oh hell, that's a shame. I bet it was the first night he'd ever slept on a boat."

"Poor kid," Gus said. "I hope he didn't die in much pain."

"Didn't the medics say they thought he'd been knocked out by the force of the explosion?"

"I think you're right. I sure hope so"

There was a long silence.

Finally Smitty said, "Well, Carpenter got what he deserved. Doesn't make me feel any better though. I wish to hell we'd never gotten involved with all this in the first place."

I'm sure he didn't mean it that way, but what he said made me feel guilty. If I hadn't screwed up with the boat slip, maybe he wouldn't have gotten involved in the first place. I guess how I felt showed on my face because Josie sidled up to me and whispered,

"It wasn't your fault that the guy got murdered on the boat you delivered. And Dad would have gotten roped into it some way anyhow, with that damn sergeant being there."

More silence from Smitty, then a huge sigh and, "I guess we better move on."

CHAPTER 70

Right after breakfast Smitty took charge. He became a detail man.

"Casey, for your IRS interview – wear your old boating clothes so you look the part. And Gus, go out and buy an IRS suit."

"What the hell's an IRS suit?"

"You know what I mean. Go to a used clothing store and buy the best conservative suit you can buy, one that looks like it's been worn, not brand new. Think of it as camouflage."

I looked at the pen slash camera. It really was a thing of beauty, like Smitty said. It had a rechargeable battery. When plugged in, it lit up green, meaning the battery was charging. I tried writing with it and it wrote just fine. Unplugged, the light went out.

Josie and I played with it again for a few minutes. I took pictures of dark corners and across the room to see how well it functioned.

Next we connected it to the computer to see the results. Damned if it didn't work. In no time we had downloaded the sequences. They were clear as a bell. I erased our pictures from its memory. The pen and I were ready to go.

"Satisfied?" Smitty asked.

"It's really neat! So, how am I gonna use it?"

"Here's what you're going to do. Call the IRS office and say that you want some help with your personal taxes. Tell them that you need to talk to someone in person, that your income is mostly cash and you don't know how to declare it. They'll probably try to fob you off to someone on the phone, but don't let them. Tell them you're afraid or something. Insist on seeing someone in person. I called my accountant. He said if you're insistent enough, they'll see you. So the first step is to get an appointment, for this afternoon if possible. Clear?"

"Got it."

"Good. Rehearse with Josie what you're going to say to the receptionist or whoever it is that answers the phone and then get on it.

Josie was a little more than cooperative.

"Good afternoon, she said. I'm the very pretty, young, single lady with whom you want an appointment this afternoon."

I had to laugh.

"Why are you laughing, young man? Don't waste my time. I'm expecting a serious answer."

I slid my hand down over my face as if I was wiping the smile off and replied, "I've been earning a fair amount of money this year delivering sailboats, ma'am, and I don't know how to report it."

Smitty interrupted and said, "C'mon Case, let's make the call."

Thinking back later, I should have realized the call would be easy. After all, that's what the IRS did. They held interviews with nervous taxpayers.

A melodious voice answered after four or five rings. "Good morning, Internal Revenue Service. How may I help you?"

"Uh, I think I need to talk with somebody about my taxes?"

"Yes sir. Do you need help preparing them?"

"Uh, I don't know. I don't think I've ever paid any."

"So this is the first year you've had earned income?"

"No – well – see that's the problem. I've been earning a fair amount of money the last few years, ferrying sailboats up and down the coast."

"Sir, have you been filing returns yearly?"

"Actually, I haven't. I don't think I've earned enough to pay taxes up till this year."

"Can I have your social security number?"

"Do I have to? You'll probably nail me for some back taxes."

"There's no way we can tell you if you owe back taxes or not unless we have your social security number."

"Can't I just come in and find out how to report income?"

"Well, I guess you can come in, but you're not going to get all the information you really need."

"But I think that's what I'd like to do."

"All right sir, hold on. I'll get the first available agent for you."

I waited for a few minutes until a young sounding female voice asked me if she could help me.

"Yes, I'm waiting for the next available agent."

"Yes sir, that's me. My name is Rachel. How may I help you?"

I went through the whole story again. Again, she wanted me to handle it on the phone. Again, I said I wanted to come in and talk to somebody. She set up an appointment for that afternoon at four-thirty and gave me directions. "Take the elevator to the fourth floor."

So I was set for the appointment and had nothing more to do.

By now, in spite of all that'd happened this morning, it was still only a little after eleven. I was nervous about my afternoon appointment. I wished I'd been able to make it much earlier. I was more than ready to go. Josie, tuned in to how nervous I was, suggested we go out for a long lunch and maybe a walk or something.

As we left, she suggested getting a quick sandwich and going over to visit Old Fort Sacramento. "Little George says it's only a few blocks away," she told me.

"What's Old Fort Sacramento?"

"It's what's left of early Sacramento. Like from the early days. It's really a museum, with lots of interesting California history stuff in it, he says. He thinks we might enjoy it. It'll make the afternoon fly by, he says."

So that's what we did. It *was* interesting, and it certainly helped make the afternoon fly by a *little* more quickly. We got back to Little George's home about three-thirty, late enough for Smitty to have gotten nervous about us.

"You sure you're ready? Just be yourself and remember to act dumb so you can be there long enough to get lots of pictures."

"Smitty, I'm ready," I griped. "We've been over all this, three times now. I'm ready!"

I think he was more nervous than I was.

We went in Smitty's car and in a short time, we were there. It was a fairly large, kind of nondescript building. Typical government mid-twentieth century-architecture, now showing the ravages of time. You know the type: big, old, square, dirty, tired, ugly. It was sure busy though. Lots of traffic through the huge brass front doors.

Smitty pushed me out the car door, pointed to a public parking lot across the street and said he'd be waiting for me there.

The first thing I saw was an information kiosk in front of the elevator banks with a sign on it saying, "All Visitors Sign In." The uniformed attendant directed me to the sign-in book and wanted to know who my appointment was with.

"Uhhh, I don't know her last name. She's with the IRS."

"Most of the building is IRS, sir," he said. "You'll have to be a little more helpful than that."

"Um. I think she's on the fourth floor and I'm pretty sure her name is – Rachel? Does that help?"

"Is this about personal taxes?"

"Yes, sir, it is. Rachel."

"Okay, you must be seeing Mrs. West. Rachel West. She's the only Rachel we have. I'll call up and verify your appointment."

My immediate thought was how is Gus gonna get past this hurdle? On top of that, how do we get our target past this hurdle?

He told me to wait where I was, that someone would be down to get me. Great.

However, as I was waiting, I noticed that most people coming in headed right for the elevators instead of going over to the kiosk as I had. Okay, that's good information. My faith in Plan B started to return.

In a few minutes a plain-looking, fortyish, brown-haired lady emerged from the elevator and headed toward me.

As I stood up, she said, "You must be Mr. Alton?" She looked much older than her voice had sounded.

I admitted I was, and she asked me to follow her into the elevator and up to her office. I asked her if I was getting special treatment since it looked like most other people just went to the elevators on their own.

"Well, I guess in a way. You told me that it was your first time here, so I thought I'd come down and get you. Most people are here for their second or third meeting. They just come right up."

Pass kiosk. Ignore the sign. Go right up.

"I think on the phone you said you're on the fourth floor?"

"That's right."

"Does that mean that you're more important than the people on the lower floors?"

I was being so clever. I hoped she'd tell me what the other floors were used for, and she fell for it— she fell right into my cunning little trap. Oh, I was good. Or was she just humoring this idiot taxpayer?

"No, Mr. Alton, it doesn't work that way," she said. "Except for seniority and occasional special assignments, we are all considered equal. The IRS doesn't use all five floors, though," she said, loosening up a notch. "We only use the third and fourth. The rest of the space is rented out to private businesses."

At the fourth floor we stepped off the elevator directly onto an open floor of cubicles. A small reception desk and waiting area sat off to one side. Apparently it would be easy to bypass, just as we now did. Mrs. Rachel West led me, a bit self-consciously I thought, to her desk. As I'd been led to expect, she didn't have an office. She barely had a cubicle. The walls couldn't have been more than five feet tall.

On the way I kept fiddling with my pen and got a bunch of pictures of the entire office area.

"What an unusual pen," said the observant Mrs. West. "Can I see it?"

CHAPTER 71

I didn't panic, did she know about these pens? I decided to ignore Mrs. West's question.

"What? Oh – oh, I'm sorry. I guess I'm a little nervous. I tend to twiddle. It's a bad habit. I better put it in my pocket or I'll drive you crazy." And I stuck it in my jacket pocket.

"People do that," she said, sat down, looked up, smiled mechanically, then gestured to a chair in front of the desk. "Have a seat?"

When I was seated facing her, I continued to act the wide-eyed boob, as per Smitty's instructions. "I guess I thought you'd have a private office for interviews?" I said, looking around. "This isn't very private."

"Well, this is as private as it gets at my level, senior agents and management get those offices over there," she said, pointing to a row of offices next to the windows.

"So how do you get an office like that? Do you move from desk to desk till you get a desk next to them, and then your next promotion is from the last desk into an open office?"

She looked up at me, probably trying to figure out if I was trying to be funny or if I was just plain stupid. I think she went for stupid. "It sure doesn't work like *that*," she said, a bit grimly, I thought. Bitterly, perhaps? I waited her out, looking expectant, and again she fell for it. "No," she said finally, "promotions like *that* come from breaking a big case. Or, eventually from hard work, perseverance – and luck. If you live that long."

Now I looked at her to see if *she* was going for humor. She wasn't.

"If it was as automatic as that," she added, "we wouldn't have those empty offices near the front door."

Ha! This was turning out to be easier than I thought!

"Why can't you use one of those offices?" I asked, like some indignant life-long taxpayer. "You do important work. They just let those sit there unused?"

"Well, I can use one if I have to. If I had a large family in, for example, I could use that larger space. Even three people. But not today."

"Now, Mr. Alton," she said, glancing down at a paper in front of her, probably checking that she had my name right. "How can I help you?"

I re-explained the whole scenario to her. She sat there nodding like someone who'd heard it all before, which she had. It was, word for word, the same story I'd given her that morning on the phone. Finally, she got my Oakland address and my social security number and looked me up on the computer. After checking and rechecking the data, she finally looked up.

"You're right," she said, seeming mildly surprised. "There's no record that you ever filed before."

"I know," I said. "That's what I told you."

"Mr. Alton," she said, "It's good you came in today because the IRS is making a special effort to help people like you who have never filed before. Tell me again what the circumstances are?"

"I went ahead and delivered the story I'd made up, about the few thousand dollars in delivery charges I'd been paid over the last year. I told her I didn't know if the boat owners had ever reported paying me or what. The only records I had were the delivery contracts, and they usually didn't mention the money.

With little interest and about as much patience, she advised me that I should treat my business, small as it was, as any other businessman would. Keep records of all my income. She also told me to keep records of expenses, that, depending on how much I made, some of my expenses might be deductible.

"The best advice I can give you is that you should start filing, even if you have no taxes to pay. And based on what you've told me I doubt very much that you'd be paying any taxes at all." Her tone was dismissive. She handed me some papers and a couple of brochures, and we were done.

As she started to escort me out, I told the lovely Rachel that I could find my own way. She ignored me. I got my pen out again, but carefully kept it clear of her field of vision. I succeeded in getting the offices on the camcorder. That plus the recording of everything she'd said should work for Gus, at least for the fourth floor.

"So – do you hold all your interviews on the fourth floor?" I asked, like I was making small talk.

"No, we use the third floor too– but not for people like you," she said, her tone now distinctly dismissive. "Most personal interviews are done on the fourth. The third floor is mainly task force offices." Whatever those are.

With that she thanked me for coming in, told me she'd be "happy" to see me anytime again and said goodbye at the elevator door. All in all, a rather nice lady.

I wondered if Smitty was going to report my hundred a week salary to the IRS.

Smitty was double-parked in front of the building.

"Jesus, Casey, what took you so long? It's been almost an hour." I thought I'd pulled it off fairly quickly.

"Hey, Smitty, you can't hurry the IRS. Wait'll you and Gus get all the information and the pictures. You'll love 'em. I got a regular travelogue for you here."

Back at the house, Smitty grabbed the "pen" out of my shirt pocket and said, "Okay. Let's download this baby and see what you got."

In a short time he agreed with me that the fourth floor was our target of choice.

"So you think we can use one of those empty offices?"

"Should be easy." I said. "I got the impression that any of the agents might grab one of them and use it, if they had more people than they could handle in their cubicles."

"You think if we grabbed one and closed the door, anyone would bother us?"

"I don't think so. If anyone pokes their head in you can say one of the agents told you to meet him there. Something generic. Should work."

"Yeah, I think so too. Let me tell you what Gus and I've come up with for getting the lady at the AG's office to come in."

"Uh – does the lady have a name yet?"

"Oh, yeah, forgot to tell you. She's a Mrs. Jane DeHaven. A fortyish widow and guilty as hell."

"I sure hope she's the one. She's the only lead we've got," I said.

"What we're planning on doing is a little complicated, but we can't think of any other way to get her in. We're planning on calling her at the AG's office and telling her just enough so she'd almost have to come to the IRS offices. Not so much that she'd panic, but enough so that she knows if she calls her boyfriend it could get worse for her. Okay so far?"

"Guess so."

"Okay. So we call Mrs. DeHaven at the AG's office and advise her that she's under investigation by the IRS and that we need to see her at the local IRS office either this afternoon or tomorrow morning, latest. We'll tell her that she may not be in any trouble, as long as she can explain away some apparent unreported income."

"Sounds like it might work. Who's 'we'? Who's making the call?" Josie spoke up, "I am."

"We thought it'd sound more convincing, and maybe a little less threatening, having a woman call," added Smitty.

Just then Gus came waltzing in wearing his new suit, shirt and tie combo. He looked perfect, every inch the business employee. Good shoes but slightly scuffed. A pair of glasses. He'd even had his hair cut short. His normal dapper look was completely gone.

"You look like a new man" Smitty said, "A regular nine-to-fiver, ready to take the family car home to the wife and three kids in the 'burbs. Maybe a little old for the three kids…"

"Second marriage." Gus said. "Cripes, I look like an old man!"

"Third," I said.

As a finishing touch Gus showed us an old but expensive looking briefcase packed with important looking papers.

I asked him about IRS identification. He whipped out an official-looking badge case from his inner jacket pocket and flipped it opened displaying a very official-looking badge and ID card.

"Will it pass a close inspection? Remember she works for the state and may really look at your ID."

"Funny you should ask," he said. "The case is a passport case, but nobody'll notice the difference. The badge and ID are the real deal."

"You mean they'll pass – real good forgeries, right?"

I got back an indignant, "No sir, these papers and the ID are the real thing. The original owner may be dead or missing, but the papers are good as gold!"

I decided I didn't need to know the rest of *that* story.

"Anyway, that's how we intend to get her into the offices, maybe tomorrow if possible," Smitty said

"So you're going to call her this afternoon and try to get her in tomorrow?"

"Depends on Josie. If she's ready to make the call, I'm ready."

Josie spoke up. "The longer we wait, the longer we wait. I can't see any reason to not go ahead right now. Let's find out if our plan's going to work or not."

Her dad spoke up. "You sure what you're gonna say, honey? You have to sound very sure of yourself, like a professional IRS agent would. Seems to me an agent would fully expect people's cooperation and her attitude on the phone would reflect that. You ready to do that?"

"Da-a-ad," she said, dragging the word out peevishly, "I really *am* an IRS agent."

"Damn, that's the right attitude! Take a deep breath and let's do it."

Smitty kicked everyone out of the kitchen except the four of us, sat Josie down at the table, and had her dial the AG's office.

"Attorney General's office. How may I direct your call?" Josie had no trouble getting Mrs. DeHaven on the phone after she said it was a call from the IRS.

As soon as Josie identified herself as an agent and said that the IRS would like her to appear at their office to talk about some perceived irregularities in her income reporting, our gal started sounding antsy.

However, none of our anticipated problems surfaced. She agreed almost immediately to come to the IRS offices at ten-thirty the next morning. She became more and more agitated as the conversation continued, but seemed afraid to say no to an appointment.

Josie calmly confirmed the ten-thirty appointment once again and told her that her appointment would be with Agent Levy. She told her she should bypass the information kiosk on the main floor and proceed directly to the IRS offices on the fourth floor. Agent Levy would meet her there. She also told her to not speak to anyone except Agent Levy. "We want to keep this as low a profile as possible," Josie said. "For your sake, ma'am."

Believe it or not, Mrs. DeHaven thanked her for calling.

Josie hung up and breathed a huge sigh of relief.

"Wow," Gus said. "Wow! It went so easy! Josie! You were spectacular! Tomorrow should be a breeze!"

"Well, Mr. Levy, the rest is up to you," Josie grinned at him. "I got her in. The ball's in your court now."

"I wonder what the real Levy looked like. It's a good thing his ID didn't have a picture on it. Now I got overnight to become an IRS agent."

"Method acting," I said.

"For Christ's sake guys," Smitty interjected. "Quit fartin' around. It's damn serious. Gus, if you blow this, if we lose her we don't got nothin'. You got tonight and tomorrow morning to think about it and you gotta be letter perfect. You got me?"

CHAPTER 72

Josie grabbed my arm and said, "Let's get out of here. Gus is going to be busy rehearsing and we don't really have anything to do. Let's do something together tonight. Maybe a play or a movie. Just the two of us."

We ended up going to a live play. Shakespeare! I'd never seen any Shakespeare before except that movie about him falling for Gwyneth Paltrow. This play was fun. They said they were gonna summarize every Shakespeare play in ninety minutes. Actually it was hilarious and we both enjoyed the heck out of it. Josie told me I still hadn't really seen Shakespeare yet and, "don't claim you have!"

After the play, we found a spot that made waffles 24/7, shared a strawberry cream one, had coffee and went back to the hotel.

In the lobby it suddenly became awkward. I think we both were getting close to sharing a room but neither of us actually vocalized it. I ended up escorting her to her room, got a very warm good-night kiss and went to my room. Alone. Again.

Next morning, surprise, we weren't awakened by Smitty. Josie called me about seven and asked if I was ready for breakfast. Kiddingly, I asked her if she wanted another cosmo like the other night.

She said, "About that. Did I propose to you?"

"I'm not sure, did I answer yes?"

"The last thing I remember is you knocking your drink over."

"We need to continue that conversation, don't we?"

"How about now for breakfast?"

We met a short time later in the hotel dining room and unfortunately had Gus sharing our table.

On the way to Little Georges' house we talked about Gus.

"I get the impression that Gus is looking forward to his acting debut," I ventured.

"Gus? He's a real hambone at heart."

Bustle, bustle, bustle. Gus was getting dressed with lots of friendly ribbing from the other guys. Things like "Hey, Gus, you got a little gut there, wanna' borrow a girdle?" and "Good God, Gus, you color blind or something? That tie's bilious." and "I think accountants always wear white socks with their suits. You should change!"

Gus just laughed and kept on dressing. Well ahead of the time he planned to leave, he was fully dressed and into his a final crowning touch: a pair of horned-rimmed glasses. In spite of all the ribbing, he certainly did look the part.

Smitty said, "Okay. Talk accountant to me."

"Debit is the side toward the window."

Silence.

"It's an old accountants joke," Gus said. Nobody laughed.

"Don't worry about the CPA talk. I used to be an accountant in a previous life. Not for long, I was just out of college. It's too boring. That's the real reason I volunteered for this gig. I get to revisit my inner CPA.

"Hell, Gus. As long as I've known you, I never knew that!" Smitty said, looking pretty impressed.

"Ah, and who knows what all else you don't know about me," Gus said, enjoying his role as mystery man. But then it was back to business. "I need to borrow a car and get over there pretty soon. The pictures are great but I'd like to reconnoiter the place on my own before our Mrs. DeHaven gets there."

Smitty told me to drive him over and wait for him.

"So what do you expect will happen?" I asked Gus. "Well, I'm going to' hit her with a shit load of scare tactics. I'll tell her we know all about her pilfering information from her office. At the very least we can prosecute her for income tax evasion, but that's the least of her worries. Whoever she's been feeding this stuff to has committed murder. All of which makes her an accessory to murder. I'll tell her that the FBI is interested in her too!"

"That'd scare the heck out of me," Josie said.

"But that's just the hook. When I give her an out, I think she'll jump at it."

"An out?"

"Yep, I'll tell her we think she's been a somewhat innocent pawn in this thing. I'll start with we know you're guilty of stealing information. Then I'll follow with we don't think you're involved in the way the information was used. Also we don't think you knew anything about the murders. Then I'll tell her, if she'll ID the guy and testify against him we can probably get her off the hook on accessory charges."

"You think she'll cave?"

You know what I expect? I expect I'll emerge from the IRS building with Mrs. Demavend in tow, and that I'll be dropping her off at a safe house for her protection within the hour."

Safe house? I couldn't believe what I was hearing. I had to say it. "Safe house? Who has a safe house?"

"We're talkin' makeshift," Smitty said with a patient sigh, like having to constantly educate me was wearing him out. "We have to get her off the street while we decide what to do with the dope she gives us. Little George has some empty real estate we can use to get her out of sight, and one of the wives is gonna play 'matron.' It's all set."

I was silent for a couple of minutes, digesting this information.

"Gus, that's kidnapping."

"Not if it's her idea. She'll ask for protection. I just have to play her right."

We got to the IRS building about nine forty-five, over a half hour early.

"Perfect," Gus said. "Try to get a parking space where you can watch the front door. You'll have to be on your toes. I'm gonna be improvising when she and I leave. I might take a taxi instead of using you. Somehow I feel that'd be more in character with what she thinks we're doing than using our car. It doesn't look very official. If I do take a cab, follow me."

With that he left. From behind he looked mighty convincing to me. Wading into a sea of suited and briefcased men, he fit right in. What a ham!"

Time went by. I did a crossword puzzle. Then I did another crossword puzzle. Finally he came through the double brass doors. I'd never seen our Mrs. DeHaven but had to assume that the lady he was escorting was her. No police right behind him, just her. I breathed a sigh of relief over that. He completely ignored me and hailed a taxi.

I pulled out two cars behind the cab. I'd never tailed anyone in my life so I did like the detective books said, stayed back a couple of cars. I followed the cab to what I assumed was her place. She and Gus went in. After a ten-minute wait she came out with a couple of suitcases and I followed them to a small tract home on the north side of the city. Gus dismissed the cab and took her and the suitcases in. After a few minutes, he came out and jumped in our car.

"Like clockwork! She's really a simple woman. All I had to do was prime her and she started unloading. In fact, I think she was relieved to be caught. She said she'd started doing a couple of small favors for this senator and then he wouldn't let her quit. He's been sleeping with her for years. Anyway, he's our guy. He's the bastard behind all this stuff!"

"Back to the house?"

"Yeah. Let's get everybody together so I don't have to tell it over and over." We called ahead.

Approaching Little George's house, there were a lot more motorcycles than had been there in the morning. Inside, Smitty told us he'd called down to Oakland and asked several of his guys to come up. They were all waiting to hear from Gus.

"Okay, Gus," Smitty said, "get to the meat. What'd you find out?"

"Well, first off, you were completely right. She was the one feeding information out of the AG's office. She said she fielded most of the tips and complaints that came into their office, and was the one who kept the records, so she had no trouble siphoning off an occasional tidbit and getting it to her friend. Once she got a tip to him, all he had to do was a little private investigation of his own. Voila – blackmail material."

"Did you get the name of her friend?"

"Of course," Gus said. "What do you think I am? An amateur? Our guy's a senator, just like we thought. In fact he's a long-time, senior senator."

Little George said, "If I were a bettin' man, I'd say it's Senator Goldberg."

"You know him?"

"I don't know him. I know *of* him. Everybody does. That son of a bitch!"

I flashed back to when I'd read his name a few days ago in the San Francisco newspaper. It seemed like a year ago.

Gus continued. "She told me she'd been doing it for years and had no idea how the tips were being used. She'd been told that because the information was being passed on to someone high up in the government, it was okay. When I told her how the information had really been used, she burst into tears. She said she had no idea."

Smitty said, "She's that gullible?"

"I reminded her that she'd been receiving expensive gifts plus cash and travel perks for many years, she must have suspected something. She told me that the senator was a 'personal friend' and that she'd separated the gifts and the tips in her mind. I said, 'Come on. How could you possibly do that?' That's when she finally admitted she'd been sleeping with the guy. She thought he loved her. Which was when she completely caved in. She wanted to know what she could do. I told her what we'd agreed on and it worked like a charm. The senator was gonna be investigated for murder. She'd be charged too unless her skirts were clean. Our investigation was leading us to believe that he'd kept her and his blackmail empire completely separate. If she'd help us, we'd help her. Anyway, it worked. She jumped at the chance to get out from under the senator."

One of the guys snickered. "Yeah. Out from under!"

"The rest was easy. I pretended to make a call and set up a safe house for her protection. She went with me to her house; grabbed some personal stuff and I took her to Little George's place. And, to date, that's where we are!"

"Gus," I said. "I still think that's kidnapping! And she's a government employee! And she works for the Attorney General! She can put us all in jail."

Gus looked over at me and said, "Going to the safe house was entirely her idea. I just told her it was available."

At least we now knew for sure about the senator.

CHAPTER 73

Little George was still furious. "That lousy bastard! I knew he was dirty. He's been screwing the public for years. We need to get rid of that guy. And you know what? The Senate won't do it. Something should happen to him!"

One of the Sacramento gang said it'd be nice if "somebody" kidnapped the senator and he just disappeared.

Another guy said, "We could do that. Nobody knows what we know about him. Nobody'd connect us with him." He was serious.

The first guy said he thought it'd be better if Goldberg just disappeared, like on a fishing or hunting trip. Or maybe in a fatal car wreck.

Josie poked me in the ribs and whispered that she didn't like the way this was going, that she was worried.

"What is it?"

"Dad. He gets wound up by a group like this and he sometimes makes bad decisions. We need some alternate ideas."

I spoke up. "Why don't we find out everything we can about the senator before we jump to conclusions? We need to know where he lives, where he works, where he might be vulnerable. *Then* come up with ideas. Besides, what would we do with Mrs. DeHaven? Kill her too?"

That suggestion seemed to get some traction. Smitty seconded it. Then he turned to Little George. "It's your town," he said. "How do we get that type of information about a state senator?"

"A lot of it's gotta be in the public domain, don't you think?" Little George said. "I'll get my guys working on it right away. Exactly what d'ya think we need?"

"Anything. Everything. Where he lives. Where his office is in the capitol. Does he have digs in Sacramento? Stuff like that. D'ya know what part of the state he represents?"

"Somewhere south. We'll find out. I don't think he's married, but I've heard he's got some nasty habits."

"All the better." Smitty smiled grimly. "We should find out who he hangs with, too. Can you find out where he banks? Something else. Find out what kind of car he drives. Does he drive himself? Remember the big black sedan that DeHaven's neighbors described? The one we got the license number on? Find out if that's his car."

"We can get all that pretty easy, I think. We should also find out how often he goes back to his district."

"Can you get all that in the next couple of hours?"

"Should be a piece of cake," Little George assured us.

The local newspaper was very helpful. Through a friend of a friend, we got his Sacramento address and a sampling of who he hung out with. We also found out that he seldom spent much time in his own district except when it came time for re-election. Evidently he didn't fish or hunt. He did go to baseball games occasionally, but he was best known for marathon poker parties. His invitees included a number of local wealthy businessmen. No other senators. Our source told us Goldberg definitely had a secretive side to him, that not a lot was known about his personal life.

He also had a reputation of being a dangerous person to cross. Very vindictive and not liked by his fellow Senators.

These Sacramento bikers had lots of contacts. It didn't take long at all to gather piles of information. Some of it was trivial, like what his favorite dessert was. Other items were potentially useful, like the report that he was a member of Alcoholics Anonymous. We also found out he drove his own car, a current model, black Cadillac.

"If we decide we need to kidnap this guy, we still need to know more," Smitty said, goading them on. "We need to know the routes he drives, when he might be alone and so forth."

Josie nudged me again. "I told you. He's so willing to take chances. He jumps before he looks. We can't let him get involved in any kidnapping!"

"Nothing's gonna happen right away," I said, trying to calm her fears. "We'll just have to keep close to him and try to influence his thinking."

"Maybe, maybe not. I know Dad, Casey. If he wants to do something he thinks I'll disapprove of, he'll just start excluding me. I think the best defense is a good offense. You need to come up with better ideas than his. He listens to you! We can't let him take the law into his own hands."

I said, "There's something else too. That sniper. Just because nobody from Little George's gang has spotted him or heard anything about a sniper doesn't mean he isn't around." I asked Little George what he thought about the sniper.

"I wasn't going to tell you anything, but since you asked— We located a guy we think may be your sniper. He's holed up in a fleabag in West Sacramento asking a lot of questions about motorcycle gangs. We gotta be careful and sure. He might just be some kid wanting to join an outlaw gang, but he's acting pretty suspicious. Personally, I think it's him."

"If it's him, what'll you do?"

"Don't ask. Let's just say professional gunmen don't last long around here."

Smitty was hyper active now. He said that tomorrow morning he wanted members of both gangs to fan out and physically see all the places that Goldberg frequented.

"Take pictures if you can. Where does he eat? What does his Sacramento home look like? What roads does he take? Find out if he's a creature of habit or if he takes a different route home every night, for instance. Let's find out everything personal we can about him, and then decide what to do."

Protecting Josie, I spoke up. "Smitty, it sounds to me like you're proposing a kidnapping of a California state senator. If you are, I'm out. We've skirted the law a lot these last few days, but I'm not into the kidnapping of anyone, let alone a senator."

"Who said anything about kidnapping?"

"You did, just a few minutes ago!"

"No, I said *if* we decided to kidnap him."

I wasn't sure I believed him. Smitty was hard to read. Glancing at Josie, I could see she wasn't buying it either.

Smitty went on without a pause. "What we need guys, is more personal stuff about him."

"You know," drawled one of the Sacramento guys, "the people that'd probably know most about his dirty little secrets would be his staff."

"Okay, so how do we get next to one of his staffers?"

Questioning sounded better than kidnapping to me. I thought for a minute or two and came up with an idea.

"I bet they'd open up to a friendly columnist," I said. "A columnist who wants to profile the staff of a prominent senator, for example."

Smitty loved it. "Perfect, how could they say no? Let's do it. Casey, it's your idea. You, Josie, Gus and Les make it happen." We adjourned to the kitchen.

Gus said, "You got a Sacramento columnist in your hip pocket?"

"Don't need one. I had a nice blurb about me and my delivery service in a San Diego column once and never even met the columnist. I got a call from a staffer saying they'd heard about me and would I give her a little info. Next thing I knew, there I was in his column."

"Okay. I see where you're going."

"Good. All we need is for someone to call his staff, tell them they're an assistant to some columnist and the rest should be easy.""

It's worth a try," Gus said. "The worst that can happen is they say no."

"I ain't no actor," Les said immediately. "No way could I pull off any of this shit. I nominate one of you three." He was pointing at Gus, Josie and me. After a quick conference, we stuck Josie with the job. The odds were higher that a columnist's staffer would be a woman, we all agreed. Plus Josie'd already proven she was a good actress. She thought it's be a gas.

The newspaper call to the senator's office went just fine. When Josie introduced herself as a staffer for a columnist whose name was a household word in northern California, the senator's staff was more than receptive. When she told them that part of the article was to be about the staff and how important a good staff was to a successful Senator, they were hooked. They told her to come on over. The only problem she had was convincing them that her first interviews should be on the phone. When she shaped her questions so that a lot of them were about the staff, they totally capitulated and answered all of them quite willingly. In the middle of it all, she was able to slip in all the questions about the senator we wanted.

"Thanks so much," she told the last of them, "and please thank the rest for me too. I'll put all this into a report to my boss for his review. He'll probably want to talk to each of you personally. It might be a while. You know how long these things take."

What we found out was interesting. The senator was in his sixties, but appeared and acted younger, particularly around younger women. In some other ways, he acted older. For example, he was completely predictable, like when he got to work each day and the routes he drove to and from work. Also he was very vain about his appearance. He would never allow himself to be seen in public in anything but a suit and tie. No one seemed to know much about the poker games we'd heard about, except that they were usually held on Tuesday nights.

Reading between the lines, his staff saw Goldberg as a lazy senator, one they really didn't like. Any one of them would leave him, given the opportunity. Each and every one of them thought they did most of the work. None came out and said so, but you definitely got the impression they didn't feel they were appreciated or treated very well. Maybe that's why they were so eager for the interview.

When we got back to Smitty with our results he told us to get together with the rest of the guys and make some sort of a chart of the senator's average day.

"By tonight or tomorrow morning, latest, I'd like to be able to see where he usually is, all day, every day."

Being curious about what Smitty had in mind for tomorrow, I stayed behind with the rest of the gang. Everyone had questions, particularly the guys from Oakland who were anxious to avenge Red and the young kid killed on Smitty's boat. Smitty said he also was pissed about his boat neighbor's death.

"He was a total innocent. Probably just woke up and accidentally saw the bomber. And for that he got killed?"

As they talked, the temperature in the room kept rising. The threats became more vicious, the ideas more outrageous.

Looking at Little George, I could see he didn't like the way the meeting was going. Finally, I guess he couldn't stand it any longer. In a loud voice he said, "Smitty, shut up and sit down!"

Amazingly, that's exactly what Smitty did.

"I gotta tell ya, I got a real problem with what you're doing now. You're talking about doing physical damage to a state senator in my town. I know I said I hate his guts and something should happen to him, but not—by—us! I, we, gotta live here. You guys think you can waltz in here, do something totally illegal and then waltz right out, leaving us holding the bag."

"I hear you, George," Smitty said. He sounded like he meant it. It was a come to Jesus moment, and Little George wasn't finished, either.

"Good, because it's your fault that you're letting these ideas even see the light of day. They're dangerous, and it's up to you to draw a line. I totally understand your outrage at these murders, but I gotta protect the future of the club."

"You're absolutely right. Guys, listen up. Little George is absolutely right. We gotta tone down the rhetoric – me first. We are not – repeat *not* – gonna do anything that'll reflect badly on our hosts here. Agreed?"

He got no argument. Little George carried a lot of weight – more than just his body weight.

Smitty suggested that he and Little George pick out three or four guys each and have a planning session first thing in the morning.

Little George agreed. "We can tie a shit can around the senators' neck without becoming a lynch gang. We'll figure out a way."

Gus and I breathed a sigh of relief. I asked Gus, "Did you put Little George up to that?"

"No way, Jose. I had nothing to do with it."

CHAPTER 74

Next morning, by the time Josie and I reached Little George's house, he, Smitty and the guys they'd chosen were huddled up in a back room, by themselves.

Conspicuous by their absence in that little group was us. Not only were we not invited, they were taking pains not to let us know what they were talking about. Gus and Les were miffed. Josie was miffed and worried. I wasn't. I'd just as soon be left out of whatever it was they were planning.

Occasionally one or two of the group came out to get coffee or a beer. When they'd pass Josie they'd glance at her surreptitiously as if they were embarrassed that she wasn't included. At one point one of them accidentally left the door open, allowing us a glimpse of waving arms and loudly arguing. It looked like Smitty was working hard, trying to convince them about something.

Finally they broke up, but they still didn't tell us anything.

"I think they're still planning to waylay the senator and do something to him," Josie said. "Their idea of breaking laws is different from most people's idea. I have to talk to Dad."

As Smitty came out of the room he looked surprised to see us standing so nearby. Josie cornered him.

She didn't mince words. "Dad, I'm really worried about what you guys are planning. You can't kidnap anybody. It's against the law. I don't want to have to visit you in jail. And don't forget your promise to Mom."

"Don't worry, little girl. We know exactly what we're doing and it's nowhere near kidnapping."

The next thing we knew, he'd had a large blackboard brought out from the rec room. This time, the door stayed open. On it, he scribbled all the observations the guys had made the previous day and taped up pictures to support them. By the time he was done, the senator's entire day was outlined, at least for most days. What they seemed to be most interested in was his morning and evening driving habits.

"Those condos there on the right are where the senator spends his nights. He was pointing at a picture one of the guys had taken. You can't see it. It's in the rear, with a lake view. As you can see, the development's new and all by itself out there, at the very end of the road."

"Real isolated, isn't it," someone commented.

"Yeah, and look at the road. It runs alongside that canal for about two miles before meeting the highway."

Then he put up more pictures of the streets the senator usually took on the way to and from his home.

After everybody got a good look at the pictures, Smitty said he wanted all the Oakland guys to come with him. "We're gonna go somewhere and get some lunch. We need to do some planning."

As they filed out of the back room, Josie and I start to gather our stuff together to join them. "Not you two," Smitty said, noticing us. "You've worked hard enough. You deserve some time off." He handed Josie a hundred dollar bill and said, "Go have a real fancy lunch somewhere. Ask Little George to recommend some place expensive." Turning his back on us, he headed outside.

Josie closed her eyes, and I don't think she was counting to ten. "I told you so. All of a sudden he's cutting me out. He's planning something he doesn't want me in on. Dammit! I don't know what to do."

"What about Gus?" I asked. "He was in on the last part of the meeting and they're taking him along this afternoon. Maybe he can find out what they're planning and let us know?"

"That's our only hope. I'll try to catch up with Gus and see if he'll do that. Maybe if Dad knows I know what he's planning, he might reconsider"

We caught up with Gus and she whispered her request to him. With a quick glance at Smitty, he whispered, "It's gonna be okay. No kidnapping, just some scare tactics and pressure. Your dad thinks we got enough info' that he'll cave if we push hard enough. Do what your dad said, have a nice lunch, relax. I'll keep an eye on him."

Little George was standing next to Gus. "You two want a good place to have lunch? Have you been to the Firehouse in Old Sacramento?"

"I don't even know where Old Sacramento is, let alone any Firehouse," Josie told him.

"Okay, then you should definitely go there. It's a little touristy, but the restaurant's good and the area's a great place to while away an afternoon."

"I don't want to while away the afternoon," Josie said. "I'm worried about what you guys and my dad are going to do."

"We spent the afternoon wandering through shops at Old Sacramento, even took a tour of a river sternwheeler. I don't know if it really still paddled up and down the river, but it served meals so we had lunch there.

When we'd had it with wandering, we found our way to the Firehouse for dinner. As Little George has promised, it was really nice. The weather was warm so we ate outside on a large patio. We tried our damnedest to not think about Smitty, but he certainly was the elephant in this outdoor room.

Gus had told us that the group expected to be out real late, so we tried to pace our evening accordingly, drawing it out with a cocktail before dinner and deliberately ordering a multi-course meal. Even following dinner with a leisurely dessert and coffee, we were still through and out of the restaurant by about eight-thirty.

Josie said she didn't want to go back to the hotel. She wanted to do something to keep her mind occupied. We checked all the movies, but didn't see anything interesting.

"What do you think of live comedy shows?" Josie asked.

"I don't know. I've never seen one," I admitted. "Seen them on TV, of course. Those seem to be pretty dumbed down and foul mouthed."

"I noticed a billboard on the old sternwheeler about a comedy show on board tonight. It said bring the family, so I imagine it'd be pretty clean, at least."

We found the boat again, were able to get tickets and, as it turned out, the show was a riot. The sternwheeler had a pretty good size theater on board. It wasn't filled but almost so. The ad hadn't lied – it was a family show and it certainly diverted Josie.

We got back to the hotel about midnight and Josie immediately made a beeline for the desk to check if there were any messages for her or me. There weren't.

She tried to reach Gus but got no answer. Same with Smitty. The automated message said that neither of the cell phones was in service. We were completely stymied. Evidently the gang had, for some reason, turned all their cell phones off.

I told her there wasn't anything we could do except wait. "The best thing we can do is get a good night's sleep. The only link we have is Gus and we have to believe he'll call us as soon as he can. Probably he'll call you on your cell. You might as well try to sleep. He'll phone when he can. Whatever they're up to, all we can do is wait. Does that make sense?"

Reluctantly, she agreed.

"But if you hear anything, you call me right away, okay?"

"I guess you're right. How about a big hug and a kiss before bed?"

Sounded like a good idea to me.

"Did you hear anything?" were the first words I heard from Josie the next morning. She'd knocked on my door just as I was finishing dressing. I wasn't surprised. I'd expected her to be up early.

"Not a peep." I replied. "You?"

"Nothing. Let's get over to Little George's house and find out what's happening. Maybe they're back."

In no time at all we were there, only to find no one was in except a rather old Mexican lady who served as a maid and cook, and she didn't know anything except that no one was there when she arrived.

She asked us if we wanted to wait, and offered us breakfast.

Josie said "absolutely," and that some breakfast would be appreciated. Nervous and fidgety, we had *huevos rancheros* – fried eggs, Mexican style – and toast with lots of coffee.

I was just starting my third cup when we heard several cars and motorcycles pull into the driveway. As bike after bike cut its engine, that noise was replaced by a fifty-fifty mix of laughter and cursing. In a minute or two they started piling into the house.

First in was Little George, with Smitty right on his heels. Both seemed real pleased with themselves. I'd expected Smitty to be upset when he saw Josie but it was just the opposite. He dashed over to her, grabbed her by the waist, picked her up off her feet and swung her around in a circle. "It was great! Couldn't have gone better!" he told us. "We scared the livin' shit out of him!"

Little George and every one of the rest of the guys tried to tell Josie just how great it had been, all together, each trying to out-talk the rest. Total pandemonium.

Finally, Smitty let out a loud shout. That did the job. "Shut up, you guys!" he yelled. "Shut up and grab a seat. Maria, can you rustle up some grub for this gang of miscreants? They've been workin' all night without a bite to eat. Their bellybuttons are probably rubbing on their backbones by now."

She scurried off, the guys all sat down at the dining room table and Smitty said he'd recap the whole night for us.

"Okay. First off, we got in touch with the chief again to see what kind of legal pressure we could bring to bear on the senator. We filled him in on all the stuff we'd found out about him. He told us that we had plenty of stuff to take to a D.A. But then he asked us how we got all the information. I told him about the fake job interviews and the reporter impersonations, and he reversed himself – he said there was no way a D.A. could use that stuff. Hell, I hadn't even told him about what we did with the gal from the AG's office."

"So…?"

"Upshot? We decided we had no choice but to take things into our own hands. That's what the meetings yesterday were all about. I left you three out of it 'cuz I didn't want the guys intimidated by you. Well, fat lot of good that did! We hadn't been in there more than a couple of minutes when one of the guys said we should listen to what you'd been saying about avoiding violence. Hell, you might as well have been there. Anyway, that's what they decided."

"Pretty soon most of the guys came 'round to the idea that death was too good for him, anyway. We decided complete humiliation would be the best punishment. Not everybody agreed, of course – there were still a couple of holdouts who thought death was the perfect solution, but they were outnumbered."

"Question was how could we humiliate him without resorting to violence?" Smitty continued. "One of the guys said, there's violence and then there's violence. Another guy says, the senator doesn't have to know we're not gonna use violence."

Josie's back stiffened. "I hadn't promised to *avoid* all violence," Smitty continued in his own defense. "I'd promised to avoid the *type* of violence that had led me into trouble before."

"Dad, you're splitting hairs!"

"I know, I know, but be patient." Josie slumped back in her chair. Smitty looked relieved. "Anyway, we came up with a plan. You know we'd been charting his daily routines and had a good idea where we might isolate him and get his attention. One thing in our favor was that he was a loner. He lived by himself, drove himself to and from the office, and often took work home with him.

"Dad, I don't like the way you keep referring to him in the past tense. Tell me you didn't do away with him. Is he still alive?"

CHAPTER 75

"No, no. He's very much alive," Smitty insisted. "Maybe not too happy, but he's definitely alive!"

Gus added, "He's right, Josie. We never hurt him. We just spent the evening with him and did some convincing."

Smitty continued. "We decided that in order to get his full attention we needed to get him isolated, scared and helpless. The best place to do that, we all agreed, was in his own home, so that's what we did. One of the guys tailed him from his office to his home and phoned us when he was getting close. We were parked near his front door but ducked down in our cars so as not to be seen."

One of the guys spoke up, "he never even looked around."

Smitty continued, "As soon as he was out of his car, we surrounded him and told him we were from his home county and asked him if we could come in to discuss something with him. He fell into our trap and invited us in. But as soon as we started talking about blackmail, he invited us out. When we refused he started to struggle. Course with nine of us that didn't work out too well for him. See Josie? It wasn't a kidnapping. We met him outside his home and he invited us in. How can you be kidnapped in your own home?"

He didn't wait for an answer. "Remember when I told you what Dan said 'there's violence and then there's violence?'" That got me to thinking and I remembered reading that the fear of violence works on some people better than actual violence. I asked Dan to look into that and he came up with some ideas."

He turned to one of Little George's young guys, "Dan, tell them what you told me."

Dan said he'd read that the first thing to do to make prisoners lose their confidence was to strip them. He said the prisoner would react worse to that than they would to real violence. "Most people, unless they've been trained in resistance, start imagining the worst. Their imagination becomes more effective than actual torture."

Dan struck me as a bookworm type. I later found out he was a computer nerd. Little George had used him for some research before.

Smitty went on, "So the first thing we did, was the x-rated part. We closed and locked the doors, pulled down all the shades, made him take off all his clothes and sit in a kitchen chair in the middle of the living room. But Josie, we never touched him. Besides, he ain't gonna tell nobody nothin' about last night, you'll see."

"So by this time he was scared shitless. The first thing that came out of his mouth was an offer to buy us off. Offered us money and all kinds of shit. All this time, none of us said a word. Dan said the other thing he'd read was to leave them alone and helpless. We'd already figured it'd probably take all night, so we just left him, naked as a really fat jay bird, except for his shoes and knee high socks held up with garters. Dan was right about him being naked. Even with just one guy watching him, he never tried to escape. Remember what his staff said about he always wears a suit? I think he wore it as a kind of protection. Anyway, he sure fell apart as soon as he was naked."

"We split up and started searching the house. I was willing to bet he'd been crooked so long without being caught, he'd become careless. Turned out I was right. We found a hidden file in his upstairs office that all by itself would end his career if any of its contents became public."

"You searched a State Senator's home?"

"Only after he invited us in. Anyway, after about an hour or so of letting him stew in his own juices, I went in to him and asked him a question. 'What would you do to someone you knew was responsible for murdering two of your friends?' Then I walked back out. Half hour later, I went back in. 'We know all about your friend Carpenter and how you had him killed. And walked out again. Next time I went in, he said he had to pee. I told him to go right ahead and walked out.
Here he was, this hot-shot state senator, accustomed to being kowtowed to, used to hiding behind five-hundred-dollar suits, now stripped naked and forced to urinate in public. I figured he'd cave before long, and we weren't in any hurry. We had all night.

A little later, I came back in and asked if he'd missed his girlfriend over at the Attorney General's office yet? That one really got him. I could see he was shaken. This time we left him alone for a couple of hours. We kept peeking at him through the kitchen door, but he didn't try to move or anything.

It was still dark when I went in the next time. Sure enough, he'd peed in the corner of the room. I told him that his girlfriend was singing her head off into a tape recorder, all about the lies he'd told her and all the stolen stuff she'd given him. Still later I told him we'd found all his papers plus we had all of Carpenter's papers, including his personal diary We left him like that all night, nobody talking to him except me, but he knew there were a lot of us there.

"So Josie, we never kidnapped him, he was in his own home all night. We never touched him except to make him take his own clothes off. We didn't even tie him up. On top of that he knows we found his private papers stash, he ain't gonna say nothin' to anybody about anything. We really got him by the short hairs",

Smitty continued. "Early this morning we decided it was time to tell him our demands. We let him get dressed, sat him down at his kitchen table and surrounded him. I told him. 'Because of you, two of our friends are dead. It took us a long time to find you. We had to find Carpenter first and deal with him in order to find you. It really doesn't matter who we are, except we have our own set of laws. One of the biggest of them is a life for a life."

"He said, 'I never killed anyone. I said, 'Maybe not personally. But you ordered the killings and that's the same thing.' I told him, 'Look, we're just wasting time. We know you had Carpenter murdered before we could do it.

Of course we hadn't been planning on doing away with Carpenter, but it wouldn't do any harm to plant the idea.

I told him, now it's your turn. We could just find a way to do away with you like we were gonna do with Carpenter, or – we can ruin you and let you live.

He tried to bluster. 'You'll never get away with this. When I get out of here I'll get the law down on you so fast you won't know what happened.'

What makes you think you're going to get out of here? At least alive?

He caved.

'Okay, okay. 'I'll do anything you say.'

I didn't trust him, but went on with our plan. You've got a choice: life or death. Right now. Plan A: you can agree to resign from the

Senate, and admit everything we have records of to your fellow senators and the press, or Plan B: we just put an end to your miserable little life right now. We'll make it look like suicide.

I added, 'Before you make your decision I want you to know, this being a democracy and all, we had a vote on whether we should just go ahead and kill you now. The vote was really close.'

There was no hesitation on his part. He went for Plan A, saying he'd do whatever we asked. I asked him if he was sure and he assured me he'd never been so sure of anything in his life. I told him he had a week to get his act together and publicly resign or we'd start publishing his papers and he'd have to walk in fear of us the rest of his life, which probably wouldn't be very long. He got the message loud and clear and agreed, reluctantly, to everything.

"By this time it was daylight, time for us to get out of there. Goldberg was a complete mess. He'd peed on the floor, stank of fear-induced sweat and looked like what he really was. An old, wrinkled shell of a man. I told him we'd be keeping an eye on him every minute of every day. That if we caught him deviating from the agreement in any way, we'd be on him like a ton of bricks. I also told him he'd get a list of everything he was to admit to in the mail. He nodded his agreement, but I told him he had to say it! He croaked out a, 'Yeah, I understand. I guess I have no choice.' I assured him he was right on that point.

Everything went pretty much as we'd planned. But I've still got some reservations about him. Looking back at his reactions to us, I had a feeling that a guy like him wasn't gonna give in that easily. He gave me the impression of a wily old fox of a politician, the type of crook who probably thinks he can weasel himself out of almost any predicament. Given that he'd spent a lifetime as a politician, blackmailer, thief and murderer, I had a lotta trouble putting any faith in his word. I couldn't shake the feeling that his word's worthless, even if his life is threatened.

Anyway, that's what we did. On the surface it looks like we're gonna completely ruin Goldberg. Once he resigns and goes public with all his misdeeds, he'll be totally disgraced and on his way to jail. He'll be as good as dead. He'll be *better* than dead. So – that's what went down last night. We left him sitting there in his kitchen, an empty shell. It was beautiful!"

Then Little George added, "And Josie, just like your Dad said we never laid a hand on him. He walked into his house with us on his own, even undressed himself. He's guilty as hell and we simply let him know his time is over. We scared the crap outta him, but we never touched him. Right guys?"

A chorus of agreement and one guy said, "Just the way we hoped it'd go."

CHAPTER 76

"Anybody want to add anything?" Smitty asked.

One of the guys spoke up. "Yeah, Smitty. You didn't say anything last night about having doubts whether this would work or not?"

"Well, truth is, while we were planning it and during the early hours of the night I didn't have any doubts. But toward morning, I thought I was seeing something in his behavior that gave me second thoughts. It kind of looked to me as if he was more *acting* being afraid than actually *being* afraid, that he was faking it. Maybe we'd dragged it out too long. Once he figured we weren't gonna kill him right away, maybe he thought he could outsmart us somehow. Did any of you guys get that feeling?"

There was a long silence.

Finally Gus spoke up. "Looks to me like you covered that anyway, with your one-week deadline. If he doesn't follow through, you just unload everything we know onto a few newspapers and his goose'll be sizzlin'. In fact, why don't we just go ahead and do the newspaper thing right now? Why wait?"

Smitty replied that the group had looked at that option before. "When we decided not to kill him ourselves, we decided we needed to get him out of politics and into jail in the most humiliating way possible. What's he most proud of, what does he value most? We decided it was his seat in the California Senate."

"We thought if he had to get up before his fellow senators and publicly admit that he was a blackmailer, had stolen information from the Attorney General's office and was under investigation in cases having to do with murder and sex with a minor, if he was forced to do that in front of the entire Senate, it'd be something he'd never recover from."

Smitty wanted to wrap it up. "Well, we are where we are," he said. "What we need now is that demand letter for the senator. It can be pretty simple. All we have to do is list everything we know about him and demand that he confess it all to the entire Senate."

"While it's in session and being televised," I added.

"Right. In session and televised," Smitty said. "So, Casey. Can you whip up a letter like that in an hour or so?"

"Piece o' cake."

And it was. We had so much – Carpenter's diary and papers, Mrs. DeHaven's confession, the connection between the senator and the murders, plus all the new incriminating paperwork they'd found in the senator's home. Just for starters, he'd been caught molesting a page boy by another senator's aide. The aide had tried to blackmail him. From what we could piece together it looked like the senator had bought the aide off, but kept his letters – an unfortunate decision for the senator because now they were in *our* possession. On top of that we found a stash of the files he'd had Mrs. DeHaven steal.

An hour later I had a handwritten sample letter. I gave it to Smitty. He glanced through it, then said, "Let me read it aloud. See what you guys think." Everyone settled down to listen.

"In order to avoid the consequences we spoke of yesterday, you must do the following. You must stand up in the Senate within one week, while it is in session and being televised, and request time to make a statement. In the statement you will admit to the following:

1. You have stolen files from the Attorney General's office.

2. You have used those stolen files to blackmail prominent people out of untold thousands of dollars.

3. You have used your position to coerce an employee in the Attorney General's office to help you steal those files.

4. You had an ongoing business relationship with one Peter Carpenter of El Cerrito and supplied him with blackmail information so that he could be your front man in the blackmailing.

5. That you were responsible for Peter Carpenter being murdered because you were afraid he would give you up.

6. That some years ago you were caught molesting a page boy and bribed your way out of the charges.

After admitting to all the above, you will resign from the senate. And, do not forget, we have documentary evidence of everything you are going to admit to. You either do as requested or all that evidence will be made available to every major newspaper in California.

The last thing for you to be aware of is the second half of the promise that was made to you. You were given a choice: cooperate with our request to the letter, or suffer the consequences we discussed. If we have to release the information – which is to say, if you don't – then you will be signing your own sentence.

Smitty paused for several seconds for people to digest it. "I like it," he said, then asked if anyone thought it should be changed in any way.

"About the one week deadline," Gus asked. "I've got a question about that. We're demanding that he does it when the TV camera's rolling. How often do they do that? What do we do if they don't televise within the one week window you've given him?"

"Okay, we need to find that out first," Smitty said, nodding. "I've seen the Senate in action on the tube a few times channel-surfin', but I haven't a clue how often they do it. Is it always televised? Little George, can one of your guys find out?"

"Should be a snap. If we have a television guide around here anywhere, it should be in there."

It only took a moment for Little George to find it.

"Here it is. It's called Live From Your Capitol and it's on Tuesday and Thursday afternoons from two to six on PBS. It doesn't usually get much of an audience unless something major happens. I think this would be major, major. Every TV station and newspaper in the nation would snap it up."

"So it's only twice a week? Maybe we should say two weeks?"

.Reluctantly, Smitty agreed to the change. "Type it up and get it delivered to his office."

Josie was cryptic. "Done!"

We all thought that was it, the end was in sight. We would be exonerated and Smitty and I could thumb our noses at his detective nemeses.

CHAPTER 77

"Let's go home," Smitty said. "There's nothing we can do here except keep an eye on Goldberg and wait."

"We can keep an eye on him if you want," Little George offered.

"Thanks, but no," Smitty said. "I want two or three of my guys to stick around and take turns watching him 24/7. Like I said, I don't really trust him. I want my guys to keep tabs on him."

He picked four of our guys to stay and arranged for them to take over our hotel rooms.

"And guys, you can watch him in shifts. Two of you on him 24/7, got it?"

Little George stopped us before we could leave. "Smitty, something you should know. Your sniper? You don't have to worry about him anymore."

"What happened?"

"It turned out he was local. He was a tough case, wouldn't admit to anything. But as soon as he found out what was going down with the senator, he decided to leave town for a while. We kind of helped him come to that conclusion. Anyway, he's gone."

Back home, Smitty had Josie drop me off at my place. He told me to take my time getting caught up with my business, but he wanted to see me the next day at his home. Josie told me to call her, that she'd come get me. I spent the rest of the day reading Latitude 38, having tea and scones with my landlady and apologizing to her.

Next morning I had nothing to do. Normally I'd hop on my bike and visit a lot of the local marinas and the local boating store to BS with the locals and check out the bulletin boards for jobs. I was up and ready to call Josie by seven, but thought better of calling that early. Grabbed my cell phone and went to a nearby coffee shop, thinking I'd read a newspaper and call sometime after eight.

Maybe I wasn't the only one with time on their hands. Shortly after seven my cell phone rang. It was Josie.

"Aren't you up yet? I've been waiting for your call for the last hour or so. Dad's got something important for you to do and he wants you to get on it right away."

"He wants me to murder somebody?"

"Don't be silly. He's got something serious for you to do. Something you'll really like. Besides, I need you up here. Can I come and get you now?"

"Sure," I said. "I'm ready. I'm out having breakfast already. So what's the big job he's got for me? Give me a hint."

"Nope, I promised Daddy I wouldn't tell. Get into some decent clothes. I'll be there before you know it."

I dashed back to my rooms. I wasn't sure what she meant by decent clothes. She knew all my new clothes were up there. I didn't have anything fancy, so I ended up jumping into clean khakis, a shirt and a light jacket, plus boat shoes. I hoped she came in a car, not her cycle. I certainly wasn't dressed for a motorcycle ride, but I figured she knew that.

Much sooner than I expected I heard Josie honk her horn and rushed downstairs.

"How the hell'd you get here so fast?"

"That wasn't so fast," she laughed. "I've done it faster."

I looked to see if she was kidding me and got a big wink for my trouble.

"Actually, I got lucky," she admitted. "I was already in the car when I called you, so I just took off. And then, more luck, I caught every green light on the way. I didn't have to stop once. Anyway, I'm here. You're here. Let's get going. Oh, yeah, Daddy said for you to bring your latest sailing magazine. *Latitude* something?"

"*Latitude 38*? Why does he want that?"

"I don't know. You'll have to ask him yourself." She didn't look like she didn't know.

On the way I tried to trick her into telling me what Smitty's big secret was, but she outsmarted me every time. She asked me if any jobs had turned up for me while we were in Sacramento and I had to tell her no.

Her response surprised me. "Good!" she said, but wouldn't elaborate, just a, "Wait till we get home!"

A short time later we were there and I went in, wondering what kind of cuckoo idea he was going to lay on me this time.

"Casey, everything okay? You all rested up and ready to go to work?"

"Uuuuuh, I guess so?"

"Josie, grab him and wait for me in the dining room. Does he know what we're talking about?"

"Not a word, Dad!"

"Okay, I'll be there in a sec."

"C'mon you, I'll get us some coffee."

I followed Josie into the dining room and dropped myself in a chair, wondering what in the hell I was getting into now.

Smitty and the coffee arrived at the same time. His first question caught me entirely off guard. I'd been mentally preparing myself for a whole list of nasty options, but nothing remotely like what he wanted to talk about.

"Have you been down to see my boat since the explosion and fire?"

I had to admit I hadn't.

"What'd you think of her condition that night?"

"Jeez, I don't know, Smitty. She was still floating, which is a good thing. But her whole topside was either burnt or blasted into the stratosphere in the explosion."

"A couple of the guys have been down there and they're telling me she's still afloat, that she looked better now than she did that night. They said she's a horrible mess, but the mess is almost all above the water line. They think she could be salvaged and rebuilt. What do you think?"

"The truth? I think she should have been hauled right away. I doubt it'd be worth your while to rebuild. I can go down and look at her but I really don't expect much."

"Okay, that's what I want you to do. She wasn't insured, so I can't just go out and buy a new one. If she's salvageable that's what I want to do."

I nodded.

"So here's my proposition. I'll pay you five hundred bucks to do a complete survey and see what you think. If you need to have her hauled, I'll pay for that too. Take a week and see what you can find out. If you think she can be saved, I'll give you five hundred a week to oversee the job. What d'ya think? Oh, wait. Before you answer, there's one more thing. I've got a two-year-old Toyota pickup you can have. You'll need wheels to get around in and pick stuff up with. So…what d'ya think?"

I was shocked. We'd gradually come to trust each other sort of. But I'd had no inkling that he might trust me this much. It was an exciting offer, but go to work for an outlaw gang chief? On the other hand there was Josie.

CHAPTER 78

I looked at Josie. She was beaming.

Rebuild a 40 foot yacht? I wasn't sure I was up to that.

"Smitty, you know I've got a lot of experience with sailing, but I've never built a boat. It sounds exciting and I really want to do it, but are you sure I'm the right guy?"

"Casey, lad. You've got common sense, a lot of boat experience and I trust you. We can buy the expertise we need, so don't worry about that. Say yes!"

I hemmed and hawed, even though I knew I was going to jump at his offer.

He threw in a cincher. "Look, I'm gonna do it anyway and I'd rather spend the money on you than a bunch of strangers at the boat yard. Okay?"

"Okay. Yes. You got a deal! How about if Josie and I take a run down there right now?"

"That's my man!"

He handed me five hundred dollars cash, and said, "You're hired! Oh, and by the way, Casey, you're pickup's waitin' for you in the garage."

Talk about confidence in your own plans.

In the garage, just like Smitty said, was a blue two door Toyota pickup. It'd be perfect for boat work.

"Surprised?"

"Overwhelmed! Where'd he get the pick up? Does he own it? What if I'd said no?"

"He's had a guy cleaning it up at the shop for the past week, and it's already registered in your name."

"Did you know about all this?"

"Not until this morning. Can you imagine? Dad can really keep a secret!" She added, "We have to talk!"

"Sure, what's up?"

"I want to work with you, on the boat and stuff! And besides, like the old song says, 'I've grown accustomed to your face.'"

"You really mean it? Me too! The accustomed to your face thing. It'll be much easier with two of us."

"Next, where are you going to stay? I'm moving back to my house."

"I'd planned on going back to my digs. It's pretty handy to the boat."

"So is my place!"

"Is that an invitation?"

"Maybe. Let's think about it."

Wow, suddenly, out of the blue, I've got myself a job, a vehicle, a business partner, and maybe a move-in girlfriend! I'm really flying!

My first impression was pretty demoralizing. The *Jezebel* was lying just as she had been immediately after the fire. Smitty's neighbor's boat was gone. The boat wasn't insured and no one wanted it, so the yardmaster had it towed away and destroyed.

Josie took one look at the *Jezebel* and threw her hands up. She couldn't see any hope of restoring it. I wasn't so sure. Smitty's gang had pumped a lot of water out of her, but I hoped that most of the water had come from the fire hoses. She'd been sitting there for over a week and was still afloat. Should be a fairly good sign the hull was intact.

"Josie," I said, maybe she can be saved. We need to clear all the burnt crap off the topside so I can get in, and then probably put her on the hard and get a good look at the hull."

"On the hard?"

"Yeah, get her outta the water."

"How do you do that?"

"Good question. There's a hoist here. I'm not sure it's big enough to handle her though. Tell you what, let's find out."

We walked up to the dock master's office. When we told him what we were thinking of doing, he assured us that the hoist had lifted boats bigger than Smitty's— but that he didn't have insurance any more and was reluctant to let us use it. After some friendly talk and a cup of coffee, he decided that if Smitty'd sign a release, he'd let him use it.

"One obstacle down. Josie identified– and solved– another one: she said she was positive a bunch of the guys would happily come down and help us clean off the top of the boat. I pointed out that she didn't know how big a job that'd be. It wasn't just the fire-damaged cabin. The masts, the spars and all the rigging had to be carted away too. On top of that, I had to figure a way to tow the hull over to the lift.

First thing, though, we had to get the mess off the deck. Josie made two calls and, within an hour, a half dozen bikers were lined up, ready to come right down and get started. I had to delay them.

Port authorities are real strict about working on boats in the water. We had to figure out a place to put all the burnt wood. Walking up and down the two docks, trying to think of a place to put all that stuff, I noticed an old World War II landing craft in one of the berths – the ones with the hinged front that dropped down so the troops could disembark.

It took all morning, but we finally located the owner and he agreed, for a price, to let us use it to as a floating dumpster. We had to promise him to clean it up and restore it to its original condition after we were done with it. Which was kind of a joke. It was in pretty lousy condition.

Once that was set, I told Josie we could go ahead and have the guys come down that afternoon. "In the meantime, if I can get hold of some good bolt cutters, we can start cutting the mast and back stays away. However, I do *not* want you on the boat – or the dock even – when I do that," I told her. "Some of those stays may be under tension and whip around when I cut them."

"What are stays?" And so began Josie's nautical education.

"Stays are the heavy wires that support the masts and rigging. The mast's down, but it's still fastened to the stays and the rigging." I pointed to a few examples.

Borrowing a bolt cutter from a neighboring boat, I set to work on the rigging. The mast was mostly in the water, having fallen sideways over the boat that'd been towed away. The forestay was still attached and taut as a drum, but the rest of the stays were slack and cutting them was no problem.

The forestay worried me. There was no way to relieve the pressure on it. If I simply cut it with the bolt cutter, I had no idea where that quarter inch thick wiring might end up. Wire that thick under that much tension could snap your head off. Frankly, it scared me. Smitty had given me the name of a rigger nearby, and I decided I'd better ask for help. I gave him a call. He said he'd be right over and thought maybe he could handle the problem.

The rigger, a guy named Harry, got there in about half an hour, took a long look at the problem and said, "I dunno'. That stay's tighter'n a drum. I cut that and she's gonna kick back and kill somebody, sure as shootin'."

"That's why I called you. Smitty said you were the best. How about moving the mast to relieve the pressure?"

"Thought of that, wouldn't do no good. That stay's too rigid."

"We gotta do something."

"I'm thinkin'. Maybe there is a way. At least it's worth a try. Run up to my truck and grab my come-along outta the back," he said, recruiting me to be his helper. "You know what a come-along looks like?"

"Yeah."

"Then you'll know this one when you see it. It's bright yellow. Looks like a regular come-along on steroids. I'm gonna stay here and clear away some of the sail debris and junk so we can see what we're doing."

It was immediately apparent why Harry sent me to get the come-along. This thing was *very* big and *very* heavy. It was an industrial-strength come-along. No– make that the mother of all come-along. I couldn't see how he could cut the stay without killing someone.

"Okay, here's what we're gonna do," said Harry. "Clamp these wire clamps on the forestay. Make sure they're really, *really* tight. When they're on, we'll attach the chain from the come-along to them, and the other end to the deck plate at the bow. When we're very, *very* sure that the connections are secure, we can gradually transfer the load from the forestay to the chain on the come-along."

"Got it," I said. "When the strain's on the come-along, we cut the forestay then gradually release the strain on the come-along. Great idea."

"If it works. gotta make sure we have plenty of chain to tighten, that stay's really taut." Sounded good. We were in good hands. However, what he said next put me back on full alert.

"Okay. Get everybody off the dock. That damn stay's thirty feet or more. With the mast on its side like it is, I have no idea where that stay might go if the come-along let's go. That thing could be a killer."

CHAPTER 79

I helped Harry get everything rigged up, then took Josie and retreated to the head of the dock. Very slowly he took the tension up with his monster come-along. Nothing seemed to be happening for pull after pull. I was afraid he was going to pull the deck plate off the bow. Gradually, oh so gradually, a slight sag in the stay developed. Without hesitation, he grabbed the pair of bolt cutters and cut. The portion of the stay from the masthead was still taught but now it was secured to the come along and Harry could gradually release it. In a short time the head stay was loosened and we were in no danger

I didn't find out until later that Harry had never tried this particular maneuver before. But that's what riggers do. He gave me his card and said to get in touch with him when we got to the point of replacing all the rigging.

Nothing was worth saving. The stays were cut up with bolt cutters. The mast had to be sawn into pieces using a reciprocal saw. It was all junk now and ended up in the converted landing craft.

One of the old timer live-aboards sidled up to me and asked a question.

"Did I hear you're gonna use the old lift on her?"

"Yeah, if I can figure a way to get her there."

"Fifty bucks and I'll get her there."

"Really? How?"

He was cagey. "If I tell you, you'll do it yourself. Give me a handshake on fifty bucks and I'll tell you how I'll do it."

If it worked, fifty bucks was cheap, so I stuck out my hand and shook his. "You got a deal – if it works."

"Okay, here's how it'll work. 'See that old scow over on the next pier, the *Dixie*? She don't look like much but she's strong as an ox. She's mine. She's longer than the *Jezebel*. I figure you guys can push the *Jezebel* outta her berth. Then I'll side tie her up to me and slowly jockey her out to the bay, turn her around and bring her back in to the lift. It's gotta be done slow and careful, but my boat can do it jest fine."

Of course. No reason it shouldn't work, if the scow's captain was as good as he said he was. Side tying used to be used a lot. Not so much any more, but not because it wouldn't work.

By then it was darn near dark. Josie grabbed my arm. "Let's quit for the day," she suggested. "Come on up to my place. We can clean up and get some dinner." No way was I going to say no to an offer like that.

At her place, she made me a drink, then headed upstairs for a shower. I took the opportunity to call Smitty and fill him in on our progress and what my current thoughts were on fixing his boat. He was tickled and wanted to know when the boat was coming out of the water. He wanted to be there. He made me promise to call him first thing in the morning and we hung up.

Sitting back, I thought how lucky I'd been. Good thing he'd been so excited about his boat, he hadn't asked about Josie. What if he'd asked me where she was? She's upstairs taking a shower? I don't think I'd tell him that.

I hadn't finished imagining that conversation when Josie appeared in a big robe, toweling her hair. She suggested I might want to take a shower too and I readily agreed.

"Tell you what," she said. "You take a shower. I'll fix a steak for dinner. That sounds more relaxing to me than going out. Okay?"

"Sounds perfect. Wish I'd stopped off at my place and gotten some clean clothes."

"Take a look in the hall closet upstairs. I think there's a gigantic robe in there. Should fit you fine."

The evening was beginning to look interesting, what with showers, robes and a home-cooked dinner, and as it turned out, it *was* interesting. For that matter, the whole night was interesting. The shower gravitated into another cocktail, the cocktail gravitated into dinner, dinner gravitated into dessert, dessert gravitated into after-dinner brandies and brandy gravitated into bed.

And all that gravitating turned out to be gratifying. Very gratifying indeed. The last thing it felt like was a one-night stand. It was more like coming home. At one point, Josie cried, saying she'd been afraid that going to bed with me would somehow cheapen our relationship. But we'd both felt a natural attraction to each other almost since our first meeting, an attraction that had only deepened, an attraction that needed to go where it needed to go.

We ended up, side by side in bed, talking about the future – which now included marriage – until the wee hours. Finally we both drifted off to sleep, but not until we decided it best to keep our plans to ourselves for now.

CHAPTER 80

Next morning we drove down to the docks bright and early. I wanted to catch the scow guy and see what he had in the way of bumpers to protect the boat with the side tie. It turned out he had plenty. He'd obviously done this before, probably many times. He also had plenty of lines to tie up with.

"If ya get the durn thing cleaned up so's we can move it, I kin probably get her done this afternoon."

I told him I had to get the boss down to sign the release papers and then we'd be good to go. I called Smitty and told him I needed him.

Just as I was putting the phone down, I felt a hand on my shoulder. Turning around I saw the landing craft owner.

"What're we gonna do with all that crap in my boat?"

Thinking fast, I said, "One of my guys is trying to find a place to dump it legally. How about we pay you twenty-five bucks a day till we can get her cleaned out. That okay with you?"

"Thirty-five and you got a deal."

This was turning out to be a bigger job than I'd imagined. At five hundred a week, I was beginning to think Smitty was getting himself a bargain.

By late that afternoon, the papers had been signed, the *Jezebel* was side-tied and on the way to the lift. Once we got her in place and the lifting bands under her, the rest was easy. Before dark we had her safely on land in a cradle, drying out.

At first light the next morning I had my first chance to examine her closely. Her bottom was filthy. Barnacles, moss, blisters – a real mess. Smitty said she hadn't been out of the water for a couple of years and she looked it. Other than that, though, she looked pretty good, at least no damage I could see. Inside was another matter. 'Still a real jumble of junk to clean out before I could start checking for interior damage.

Several of the guys and Josie helped me clean out below decks. We decided early on that nothing was worth salvaging. We just threw it all away. I finally got down to the floorboards and found the bilge was still full of water. I'd have to locate a land pump and clear that out before I could take an ice pick and start checking for wood rot or other failure.

There was a lot to do, but we got the water pumped out and after checking out the hull thoroughly, I began to think she was worth saving and called Smitty and told him so.

"But it's gonna take a lot of time and money to do it." I said. "Probably the best way would be to have her taken to a professional yard and let them do it. It'd be costly, but much faster."

"Nope, no way!" Smitty said without hesitation. "First thing, I'm in no hurry. Second thing, we've got a verbal contract and I expect you to live up to it. Like I said, I'd rather spend money on you than on a shipyard."

Shortly after lunch Josie and I went up to Smitty's house and he cleared the air about the whole project. We made up a little employment contract between us for me to oversee the rebuilding of the *Jezebel*, with him keeping control of the design but leaving most everything else to me. He set up an open account at the shipyard so I could buy anything I needed, and asked me if I knew that he'd transferred ownership of the pickup to me.

"Yeah, Josie told me. It's perfect for the job. I'm kinda' speechless."

"Well, there's more. In my *considered* judgment...harrumph..." he said, openly winking at me, "you'll need office help to keep records and so on. And I *should* have someone looking over your shoulder. So I'm hiring Josie to be your amanuensis."

"My – amanuensis?"

"Secretary," Josie said.

"Unless you object to having her around all the time?" Smitty said, rhetorically. If I didn't know better, I'd almost swear he was leering at me. And who was I to say I knew better? I had the distinct impression he already knew I'd spent the night at Josie's house.

That afternoon I went over the boat with a fine-toothed comb to see what she needed structurally and the three of us drew plan after plan for the superstructure above deck. Everything from the waterline up was up for grabs. It would be a completely redesigned boat. Smitty found an evening class in boat design on line and suggested I enroll in it to make sure our designs were sound.

The only fly in the ointment was Sergeant Horning. Smitty and Little George were keeping tabs on the Senator. One of the broadcasted Senate sessions had come and gone without Goldberg saying anything. There were only two more session scheduled to be broadcast before the two week deadline. The four guys watching him said he hadn't made any suspicious moves; in fact he wasn't doing much of anything, except drinking.

The sergeant of course, didn't know what we knew. Smitty wasn't about to tell him anything, he wanted Horning to fall flat on his face when the truth came out. Horning kept needling him. Somehow he'd found out that we'd been out of town in spite of his warning us to stay close, but he couldn't find anyone to corroborate his suspicions. We heard he was after Smitty day and night. He'd told somebody that this time; finally, he had Smitty dead to rights and was going to put him in jail where he belonged.

Smitty, for a change didn't say much about Horning, but Josie and I could tell he was pissed.

Josie said, "Let him rant and rave, it'll just show him for the fool he is when the whole story comes out."

But Smitty was getting tired of waiting.

So was Josie, it turned out. But for a different reason.

It had been a long day for us. We were relaxing in her house, talking about everything that'd happened since that morning. After a while, conversation abated, I thought that Josie had fallen asleep. Suddenly she blurted out, "Why don't you let go of your apartment, move your stuff in here and let's get married," all in one breath.

I think we'd both been skirting the idea for some time, so it didn't take much to convince me.

"What about your dad?" I asked.

"Dad? He's way ahead of you!" she laughed. "He knows we've been together since the very first. Why do you think he hired me for you? Actually, if you want to be on his good side, you better make an honest woman of me pretty soon."

I was struck by the humor of the moment. First Smithy's thrown Josie at me, Then Josie's proposed to me – and I loved it.

"Okay, you and your dad can get up off you knees. I accept your proposal." And on that romantic note, we were officially engaged.

In bed that night, I reflected on the fact that we'd only known each other for less than a month. Did I have any second thoughts? Absolutely not! I thought we felt totally right for each other.

Things were going awfully well for me. So well I began worrying. My experience at sea told me that smooth seas were followed by storms.

CHAPTER 81

Sanding hulls is a dirty job. The port authority demands that boats be draped to minimize dust and other particles. That meant we'd be working under the boat, inside what amounted to a tent, wearing coveralls and masks, power-sanding the entire bottom– in short, a dirty, tiring, hot, sweaty, messy job.

Next morning we got started. Josie was terrific. She never complained once. We started early, before it got too terribly hot, and by eleven in the morning had made a lot of headway. I could see she was wilting.

"Let's quit for the day," I suggested, and Josie looked relieved. "This doesn't have to be done all in one day. We've got lots of other things to do. Let's go home, clean up and do some running around. I want to meet the guys at West Marine and see what kind of deals we can get."

"Theme's the kindest words I've heard all morning," she admitted. "And sumpin' else, my man. We have to think about when and where we're going to let Dad in on our little secret."

"That's another errand for this afternoon. Thanks to your dad, I've got enough money to make a down payment on an engagement ring. There's a nice little jewelry store in Alameda near a chandlery I want to visit. I thought we might drop by there if you're interested, unless you'd rather go to the chandlery first?"

"Idiot!" she laughed and added, "What's a chandlery?"

Needless to say, we ended up at the jewelry store first. Actually, I knew the owner through sailing and he gave us a really good deal. Josie was the practical type when it came to jewelry. We were able to get a ring she loved for just about every cent I had.

Outside the store, she gave me a big hug and said, "I can't wait to tell Dad!" I wasn't as enthusiastic as she was about confronting Smitty, but it had to be done sooner or later.

So I said, "Do you want to call him and tell him right now?"

"Ummmm, I don't think so," Josie said. "I'd rather surprise him. How about if we take him out to dinner tonight? We'll tell him we have a surprise for him. He'll assume it's about the boat. Then we can spring our engagement on him. He'll love it!"

I wasn't so sure. I hadn't gotten the impression that Smitty liked surprises too much. But he was her dad and it was her engagement so I let her call the shots.

He agreed to meet us for dinner down at Jack London Square and kept pestering Josie about what the surprise was. Then he wanted to bring a couple of the guys along with him. Josie finally settled on letting him bring Gus.

At dinner Josie deliberately left her new ring off until dessert was served. Smitty kept asking, "So what's the surprise?" and she kept putting him off. As dessert was being served, she surreptitiously slipped the engagement ring on under the table, and at the proper moment she waived her ring finger under Smitty and Gus's noses and said, "Casey and I are engaged to be married!"

Smitty said, "That's nice. But what about the surprise?" Then he and Gus cracked up.

"You guys!" Josie said. "I bet you had us all figured out, didn't you?"

"Of course we did," Smitty laughed. "And we had a bet going, whether you'd tell us right away or after dinner. Didn't know you'd already got a ring though. So, I guess you're really serious about this?"

I looked at Josie and she said, "I think he's perfect. Don't you, Dad?" She really put Smitty in the hot seat.

"Weeeeellll, I guess he's okay." Pretty high praise indeed from Smitty!

"Congratulations, kids," Gus chimed in. "When's the date?"

"We have to finish the boat first!" Josie said.

"Forget the boat!" Smitty said, "I want a grandchild!"

Gus said, "I'll drink to that," and calling the waiter over, ordered champagne.

We finished two bottles of champagne, moved into the bar area and had some after-dinner drinks as well. At one point Smitty got me off to one side and told me he was really pleased to have me as a soon-to-be son-in-law.

I was really touched until he followed that by telling me that he'd probably have to fire me as his boat builder.

All three of us looked at him with surprise.

"Wouldn't that be nepotism?" he said and then burst out laughing.

Shortly after, we all decided we'd better head for home. Smitty insisted we'd had too much to drink and called for a cab to get us home. Oops. Did Smitty know we were living together? Would he care? Josie gave the driver her address for both of us. Smitty never said a word.

In the house, Josie said, "I'm not really sleepy. How about some coffee?"

Halfway through the coffee, Josie said, "What do you think?"

"About what?"

"About setting a date, goofus!"

Trying to lighten the moment a little I said. "We don't *have* to get married, do we? I mean you're not PG or anything, are you?"

"Don't be silly. I'm serious. Why wait? I know I love you. Do you?"

"Do I what?"

"Do you love me?"

"Seriously? No question. I do love you. You want to get married tomorrow?"

"Not tomorrow, you idiot. How about soon, like next Sunday?"

"Like drive up to Reno or something? I asked.

"No, no. Right here, a big regular wedding in a church."

"Can we really get married that fast? There're licenses, churches, people, receptions and everything. I don't think it's possible."

"Dad can do it, if we really want it."

"Then there're *my* parents. I think they'd be a little miffed if I didn't invite them to my – our – wedding. I'm not sure we can get them here that soon."

"We can send a couple of the guys up on motorcycles to get them."

"Seriously."

"Seriously? Dad can do it. Dad can do anything. Seriously!"

We agreed we'd talk to him first thing in the morning.

Sunday morning, bright and early, Josie cornered her Dad at his house.

To say he was startled would be the understatement of the year. "You want to get married next *Sunday*? Like maybe Reno?"

"Nope. Not Reno. Right here. Today's Tuesday, you've got five days to get it done!"

"*Me*? Five days? I suppose you want a church wedding and all the trappings too – by Sunday?"

"Yep. I told Casey if anyone in the world could do it, you could."

"Jesus, let me think. You're really sure about this?"

"Absolutely."

"Okay, okay, okay. Let me think. I'm pretty sure I can get the church, but I better call Father Murphy right now."

In a few minutes he had the church lined up. Three o'clock, Sunday afternoon. One little hiccup: Josie and I had to have a meeting with the priest before the wedding. That was okay with Josie who's what you would call a part-time Catholic. For me, I really didn't care. I could go along with whatever was necessary for the wedding. So that was set.

Then there was a whirlwind of planning to do. I called my folks and a few friends. Smitty called all the Devils. He told them they had to rent tuxes for the event – he'd accept nothing less. I quickly called and made an appointment to get a tux, seeing how there was gonna be rush on them. Josie called a bunch of her friends and was agonizing over her choice for maid of honor.

I asked Smitty if he'd be my best man, but he respectfully declined. "Thanks, Case," he said. "I'm honored, but I'm already taken. Father of the bride, remember? How about Gus?"

When I asked Gus, he jumped at the chance. Turned out, he had plenty of experience. He asked me if I wanted references.

Josie called her dad. "You need to plan a rehearsal dinner for after the rehearsal Saturday night."

"Jesus, Josie. A rehearsal dinner? Your mom and I never had one of those. You're sure it's necessary?"

"Come on Dad. You know what they are. Nowadays it's expected."

"Okay, I give up. Who's supposed to come to that and where should it be?"

"Well, the parents of course. And everyone in the actual wedding party."

"Okay, I'll find a place. You invite everyone. And Josie? I'd like to invite Chief O'Meara and his family. What do you think?"

"Great, perfect! Do it!"

I asked Josie if maybe this wasn't too much of a financial load for Smitty. Her answer was as clear cut as the rest of her planning. "Are you kidding? I do his taxes. He could afford a wedding like this every other month without batting an eye!"

The boat got neglected in favor of wedding planning and the next morning I apologized to Smitty for the delay. His response brought me up short.

"Don't worry about the boat. First the wedding, then the honeymoon and then the boat. I panicked.

"Oh my god, Smitty. A honeymoon! I clean forgot about a honeymoon! What'll I do?"

"Casey, my boy, would you trust me to handle that for you?"

"But, Smitty, I'm broke! The engagement ring took all my savings. I never expected all this to happen so soon."

"Yeah, I know – you and me both. But Josie and you are gonna have a nice wedding and nice honeymoon. When you get back, we'll work on the future."

In spite of his upbeat attitude toward my problems, I could see that something was still eating away at Smitty.

"Something else bothering you?" I asked

"Yeah, but nothing you can do about it. It's that god damn Horning, again"

"Horning?"

"*Sergeant* Horning, one of Oakland's finest? Remember?"

"I'd hoped to not hear anything about him for a while."

"Son of a bitch doesn't have the slightest idea that we've solved his murder case, and I don't see any way of telling him. Now he's gone and convinced some judge," he paused for a moment, "he's got a murder warrant out for my arrest."

"No way!" I was flabbergasted. "No way can he prove that. There has to be a way we can get rid of him."

"Sure, given enough time. But you know what I just found out that rotten, good-for-nothin' S.O.B.'s planning on doin? He's plannin' on waiting to the last minute to get a warrant and then serve the warrant on me at your wedding. One of my old buddies at the station said he'd been bragging about his plan. He said there was no way I could stop him 'cause he wasn't getting the warrant until Sunday morning. The prick must have some judge in his pocket. And then he's gonna haul me away right in front of Josie's eyes! What a shit!"

CHAPTER 82

"Jesus Christ, Smitty. That'll ruin the wedding for everybody – and you in particular. We gotta do something!"

"Yeah, but what? I called an attorney friend and he said there's nothing he can do until there's a warrant."

"I wonder if Chief O'Meara could help. He knows the score. Maybe he could talk to the Oakland chief? It's worth a try, right?"

"Can you call him? We got a call back from his wife saying they're coming to the wedding. Maybe you can pull one of your famous stunts and get me out of this mess. And for chrissake Casey don't tell Josie!"

I called the chief and brought him up to date on Sergeant Horning's plan. He asked me a lot of questions about the long-lasting relationship between Smitty and his nemesis the sergeant. Finally he said, "Give me a day or two. I'll see what I can do."

I left it at that, crossed my fingers, then set to work trying to come up with a whole alphabet of fallback plans. There had to be some way to stop Horning in his tracks. I even went so far as to conjecture one of our gang breaking Horning's leg if the Chief couldn't come up with something. Anything to keep him from spoiling Josie's day.

Thursday morning started out like any other day. I was in my apartment, planning a rather quiet day – perhaps the last day I'd ever have to myself before getting married –

I was still worrying about Sergeant Horning and hadn't giving up on the idea of breaking his leg, although I hadn't told any of the gang about that, they'd be much too likely just to make it happen.

The phone interrupted my planning.

"Case, its Nips. We're gonna pick you up around two this afternoon. The gang's got something special planned"

"What's going on?"

"Nothin' to worry about just be ready at two."

I spent the whole morning worrying. No telling what the gang had planned for me, but I couldn't say no.

As it turned out, it wasn't too bad. They took me to the warehouse, plied me with beer and told me stories about their past escapades. The stories got wilder and wilder and they kept giving me beer after beer. I'm pretty sure they were giving me boilermakers, not plain beer. It gradually dawned on me their goal was to get me blind drunk. They didn't know I can't drink beer after beer. Consequently a couple of nearby potted plants probably got blind drunk. I didn't.

The gang was having a blast. I was too. This was turning out to be one of the parties that Josie'd warned me about. The guys don't know when to quit. So far, so good. Some happy beer drunks, nothing to worry about. A couple of the guys from Sacramento were there along with Little George.

The party got more and more raucous and I was just thinking they wouldn't miss me at all if I slipped out when I saw Little George headed towards me.

Looking around to make sure he wasn't overheard, he said, "Meet me in the head."

"What's going on?"

"Big trouble. We need to talk, now!"

I walked to the head, Little George right behind me.

Little George locked the door behind him very, very carefully, the way a drunk does. With exaggerated movements. Putting his finger to his lips, he said, "I probably shouldn't be telling you this. I'm only doing it because I'm worried about Smitty."

"Smitty's okay," I said. "Except for that damn sergeant"

"That's not what I'm talking about. I'm worried about what's going on in Sacramento."

"Sacramento? What's going on up there?"

"I think your guys and a couple of my guys are out of control. I heard they've planted a bunch of evidence in the senator's car and they're gonna set the guy up for a fatal car accident tonight. They don't care what Smitty ordered. They just want to avenge Red."

"Oh, man. This is *not* good," I said.

"Got that right. If they do it, Smitty's gonna be wicked pissed. On top of that, I don't trust these guys to get away with it. If they get caught, the whole thing may get laid on Smitty. Look, I'm caught between a rock and a hard place here. I think Smitty should know, but I don't want to rat on my guys. That's why I'm telling you. Now I'm out of it."

Oh, great. With that, he unlocked the door and started out, only to be pushed back in by Gus.

"Did you tell him?" he demanded of Little George.

"Yeah, I told him the same thing I told you. Now it's up to you guys." And he left.

"What do you think?" Gus wanted to know.

"I think we gotta stop them, for Smitty's sake. Don't you?" I replied.

"Yeah. But how?" he asked.

"Don't ask me. But I think we need to get up there ASAP, and try and get control of the situation. Maybe we'll get an idea on the way."

He deliberated for a moment, then, "Motorcycles the fastest way. As soon as Little George told me what was going on up there, I quit drinking. If you're up to it, we can double up on my bike and get up there in an hour easy. Trouble is I don't know where our guys are hanging out up there. Do you?"

"No, but I bet Little George does. Is your bike here? What'll I do about a jacket and helmet?"

"Yeah, my bike's here. I'll check with Little George and find out where they're hanging out. I'll tell him to tell the gang you can't hold your booze. You're sick and I'm taking you home. Wait here. I'll be right back. While you're waiting, find a jacket and helmet from that pile over there. A couple of the guys are about your size. Lord knows, they won't miss them for hours!"

In a short time we were mounted up. For an old guy, Gus really tore up the ground. Up Highway 80, over the Carquinez Bridge, he wove his way through rush-hour traffic until we were nearing Sacramento, covering the distance in about fifty minutes. It was almost six o'clock.

From what Little George had told Gus, the senator had taken to stopping at a particular bar and getting well lubricated each night on the way home. Each night he stayed a little longer, as if he was afraid to go home. The guys'd been cozying up to the senator, setting him up for tonight's operation. Little George had told Gus that the guys weren't planning to do anything until after dark, so we thought we were in time. *If* Gus could find the bar. We knew the name, Oasis Bar.

"I think I can find it. It was in the south end of town and was on an alphabet street. Like A or B or something. C? I just hope we're not too late!"

We roared up and down alphabet streets looking for the bar.

CHAPTER 83

It took us a little over a half hour to find the place. When we walked in the first thing we saw was the senator sitting at the bar. His suit was rumpled; tie loose and hanging to one side, the man was the picture of dejection. Several empty glasses before him. Unkempt, unfocused, a total loser.

Over in the corner, surrounding a pool table, I spotted the cycle gang. Four of them, two from our gang and two from Little George's gang. I remembered that Smitty had told his four guys to take turns watching the senator, two by two. Why were the other two guys here? Gus and I casually wandered over to them and asked, "What's going on?"

They were shocked to see us. One of them replied somewhat belligerently, "Just keeping an eye on the senator, like we're supposed to. We keep sending drinks over for him and he keeps drinking 'em."

"Every night?"

"Yep. Same thing, every night."

"How does he get home?"

"Believe it or not, he drives! Guy must have a hollow leg. One of these nights he's not gonna make it. They'll find him drowned in that ditch out by his place or something."

"You guys wouldn't be planning on helping that happen, would you?" I asked.

Gus and I'd devised a skimpy plan on the way up. This was Step Numero Uno.

The same guy pretended to be outraged at that idea. He was a lousy actor.

I told them about the bachelor party and they all griped that they'd missed it.

"Well that's what Smitty was thinking too. You guys, stuck up here and missing all the fun. From what we've heard, the senator's mostly blind drunk and hasn't been able to get at his money or buy an illegal passport. He ain't going anywhere, just waiting for the other shoe to fall."

"That's about right!"

"Well, Smitty and Little George want you guys to hightail it down to Oakland and get in on some of the fun. There's nothing for Gus and me to do before the wedding except the rehearsal and the dinner Saturday night. I think Smitty really wanted to get me out of his hair for a couple of days."

The two guys up from Oakland didn't know what to say. They looked at each other for a moment or two, then finally one of them said, "Geez, we had something sort of planned. Hang on a sec." They walked to the end of the bar and huddled. One turned to me and said, "He wants all of us to quit watching the senator?"

"That's right. Gus and I'll keep a loose eye on him until Saturday morning and then we'll just leave him. Like Smitty said, 'He ain't going anywhere! Besides, Little George and Smitty said I needed some going-away clothes and they got Gus to volunteer to outfit me at a place Little George recommended up here."

"Oh yeah, we know the place. Over on D Street. Great store! Listen, with Gus being the dandy he is and goin' to that store, you're in for a treat!"

"Plus you guys are all going formal. So you two have appointments at the tailor's tomorrow morning."

The other two wanted to know where the party was. Our guys said, "follow us," and they left.

"Whew!" "Now we gotta phone Little George and bring him up to date. He better intercept them before they see Smitty. Smitty'd smell a rat, for sure!"

Part one of our plan worked. On to Part Two.

Gus and I grabbed a booth and watched the senator. He was really sloshed. I couldn't see how he could drive home. "How do you want to handle the next part?" Gus said.

"I think we need to sober him up some first. He's not gonna understand anything we say, drunk as he is now."

"Let's slip the bartender a hundred and get him to cut the senator off," Gus suggested. "He can tell him that under the law he's responsible if he lets a customer leave drunk and the customer gets in an accident. I think that's true anyway. Get him to start servin' him coffee. That'll keep us out of it until we make our move."

It took almost an hour, but eventually the senator seemed a little more coherent. It was time to make our move.

"Gus, I think you better make the first contact. You're older and more believable than me."

"Yeah, I'm older, but it's your idea!"

"Doesn't matter whose idea it is. I think you're the man for the job right now."

"Okay. Here goes!"

Gus wandered over and sat on the stool next to the senator. We'd bribed the bartender to spend his time at the other end of the bar. Gus and the senator were all alone.

The bartender had told us, "He's a mean drunk. Senator or not, no more booze for him."

Gus could hear Goldberg mumbling under his breath. "Son of a bitch's got no right to cut me off, I'll have his job."

"Senator," Gus said, leaning over to make it feel like he was confiding in the man, "it wasn't the bartender's idea to cut you off. It was ours."

His answer was slurred. "What the hell you talking about?"

"I said it was us that had the bartender start serving you coffee instead of booze, 'bout an hour ago."

"Well, tell him to start the booze again! I'll have his license and yours too."

"No you won't. I'm trying to save your life."

"Too late," he said belligerently, and tried to push away. He was still a little sloshed.

"Did you happen to see those four guys leave a little while ago, those guys who'd been buying you drinks?"

"Yeah. They were buying me drinks. Nice guys."

"Nope. Not so nice. They were planning on killing you tonight."

"You're shitting me."

"Nope, and I can prove it."

"Kill me? Here in a public bar? What're you trying to pull?"

"Stop and think about what you're saying, Senator," Gus said, sounding like he was trying to explain something to a two-year-old. "Really, would I try to sober you up if I was trying to pull something on you?" The senator appeared to be trying very hard to follow the logic, but he seemed to be getting tripped up by so many words.

Finally he gave up and yelled to the bartender who was busy drying glasses at the other end of the bar. The bartender made it clear he was listening, but that he wasn't coming back up to the senator's end. Frustrated, the senator had no choice but to yell. "Bartender! Is what this guy's saying true? Did he get you to cut me off?"

"Yep, Mr. Senator, he did."

Goldberg turned back to Gus. Slowly and drunkenly he said, "Okay, say I believe you so far. How can you prove they were trying to kill me?"

"Simple. Let's me and my friend take a stroll with you to your car and we'll show you what they had planned." He pointed me out to the senator. I waved a cheerful, innocent hello.

The senator looked back at Gus and still slurring his words "I should go with you two to my car? Whaddya' think I am, some sorta' nut? Leave here alone with two strangers after you've been talking about me getting murdered?"

"For Christ's sake senator, you got the bartender watching the whole thing. He'll vouch for us."

"Will do," agreed the bartender with a shrug.

Countless cups of coffee later together with the shock of being told he was being targeted for murder seem to have at least partially sobered him up. He finally agreed to go out to his car with us.

"I got to' pee first," Goldberg said. Gus went with him to make sure he didn't pass out or try to get out.

After that the three of us walked out to his car. Before any car doors were opened, I pointed out a pile of papers on the back seat. "Were those there when you left your office to come over here?" I asked him.

The senator blinked several times, then finally, reluctantly, said no.

"Let's get in and talk," I said.

Goldberg got in behind the wheel. Gus sat in the front passenger seat. I sat in the rear. And there were all the papers the gang had planted, on the seat beside me, just like I'd expected. Now all I needed to know was if the really damning ones were among them.

Gus told me to pass the papers up front to him. One by one, I handed them to him, and one by one he started handing them over to the senator. "Recognize this?" he asked as he put the first one in Goldberg's hand. "Or this? Or *this*? Surely you recognize *this* one."

"Where the hell's you get hold of all these?" Goldberg blustered, turning redder with each new page.

"On the back seat, just where you saw us find them."

"Who put 'em there?"

"The four guys we got rid of. Their plan was to force your car off the road and make sure you died in the wreck. When the police found you and the papers, you'd be dead and your reputation would be deader."

"Tonight?"

"That was their plan."

"So what are *you* gonna do? Can I have my papers and go?"

"Good god, man, no!" Gus laughed. While he laughed, I quietly sorted through the rest. The guys had done their homework – the absolute worst was there. I shuffled it to the bottom of the stack.

"We keep the papers," Gus said as I finished up my reorganizing. "But we're not gonna kill you. We can't save your reputation, but we can save your life. When these papers go public, there's nothing nobody can do to save your political hide. As they say, you're toast."

"But we have an offer," I spoke up. "If you don't take it, those guys'll be back, buying you drinks, and you get killed. Your choice."

A long silence. Finally a resigned, "What's your offer?"

"Believe me, it's your only chance. Otherwise you're a dead man," Gus said, relishing his role. "You take all these papers, walk yourself into the nearest police station and voluntarily give yourself up. We go with you, to make sure you make it there safe and sound. Then you're on your own."

"Jesus H. Christ! I can't do that. It'll mean the end of everything"

"Yeah – but you'll be alive!" I pointed out.

"I'll have to go to trial. Everything will be public. I'd be ruined!"

"Yeah, but you'll be alive," I said again.

"And maybe, with luck, you might get out of jail in time to enjoy life again," Gus added.

"This way – our way – you'll have a chance," I said with exaggerated patience. "The other way, you're dead. That's pretty final. Again, your choice."

"What about my money?"

"Keep your money, we don't want it. You can use it to get yourself a good lawyer. The main thing is – you'll be alive."

The senator suddenly whirled around to look at me. To *really* look at me. "Are you part of the group that tortured me in my home last week?" he asked suspiciously.

"Someone tortured you in your home last week?" Gus deadpanned. "Hey – we don't know anything about that. But wait – the four guys. Maybe they were part of that."

A long silence then more to himself than to us, "Do I have any choice? Death or dishonor? Dear God, I don't want to die!"

"Yes, you have a choice – yes or no. Right now," I said.

"Now?"

"Yep, right now. Get it over with. Before you lose your nerve. You're here, the papers are here, and we're here to make sure you get to the police station safely. Except for one stop on the way. We'll need to stop at a copy place and get these papers copied, just to be safe. You of all people know how easily officials can lose important papers. These are never going to get lost, no how!"

Within the hour, it was done. Papers all copied. The senator locked up. We were ready to head back to Oakland. One last little detail to finish up: Gus and I called every newspaper in and around Sacramento and made sure they had the story. Nothing could save the senator now.

So much had happened it was hard to believe it was only a little after nine. We debated about staying over for the night but finally decided to have a quick dinner and head back on Gus's cycle that night.

Over dinner we tried to figure out what Sergeant Horning was planning.

"That idiotic asshole! He's the world's worst detective. He couldn't find a manhole if he fell into it! What's Smitty doing about it?"

"Nothing! He's left it up to me. I've called Chief O'Meara for help."

"You know what? I think you better call O'Meara right now and let him know what's just happened here," Gus said.

The chief was still at his office. It only took a few minutes to get him up to speed. I left out a few things I didn't feel he necessarily needed to know. As soon as he found out that the senator had confessed to everything, he said, "That's great, but I still don't have any idea about how to forestall your sergeant. Your wedding's only a couple of days away and the sergeant has complete charge of the case. And didn't you tell me he already had a warrant? I'm still trying to come up with ideas but it may be hopeless. He might still screw up your wedding.

One disaster after another, Poor Smitty!

CHAPTER 84

By eleven we were back at the party, it was still going strong. Smitty wanted to know if I felt okay. I didn't know what he was talking about until I remembered that Gus had taken me home sick earlier that day. Or so everyone thought.

We'd raced up to Sacramento, nipped a murder plot in the bud, convinced a senator to give himself up, accompanied him to the police station, notified all the local papers, had dinner, raced back to Oakland and hardly been missed.

Little George pulled Smitty off to one side and started explaining what'd been going on the last three or four hours.

"It was one of them catch twenty-two things for me, you know— damned if I did, damned if I didn't. I wanted to tell you, but I didn't want to rat out my guys. I finally decided I had to protect you so I told Casey about it. I know he's smart and I know he's completely loyal to you. I kind of thought he'd figure a way out. I knew I went to the right guy!"

Turning to me, Smitty said, "What's he talking about?"

Starting with the episode in the head, Gus and I took turns relating the whole story. When Gus told him about my idea of making the senator give himself up to the police, Smitty said, "Did it work?"

"Ab-so-lute-lee! We followed him into the police station and saw him turn over the papers to the cops. Then we made sure every paper in town was tipped off to the story. Tomorrow mornings' papers'll crucify him. I can't wait to see 'em.

Smitty was silent for a minute then, "So it's over. The Senator's a goner. Little George said they'd taken care of the shooter and now we got the Senator behind bars and Carpenter was murdered. I wonder if that's the end of it all.

"Should be," I suggested. "We gave almost all the blackmail records and information to the police. There's gonna be a big stink involving a whole bunch of people named in those papers. We also got rid of some of them, like the donut shop owner and the police chief. They're gone. I think we did what we set out to do."

"No question." Gus answered. "But I gotta give credit where credit's due – this was totally Casey's idea. See, he fed me a sampling of what was in the pile to show to the Senator, but he hid the stuff about him being a pedophile down at the bottom of the pile. The Senators gonna have conniptions when he realizes what he's actually confessed to. It's gonna be real juicy."

"Well, I'll be damned. Casey, looks like you're really earning your keep. I had no idea this would all end this way." Smitty sat back. "This calls for a drink, something other than beer." A couple of bottles of champagne were produced and we toasted.

A little later he leaned over to me and whispered, "What about that other thing, you know, Horning.

I lied to him. "I talked to the chief and he said not to worry."

"Not worry? How in hell can I not worry? I want Josie's wedding to be perfect and that little shit's gonna screw everything up, I just know it."

I grabbed his arm, "Relax," I whispered. "Go get some sleep. It'll all work out. The chief's on your side, he'll come through."

I didn't believe myself. The more I thought about it, the wedding only a couple of days away and the Chief doubtful, the more I was convinced that the wedding was going to be a big fiasco. Especially for Smitty. Arrested for murder at his only daughter's wedding.

Gus and I were still keyed up. Too keyed up to sleep. We made some coffee and sat down to try some of that relaxing ourselves. All of a sudden it hit me. Oh boy was I ever in trouble. I wondered why Smitty hadn't said anything about it.

I caught Smitty just as he was leaving.

"What now?" he sighed.

"Smitty," I groaned. "Josie's gonna kill me. I forgot the meeting with the priest."

"Oh hell, Case, I forgot to tell you. It was postponed. Some sort of emergency at the church. Anyway, it's on for tomorrow morning instead."

A miracle!

So much was happening in such a short time. Josie and I were going to be swamped on Friday. Meeting with the priest in the morning – who knows how long that'd take. Tuxedo fitting in the afternoon. Meeting my parents and getting them settled. They hadn't even met Josie yet. The wedding rehearsal in the late afternoon. All that followed by the rehearsal dinner that night.

The first thing Smitty said he did the next morning was to turn on the news looking for the latest on the senator. He wasn't disappointed. It was all there. How he'd given himself up, saying he just couldn't live with himself anymore, that he wanted forgiveness for his sins. Reading the list of all the sins uncovered in the papers he'd volunteered, I didn't think he'd get much of any forgiveness. The reporters said he'd appeared shocked when the cops quoted what his papers documented about his dalliances with minors.

What wasn't in his private papers he gave up when interviewed by the police. The blackmail, his lover in the AG's office, the hired killer, he told everything except about what'd started the whole thing, the murder on my boat. Maybe they'd get to that in a later edition. Meantime, we weren't exonerated yet. We knew, the chief knew and we had the papers to prove it but no one else knew we were innocent. Most importantly, Horning didn't know it yet.

Thinking about Horning and his promise to arrest Smitty at the wedding, it seemed like I was watching two trains approaching each other at full speed on the same track. The collision would occur and it would be at our wedding.

The tuxedo place called and wanted to know if I could come in on Saturday instead of Friday and I agreed. As long as it was ready for Sunday and it fit really well, why should I care?

We went and met with the priest, Father Murphy, who turned out to be a youngish, rather casual basketball-playing type of a guy. He felt more like a brother than a father, age-wise anyway. And he was really easy to get along with. We invited him to the rehearsal dinner, which turned out to be a good thing.

My parents. Did I mention they'd originally come from the Midwest. They also came with a bias against motorcycle gangs. During the rehearsal it was very apparent, at least to me. My mother even physically drew away a little from Smitty when she first met him. Fortunately Father Murphy noticed it too and went out of his way to smooth the ground between them. At one point he put his arm over

Smitty's shoulders and led him over to my mom "You know, Mrs. Alton, Smitty's been a great source of aid to our church. I can't tell you how many times he's helped out some of our neediest families."

Then, just to further confuse my folks, Chief O'Meara introduced himself to them, and of course, he had nothing but high praise for Smitty. First a priest? Then a police chief? Not at all what they'd expected.

By the time we arrived at the rehearsal dinner, Mom had warmed up to Smitty. Enough so that he could turn on his charm and win her over. The crowning touch was when he kissed her hand. I don't think anyone had ever done that to her before. I know it sounds corny, but she loved it.

So the dinner was a success. Gus acted as Master of Ceremonies and ended the dinner choreographing a very nice series of toasts. The last thing he said got a lot of laughs from the party – and a huge sigh of relief from me.

"Casey, you have no idea how lucky you are! If we'd just had one more day! One of the traditions in our group (I think he said group instead of gang out of deference to my mother), is to give the groom an all-night bachelor party. I've been to lots of them and let me tell you, they're something!" A long pause, then he added, "Something to avoid, if you possibly can!"

Smitty had arranged lodging for my mom and dad at a nearby inn. After dinner, Father Murphy insisted on taking them there and picking them up for the wedding the next afternoon.

Smitty insisted that I stay with him at his place. It wouldn't be seemly, he said, for me to stay at Josie's place the night before the wedding. As it was, Josie had a couple of her bridesmaids staying with her. I couldn't help thinking that someone should write a book about Smitty. What a study in contrasts! From Devil chief to worrying about appearing seemly."

He was still going nuts, worrying about being arrested during the wedding ceremony. I called the chief again and he said, "Casey, I'm doing my best. Trouble is I don't really know anyone over there that well. Horning's still got an arrest warrant he can serve anytime he sees fit. He can serve it on Sunday and say he just found Smitty. That's completely legal. If only the papers had said something about Carpenter being behind the murder on your boat— but they didn't. I can't promise anything but I'm still trying."

He'd been on my speaker phone and Smitty heard it all.

"Maybe I just shouldn't go to the wedding," he mumbled as he was about to hit the sack. "If I'm not there, he *can't* arrest me."

"You can't miss your daughter's wedding, Smitty. You're giving her away. You *have* to go!" I protested.

"But if her wedding's ruined, that's all she'll remember for the rest of her life. Her dad arrested for murder at her wedding!"

"Smitty – something'll happen. If I have to, I'll tackle Horning myself!"

"Oh, sure, and get yourself arrested too? Some wedding!"

However he did get a chuckle at the thought of little me tackling a policeman. His mood lightened up a little.

CHAPTER 85

Saturday was a complete blur. Tuxedo fitting, time with my parents, showed them Smitty's boat and Josie's house, got a haircut, totally forgot about lunch until my parents dropped some hints. Somehow I got through it.

Our wedding day dawned with beautiful weather. Smitty got me to the church on time. Josie was already there, making the final adjustment to her wedding gown. Smitty, my parents and I were waiting outside in front of the church.

Chief O'Meara and a friend of his were standing off to one side. The chief in full uniform, his friend in a conservative blue suit. His wife and kids were already in the church. I wondered why the chief was standing outside. Smitty spotted several Oakland police cars parked in the street He asked me if I thought they were for him. I turned to the chief and he called me over.

"Chief, I'd like you to meet the groom, Casey Alton." His use of the word Chief momentarily confused me. He continued, "Casey, this is Chief Jordan of the Oakland police," and he gave me a huge wink. I could only hope.

As I was starting to wonder where all the gang was, I heard the unmistakable rumble of lots of motorcycles.

In a moment they rounded the corner and approached the church, two by two, the same formation they'd used at Red's funeral. They parked across from each other forming an aisle way from the church to the parking lot. As they formed, I counted them: twenty-four beautifully shined bikes, each one mounted by a tuxedoed rider. I knew they'd be wearing tuxes, but I hadn't expected this.

So far there'd been no sign of Horning, except for the police cars parked beyond the parking area. Smitty was now utterly beside himself with worry.

The gang filed into the church and took their places escorting the guests to their seats. My parents were escorted to the front row and I was more than ready to walk to the front of the church with Gus beside me. Josie and her bridesmaids came through a side door. Smitty went and took her arm, ready to follow us into the church. He was obviously very nervous, kept glancing around as if he was expecting Horning to pop up in the church.

A little jostling went on as everyone settled into their proper places, then the organ started. Gus and I started our marathon trek to the altar, and the bridesmaids followed.

Just as Smitty and Josie started down the aisle, there was a loud commotion at the door behind them. The whole audience turned sharply around to see who was destroying the ceremony. The swinging doors at the rear of the church were rudely thrown open and Sergeant Horning, along with two uniformed policemen, strode through the door. Horning bulled his way past the ushers and reached out for Smitty's arm, saying loud enough for everyone in the church to hear, "Eugene Smith, I have a warrant for your arrest for the murder of Joseph Mitchell. Officers, handcuff him!"

I could hear Smitty clear from the end of the aisle. "You miserable prick. I'll get you for this!"

Josie turned pale and tried to hit the sergeant.

At that moment, Chief O'Meara and his friend stood up in the last row of pews. The chief's friend, in a loud official sounding voice, said, "Officer Horning!"

Not turning around, the sergeant said, "Everybody shut up! This man's a dangerous criminal. I don't care what's going on here. I'm cuffing and arresting him." You could see how pleased he was at humiliating Smitty.

"No, actually, you're not, Horning!" again from the Chief's friend.

One of the uniformed police swung around to shut the speaker up. Instantly, he grabbed Horning's arm and whispered into his ear.

"What the hell?" Horning said as he swiveled toward the speaker. His jaw dropped down as he instantly recognized the Oakland Chief.

"Chief, what the hell are you doing here?"

"What the hell I'm doing here is arresting you!"

"Arresting *me*? You can't do that."

"Oh, yes I can. Officers, I'm officially ordering you to arrest Sergeant Horning for disobeying orders and concealing evidence, among other things."

The looks on the uniformed policemen's faces was the stuff of high comedy: conspicuous relief, followed almost immediately by gut-level satisfaction. They obviously enjoyed cuffing the sergeant. The San Francisco Police Chief ostentatiously held the warrant high in the air and deliberately tore it up.

The church was paralyzed into silence. Everyone had heard Horning's charges against Smitty, followed by the Oakland police chief's charges against Horning. The gang recovered first. They broke into applause, and it wasn't long before the whole congregation joined them – with the notable exception of my parents and the priest. They were simply bewildered.

The gang left their seats and gathered around Smitty and Josie, anxious to shake his hand and congratulate him on finally getting rid of his nemesis. The two chiefs insisted they hadn't planned the timing of the arrest to embarrass the sergeant or to benefit Smitty. It has just happened that way. The Oakland chief said that Horning had been under investigation for some time for any number of department infractions. This thing with Smitty was the last straw.

Smitty was bouncing back and forth from hilarity to about as close as anyone could remember seeing him come to tears of relief. He thanked both chiefs effusively and hugged Josie over and over again.

It took some time to restore order, but finally everyone was reseated and I'd had a little time to explain enough to my parents to get us through the moment. Josie and Smitty backed up to the rear of the church and the organ started again. The priest, Gus and I took our places and the bridesmaids resumed their procession.

From that point forward, everything went exactly as planned and much faster than I'd expected. A pair of "I do's", a juicy kiss, and the daring deed was done. We were Mr. and Mrs. Casey Alton.

In the lobby of the church, we kissed, hugged, and shook hands with all our guests. After that Smitty drove us to the reception. He was at once exuberant and relieved. He'd been expecting the worst and received the best. His daughter married and his enemy vanquished in front of his friends and in church.

Toward the end of the reception, amidst champagne bubbles and many toasts, Smitty got up and proposed his own toast.

"Casey, in spite of the terrible first impression you made on me, I've come to like and respect you. I'd like to welcome you into my family. I just wish Josie's mother and our good friend Red were here to welcome you too. The past few weeks have been tumultuous to say the least . Now, to make this wedding completely legal, I have two all-expense-paid tickets to Hawaii, plus a check for two thousand dollars for your honeymoon. And, a word of warning. You better take damn good care of both Josie and my boat. Here're the tickets, you leave tomorrow morning! Aloha!"

I turned to Josie, "Did you know about this?"

"Sure did, partner."

Together, we gave Smitty a big hug.

More toasts and more champagne, then someone said it was time to cut the cake.

We each had our pieces. Josie squared off and said, "If you dare smash that cake on my face, I'm gonna kill you." I was no fool. I took a big bite. While I was chewing it, licking my lips in appreciation and grinning like the happy fool I was, she smashed her cake on my face.

I asked her if this what our marriage was gonna be like. She said, "Wouldn't you like to know," and laughed.

CHAPTER 86

So, that's what happened. The guy who'd hired me to deliver his boat, dead. Red killed. A young guy killed on Smitty's boat. Carpenter assassinated. The senator headed for prison, his reputation destroyed. Josie and me married. My mom and dad in-laws with a notorious motorcycle gang chief. The *Jezebel* almost completely destroyed. Sergeant Horning's career destroyed. All because two little numbers had gotten smudged on a piece of paper.

The adventure ended, but the story went on. When we returned from the honeymoon, we went to work on the *Jezebel* in earnest. Six months later, she was back in the water, rigging all installed and a thing of beauty.

Another thing of beauty by that time was Josie's belly. Three months pregnant and showing. I was tickled, Josie was tickled, my mom and dad were tickled, and Smitty was way more than tickled. I'd made a start on going back to college, majoring in Oceanography.

Smitty was so pleased, he bought us a sailboat. Actually, not just any sailboat – he somehow managed to find the boat that'd started the whole thing, the one I'd ferried up from San Diego. No one claimed it, so the city sold it at auction. He bid for it and got it. Not huge, but big enough. And the boatyard where we did most of the rebuilding on Smitty's boat offered me a good-paying, part-time job so I could go to college. Everything was rosy.

One afternoon Gus called and said the guys felt kinda' bad that they'd never had time to throw a real bachelor's party for me.

I was immediately reminded of what Gus had about how lucky I was to have avoided the gang's traditional bachelor party.

"Tell the guys how much I appreciate the gesture but it really isn't necessary."

"Yes it is" he assured me. "It's a tradition. It's on for tomorrow night. Seven o'clock at the Seaside Inn. Be there!"

"Aw, c'mon, Gus. Do we really have to do this? Josie's got a special dinner planned for tomorrow."

"Quit weaseling," Gus said. "We've already cleared it with Josie."

Seeming to have no choice in the matter, and seeing that Josie was complicit in the trap, I gave up.

They'd reserved a private room big enough for the whole gang. And they were all there, more than thirty of them. In addition, Chief O'Meara and Little George showed up. I was particularly glad to see the chief there – hoping his presence might tone down the proceedings a little.

And as it turned out, it was a great party. An open bar, cocktail waitresses, canapés – they even had entertainment in the form of a three-piece swing band. No tuxes this time, just casual biker wear. In terms of what I'd been expecting– dreading?– the event was fairly tame. All thirty-plus tried their damnedest to get me drunk. I lost track of the number of drinks I surreptitiously dumped into the potted plants, but I imagine most of the gang woke up the next morning feeling pretty grim.

Finally dinner was served, but the drinking continued. At the end of the dinner, Gus stood up and made a little speech.

"My dear friend Casey! I hate to bring it up, but I've got a list – a *partial* list – of your very serious and very numerous transgressions in the short time we've known you," Oh boy, I thought, here it comes." he continued "You caused Smitty's boat to be bombed. You made us waste a lot of time in Sacramento. You almost got Smitty's house invaded. You got us mixed up with a blackmailer and a murderer. You got us mixed up with a dirty, dishonest senator. You got Smitty under suspicion for murder. We had to rescue you from being kidnapped. The fact is – you've been a hell of a lot of trouble to us."

"Hear, hear!" from the gang.

"Now then, young man. We were pretty willing to forgive you for being such a problem, but then you committed something so vile, so intolerable, so offensive, so unforgivable, we feel we have to punish you with something you'll have to live with the rest of your life!"

A small spattering of applause.

"Do you have any idea what terrible thing is you did?"

I had a suspicion but I went along with gag. "No, sir?"

Gus turned to the gathering and said, "Do you?"

In unison and well rehearsed, they boomed out, "YOU STOLE OUR JOSIE!"

Then Gus added, "And on top of that, you got her pregnant! How can we ever forgive you? Do you have any thing to say in your defense?"

"I didn't know what I was doing?"

One of the guys called out, "When you got married or when you got her pregnant?"

"Maybe neither? Or maybe both?"

Everyone enjoyed a laugh at my expense. I acted hurt. Then Gus said, "Okay. On to the punishment phase of the evening. Do you, Casey, realize that none of this would have happened and we'd still have our Josie, if you hadn't made one little slip?"

"One little slip?"

From the audience: "Yeah, you slipped up."

Another: "You slipped into the wrong slip!"

And: "You're on a slippery slope!"

Yet another: "What can you expect from such a little slip of a guy?"

And: "His navigating must be slipshod."

Then: "You slipped up when you slept with Josie!"

That one got both laughs and boos.

Gus quieted the room down and asked, "Would you like to know what your punishment is?"

"Do I have a choice?"

"Nope."

And with that he signaled one of the guys to bring a large, wrapped package to the front of the room. It looked like a fairly large painting, two feet tall and maybe six feet long. They plunked it down in front of me and told me to unwrap it.

I took my good time unwrapping it as slowly as was physically possible. The back was exposed first. Turning it over, I saw it was a very professionally rendered hand carved wooden sign in bright yellows and oranges.

In large letters, it said, CASEY'S SLIP.

"That sign's going up over slip number 7," Gus said. "That's the slip you were *supposed* to slip into when you slipped up, and from this day on, it's *your* slip. Maybe with this sign you'll be able to find the right slip. And, it's gonna stay there forever, my friend!"

Gee, I'm famous! Or is it infamous?

They wanted me to make a speech. I told them I was overwhelmed, and had no doubt that I would be forever blessed – or forever cursed – by that sign. I also said that Josie and I were trying to figure a way to use Smitty as a first name for either a boy or a girl.

Then turning back to Gus, I thanked him for all his help and told him that as much as Josie adored him, there was no way we were gonna name any kid of ours Gus.

That got a lot of laughs. Then the party gradually broke up.

Smitty, who'd been pretty quiet during the evening, gave me a big hug as we were leaving. I felt pretty sober and offered to drive him home. He looked a little bombed and he accepted. On the way, he told me again how proud he was of me and hoped I wasn't offended by the sign.

"Offended? Hell, no! I'll be able to show that sign to our kids and tell them the whole story, over and over and over again. 'Casey's Slip!' I love it!"

But the final icing on the cake for Smitty didn't occur until a few days later.

That was the day when the Oakland police department officially stripped Horning of his badge. They cited numerous crimes against citizens, along with his obvious bias and dishonesty. Bottom line: they said he let his own personal feelings influence and interfere with his performance in the murder case on my boat. Horning's days as a corrupt policeman were over.

Several of Oakland's finest went out of their way to drop by the warehouse over the following days and tell Smitty how glad they were to see the last of Horning.

"You weren't the only one he was a pain in the ass to," they said. One of them wanted to know how in hell Smitty got the Oakland and El Cerrito chiefs to work with him.

"Ask Casey," he said, and ducked out.

"I'll never tell," I thought to myself. And I never did, until now.

END.